KINGMAKER
THE RAVEN'S BLOODY CROWN

Kingmaker – The Raven's Bloody Crown by Axel Martens

Copyright © 2025, ProjectWitchcraft LLC.

ISBN: 979-8-9901842-4-4 (Paperback)

979-8-9901842-5-1 (Hardcover)

Visit us at project-witchcraft.com

Be Careful What You Witch For!

AXEL MARTENS

KINGMAKER
THE RAVEN'S BLOODY CROWN

BEWARE YOUR DREAMS – THEY MIGHT COME TRUE.

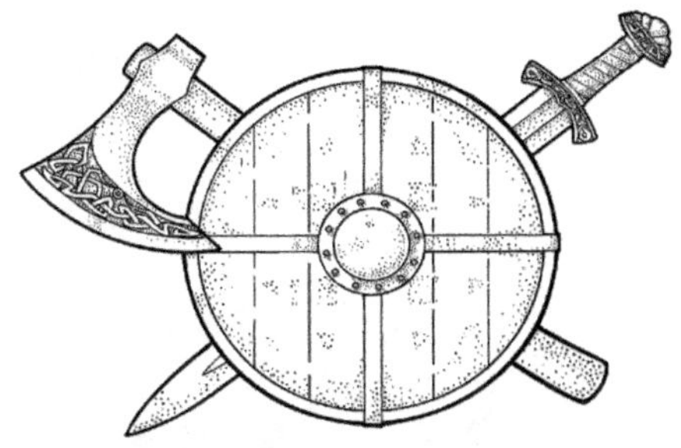

"I do not kill with my gun;
He who kills with his gun has forgotten the face of his father.
I kill with my heart."

– Roland Deschain[1]

[1] Stephen King (1982): The Gunslinger, Book one of The Dark Tower series

FOR MY DAD

Table of Contents

Back Cover Blurb

The Norns haven't been kind to Bergrún.

In a world that scorns ambitious girls from poor families, Bergrún was never given a chance. Bullied, humiliated, and cast aside, she turned to the dark powers of ancient Norse magic not just for revenge, but for justice.

To forge a new order from the ashes of the old—a future she would rule—the witch seeks a Viking chieftain to conquer her homeland and crown her queen.

But when the capricious Norns throw her into the path of the young and idealistic warrior Rikard, Bergrún must choose between her ruthless mission and an unexpected alliance.

Can she manipulate the threads of fate and claim her bloody crown, or will the old gods and her own heart conspire against her?

The Doom of Hamarrfjold

Once full moon bleeds and sky turns red,
Vile shadows crawl upon the land.
Old foes and new strike, forces blent,
Like wolves of Fenrir's bloodthirst pack.

As brothers clash, and kin slays kin,
Hel's lies spread deep like deadly thorns.
A woman bold defies the Norns,
breaks customs old, absorbs black sin.

Her zeal flames ash to bright renown,
With warrior's strength to seize her goal.
Yet fate shall mar both heart and soul,
to raise her queen, without a crown.

Ten Years Earlier

SVARTVIK BURNED. BILLOWING swaths of smoke rose into the air, weaving between the banks of low-hanging clouds. Orange flames danced on the roofs, tendrils reaching skyward despite the ceaseless rain. The acrid smell of burning timbers, livestock, and worse clung to the wind. It reached far out to sea, where Bergrún's ship pulled against the tide with mighty oar strokes. She stood at the stern, her long, raven-black hair whipping in the wind. Her hands gripped the railing, her muscles taut, her gaze fixed unwaveringly on the destruction of her home—the last vestiges of her human past.

She had tried, hadn't she? Despite the humiliation of being looked down upon her entire life—a girl daring to have ambitions, a sharp tongue from the lowest rung of a backwater society, an outsider in looks, dreams, and nature—she'd given them a choice. No longer powerless, no longer weak, she'd offered a path forward, requiring only the necessary retribution. They must've known what consequences their refusal would bring. Hadn't they felt how the power had shifted and seen the lines drawn in the sand, never to be crossed?

She hadn't demanded their feigned adoration. No one was forced to grovel in the dirt. In fact, very little in their pitiful lives needed to change. Still, they chose to poke a dragon in the eye, blinded by their stubborn pride and bitter prejudice. And then, when the inevitable happened, they screamed in panic. Begging for mercy, they pleaded utter ignorance as its fiery breath engulfed them.

The deed was done, the rotten tree chopped down, and from the ashes of its smoldering timbers, Bergrún would build a better world where the random luck of birth counted for nothing against the power of will and the will of power. But first, she must leave. The fires devouring her childhood still blazed too hot. The smoke's noxious odor stole the air from her lungs and stung her eyes, causing tears to pool in the corners.

The witch swiped the moisture away, disgusted. Her jaw was set, her shoulders stiff. She jerked her gaze away. Behind her, the oars creaked as eight men labored to propel the ship. With their eyes downcast and their voices reduced to grunts, they were nothing but sheep—frightened animals, yet with enough sense to protect their hides. Soon their toil and sweat would move the vessel past the shallows, and she would order the mainsail hoisted.

Her gaze sought the horizon. Beyond the restless sea lay a world of hidden secrets, daring ventures, and limitless opportunities. The wind would guide her destiny for a while, until she returned, ready to claim the rightful place her new nature demanded.

PART ONE

Silver-gray Dawn

"War, my friends, is a thing of beauty.
Those as says otherwise are losing."

– Jorg Ancrath[1]

---

[1] Mark Lawrence (2011): Prince of Thorns, Book one of The Broken Empire series

CHAPTER ONE

Raiders

THE LATCH RATTLED, but the wooden bar remained stuck—the warped boards refusing to relinquish their hold. Cursing and grunting reached Bergrún's ears before a forceful kick shook the frame. Another kick and the door creaked open, letting the gray light of an overcast sky seep into the tiny shed. Bergrún crouched in one corner. Huddled into a ball, she'd tried to preserve her body heat. Mud caked her bare legs, and straw clung to her soiled dress. Wearily, she raised her head to face the figure standing in the doorframe.

"The men left three days ago," Grimarr said in his rasping voice. The aging warrior had suffered a stab to his throat during his last campaign. Clinging to life like lichen to a cliff, he'd crawled from the battlefield and returned home, using the axe that split his leg as a crutch.

My opponent didn't need the weapon any longer," he was fond of telling everyone. With his pillaging days over, the battle-scarred Viking taught the village boys, advised the jarl, and acted as the thane of the village when the warriors left on a raid.

"Why don't you step out? No need for you to freeze in here and for me to freeze over there." Grimarr pointed to his house across from the chicken yard. His eyes roamed over her body, lingering. "You cook for me and see to my *other* needs, and no one will care that I let you out before the fortnight was over. It's getting cold at night this time of the year. What say you?"

Bergrún lowered her gaze and rose to her feet, her muscles stiff. Her right cheek still throbbed where Stígur had backhanded her. Without a word, she shuffled toward Grimarr.

"He got you good," the old man chuckled as the light touched her face. "Count yourself lucky. If a karl had used that tone with our chieftain, he'd have been strung up and whipped bloody. A thrall? Stígur would've killed him on the spot," he added, stepping aside. "You've just received a friendly reminder of your place, seeing that you've been Stígur's 'honored' guest. But by Thor, woman, what came over you to scream at him?"

Bergrún remained quiet, waiting for Grimarr to lead the way. He looked her up and down, sniffing in disgust.

"You will wash before you enter my house—your clothes, your hair, and your body. I can't have a filth-covered scarecrow preparing my dinner, can I?"

Bergrún crossed the yard to the rain barrel and poured a bucket of water into the low tub resting on a bench beside it. Untying the drawstring on her dress's neckline, she let the shapeless garment slide off her body. The coarse soap stung her hands as she rubbed the thin linen over the washboard, and the icy October wind raised goosebumps on her pale skin. Seagulls circled overhead, their shrill cries breaking the monotonous rumbling of waves against the rocky shore.

Grimarr leaned against the shed. Chewing on a strip of dried elk meat, he ogled the young woman's naked body. Then he hawked up phlegm and spat on the ground. She whirled around. For a single heartbeat, their gazes locked—a flicker of crimson igniting in Bergrún's onyx eyes. She pulled her lips back, baring her teeth as her balled fists shook.

A wave of her cold fury washed over him. He stumbled backward, gasping, as if she'd doused him in icy water. For two heartbeats, he stood frozen before he shook his head and limped toward his hut.

"Fetch fresh water and boil the oats when you're done," he mumbled. "Don't you dare keep me waiting for supper!" With that, he went inside, slamming the door behind him.

Bergrún rinsed and wrung her dress before hanging it under the eaves to dry. She washed her long, raven-black hair and scrubbed her skin, wincing as the horsehair brush scratched her bruised ribs. A bundle with her possessions lay next to the hut's door. After slipping into her spare dress, she tied leather wraps around her feet and fetched the water from the well for her new master's supper.

Like most houses in Fårosünd, Grimarr's hut had been built from a simple wooden frame filled with mud bricks and covered with soil and grass. The dwelling had no windows, just a wooden door and a hole in the roof over the open fireplace. Bergrún stoked the embers and added new logs. As the flames caught, she hung a blackened pot onto a metal hook, adding the oats. She let the gruel simmer before adding nuts, mushrooms, and slices of smoked elk. Grimarr sat in a driftwood chair, tapping his good foot with impatience yet not meeting her eyes. Finally, she filled his bowl, leaving only scraps in the pot for herself to eat.

"Go to the lodge and fetch me a pitcher of ale from Stígur's stock," Grimarr ordered halfway through his meal. "I'm in the mood for a drink tonight. He won't mind." Taking a crude iron key from under his tunic, he tossed the heavy object to Bergrún, hitting her on the leg.

Night had fallen, and low clouds rolled in from the sea, blanketing the village in dense fog. Bergrún pulled her cloak tight. The cluster of low houses looked ghostly in the swirling mists. Two braziers burned in front of the longhouse, the diffused light glowing like the fiery eyes of a fearsome beast. Folk said witches and demons roamed the world on nights like this. Bergrún didn't fear anything out here, knowing that the monster waited in the house, eager for her return.

He'd let me out too early, she thought. *Five days might not be enough. Have my ravens even reached Hrafney?* They had better; she wouldn't endure this filthy warrior's touch.

Entering the large, square building, Bergrún needed some time to find what she was looking for. Occupied with vicious thoughts on how to deal with her new master, she almost forgot the ale. Smiling to herself, she contemplated pissing into the pitcher instead. But then, these backwater pigs might not even taste the difference.

"What took you so long?" Grimarr yelled as she entered. "I should whip you for your tardiness. Remind me in the morning!"

Bergrún poured the ale into a horn, and he snatched it from her hands, drinking deep gulps. Much of the ale ran down his beard and sweat-stained tunic. She refilled his horn.

"That's better!" he belched, wiping his beard. "Now, sing for me. You can sing, don't you?"

Bergrún sucked in air through her nose, trying to cool the rage bubbling in her veins like molten lava, when the bell over the village's gate rang the alarm.

* * *

RIKARD STOOD AT the bow of the longship, staring into the fog. He pulled his wolf-pelt-adorned cloak tight around his skinny shoulders. The unfamiliar leather armor creaked with every move. His wavy blond hair swayed in the wind, willful strands flicking into his eyes, the locks still too short to be braided.

The boat had slowed since the men struck the mainsail, propelling the vessel forward with cloth-wrapped oars instead. Choppy waves slapped against the hull, and the smell of seaweed clung to the air. Squeezing the hilt of his shortsword, Rikard wondered how anyone could steer toward their destination on a night like this.

Footsteps approached. Turning, Rikard saw Harold and Thorstein.

"Shitting yourself yet?" the taller warrior jeered. Thorstein was over six feet tall. Braids of thick red hair spilled over his massive shoulders, and a permanent sneer clung to his lips, aided by a scar on his chin.

"Keep your voice down, idiot!" Harold hissed. "Want to give us away?"

"Relax, Harold. There are only women and children in that village. Let them have some excitement. It's much more fun to see your victims flushed with fear. Like this one." He punched Rikard on the shoulder. Ignoring the taunts as best he could, the young man turned to his brother.

"Are you certain the warriors left on a raid to Inglandia?" Rikard asked.

"I wouldn't come here with only one longship if I weren't convinced," Harold explained. "Two ravens carried the message. Odin had two ravens—a potent omen. Still," he whispered, leaning toward the lanky youth beside him. "Some men might have stayed behind. That's why I brought my fearsome little brother on his first raid. You shall have a chance to wet your axe."

"Or his britches," Thorstein jeered. Rikard turned away, and a strong hand clamped on his shoulder.

"Listen, brother," Harold said, his tone earnest. "We've all soiled ourselves once, maybe twice, before a battle. That doesn't matter. Your sweaty hands, your ragged breath, your doubts—everything will vanish when your bloodlust starts boiling and your lessons kick in. You've bested many fighters who were older, taller, and stronger. Odin is with you!" The warrior squeezed Rikard's shoulder, and the youth nodded.

"Get ready now," Harold ordered. "Thorstein, you take twelve men and assault the main gate. Make a ruckus, draw their attention."

"And their arrows," the tall warrior interjected with a scoff.

"Use your shields. Just keep them focused on you. Einar and I will lead another dozen men to swing around. We'll scale the ramparts and pay a surprise visit to the village square before opening the gate for you."

"Which of you shall I join?" Rikard asked.

"Neither," Harold declared. "You and Bjorgen will follow Gundloff around the other side. Head to the sheep pens and secure the animals." Seeing his brother's face fall, Harold explained. "The animals are the reason we raid this village..."

"Besides kicking Stígur Asmundsen in the balls," Thorstein snickered.

"Yes, besides that. But there's more. Everybody fleeing will go that way. Make sure no one escapes!"

"I'm to butcher defenseless women and children?" Rikard protested.

"Children grow up to be men, and women are not defenseless, believe me. They'll butcher you without blinking an eye if they get a chance. These are our enemies; always remember that. Their kin murdered our mother and sister." Harold's voice turned to ice. "We owe them *blóðhefnd!*"

"It's time," Thorstein growled. A gap opened in the fog, revealing the craggy shore of Brótinholm a mere ten boat lengths out to starboard. A low outcrop barred the direct path to the harbor, from where a steep path led to the fortified village. Harold contemplated ordering the men to row the boat around the obstacle when alarm bells sounded from the village.

"*Skítr!*" Harold cursed. "Gundloff, beach her here!"

"To the weapons, men!" Thorstein shouted. "For kin and jarl!"

"For blood and glory!" the men replied, grabbing their shields and axes.

* * *

"By Hela, what's going on?" Grimarr barked. Tossing his horn to the floor, he pushed himself upright. "My shield and axe. Hurry, woman, bring me my weapons!" Bergrún had already reacted. Throwing the lid of his war chest open, she snatched the double-sided axe, ripping apart the leather straps holding the weapon in place. Taking a running start, she swung the gleaming blade in an elegant arc, splitting Grimarr's head to the collarbone.

Bergrún let go of the handle and stepped back to avoid the spray of blood gushing from the corpse. She rushed back to his chest and scattered the contents on the floor. Finding two coin pouches, she ripped a shirt into strips and tied them to her inner thighs. Then, she dressed in the dead man's pants and tunic as best she could. A dagger went into the shaft of her new boots.

Should I take the axe? Too dangerous! Better, she looked unarmed and defenseless. With a grim smile, Bergrún kicked the hearth's glowing embers onto the furs and blankets before leaving the house.

Chaos had already engulfed the village. Grunts and cries filled the air, accompanied by the clang of weapons. The mighty boom of a battering ram sounded from the front gate. Bergrún looked around, and an arrow struck the wooden door frame inches from her face. From across the yard, three old women hurried toward her.

"Where's Grimarr?" the lead woman shouted. "We need the key, the lodge…" she huffed, bending over, "must bring children to safety."

"Grimarr grabbed his axe and left," Bergrún lied. "Why the lodge?"

"We can barricade the door," another woman said.

"Yes, and the raiders will thank you. They'll set the longhouse on fire. These warriors must hail from Hamarrfjord, returning the courtesy of last year's friendly visit."

"Then we must fight," the third woman declared. "Honor demands it."

"By all means, honor this clump of horse manure by bleeding into the dirt," Bergrún jeered. "I'm out of here!" She slipped past the women and had already gone four steps before halting. Turning back, she saw flames breaching the roof of Grimarr's hut. The firelight highlighted the despair in the older women's faces. Closing her eyes and shaking her head, Bergrún said, "Send the children with me if you want them to live!"

"Where will you lead them?"

"Out the back and into the marshes. They can climb the dead trees and hide. The heavy warriors won't be able to follow."

The creak and clatter of wood signaled the breach of the village's gate.

"Arne, Tjorben, go with Bergrún. Help her save our children."

"I can fight!" Tjorben protested.

"And you shall, when you're a man. Now, you must hide until your father returns. Tell him what happened. Freya be with you. Now go!" the graying woman urged. Taking a dagger from her belt, she and her two companions marched toward the gate, their heads held high.

Bergrún urged her group of a dozen frightened children to run for the back gate. Lifting two toddlers into her arms, she bellowed at the rest to run like the devil was after them. The gate was locked, but Bergrún did not slow. Only twenty paces separated her group of refugees from the exit when the thick wooden boards flew apart. The boys in front stopped, horror-struck, and Bergrún almost ran them over.

"Move!" she shouted. These raiders wouldn't leave any witnesses. Clearing the gate, Bergrún halted, turned, and spotted pursuit. She closed her eyes and screamed. A tremor ran through the ground like a *jarðsquake*, causing a landslide to fill the gap in the bulwark. The witch sank to her knees, exhausted.

"Arne, Tjorben," she croaked, "take these bairns and keep running. Leave me your bow!" Her glare bore down on the taller boy. He shuddered, not daring to protest. Leaving their weapons behind, he and Arne hoisted the toddlers and ran, herding their group toward the ghostly trees rising from the marshes.

* * *

RIKARD STOMPED UP the hill. He was carrying his father's axe, his uncle's shield, and a newly forged sword his brother had gifted him for his fourteenth name day. This was his first raid, his first chance of glory, of tasting blood, of taking a woman. But instead, his brother had ordered him to secure the sheep, together with the lisping dimwit Bjorgen and the old sailor Gundloff. How cruel the Norns could be.

Maybe some cowards will try to flee, Rikard thought. He imagined slitting a fat merchant's belly open and cutting the rings from his fingers. But no wealthy merchants lived here. Fårosünd was as pitiful a village as Rikard's home on Hrafney. This raid served no other purpose than to continue an age-old blood feud between the two clans.

The sharp sound of wood splintering grabbed the youth's attention. Turning toward the village, he saw a group of people fleeing through the back gate. Bjorgen had spotted them, too.

"They're running away!" the lanky man called.

"They won't get far," Gundloff grunted.

Both men pulled their swords from their sheaths and started toward the village. Rikard followed, struggling to keep up over the uneven ground. He felt off balance with the unfamiliar weapons on his back, swinging left and right. He passed Gundloff. Then, the earth shook. Rikard tumbled into the dirt, and the shield smacked into the back of his head.

Dazed, he pushed himself onto his knees. His comrades had remained upright, continuing the assault. Groaning, Rikard closed his eyes, fighting nausea. He was useless—too clumsy for the simplest missions. His uncle was Hamarrfjord's chieftain, for Hela's sake. What shame had he brought onto his family?

Getting to his feet, he saw the group of refugees dispersing. One figure knelt near the village's earthen wall. Rikard pulled the shield and axe off his back. Holding the weapons in his hands allowed for easier running. He sprinted downhill, screaming his frustration into the night. Faster and faster, his feet pounded the soft ground, racing to the ferocious drumbeat of his heart. Catching up with Gundloff, Rikard turned toward the older man in time to see an arrow piercing the sailor's eye. In shock, the youth skidded to a halt. He raised his shield in time to hear an arrow bury itself in the wood with a loud thwack. Peering over the shield's rim, his eyes widened. The figure near the village loosed another shot. Bjorgen fell, struck by an arrow. Three hundred paces, uphill, in the night—what foul magic was this?

A foe worth killing, he thought, his eyes on the figure below, *a battle the bards will immortalize in song.* Shouting at the top of his lungs, the young Viking sprinted toward death or glory.

* * *

BERGRÚN SWAYED, LETTING the bow drop from her numb fingers. A vicious pounding behind her eyes caused vertigo. Sinking to all fours, she fought to stay conscious. She'd spent all her energy to save the children.

Why? she berated herself. *What are these brats to me?*

Had her sentimental weakness ruined her entire plan? Too late to worry now. Once the Norns have woven the threads, the pattern cannot be undone.

One Viking had evaded her arrows. Bergrún needed to deal with him. Her left hand sought the knife in her boot, fumbled, and slipped. She fell over. Lying in the dirt, she saw the yelling warrior closing in, raising his axe for a deadly strike.

"No, please," she croaked, pitiful even to her ears. She looked into his eyes and raised her right arm to stop his momentum. He froze. He looked young, a youth on the cusp of manhood.

"I don't belong here," she whispered. "I was a thrall in this village. I'll be your thrall. Take this," she said, trying to pull a wrapped bundle from under her cloak. "You'll be a hero."

His glare hardened, his hand squeezing the axe handle. Moisture pooled in her eyes.

"Please, have mercy," she mouthed before her energy reserves ran dry and she fell unconscious.

CHAPTER TWO

Taken

RIKARD STARED AT the woman at his feet. She lay in a heap like a corpse tossed off the death cart. Long black hair obscured half of her pale face, and her body looked small and slender.

Had she fired the bow? Had she killed Bjorgen and Gundloff? Impossible!

Yet no one else was there.

Rikard should finish her—kill her to avenge his comrades. He couldn't. The memory of her pleading, mystifying eyes stayed his hand. What glory was to be gained from killing an unconscious woman? What honor in slaying a defenseless foe? Lowering his axe to the ground, the warrior approached.

He pulled a dagger from his belt and knelt beside her. Pushing her over, he braced for trickery. Her body rolled limply and rested on her back. She seemed only a few years older, perhaps in her early twenties. The woman wore ill-fitting men's clothing, and the thin linen tunic left little to the imagination. Careful to avoid brushing her breasts, the young warrior pulled the bundle from under her arm. Then he cut strips from her cloak and bound her hands and feet.

He was about to open the bundle when a rock struck his ear. Pain exploded. Ducking sideways, the dazed Viking saw a man running toward him. The newcomer bent to pick up the discarded axe while another stone hit Rikard's knee. Howling in pain and frustration, the young raider scrambled to pick up his shield just in time to deflect the approaching foe's first blow. The attacker had swung the heavy war axe one-handed, leaving him off-balance and exposed. Lying on the ground, Rikard kicked the man in the groin. The attacker stumbled backward, a satisfying moan escaping his lips.

Rikard dropped the shield and jumped to his feet. A second, much smaller figure sprinted toward him, a blade glinting in the hazy moonlight. Rikard pivoted to avoid a fatal wound, and the knife sliced his left arm. He punched the knife wielder, and the second assailant dropped with a high-pitched wail.

The first man had gotten back up and hefted the axe one-handed.

He only has one arm, Rikard realized, astounded, *and he looks old.*

Gaining confidence, the young Viking drew his sword and stepped in, widening his stance. The man swung. Rikard caught the expected axe blow with the cross guard and punched with his left. His fist connected, and the attacker dropped the axe. Rikard punched him again and again, kicking him to the ground. Without conscious thought, he thrust his sword, slicing through the fallen man's neck. The blade crunched six inches into the rocky dirt, cutting his opponent's cries short. Pulling his sword free, he stared in disbelief at the blood coating its tip.

I've killed a man.

The thought paralyzed him as the gurgling from the fallen foe grew faint. He had done it—not in the practice pit with blunted steel, but in a real battle.

I've cut a man's throat, and he's dead.

Looking around, unsure of what to feel, the young Viking spotted the second figure struggling to lift the discarded axe. Rikard closed the distance in two strides and lunged. His left arm shot back for balance, his right knee bending to absorb the momentum. The blade found its mark with a sickening thud. Raising his gaze from the point of impact, Rikard looked into the dirt-smeared face of a girl not yet in her teens.

The Viking let go of his sword and recoiled in horror. The girl's eyes opened wide in shock. Wheezing escaped her mouth; her trembling lips tried to form words. For two heartbeats, no one moved, frozen like flies trapped in amber. Then she toppled forward, driving the deadly weapon to the hilt into her small body.

Rikard's ears rang. The sickening smell of blood filled his nostrils. His vision blurred, and nausea drove him to his knees. His body heaving, he vomited. For long minutes, the young man remained on all fours, squeezing his eyes shut and shaking his head to dispel a ghastly thought.

I've killed... a child!

* * *

THE BATTLE FOR Fårosünd raged on. The wind carried screams from the village, and the smell of burning houses fouled the air. Raising his head,

Rikard saw the settlement's bulwark backlit by angry flames. Silhouettes danced on top of the walls like pieces in a shadow play—his fellow warriors butchering the villagers.

Crawling on hands and knees, Rikard tried to escape the scene of his first kills. The elders spoke about the glory of battles, praised the rush of victory, and toasted the honorable deaths of warriors. Rikard saw no honor in butchering a child and a one-armed pig herder. He returned to the unconscious woman. She was moaning, and her eyelids fluttered. He slumped next to her, his head between his knees.

Hurried footsteps drew Rikard back to his reality. Two figures ran from the village below, illuminated by the spreading fires. The hulking shadow of a demon followed what looked like a woman clutching a bundle. Less than twenty paces away, the predator caught up with his prey. He swung his axe. Rikard squeezed his eyes shut, yet he was unable to block out the woman's screams. The bundle slipped from her arms as she fell. The high-pitched cry of an infant forced Rikard to look against his better judgment. Frozen and numb, he witnessed the pursuing killer's axe silencing the babe.

The executioner spotted Rikard. He rushed up the incline, eager to find another target for his blood-dripping weapon. Rikard clambered to his feet and stood with hands raised, awaiting his fellow monster.

"Rikard? Is that you?" Thorstein called. "Don't move until I can see you!" Hefting his axe in two hands, the tall warrior approached, his gaze sweeping the surroundings.

"It's me," Rikard croaked.

"You're alone? Where are the others?"

"Dead."

"Feasting in Odin's halls, huh? And these here? Your kills?" Thorstein lowered his axe as he took in the scene, giving the young man a grim nod of approval. "Three dead on your first raid... Not bad for a start." He tried to clap Rikard on the shoulder, but the younger man dodged.

"Two dead," Rikard spat. "An old cripple and a young girl. The woman is still alive."

"Well, blame the Norns, not Odin," Thorstein chuckled. "There wasn't an able warrior in the whole stinking village. Next time, you'll..."

"You think I'm angry because I didn't spill the *right* blood?" Rikard's voice cracked, raw with emotion.

"You'd better," Thorstein growled, stepping close. "Otherwise, your words test my patience."

"Then let me praise you instead. That woman has surely done evil to deserve your axe," Rikard said, nodding toward the fallen villager. "And your valiant slaughter of her babe."

"Enough!" Thorstein roared, backhanding Rikard with enough force to send him sprawling. "Disrespect me again, and you'll learn the meaning of pain."

The young man lay on the ground with stars blazing in his vision. "What honor is there in killing the innocent to avenge the innocent?" he called, defiance mixing with pain. Thorstein loomed over him, a sneer curling his lip.

"I always knew you were a coward, a weakling!" His hand closed around Rikard's throat, squeezing. "Daring big words when you can hide behind your brother." He squeezed harder. "Questioning our ways, the right of conquest. I should've cast you into the sea long ago. You're a disgrace to the weapons you wear. Still, it's not too late to right a wrong now."

The woman stirred, causing Thorstein to loosen his grip. Rikard gasped for air. The tall warrior regarded the captive with a predatory gleam in his eye. He approached, crouched down, and pulled her hair to get a better look.

"But if your tender soul weeps for that babe," Thorstein shouted over her cries of pain. "I'll make a new one right now."

"Get away from her," Rikard croaked. "She's mine."

"Yours?" Thorstein laughed. "First, you need to grow some balls, boy."

"I said get away, you pig. I claim her by right. You'll have to challenge me."

Thorstein jumped to his feet in one fluid motion despite his size. Anger flashed in the tall warrior's eyes, but his voice became sweet as honey.

"Say that again, Rikard Thure Svensen. You want me to challenge you?"

"You can leave her and walk away," Rikard replied, struggling to regain his feet. His body shivered, but he managed to keep his voice steady. "But by our laws, you can't touch her without challenging me."

"Knives," Thorstein growled. "Here and now. Odin shall witness." He pulled a dagger from his boot. The wicked weapon had a serrated blade. Forged from a fallen star, the eight-inch-long knife was pure black, swallowing the diffused moonlight. Rikard walked to his fallen dagger and hefted it in a shaking hand. His weapon was several inches shorter.

"Agreed!" Rikard shouted, squaring his shoulders. Thorstein attacked before the younger man could fall into a proper stance. The tall warrior kicked Rikard in the chest, sending him sprawling. White-hot pain jolted his body.

Rikard found himself pinned to the ground, the weight of a walrus constricting his bruised ribs. Baring his teeth, his assailant sliced his knife across the young man's cheeks, drawing blood. Rikard couldn't move, couldn't breathe. What had he thought? He hadn't lasted two seconds in this fight. With obscene pleasure, Thorstein licked the blood off the blade.

"Now, where to cut first?" He moved the tip within a hair's breadth of Rikard's left eyeball. "What beautiful eyes you have," he crooned. "You should wear a dress and entertain the men. What a pity no one will go near you after I'm done."

"Please, don't," the woman called. Having managed to sit up despite her bound wrists, she looked at Thorstein with pleading eyes. "I'm yours, brave Viking lord. I choose you for your strength and prowess. Let the unworthy child go and allow me to pleasure you. I'm well-trained in the female arts."

"Won't cost a raven's caw to finish him." Thorstein's lips stretched into a sinister smile.

"But his dying soul might spoil the mood. He's kin to you, is he not?"

"Perhaps you're right." Thorstein stood and spat on Rikard. The woman raised her hands for the warrior to cut the rope. He ignored her gesture. Sheathing his knife, he knelt beside her and ripped her shirt open. "I hope you're worth the trouble," he threatened.

The faint moonlight reflected on her smooth, pale skin, bathing her in a soft glow. She placed both hands on his cheeks and whispered, "I'm worth more than you can imagine."

He squeezed her breasts and licked his lips, his eyes burning with desire. Then his body jerked once, and he toppled lifeless to the ground.

* * *

THE NEXT MORNING, the sun rose behind thick clouds, painting an orange glow on the horizon as two ships set sail to leave Brótinholm's craggy shore and the burning village of Fårosünd. Rikard sat dazed on the deck of the Wave Dancer, the invader's longship. His horn of mead still filled to the brim, he stared back at the pillar of smoke growing fainter in the distance. Warriors cheered and clapped him on the back. Someone had draped a faded red banner with a wolf's head around his shoulders. Rikard grunted and nodded, which seemed to be the correct behavior for the hero of the battle.

The young man didn't feel like a hero. He hadn't found and recovered Hamarrfjord's most prized heirloom. The girl had handed him the bundle. And he hadn't bested Thorstein in an honorable duel. He had lost, lain helpless in the dirt like a babe, until the girl...

"Here he is!" Harold's voice boomed with pride. Rikard's brother's face looked ruddy from drink, and his eyes glowed like comets. He grabbed his little brother by the arm, spilling half of his mead over the younger man's boots. "You should celebrate with the others! You can have your pick."

Rikard looked to the stern. The Vikings had taken about a dozen women captive on this raid, ranging in age from girls on the verge of maidenhood to gray-haired ammas. Most sailed trussed up like animals with the livestock and plunder on the second ship. Yet, Harold's most infamous warriors had picked a handful for entertainment during the return journey. The men's jeers and grunts almost drowned out their pitiful whimpers. Rikard's jaw tightened, but he did not respond. Harold crouched before his brother, a wry smile on his lips.

"I understand. You don't want to take your first woman here, in the open, waiting your turn. I saved you a treat." He gestured to the ship's bow, where a makeshift tent fashioned from sailcloth provided the only privacy. "You had a tough night: Thorstein's betrayal, the death of your comrades... But by Odin's remaining eye, you recaptured the banner of Leif Rødskæg—the first jarl who united all the tribes, your great-great-grandfather."

Rikard replied with a noncommittal grunt.

"Go and rest for a bit." Harold nodded toward the tent. "Let it sink in. Let it sink in deep!" he chuckled, gesturing his drink horn toward Rikard's groin while spilling the last drops of his mead. Then Harold stood, pulled his little brother to his feet, and, with a grin, shoved him toward the bow.

* * *

RIKARD'S HEART HAMMERED against his ribs as he pulled the tent flaps open and ducked inside. The space was tiny, filled with the scent of animal hides, salt, and sweat. Furs covered the ship's planks. A small lamp cast flickering shadows, revealing the young woman tied to a center beam. She was gagged. Her shirt hung torn open, exposing a strip of pale skin from her neck to her navel. He forced his gaze away, as if he had intruded on her bathing. Then dragged his eyes back to her face, angry at his childish hesitation. She was his captive, his prize.

The woman raised her head, worry creasing her brows. When her onyx eyes met his, some of the tension in her shoulders eased, and a slow breath escaped her nose.

Rikard stiffened. A muscle twitched in his cheek. Unsure what else to do, he knelt, and his hand found the hilt of his dagger, squeezing until his knuckles turned white. The banner of Leif Rødskæg got in his way, and he tore it from his shoulders, tossing the priceless relic to the side. His gaze remained fixed on her. Staring into the witch's unusually dark eyes, he tried to gauge how dangerous this creature was.

After several tense heartbeats, he approached, reaching for her gag. She flinched, but held still. An almost imperceptible tremor ran through her body. Rikard pulled her gag down, and she spat a piece of soaked cloth on the floor. He recoiled, startled.

"Thank you," she croaked after working her jaw. She tried to smile. Strands of spittle clung to her mouth.

Rikard leaned forward and raised his hand. She pulled back, expecting a blow. Instead, he wiped the moisture away with his sleeve. Her smile widened.

"I don't trust you," he barked, his voice too loud in the small space. He pulled back and crossed his arms in a clumsy attempt to undo his moment of gentleness.

"A wise choice," she replied in a low, melodic voice. "I have no reason to trust you either. Yet..." she paused. Tilting her head, she let the lamplight play across her features. "I have no choice."

"You're a witch!" The angry hiss carried a hint of fear. "You killed Thorstein with dark magic."

"Do you prefer I hadn't?" She raised her eyebrows. Rikard's actions had pushed her shirt to the side, exposing one breast. Heat flooded Rikard's cheeks. He jerked his gaze away, fixing it on the tent pole as if it were the most fascinating thing in the world.

Her smile spread into a grin, and her eyes glinted with amusement at his discomfort.

"You won't beguile me, witch, like you did him," he stammered, still not looking at her.

"I had to do what I had to do. And currently, I'm unable to cover myself."

With a frustrated sigh, he pulled her shirt closed. Her eyes never left his face. They sat in silence for a while.

"You could have killed me, too," he whispered. "Why didn't you?"

"I could ask you the same."

"I still can." Rikard's hand went back to his dagger. She didn't flinch.

"So could everyone on this ship," she said, her voice even. "Somehow, I have the feeling you won't."

"You don't think I'm capable of killing a woman?"

"A bound captive?" she asked, a single eyebrow raised. "No. I don't think so." A muscle in his cheek twitched. "That is a compliment, Rikard."

"You know my name?"

"The other man shouted at you, remember?"

"Don't test me, woman!"

She bit her lip and lowered her gaze. Then, she arched her back to relieve the strain on her shoulders. A pained moan escaped her lips.

"Oh, this is stupid," Rikard huffed. He pulled his knife and slit her bonds, steadying her as she tipped forward. Their faces hovered inches apart. She blinked, and he swallowed.

"Thank you, Rikard," she whispered, all flippancy abandoned.

He remained motionless for two heartbeats before shoving their bodies apart with gentle yet inexorable pressure. His hands felt warm and moist where he touched her bare skin. He squeezed his lips into a thin line, but his eyes were wide open and eager.

"What's your name?" he finally asked, clearing a lump from his throat.

She did not answer immediately. Instead, she looked down. Her raven-black hair fell like a curtain, hiding her face as she tried to button up her shirt. But Thorstein had ripped it to pieces. Resigned, she pulled the torn fabric close as best she could and tied a knot at the bottom.

"Agnetha," she whispered into the charged silence. "Agnetha Lundgren. I hail from Götaland."

"You don't look Geatish to me."

"Tell me about it. I've never fit in anywhere." She raised her gaze, and he saw a fire burning in her eyes.

"Best you tell me your story. We have a few hours at sea before we reach Hamarrfjord."

"That might not be enough time. And do you only want to talk? I owe you my life."

"Yes, and I value mine. So I won't touch you."

"But I won't... Nevermind. It's probably for the best." She looked into his boyish face, and the first genuine smile tugged on her lips. Pulling her feet up, she sat cross-legged and laid her hands in her lap. "What do you want to know?"

CHAPTER THREE

Homecoming

Rikard emerged from the tent two hours later. The earlier revelry had quieted down, and the men lay strewn all over the deck, snoring. Most hadn't even bothered to string their hammocks. Hamar, the mute, stood at the rudder. Rikard couldn't decide if he held the course steady or the worn wooden crossbeam steadied him. Clambering over the tangle of limbs, the young Viking reached the water barrel midships and splashed his face. Above, the mainsail bulged in the favorable wind, stretching the sheets and sending the *Wave Dancer* flying across the open sea. As the sun rose high, the clouds dispersed, promising a pleasant journey home. Clearing a space, Rikard sat on the well-worn wooden planks and let his back rest against a mounted shield.

"Want to talk?" Harold's voice woke Rikard. He must have dozed off, soothed by the comforting creaking of wood as wave after wave splashed against the narrow hull. Blinking, he regarded the tall silhouette outlined by the sun before his brother sat next to him.

"Not really," Rikard mumbled. His gaze returned to the tent at the ship's bow, and a flush crept up his cheeks.

"Not about that," Harold chuckled. "About Thorstein."

"Oh, him." Rikard's face fell. "He came at me without warning. He attacked as soon as he saw what I'd found. Before I knew what was happening, I lay sprawled on the ground, his vile dagger an inch from my eye." The young Viking shivered. "The girl saved me."

"The girl? How?"

"She stirred. Earlier, I'd found her unconscious, so I tied her hands and feet. She woke, and her moans distracted Thorstein. I saw the lust in his eyes, and"—Rikard swallowed and lowered his gaze—"I managed to stab him."

"More than stab, I'd say. You smashed his skull with Father's axe."

"That was later. As he lay there... I didn't want him to rise again." Rikard coughed, feeling the lies scorching his throat.

He should have been dead. He'd done nothing but lie helpless in the dirt while Agnetha killed Thorstein. It was she who'd swung the axe to cover her deed, she who'd whispered the story he was now forced to tell. With every word, he felt her hold on him tighten.

What have I gotten myself into?

"On a raid, Thorstein could turn into a blood-crazed berserker. I knew that, but I never believed he'd attack his own. Especially not my brother."

"Being your brother hasn't always helped. Many people think I had it easy because of you and our uncle."

"Well, you've proven them wrong! I didn't help you beat Thorstein. Last night, you became your own man." Harold stood and ruffled Rikard's hair. "Wait until we get home. Watch the village welcome the victorious warriors. You'll be a hero."

* * *

AFTER THE YOUNG Viking had left, Bergrún remained in the tent. He had allowed her to stay in her tiny island of solace. The ship's hull protected her from the wind, and the tanned sailcloth absorbed the sunlight. She sat with her arms around her knees, her back against the pole she'd been tied to earlier. Her head drooped with increasing frequency. The captivity on Fårosünd and her magical expenditure had left her body drained. Even the influx of Thorstein's life energy wasn't enough to restore her vigor without rest.

Yet despite her fatigue, her mind refused to quiet down. Too much had happened, and little had gone the way she had foreseen. Her ravens had worked. Her message had reached Hrafney in time to incite last night's attack. Yet instead of wooing the leader of Hamarrfjord's raid with the ancient banner of their first chieftain, she'd rescued his younger brother—a green boy, naïve and idealistic.

Now what?

Bergrún had made a snap decision to conceal her true identity.

Names are powerful, her old mistress on Heilladur had been fond of saying. *They shape a person and reveal much about one's true essence.*

The witch didn't have the fondest memories of her years toiling as the old hag's apprentice. Still, she couldn't deny the wisdom. Bergrún didn't want to draw any attention to her origin. Too deeply ingrained were the prejudices against her people. Now she was Agnetha Lundgren from Götaland; just one more lie to bring her closer to her goal.

The young woman shook her head. How often had her snap decisions led to disaster? They'd led to her public humiliation by Stígur Asmundsen and to her imprisonment in that drafty shed. And last night, her urge to save Fårosünd's children had threatened to ruin it all.

Now, she'd come across Rikard. He seemed a pliable youth. In time, she would mold him to her advantage even if she'd failed to seduce him right away. Whether he was the vessel for her glorious return to Heillaður or just a stepping stone, only the Norns knew.

Bergrún hated the meddling crones, having been trapped in their foul weaving too often in the past. Yet, given that her grand plans for vengeance could still succeed, despite all of her foolish snap decisions, she had to appreciate their wicked sense of humor.

* * *

THE FINE WEATHER held, and Njord's mighty breath hastened the homebound journey. As soon as the island's craggy outline came into sight, Harold raised the wolf's head banner. Rikard could see people gathering around Hamarrfjord's harbor. His brother climbed atop the bowsprit and raised his sword high like a hero of old. Passing the storm breaker, the ship glided into the harbor basin, and the discordant sound of horns and drums filled the air. The villagers' cheers grew deafening as they recognized the flag flying from the topmast.

Harold jumped onto the pier even before the ship had docked. Olver Agnarsen greeted him with a stern expression. Wearing his crimson cape, the Jarl's First Shield stood stiff, not partaking in the jubilations. Four of his men kept the villagers back, giving their commander privacy to address the arriving war leader.

"Where's our chieftain?" Harold asked. "Isn't the victorious return of a raiding party worth my uncle's time?"

"Jarl Gustav bade me welcome you home. He's recovering from a bout of the shivers. He asked me to escort you to the great hall."

"Escort me?" Harold scoffed. "I've lived in this village all my life; I know where the hall is. If he's too ill, go tell my uncle I'll see him after I've secured the haul and split the bounty."

"I have orders to fetch you immediately. Thorstein can take over the distribution of goods. We'll take a third. Your men can split the rest between your crew and the village."

"Thorstein is feasting with Odin." Harold took one step toward Olver. "So are four other *brave* men," he hissed. "So you won't take shit!" Harold glared at his uncle's guard dog, his hand sliding toward his sword's hilt. A tense silence followed.

"I can help with the bounty," Rikard offered as both men widened their stances, their eyes narrowing.

"I'd rather not do this here, in front of your men," Olver growled. "We'll find another time to *talk*."

"I know you'd rather not," Harold spat. "You've never dared to face a man, Olver Agnarsen. Staying back, avoiding every raid this year, is that how you weaseled your way into my uncle's ear and Toril's bed?"

The onlookers had quieted. Every eye focused on the two men separated by less than a spear's length.

"You dare big words before a crowd, Harold Svensen," Olver whispered. "Meet me alone one night, and I'll demonstrate why I'm Hamarrfjord's first shield, not you." Turning to the spectators, he shouted. "There shall be mead and meat for everyone later. Our chieftain has asked me to prepare an honor guard for the brave leader of this victorious raid on our blood enemies." Dropping the false smile, Olver glared at Harold. "Now, leave your little brother with the sheep and come along."

"Rikard is coming with me! He captured the banner of Leif Rødskæg." On a wave of his hand, two sailors hastened to lower the banner and draped it around Rikard's shoulder. Renewed cheers erupted. Turning back to Olver, Harold forced a smile and shouted. "I'm grateful for the honor my uncle has shown me. Lead the way, Shield of Hamarrfjord. I long to embrace my blood-kin and lay my men's heroic deeds before our revered chieftain."

* * *

Olver ushered Harold and Rikard through the empty feast hall toward the back stairs leading to the chieftain's private rooms. His men remained outside. Reaching the landing, he knocked on the plain oaken door but entered without waiting for a response. The room felt cold despite a fire burning on the hearth. Gustav Haakon Larsen stood with his back to the door, staring out the open window. His long, graying hair spilled over his broad shoulders and once-powerful arms.

HAROLD STEPPED INTO the middle of the room, pulling his brother along, while Olver remained near the door.

"I hear you're not well, Uncle," Harold greeted. "Let me show you something to lift your spirits." He spun his brother like a practice dummy, displaying the angry wolf's head at the center of the faded red flag.

"Leave us, Olver," Jarl Gustav commanded. "Make sure there will be drink and merriment to quell any rumors."

"*Já, herra minn.*" The guard saluted, turned on the spot, and left, closing the door behind him.

"You've trained your dog well; I must give you that." Harold chuckled.

Gustav Larsen spun around, and the icy gust blowing through the window felt like a midsummer breeze compared to the old Viking's expression.

"Have you lost your mind?" the chieftain barked. Anger burned in his pale blue eyes, and a vein in his temple pulsed. "I forbade you to raid Fårosünd."

"I am my own man, with my own ship," Harold replied, squaring his shoulders. "I've seized the chance to avenge our dead."

"So, tell me, nephew," Gustav asked, his voice becoming soft as silk. "How many enemy warriors have you slain?"

"We burned the village, took plunder and slaves, and killed everyone else."

"Plunder, you say," the old Viking laughed, clapping his hands like a child receiving yuletide presents. "And slaves. How many bags of gold? How many chests of weapons? How many strong workers?"

"We brought a dozen women, twenty sheep, bales of clothes, and..."

"Enough!" the chieftain bellowed. "You've lost men for *sheep*? You've endangered our village for bales of clothes? Have you any idea what you have done?"

"I restored our honor."

"You've doomed us, you idiot!" Gustav Larsen stepped forward, grabbed the flabbergasted Harold by his shirt, and shook him like a rag doll. "Times are changing, and the world doesn't give a crow's shit for your honor." He shoved his nephew back before shaking his hands in disgust. His chest heaving with labored breaths, the aging warrior walked to a pitcher of ale and took several gulps. Then, he sank into the chair next to the fireplace. No one else had moved.

"The Danske King is gathering his forces," the chieftain explained. "He has embraced the White Christ and is eager to spread the rule of the cross. In the East, Starvinger and Trondborg have ended their *blóðhefnd* and formed an uneasy alliance. The Gauls and the Frisians have fortified their coasts and strengthened their fleets. Even in Inglandia, rumors speak of a new king with a mighty sword gathering his warriors around a circular table. We can't waste our men on ancient squabbles. We need new allies, not old enemies!"

Rikard stood open-mouthed. But Harold had regained his composure. Tucking his tunic straight, he challenged his uncle. "What do I care about foreign lands? I care only for the wealth of my kin, the honor of my clan, and the defense of my home. Hamarrfjord needs a strong leader."

"Hamarrfjord has a leader," Gustav growled.

"But who's next? You have no son. I'm your blood."

"Aye, you have my blood. That's why you're still standing here instead of rotting on the bottom of the sea. Sadly, you don't have my daughter's wits, not a tenth of it."

"Your daughter, a woman, what can she do?" Harold laughed, drowning out the soft creaking of the floorboards, until he felt the cold tip of a blade pricking his neck.

"You're right," Toril whispered into Harold's ear. "What can a woman do? We're weak and should stick to needlework. We must remain out of sight when men discuss important affairs."

Jarl Gustav got to his feet and closed the distance. "Here is what you are going to do, dear nephew," he said. "Rouse your men and prepare your ship. You'll sail to Starvinger on the morrow. Take the new vessel as well. You'll spend the winter there, building ships and training warriors. In the spring, you'll join our eastern neighbors on their raids south. After that, you'd better return with real plunder and new allies, not more sheep. You will own what you earn, since Rikard will inherit your house. Have I made myself clear?"

Toril twisted the blade, and a tiny drop of blood ran down Harold's neck.

"*Já, herra minn*," he replied.

"Good. You'll join the feast tonight with your men and mine. Explain that I've honored you with this task as a reward for your daring raid. My thralls are already loading provisions. You'll set sail before the midday tide. Now go."

Toril pulled the knife back, and Harold left without another word. Rikard started to follow when Toril placed her hand on his arm.

"Wait," she said. "Let him go. He has been scolded by his uncle and bested by a girl. He needs time to mull things over."

* * *

"WAS THIS NECESSARY?" Rikard asked half an hour later as he walked beside Toril toward his brother's house—his house now. She wore a knee-length, green dress with intricate embroidery over tight, black leggings and soft leather boots. Twin braids circled her head, meeting at the back of her head to keep her golden hair flowing over her shoulders. Kohl outlined her large, sky-blue eyes, and a rosy flush colored her smooth skin, more likely from the recent excitement than the crisp air.

"My father told the truth," she replied. "We need allies. Otherwise, we won't stand against the retaliation of Fårosünd, especially if they find allies first. Look all around you." She stopped and raised her arms to the rain-sodden village. "We're mired in the past. Our feet squelch through mud while the world around us dances in golden halls. I want more; we need more!"

"I don't know. Haven't we always lived like this?" Rikard looked from the crude houses to his disheveled attire. Mud, sweat, and blood spattered his tunic; his breaches were torn at the knees, and dirt formed half-moons under his fingernails. Realizing how he must have looked to her, he raked his fingers through his short, curly hair, dislodging blades of grass. "This is who we are," he said, defensively. "But after today, Harold must hate you. I'd thought the two of you would end up... I mean, he was so angry when he learned your father had promised your hand to Olver."

"Harold's anger won't last. My dear cousin and I," she smiled, "we have teased and taunted each other for as long as I can remember. I love him to death. All the adventures and discoveries we've shared... but he can be a fool. In the end, we always find our way back to each other as soon as he realizes that I was right. Besides, Olver was my choice, not my father's."

"Still, tonight might have changed things. The two of you aren't children anymore, fighting over mud castles. You chose another man, and your father banished Harold."

"Banished?" Toril laughed. "My father gave him a chance to become a true leader by joining forces with the Norskar and raiding to his heart's delight. No restraints. He'll come back a rich man. It's a dream come true, if you were born as a boy, that is." Her gaze shifted toward the endless sea, and her voice trailed off.

"What if he doesn't come back?"

"Unseen to us, the Norns weave each man's thread," she said.

"Would you have said so if *I* hadn't come back?"

"What do you mean?" Toril asked, whirling around.

"The raid. I could've been killed."

"Harold led you into battle?" She grabbed Rikard by the arm, squeezing his muscles. The light was fading. Still, he could see the shock and fear on her face. "I thought you stayed behind on the ship."

"I'm not a child anymore, either," he replied, louder than he had intended. "I can fight, and I've killed… a man."

"I'm sorry, Ricki, I didn't mean… I didn't think… I know you've grown, and I'm so glad you returned unharmed." She threw her arms around him and squeezed him into a fierce hug.

"Doesn't help when you call me Ricki," he muttered as her hair covered his face. Then he hugged her back, and both chuckled about the absurdity of growing up without meaning to.

CHAPTER FOUR

THRALLS

IRRITATED, BERGRÚN SCRATCHED the scab on her left arm. She shifted again, but the hard-packed earth offered no comfort to her bruised body. A jagged rock dug into her hip, and she groaned in frustration, swatting at the offending object.

Curse these Norns! she thought, digging her fingers into the cold earth. *Must they test my patience at every turn?*

The witch would have her revenge yet. Grinding her teeth, she pictured herself seizing the hideous creature's loom, weaving her own destiny—a destiny of power.

Bergrún had been locked with the other captives from Brótinholm in a drafty shed near the harbor. Most women huddled together for warmth, yet no one approached the black-haired outsider. Instead, they shot nasty glances in her direction and conversed in agitated murmurs, not caring if the shunned woman overheard them.

"She thinks she's better than us," a willowy woman in her thirties declared, "the way she wormed her way into the war leader's tent."

"And she seduced his brother, too," a younger woman spat. Clumps of dried blood clung to her matted hair.

"Doing the devil knows what—with both of them," a crone to her left agreed. Her face was marred by deep purple bruises.

"She must be a witch," the first woman said. "Look at her hair, dark as sin."

"Aye! A reed-thin waif, still, men fall for her. She'd ensnared our chieftain. And when she pushed him too far and he dropped her, see how quickly she conjured more gullible men."

"Of course, she's a witch," another woman hissed through her split lips. Her voice sounded muffled through her broken nose. "Never seen anyone like her. Skin as pale as death with eyes like the devil's."

Bergrún shook her head, a soft chuckle escaping her lips. Like spring lambs in a hailstorm, the women fell silent, cowering in fright. The witch didn't mind the nasty rumors. She held no high opinion of her companions either. Still, the irony amused her.

These gossipmongers have no idea, she thought, *how close their arrows came to hitting the mark.*

Stretching in the relative space granted by her fellow captives, Bergrún increased her blood flow to fight off the chill. She yawned, folded her hands in her lap, and fell asleep. In her dreams, she was always so much closer to her goals.

The sun's first light had barely tinged the horizon when the shed's door banged open. Bergrún blinked, taking in her surroundings.

Am I back in Fårosünd? she wondered, before a harsh female bark cleared the haze, followed by the sharp crack of a whip that clarified the situation.

"Up, my pretties. Get out of your goose feathers and line up." A stout woman stood in the yard, flanked on either side by identical-looking, gangly boys. "So kind of you to rise early," she bellowed. "Tomorrow, it'll be the whip first. Now, line up! Bairns to my left and crones to my right. Move, for Hela's sake!"

The captives scrambled to array themselves by age, leaving a wide gap on Bergrún's either side.

"I see," the commanding woman sneered. "You're *that* one." She approached Bergrún and grabbed her face like a vise. "Think you got it made for you, do you, by plucking gentle Rikard's maiden's bloom? Think again! When Harold and his men return, I'll send them your way, one by one. Their dogs and ponies, too." She shoved Bergrún back.

"Now, listen up," the taskmistress barked. "The men are gone, off to another raid. So, there won't be any more pleasant pillow play. Savor the memories and share them with the young ones, until your masters return, all starved for attention." She followed her statement with a wicked grin.

"The name is Edda, not Mistress Edda, just Edda. I'm a thrall. I belonged to old Sven Larsen, and now I belong to his youngest son, Rikard. But don't think for one crow's caw I'm like you. I'm not your friend. Don't care if you live or die as long as the work gets done and the old men in the village remain happy. Have I made myself clear?"

A faint muttering followed. Edda shook her head. She stepped up to a woman in her late teens and slapped her hard across the face, causing the woman to cry out in pain.

"Have I made myself clear?" Edda bellowed.

"Já, Edda!" the women shouted in unison.

"See, that wasn't too hard. Now, the young ones go with Frick." She pointed to the boy to her left. "You'll work the spindles and the looms. Don't get any ideas! Get your hands into my son's pants, and by Odin, I'll strangle you with your own hair." Edda glared for two more heartbeats at the woman she had struck. "The rest of you, with Frock. You'll work the fields. There's a nice heap of manure that needs spreading, smelling just as sweet as your asses."

"Not you," Edda called as Bergrún started to join the larger group of older women. "You'll come with me. Don't know what you've done, but young Master Rikard asked for special treatment. The poor lad is so befuddled, he'd have asked for that toothless crone if she'd been his first."

Special treatment? Bergrún thought. *Have I made an impression on that boy, after all?* Yet, she stood ramrod straight, not showing the slightest reaction to the other woman's words, having learned to mask her emotions long ago. Huffing in irritation, Edda stepped closer and seized Bergrún by the chin.

"I'll find out how you've ensnared him," she hissed. "I don't care if your heat smells like honey. That boy is dear to me, more than my own dimwit offspring. You'll do him harm, and, by Freya, I'll tear you limb from limb with my bare hands."

"Yes, Edda," Bergrún replied, lowering her gaze. She balled her fists and suppressed a sinister grin. She would show the stern taskmistress whom she dealt with. Soon, they'd meet in a dark corner at night with reversed roles. But not today and not tomorrow. First, the witch needed to learn the lay of the land and move the right pieces on the board into position.

I can play along, she thought. *But I won't forget!*

* * *

Edda led Bergrún through the village and up a steep incline toward the forest stretching over rolling hills. Most houses in this settlement were built from rough-hewn logs, with soil and grass covering the roofs. The steady wind blowing from the sea had tilted many dwellings leeward.

"Behold, Hamarrfjord in all its glory," Edda explained, seeing her charge's appraising gaze. "Who knows what miserable hut you'll end up in? But, by Fenrir's teeth, it won't be Master Rikard's."

Bergrún whirled her head around, surprised. Remembering her position too late, she bit her tongue and lowered her eyes.

"So," Edda laughed. "Thought I'd lead you straight to a highborn's soft bed? No, you're too clever for your own good. We'll find you a nice brute when the men return, one who'll beat the lofty dreams out of you. For now, the healer needs help. You'll fit right in, you'll see."

The two women marched for ten more minutes before reaching a ramshackle hut surrounded by stunted birch trees. A woman dressed in gray sacks knelt before the door, working with mortar and pestle. Forewarned by Edda's noisy breathing, she looked up and displayed a wrinkled face. Burn scars marred the left side, and one milky eye stared unseeing while the other held a friendly twinkle. Half her mouth formed a smile.

"Ah, Edda Ingmarsdotter," she called. "What wind blew you here this fine morning, and who's with you?"

"A new thrall," the gruff woman explained in a much friendlier tone. "Someone to help grind the herbs and fetch wood, at least until the men return. How's your Stina?"

The smile vanished from the scarred woman's face. "Still not good," she said. "I splinted her leg and wrist, but there's nothing to do about the ribs. And the fever... Well, she'll need time to heal. Do you care for some tea? I brewed a pot not long ago."

"Another morn'," Edda replied. "The new thralls need looking after. If I work them hard, the village's women might claim some ere the men return. You'll be fine with this one? Her ladyship has some high opinions of herself."

"I'll get her sorted. Álfheimr knows I need the help."

Bergrún had peered into the forest's shadows, lost in her thoughts. Upon hearing the healer's last words, she turned with surprise toward the scarred woman. Edda regarded her with a knowing smile.

"You'll do as healer Gunhild says," the taskmistress barked. "If I hear any complaint..." With a prod of the whip, she ushered Bergrún forward before marching back to the village.

The healer stood and approached Bergrún, dusting off her hands. The left bore burn marks matching the scars on her face. "Call me Hilde," she said, smiling. "What's your name?"

"Agnetha," Bergrún said, taken aback by the older woman's friendly tone. "Agnetha Lundgren."

"Well met, Agnetha. Come, have some tea. We'll bring the stools out here. Too nice a morning to stay inside."

Moments later, Bergrún found herself sitting on a low wooden stool with a steaming mug of herbal tea in her hands, unsure what to expect.

"There's a kind soul hiding under Edda's weather-worn skin," Hilde said after sipping her tea. "She'll try to protect the new women as good as she can. If it weren't for her, Stina would've died."

"What happened?" Bergrún asked, setting the untouched tea down. She had spotted a young woman lying on a cot, tossing and moaning with sweat glistening on her forehead despite the chill air.

"Poor Stina, the Norns haven't been kind. A fortnight ago, she'd lost her babe; too early. Happens to many thralls. The hard labor and little food."

"She's your thrall?" Bergrún asked, astonished.

"She's my daughter. We're all thralls. The jarl owns me and my Stina."

"And he beat her?"

"Oh, no. Old chieftain Larsen is not as cruel as some. He'd sent for Stina to be his grandson's wet nurse. I'd thought there was at least some good in my daughter's misfortune. But then…"

"What happened?" Bergrún whispered.

"A guard," Hilde said, her voice trembling. "She'd just laid the bairn to rest, her breast still bare, when he grabbed her from behind. My foolish Stina… she shrieked in fright. I told her never to fight back."

"You fault your daughter for resisting?" Bergrún's eyes narrowed, and her jaw tightened.

"We're thralls! We have no right to resist," Hilde lamented. "By Freya, woman, weren't you on the ship? With your looks, the men must've jostled for position. How do you think Stina came with child? You fight, and things turn ugly." Lowering her gaze, Hilde whispered, "I thought my daughter had learned this lesson already—the hard way." She blew on her tea and remained quiet for a few minutes, her good eye losing focus before she continued.

"Stina's cries alerted Mistress Toril, the jarl's daughter. The lady was out-raged and had the guard whipped. She meant well… But two nights hence, the vile man attacked my Stina in the dark. He would've killed her if Edda's arrival hadn't driven him off." The healer raised her gaze to Bergrún, tears glistening on her cheeks. "A freeman can beat any thrall," she explained. "But killing someone else's property is a crime. Edda carried my Stina home, and I've done what I can. Still, the fever gets worse by the hour. Fenrir's shadow lies heavy on my little girl." Hilde's shoulders sagged, and a tear fell onto her balled fist.

Bergrún reached out to touch the woman's shaking hand. "I'll try to help your daughter. I learned healing on my home island when I apprenticed with an old... woman."

* * *

"Where was your home?" Stina asked, five days later. She walked beside Bergrún toward a clearing in the forest. A light breeze carrying the smell of wet moss with a hint of salty spray played with her curly, auburn hair. The sun was already nearing the horizon as the two women set out to gather herbs and fungi.

Over the last days, Bergrún had spent every free moment caring for the young woman. At first, Hilde was alarmed to see the witch adding black henbane leaves to the mint tea. But as the fever vanished, so did the old healer's concerns. Bergrún sat through the nights with her patient, holding Stina's hand. The witch often had her eyes closed and hummed entrancing tunes. She startled when Hilde remarked on the semblance to melodies the healer knew from her home on Heilladur.

Much faster than anyone could expect, Stina was up and walking again. No bones seemed broken. Only a slight limp and the purple bruises on her youthful, freckled face told the story of her recent ordeal. Yet her large, green eyes shone with vitality.

"I grew up in Götaland," Bergrún said, her voice sounding distant before trailing off. "And you?" she asked after several minutes of silence. "You hail from Heilladur, right?"

"Yes, we do. How do you know? Did Edda tell you?"

"No. Something your mother said; I heard that expression before."

"Have you met many people from Heilladur, then?"

"A fair few." Bergrún's eyes turned northwest, seeking the ocean. But the dense trees blocked the view.

"You must've heard the rumors about us wicked heathens, the old wives' tales of witchcraft and devil worship," Stina exclaimed, a frown replacing the smile. "What's wrong with believing in nature spirits and Mother Earth's energy rather than Odin and his violent cohort?"

"People tell tales," Bergrún said. "Doesn't mean I believe; doesn't mean they're true."

"I wish they were. I wish I were a witch! They'd never have taken me."

About three years ago, Stina's father had taken the family on a trading journey to Norskvegn. The route was deemed safe, but a storm blew the vessel off course. Sailing too close to unfriendly shores, fast longboats soon gave chase. They surrounded the laden knarr like hungry wolves circling a pregnant deer. In the brief and uneven fight, her brother and father died defending the women.

"I was fourteen," Stina explained, "and small for my age. But I'd bitten, scratched, and kicked every man who tried to grab me. My mom told me I'd fought like a berserker. Alas, there were too many. They overpowered me. I don't remember much afterward," she said, lowering her gaze. "My mom says I didn't speak for a year. I didn't cry or weep, but every night, I wet my bed. The villagers thought I was possessed by the dead. So, at least they let us be."

A long silence fell. Stina sat on a toppled tree, shredding anemone leaves. Bergrún stood behind her, regarding the young woman's bowed head. Anger boiled like magma in the witch's chest, sending streams of liquid fire through her veins. She, too, felt the urge to rip something apart.

"They fear us, you know." Stina gave a mirthless laugh. She turned her head. Tears sparkled in the corners of her eyes. "The fine people of Hamarrfjord, they climb the hill, thralls and freemen alike, making signs to ward off evil. They mutter and grumble about unnatural forces at work. Nonetheless, they come for the drafts and potions my mother brews. If it were me, I'd have poisoned them all long ago. I wish I were the witch they believe me to be."

Stina stood, brushed her hands on her worn smock, and picked up the basket. "Was it nice in Götaland?" she asked. "Do you miss home?"

"I've never fit in," Bergrún scoffed. Spreading her arms, she amended, "Look at me. I'm neither tall nor blond, no blue-eyed shield maiden. Everybody in my village looked down on me. I was glad to leave."

"And your family?"

"My parents died in a fire; I saw the whole village burning."

"I'm sorry." Stina laid her hand on Bergrún's arm.

"It's not your fault!" Bergrún exclaimed, the bitterness of her memories seeping into her voice. "Too often, the world punishes those who seek to make it better."

"True, the Norns weave as they will," Stina replied. "We may never know the pattern, but every thread is needed. Fate brought you here to save me. Now, we're bonded. I needed you, and you... You may need me one day."

* * *

Twilight had fallen over the land, and the first stars shone in the east as the two women returned to the healer's hut. A cloudless sky promised a cold night. Bergrún's cloak fluttered in the wind. She carried this afternoon's harvest as Stina's limp had worsened with the dropping temperatures. Yet before either woman reached the house, the door flew open.

"There you are," Hilde exclaimed. "This is no time for leisurely strolls through the countryside. The jarl sent for you hours ago. His grandson is teething. He needs a chamomile salve to numb the pain. Hurry, girl! The guard wasn't pleased to return empty-handed."

"The guard? Who?" Stina stammered.

"It wasn't that vile Sverre Borgersen. He knows better than to come within one hundred paces of my hut. Jarl Gustav sent his great-nephew, and I had to make him wait. By Hela, take this flask and run to the lodge, else we might not live to see the sunrise."

"The lodge?" Stina shrieked. "Why me? Why haven't you given the flask to the guard?"

"Why, why, why? I can't give a potion for the highborn babe to an ignorant guardsman. I was about to hobble down to the village myself. Now stop being foolish and go!"

"I'll take it to the chieftain," Bergrún declared, seeing Stina shaking from head to toe.

"No good!" Hilde shook her head. "Guards wouldn't let you enter. They don't know you."

"Will you come with me?" Stina begged.

Half an hour later, Bergrún neared the impressive two-story manor in the village's center. Stina clung to her arm, pale as the rising moon. Braziers with burning logs stood to either side of the massive oaken door. Their firelight revealed a lone guard with his back to the approaching women, warming his hands over the flames. The crunching footsteps on the frozen ground drew his attention. Grabbing his spear, he turned, and Stina froze midstride, standing rooted to the ground.

"Who goes there?" Sverre Borgersen bellowed.

"Is that him?" Bergrún whispered in Stina's ear. The young woman's voice sounded like a shrew a moose had trodden on. "Don't worry," Bergrún said, squeezing her hand. "I'm here with you." To the guard, she called, "We're here by the jarl's orders to see to his grandchild."

"Show yourself!" The man stepped forward, gripping his spear in both hands. His knuckles turned white, and he attempted to bar the way. Dragging a petrified Stina along, Bergrún glared. The unreleased anger surged again in her chest. A dust devil rose from the ground, sending sparks from the braziers skyward, and all around, the window shutters rattled. Alarmed, the guard stumbled backward. Then, he recognized the frightened young woman clinging to Bergrún's arm.

"Witch!" he snarled. "You're dead. Has your ghost come to haunt me? Go back! No further! The fires shall burn you!" He pushed one brazier over and kicked the burning logs onto the path.

"What's going on?" a second male voice shouted. The tall figure of Olver Agnarsen, Shield of Hamarrfjord, rounded a corner and stepped into the light. With his sword in hand, the warrior looked from the flustered guard to the approaching women.

"It's her!" Sverre answered. "The witch from Heilladur. The ghost of the healer's daughter. Hold her off! I'll call for more swords." His voice vibrated with tension, and his eyes darted between the women and his commander.

"Get a grip, man! Her name is Stina, and she looks quite alive to me."

"She can't be!" Sverre protested. "She's dead. I... I mean, she died."

"You mean, you've almost beaten her to death. She survived, and you know it. Otherwise, the jarl would have you executed."

"He wouldn't. She's a witch. How else would she be walking and talking so soon after..."

"She is the healer's daughter."

"A WITCH!" Sverre shrieked. Lowering his spear, he charged forward until Olver's sword blocked his path.

"Enough!" the commander bellowed. "Pull yourself together."

"You don't know anything!" the guard wailed. His voice had risen two octaves. "That night in the lodge, she'd bewitched me. It was her fault, but I got flogged. And the other night, she attacked me with dark magic. I only defended myself, yet I got flogged again. Now she's come to finish me off!"

Olver grabbed the smaller man by his collar and hoisted him in the air.

"Listen to me, Sverre Borgersen. Everybody in Hamarrfjord knows what kind of despicable man you are. If we weren't kin, however distant, I'd have had you thrown from the guard years ago. I almost wish she were a ghost seeking revenge. You lay hands on that woman again, or any woman for that matter, and I'll break every bone in your body."

"Lies!" he squealed. "All lies. It was her fault."

"Tell this to the devil when you meet her," Olver snarled. "Toril and Edda saw you, remember?"

"Lies! Can't trust the lies of womenfolk, you fool. Their words are poison! They are all witches!" Sverre croaked as Olver's powerful grip constricted his windpipe. With a yelp, the gasping man flew through the air and crashed against the great hall's front door.

"What did you call my betrothed?" Olver bellowed, looming over Sverre. Raising his sword, the tall warrior was about to deliver a deadly blow when Stina intervened.

"Don't!" she begged. "Not on my behalf. And not on Mistress Toril's either. She wouldn't want you to slay your kin."

Olver stood for two heartbeats, his weapon gleaming red in the firelight. Then, he kicked the fallen man in the stomach.

"Get out of here, out of the village. If I ever see you again, I'll cut you open like a pig!" Two more kicks followed before he sheathed his sword and leaned against the doorframe. His beaten opponent pushed himself to all fours and vomited.

Bergrún, who'd observed the proceedings with vindictive enjoyment, shook her head in disapproval of Stina's intervention. She would've loved to watch one vile creature slaughter another. But it didn't matter. Sverre Borgersen wouldn't survive the night.

In fact, I prefer it this way, she thought.

CHAPTER FIVE

Witchcraft

"STINA IS ASLEEP now." Bergrún pulled the wooden stool back and dropped onto the wobbly seat. Hilde bustled over, putting a steaming mug of tea in front of the exhausted-looking woman. The witch lifted the chipped cup in both hands, relishing the warmth and enjoying the rich aroma of mint and clover.

"Did you give her more henbane infusion?" the older healer asked.

"No, we just talked, and I held her hand. I don't want Stina to become too dependent on the draughts."

"Thank the Norns for your presence, Agnetha. What would I have done without you?"

"Don't invoke the Norns!" Bergrún scoffed. "Their whims are capricious. How I long to be free of their wicked weaving." Putting her tea down, she rubbed her eyes.

Three days had passed since Stina had come face-to-face with her tormentor. The unfortunate event had reduced the fragile young woman to a frightened fawn, cowering at the slightest sound and recoiling at any sudden movement. Bergrún finished their duties at the chieftain's longhouse before guiding her friend home. Every night, she spent hours until Stina fell asleep, caring for her like the child the witch never had.

"He wouldn't dare come here," Hilde reassured. "Not after the shield's intervention."

"Oh, he'll never come near her again," Bergrún chuckled. "Believe me."

The women sat in silence for a long while, sipping tea, lost in their own thoughts. The logs crackled, and the soft breeze in the rafters made Bergrún drowsy. She'd just drifted into slumber when something slammed against the window shutters with great force.

"What was that?" the witch cried, startled awake. She looked to Hilde and saw the color drain from the woman's face as shouts rose from outside, followed by a series of heavy thumps.

"Trouble!" the old healer exclaimed. "Quickly, help me bar the door." She pushed the oaken table over with surprising strength, and both women shoved the rough-hewn furniture in front of the door. They barely managed before the boards rattled and the frame cracked. Heavy objects battered the warped timbers.

"Take Stina and get out!" Hilde shouted. "Through the back and into the forest."

"Why? What is this madness?" Bergrún shrieked. The sound of an axe splintering the wood was all the answer she needed. "Villagers," she hissed. "Riled up by Sverre's twisted tales. I'll deal with them!" the witch growled, fury replacing her confusion.

"Don't be foolish! These men are armed, angry, and probably drunk. You need to get out. Please, once more, save my Stina!" Hilde's voice cracked. Her body trembled, and tears glistened on her cheek. Grabbing her frayed broom in both hands like a warrior's longsword, the woman gave Bergrún one more pleading look before turning toward the violent axe strikes devouring her front door.

Bergrún's blood boiled, the feeling of helplessness stoking her ever-present fury. Yet Hilde was right; she couldn't win an open fight against these men, not without everybody losing.

This isn't my fight! The sudden thought sprang into the witch's mind, blocking all other concerns until a profound realization flushed it away. *This has always been my fight... because these are my people, my kin, my friends!*

With a cry of anguish and despair, the witch exploded the roof, sending beams and stone slabs onto the assailants outside. She met Hilde's gaze, her own jaw set, and gave the old healer a single, sharp nod of grim understanding. Then she was off, pulling the drowsy Stina from her bed, hurtling down into the cellar, and out the obscured back door.

* * *

BERGRÚN DRAGGED HER friend into the forest. Both women stumbled over roots and rocks. Impenetrable darkness lay ahead as heavy clouds covered the moon. Behind, the flickering torchlight grew into something more sinister.

"Is it Sverre?" Stina wailed. Bergrún didn't respond. The certainty that Sverre wasn't involved provided little solace. She pushed onward, eager to put as much distance as possible between them and the burning hut.

Stina fell. Her high-pitched scream pierced the night. Lifting the fallen girl to her feet, Bergrún saw two lights detaching themselves from the glow.

"*Skitr!*" she cursed. "Come on, Stina."

Blood coated the young woman's shin, and Stina's ankle refused to carry her weight. The witch pulled her friend's arm over her shoulder, dragging the injured woman along until a bramble thicket barred the way. The sound of waves crashing into rocks hinted at a cliff not far beyond. She lowered Stina onto a rock and gathered branches to hide their presence. Yet, the younger woman's cry had given the hunters a target. Their bobbing lights grew inexorably closer. Soon, Bergrún heard the crunching of leaves and snapping of branches under stamping boots.

"How many are there?" Stina asked.

"A lot fewer, soon," Bergrún growled. She closed her eyes, flexed her fingers, and began humming strange words. With a clap and a shout, a whirlwind rose from her outstretched palms. Leaves rustled, trees swayed, and wood groaned. A dozen sharp cracks sounded as thick tree branches broke loose, hurtling down on their pursuers.

The men stumbled, screaming in pain and rage. But several got back up. They closed in, their angry footfalls squashing any hope of salvation. The witch sagged, the fire in her eyes dimming.

"They're going to kill us," Stina whispered. Her voice had lost all inflection, sounding hollow, dead. "Why?"

Because life is a never-ending misery, the witch thought. Her healing and care, her friendship and protection—they'd been nothing more than an early spring day in February, to be snuffed out by brutal winter winds.

"I'm so sorry I dragged you into this," Stina whispered, squeezing Bergrún's hand. "You were right. All too often, the world punishes those who seek to make it better."

Only fifty feet remained between the women and their executioners—three men with axes and spears. Shadows hid their faces, but Bergrún could sense their hatred emanating in waves. Her stomach churned. Her foolish actions were to blame for their attack, but Stina would pay the bitter price.

Bergrún blinked, and for a brief moment, she was back on Heillaður, alone in a dark forest, a young girl chased by laughing brutes. She'd felt so weak and powerless in her humiliation. The absolute knowledge that no one in her entire village would bat an eye over the fate of the young outcast and the despicable acts the men would do to her had scorched her insides as if someone had shoved glowing embers down her throat. Her body jerked, and she was back with Stina.

"No!" she growled like the rumbling of an avalanche. *This is not how it ends.*

The brambles rustled nearby. The witch snapped her head to the side. Letting her mind whip through the darkness, she detected a presence. A she-wolf hid in the underbrush, crouching. Separated from the pack, the animal sought shelter from the hunting party. Bergrún felt an immediate kinship. She, too, was a lone she-wolf in a hostile forest. Yet, she was no longer weak and powerless. Stina's innocent life was in grave danger.

The witch stood. Stretching her hands to the heavens, daring the Gods, she shouted in defiance.

"*Ráðast á! Bíta! Drepa!*" Her words bounced from tree to tree.

Then, she crumpled like a sail shorn from the mast.

* * *

"THERE THEY ARE," Haddur Borgersen shouted. "Lyngar, cover the right side. Mikkel, to my left. Grímnir, with me. Move, before these fiends call on more dark magic!"

"Grímnir fell," Lyngar replied, "struck by a branch."

"Doesn't matter. We'll take care of him after we're finished. Onward, men, for blood and glory!"

"What's there?" Mikkel called. He lowered his spear.

"Only a wolf," Haddur replied. "Leave it. Focus on the women."

"Eya! Ha! Fya!" Mikkel shouted. He waved his torch, leaving red afterimages in the forest's darkness and the beast's glowing eyes. The wolf dodged, avoiding the flames. Then, with a forceful leap, the animal attacked. Its fangs tore into Mikkel's forearm, ripping through the leather arm brace, tearing skin and muscle. Bones splintered like frozen timber. Howling in pain, Mikkel shook his mangled limb, trying to dislodge the vicious predator.

"By Odin!" Lyngar shouted. Taking two strides, he rammed his spear into the wolf's flank. The animal let go with a yelp. Both Mikkel and the beast fell to the ground. Lyngar twisted his spear before pulling it free. Blood coated the broad iron tip.

He bent to lift his comrade to his feet. Yet his attack must only have grazed the wolf's side. With a guttural snarl, the beast lunged. Its fangs sank into the fallen man's throat, turning his cries into gurgles.

Lyngar stood frozen in shock, watching his comrade's body twitch and fall limp. The wolf's head turned, teeth bared. Blood dripped from its muzzle. With its fur raised, an unnatural red fire burned in the animal's eyes. The Viking dropped his spear. His mighty shield slipped from his numb fingers, landing with a dull thud on the forest floor.

"What is wrong with you?" Haddur bellowed. "Kill the beast!"

But Lyngar retreated on shaking legs.

"The devil," he muttered. "It's the devil!"

"Out of my way!" Haddur shoved his terrified companion aside. He swung his axe in a wide arc, the torchlight reflecting on the gleaming weapon. The wolf evaded the blade, yet its movements became sluggish. The second swing hit, severing the animal's right front leg. Blood sprayed like a fountain, filling the air with its metallic taste. The wounded beast tried to roll out of harm's way. Too late. The next blow split its spine, severing the hip from the torso.

"There!" Haddur huffed. "Now pull yourself together. Find these witches!" He emphasized his frustration with a kick at the bloodied carcass. Another kick followed. With unnatural speed, the butchered wolf's jaw clamped onto Haddur's ankle like a vise.

"Argh!" screamed the surprised warrior. "By Hela, let go!" Over and over, he swung his axe, yet the pressure did not relent. Tendons snapped, and bones cracked. "Help me!" Haddur shrieked in agony.

Yet Lyngar was gone. Shouting at the top of his lungs, the warrior fled headlong into the darkness. "Devil! It's the DEVIL!"

* * *

THE COLD AND damp caused gooseflesh to rise on Stina's bare skin, her tattered nightshirt providing little protection. The smell of rotten vegetables mixed with the woody scent of peat. She shivered. Wrapping her arms tight around her knees, the girl perched on a fragile crate like a delicate songbird in a cast-iron cage. With eyes pressed shut and head bent, she sat as far away from Bergrún as the tiny, makeshift prison cell allowed.

The witch sat across from her on the uneven ground. Her head rested against the wet fieldstone wall. The circular pit, not more than six spans wide, gave her the impression of sitting at the bottom of a well. She felt drained; a bone-deep weariness persisted despite the recent harvest of Grímnir's vitality. She had stretched herself too far, come too close to burning herself out.

And for what? For nothing! she thought bitterly.

After fighting off the axe-wielding mob, they'd returned to the smoldering remains of healer Gunhild's hut only to be surrounded by a second group of warriors geared up for battle. The jarl's guards pried Stina away from the body of her slain mother and marched both women in a block of shields back to the village, where they led them into this abandoned root cellar.

Bergrún opened her eyes. Faint light from above seeped through the cracks in the wooden trapdoor. The scraping of objects across the floor had ended a while ago. Now, only infrequent footsteps of a lone sentry interrupted the monotonous sound of dripping water.

They'd heaped chests and barrels over the exit to keep us from escaping, the witch thought. *As if that made any difference.* She regarded Stina, her 'friend'—the young woman for whom she'd risked it all, whom she'd healed and protected. *She's too disgusted to even look at me! There's your reward for caring,* Bergrún scoffed. *Truly, no good deed goes unpunished.*

"You did that," Stina whispered after what felt like an eternity. The half-question, half-statement hovered between the women. Bergrún balled her fists, yet didn't speak. A drop of icy water landed on her bare collarbone, running down her skin and raising gooseflesh. Still, no sound escaped her lips. The silence stretched, thick and heavy.

"You caused it all," Stina insisted. She peered around the pitcher with water and the covered loaf of bread that rested untouched on a wooden block in the room's center.

"What?" Bergrún's throat was dry, adding a menacing rasp to her words.

"The wind, the branches..."

"We were near the cliff," the witch interjected. "Strong gusts often blow inland from the sea."

"And the wolf?" Stina asked, her voice thin and shaky, rising in pitch.

"Keep your voice down!" Bergrún hissed. "They're listening." Her gaze wandered up to the trapdoor.

"Do you deny it?" Stina asked in an agitated whisper.

"What do you want from me?" Bergrún replied.

"The truth."

"And what has the truth ever done for you? Did the truth save your father and brother? Did the truth stop the men from violating you? Did the truth heal your injuries?" Despite her own advice, Bergrún's voice rose in anger. "Truth is what the powerful declare it to be," she growled.

Stina recoiled.

Seeing her glowing red eyes reflected in the younger woman's frightened stare, the witch took deep, steadying breaths. She raised her hands, palms up in a gesture of peace. "I kept us alive," she finally amended. "But we're not out of danger yet. That is the truth."

"How?" Stina's voice was so low, Bergrún almost missed it. She didn't answer. Stina unfolded her limbs. She straightened up, leaned forward, and looked her fellow captive in the eyes. "Who are you?"

* * *

The midday sun hid behind an overcast sky as half the jarl's guard force, with weapons at the ready, escorted the prisoners to wooden benches in the center of the village square. Iron manacles lay ready to bind the women, and the guards formed a tight circle blocking anyone from getting out or in.

Two days had passed since the attack on the healer. Bergrún's back ached. Narrowing her eyes against the bright sunlight, she regarded the scene with growing unease. The odds were stacked against her, her options limited. Would her grand plan to coerce a Viking leader end in another pile of ashes?

The aging jarl sat in an ornate driftwood chair atop the steps to the great hall, wrapped in blankets and looking ill. His personal protector, Olver, stood to the right, his daughter to his left. Most of the village seemed in attendance, freemen and thralls alike. Turning her head, the witch spotted her fellow captives from Fårosünd with expressions of glee on their ugly faces. Bergrún realized that she must project what she expected to see; the women were too far away to make out their expressions. Close by, however, on cushioned chairs sat the two surviving men of the bloody attack. The witch had no problem reading the hatred and anger burning in the leader's poisonous glare.

Jarl Gustav raised his bejeweled war axe, and the villagers fell silent, the excited murmurs dying down as every eye turned to the chieftain.

"Proceed, Toril," the chieftain commanded. His voice, deep and gravelly with age, was tinged with a wheezing rattle. He coughed, causing renewed murmurs to erupt. Toril took a deep breath, her gaze fixed on her father, and with a slight nod, she began to speak.

"Two nights ago, unprovoked violence erupted in our village. Under the cover of darkness, vile creatures committed crimes—atrocities that demand retribution, justice, and yes, harsh punishment without mercy, for innocent lives were lost. Blood clings to the hands of murderers."

"Aye, those witches must burn!" Haddur Borgersen shouted. He stomped his bandaged leg in agitation and winced as a jolt of pain spread from his ankle. Lyngar sat next to him, motionless, his stare blank.

"I wasn't finished," Toril said. "But since you're eager to speak, let's hear your story."

Haddur shot Toril an angry look. Then he stood, turned to the assembled crowd, and raised his hand to point at the bound women.

"These fiends... these witches! They attacked us with dark magic and..."

"Yes, yes. We'll come to that. But let's start at the beginning."

"Don't interrupt me, woman! Or I will..."

"You will treat my daughter with respect!" Jarl Gustav bellowed. He had risen to his feet in one swift motion, looming over the men below.

"As I was saying," Toril continued. "We'll come to your adventures in the forest. Let's start with your reason for being there. What were you doing at healer Gunhild's hut?"

"I was killing witches," he screamed.

"You admit to killing healer Gunhild?"

"Yes!"

"Breaking her door, setting the house on fire?"

"Yes."

"Slaying a defenseless old woman and chasing her daughter into the forest?"

"I don't like your question!"

"Answer this one, and I'll ask the next."

"I was... We made sure these witches paid for their evil deeds."

"But it was your idea? You convinced Mikkel, Grímnir, and Lyngar," Toril nodded to the man next to Haddur, who still hadn't moved a muscle. "You convinced these men to aid you in your act of violence?"

"Watch your tongue, woman!" Haddur shouted, causing Olver to step forward, gripping his sword. Toril raised her hand, signaling him to stay back.

"You and your men destroyed a house and killed a woman. I've never been on a raid to know exactly where such an act would land on the scale of usual violence. Yet, from where I stand, it sure looks violent to me."

Haddur looked at Toril, his eyes wide, his eyebrows furrowed, and his jaw slack. "Wait... what?" he mumbled.

"Can you tell me why you were so eager to kill these women?" Toril spoke very slowly, enunciating every syllable.

"My brother," he stammered. Then, with more force, he amended, "These witches killed my brother!"

"Your brother, Sverre, whom the Finsgúr boy discovered in the stables?"

"He's dead! These witches killed him!"

"He is indeed dead," Toril replied. "Erik found him on the morning of your attack, face down in the water trough. Have you seen these women or the late healer Gunhild murdering your brother?"

"No, but I know because..."

"Because your brother assaulted poor Stina twice, leaving her one inch from death?"

"Thrice," Olver interjected.

"Oh yes, thrice, my mistake. Thank you, Olver. That's why you dismissed him from the guards, right?" she asked.

"THEY KILLED HIM!" Haddur shouted.

"How?" Toril asked. "We found no wounds on his body." The jarl's daughter walked toward the accused women. "Look at Stina," she commanded. "The girl weighs no more than a wet cat. Your brother was big, at least sixteen stone. How do you think she managed to kill him?"

"With dark magic!" Haddur spat. "We witnessed those fiends use their evil magic on us."

"Like what?" Toril asked.

"The house exploded, beams falling, stone slabs raining down on us."

"You mean the house collapsed after you set it on fire? Houses do that, especially poorly maintained servants' quarters."

"The wind in the forest..."

"The northern cliffs are a mere mile from the hut, the former hut, I should say. This time of year, the wind often gusts from the sea."

"Branches rained down on us..."

"Because of the wind we just discussed," Toril mused.

"And the wolf?" Anger blazed in his eyes. "The wolf attack... Was that also the wind?" he sneered.

"No, that was a she-wolf defending her cubs. We found her litter in a den nearby."

"That was no mere she-wolf; that was the devil. Ask Lyngar."

"Lyngar?" Toril asked, turning to the second man. "Can you corroborate Haddur's tale?"

Lyngar remained motionless, his shoulders sagging, his eyes unfocused.

"Coro-boro-tate?" Haddur huffed.

"Co-rob-o-rate," Toril explained. "It means to confirm a story by providing proof."

"This ain't no story, woman. I'm telling the truth. I won't stand for this any longer. You paint me the villain! These women are witches. They're on trial here."

"No, Haddur," Toril replied, shaking her head. "You are! For the unprovoked murder of my father's thrall, for the wanton destruction of my father's property, for the deliberate attempt to murder two more thralls you don't own. You are on trial, and you have been found guilty."

Spiderwebs

"WHAT'LL HAPPEN TO these men?" Rikard asked. He'd arrived late for the trial, delayed by an "urgent" matter Edda had reported, which turned out to be nothing of the sort.

"Our laws require a life for a life," Toril explained, climbing the stairs beside him. "Lyngar chose enthrallment; to be sold into exile from Hamarrfjord. Haddur..." She paused, biting her lip. "He invoked an old right. A gamble with the sea."

"What do you mean?" The two cousins had reached the plain oaken door to the jarl's chambers but signaled the guard to wait before announcing their presence.

"Haddur's father, Borger Carlov, was Hamarrfjord's foremost shipwright and a close boyhood friend of my father. His ancestry is Tatar, hailing from the East. His people brought strange customs from their lands. They tie the convicted criminal to a pole at low tide with his head one hand below the expected flood line. When the tide rolls in and he drowns, the sea accepts his guilt and washes his soul clean. If the tide remains low, however, he is granted a boat and provisions and cast into exile."

"And Haddur chose that?"

"He must prefer the risk to a life in bondage," Toril replied. Before they could discuss the issue further, the door flung open. Olver poked his head out.

"There you are," he admonished. "The jarl is waiting!" He stepped aside and ushered them in. Jarl Gustav stood at the open window, a cup of spiced mead steaming beside him.

"Father," Toril said. "You shouldn't stand in the draft."

"Are you our new healer now, too?"

"No, but I am…"

"Wiser than everybody else?" he turned. Creases deepened on his weatherworn face. His lips stretched into a thin line, and he glared at the new arrivals. "Are you the new chieftain of Hamarrfjord already? Must I bow and swear my fealty?"

"Father!" Toril huffed. "We've talked about what was best. You agreed." Turning to Olver, she amended, "Please make sure Stina is well cared for; I'll see her a little later."

"My Shield stays!" Gustav Larsen growled. "He is family, father of my grandchild, is he not? Oh, wait. Little Morton doesn't carry Olver's name, nor do you carry his wedding band."

"Forgive me, uncle," Rikard stammered. "I should see to…"

"You'll stay as well!" the jarl bellowed. A vicious bout of coughing followed, and Toril rushed to help her father into the chair by the fire. "You are my blood, son," the aging chieftain croaked. "The future of Hamarrfjord lies as much in your hands as in my cunning daughter's talons." Yet, despite the harsh words, he'd softened his tone and accepted Toril's fussing.

"Now, sit! All of you," he ordered after taking a deep draft of the spiced mead. "Today, my daughter, you made many people very angry. You might even have garnered a few mighty enemies."

"We discussed this. I was just…"

"I'm talking, woman! Must I have my Shield gag you to get a word in?" The glare of his pale blue eyes lingered on his daughter like a cold blade against a bare throat. Toril recoiled. She folded her hands in her lap and lowered her eyes. Yet the icy silence that followed hinted at a limit almost reached.

"I've convicted two men for a 'crime' most villagers wouldn't raise a crow's caw about. They'd more likely applaud the deed, if not openly, then deep in their superstitious hearts." Jarl Gustav looked from Toril to Olver to Rikard and back to his daughter, daring them to argue. No one spoke, and a palpable unease settled over the room. After a long pause, the jarl nodded, accepting their unspoken consent.

"I stand by my decision," he declared. "We cannot have baseless accusations and irrational fears divide our society. The law must stand!" Toril raised her head, but her father's unwavering glare kept her lips sealed.

"You," he continued, "in your determination to save that girl, or maybe to protect all the girls beneath Odin's gaze, you have humiliated the men. You've flaunted your wits and twisted Haddur's words. You've shown the assembled village that a warrior's prowess counts less than a woman's tongue. In doing so, you've unleashed a tidal wave of fear that'll crash down upon any woman who dares rise above her station. Think on that!"

Toril twisted in her seat, not meeting her father's gaze. Seconds passed with the viscosity of frozen honey. Only the creaking of chairs, caused by their anxious inhabitants, dared to break the silence. Finally, Jarl Gustav rose.

"What's done is done; pointless to argue about the pattern after the Norns' loom has fallen silent. You may leave now. We'll talk more on the morrow."

Toril got to her feet and walked to the door with the expression of a convict climbing the steps to the gallows. Rikard got to the door first and opened it for his cousin, eager to be anywhere else.

"Stay, Rikard," the chieftain asked, sounding tired. "Olver, you go with Toril. I'm sure I'm safe with my nephew."

* * *

Olver closed the door. Turning to his beloved, he asked, "Are you all right?"

"Don't!" Toril cried, her voice brittle. She turned away in a desperate attempt to retain her composure. "See to Stina and send Edda to my room," she said, dabbing tears from her eyes. "Tell her to meet me after the next bell."

"Where will you go?"

"Do it!" she shrieked, her voice shrill as the cry of a hawk. A crimson blush had flooded her cheeks, and her lips quivered. Then, laying her trembling hand on his arm, she sought his eyes. "Please, Olver, I'm sorry. Do me the favor. I need to go; I'll explain later." Without another word, she turned and rushed along the hallway, disappearing into the room at its end.

She closed the door and stood for several heartbeats with her back against the frame, banging her head against the wood in frustration. She'd never been so humiliated. Inhaling deeply, she squeezed her eyes shut, willing her fury to subside.

Finally calmed, she untied her wrap skirt, revealing leather leggings underneath. She kicked her boots off and climbed a shelf filled with ugly plunder. Reaching the top, Toril lay on her stomach and inched forward.

The gap felt much tighter than in her childhood days. Cursing under her breath and wriggling like an eel, she managed to squeeze into the attic space above the jarl's living quarters. Feathers and bird droppings covered the floor. Careful to avoid disturbing the loose boards, she pressed her ear against the dusty wood.

"... since your brother's departure," she heard her father say.

"I'm well, I guess," Rikard answered. "Edda tells me what to do. Sometimes, I wonder who's the master and who's the servant."

"I wonder that a lot lately," Jarl Gustav grunted. "Quite a lot."

"Toril means well... how she stood up for Stina."

"The dead bodies of well-meaning fools could raise a dam from Inglandia to Norskvegn."

"She isn't a fool," Rikard objected.

"Most of the time, she isn't. But as often as the sea smokes, she acts like the queen of them all. Listen, son," Gustav Larsen said, raising his hand as Rikard was about to protest. "I didn't keep you behind to hear me speak ill of my daughter. I love her, and I know her heart is in the right place. But I need you to help her."

"How?"

"What I'm telling you now, no one knows except for Toril and me."

* * *

DARKNESS HAD SETTLED, the candles spent, and the fire burned to smoldering ashes. Olver Agnarsen's back arched. His powerful hands clenched the armrest with all his strength, torturing leather, wood, and padding alike. His chest heaved, pumping like the forge's bellows. With every muscle taut, every tendon stretched, his entire body shook with the frenzied beat of his heart, sending vibrations into the floor beams.

The large house had fallen silent hours ago, except for the ever-present wind whistling through cracks in the wood. Fighting to remain quiet, the Viking warrior squeezed his eyelids shut. Yet pained moans escaped his taut lips as long, red nails bit into his exposed flesh. With a muffled, animal groan, he spasmed, his hips bucking. The rattle of the heavy chair reverberated through the quiet room. Then, he fell limp, spent, his breathing shallow and ragged. Yet a grin widened on his relaxing face.

Toril got to her feet, wiped her mouth, and went to the pitcher of ale warming near the hearth. She drank deep, savoring the rich, overpowering bitterness. Turning around, she smiled, seeing her consort's drained body drooping spreadeagled over the cushioned armchair like a discarded robe.

"What do you think about Stina and that mysterious Agnetha?" she asked in a conversational tone.

"You ask me now," he wheezed, "what I think? About other women?"

"I do. You fancy that little red-haired vixen. Do you imagine her kneeling before you? She can't be as innocent as she looks," she teased.

Her playful tone suggested she didn't mind whether her words rang true.

"Heart of mine," he gave a strained laugh, which turned into a cough. "You overestimate the ability of men to think of anything in moments like this."

"I often overestimate the ability of men to think," she mused, filling a second cup of ale. "Take dear Rikard, for example. Has he truly fallen for the new thrall? She feels dangerous, too dangerous for a green lad." Toril walked barefoot across the room, handing the cup to Olver. Climbing onto the overlarge bed covered in furs and goose-down feather pillows, she let her hand feel the softness of a wolf's pelt. "If we don't watch out for him, she might turn out to be a she-wolf and devour my poor cousin."

"Would that be so bad?" he asked after laying his head in her lap.

"Of course," she huffed, slapping him. "He's my favorite cousin, my blood."

"Exactly, as the jarl said, right after biting your head off today." Imitating the jarl's deep and gravelly voice, Olver recited, "You are my blood, son."

"So you can think after all, sweetling," she laughed. "There's more to you than meets the eye, or met the eye earlier, I should say," she chuckled, looking down at his naked body.

"Talking about your father's words..." Olver turned his head to look Toril in the eyes. "What's that about Morton not carrying my name?" The window shutters rattled in a sudden gust, and drafts of icy air seeped into the room. Toril shivered. Pulling the furs tight around her bare shoulders, she fixed her eyes on the faint glow of the dying embers.

"Remember the prophecy?" she finally asked. "Gustav told Rikard about it. I overheard them."

"Don't lure me onto a stroll into the marshes," he replied, a bitter edge to his voice. "What about my son's name?" The bed creaked as Olver sat upright, his shoulders tense, his eyes on hers.

"The prophecy," she said, her voice urgent. "It speaks of our downfall. A bloody war of kin against kin, all-consuming fires." She took his hand. "Only the bold actions of a woman, her vision breaking with traditions, can save our people. And she needs a warrior at her side. Don't you see, Olver?" she pleaded. "It's us, you and me. We carry this burden. And our son... he's the future, the new beginning—the true son of Hamarrfjord. His name is our hope; his name is Morton Gustav Bror Hamarrsen."

"So why haven't you told me?"

"I know how deep the roots of tradition reach. I'm not as ignorant of our people's feelings as my father proclaimed. Change is hard; too much change is dangerous. But Olver," she took his face in her hands. "Names are powerful; names shape destiny. I had to trust my intuition. Please trust my love for you." Her breath caught, causing her voice to tremble. She pulled him close and kissed him.

* * *

"Who's there?" Olver called hours later in response to an insistent knock at the door. Darkness still blanketed the room. Even the wind's constant whisper had ceased as if to rest before the new day's dawn. Yet the warrior sat bolt upright, his hand gripping the sword leaning against the bed frame.

"Hail, Shield Agnarsen. It's Holger Claassen with an urgent report."

"Come in! Is it time? How long until low tide?"

"What's happening?" Toril asked, rubbing her eyes as the door swung open. A warrior stepped in and bowed, followed by Edda carrying a tray of tea and smørrebrød.

"I need to get up and see to Haddur's punishment," Olver explained in a gentle tone. "Go back to sleep."

"Forgive me, Shield. There's still an hour until low tide. But the punishment won't be possible." The warrior lowered his gaze, shifting his feet. "Haddur is dead. Both men are, he and Lyngar," he amended. "Dead on the floor. No blood, no marks."

"Who knows?" Olver asked, slipping into his tunic and breeches.

"Bjorn was guarding the house. I found him asleep, difficult to rouse, as if he were drugged. Else, only you and..." He spread his hands, indicating everyone present in the room.

"This cannot become known!" Toril hissed, wide awake now.

"I know," Olver replied. He had finished dressing and marched across the room with sword and shield in hand. "I'll handle the men. Lead on, Holger!" he commanded. Edda stepped out of the way. Placing the tray on the windowsill, she closed the door behind the men.

"What happened?" Toril demanded.

"Quite a lot, Mistress. Quite a lot!"

Edda helped Toril dress, poured her tea, and ushered her mistress to sit and eat before giving her report. "Some tidings settle like jagged flintstones in an empty stomach," the old woman said.

"Stop fussing, mother hen, and tell me the news."

"Well," Edda started, taking the seat across from Toril. "You had worried about poking a hornet's nest with Haddur's trial. I'd say you've found a big one, smashed it clean off the tree, cracked it open, and made us all dance naked among enraged stingers. If it weren't for the tiring effect of strong ale, the tavern crowd might have set the great hall on fire last night. If they learn of the condemned men's deaths…"

"Olver will handle that. His men are loyal to the death."

"Your word in Odin's ears. Because that's not all."

"What do you mean?"

"Your father's doubts about the succession. Aren't you worried about his conversation with Rikard?" Edda asked.

"Of course, I am. I heard the whole thing. He told Rikard the prophecy and asked him to help me."

"What will the boy do? Can you bring him into your schemes?"

"No, not yet. He's growing up, starting to have his own ideas. But he glorifies his brother. Honor and honesty, bravery and tradition—all that nonsense," she scoffed. "We have to be very careful in steering him our way."

"We might not have time to be careful. The chieftain's health is failing. He coughs up blood, eats little, and sleeps poorly. And with the healer dead…"

"Are you trying to drown me in ill portents, woman?" Toril hissed. "Making up for the tide failing to claim dear Haddur?" She slammed her teacup onto the polished table, leaving a visible dent in the delicate inlay.

"I'm just honest. The situation is dire. We have limited options." Edda leaned forward. Her weather-beaten face looked ghostly in the pale, pre-dawn light. "The only choice I see," she whispered, "is risky, very risky."

* * *

BERGRÚN FOLLOWED EDDA into a chamber off the great hall. The rising sun painted the small, east-facing room orange, the gleam reflecting on polished weapons adorning the walls. The jarl's daughter sat in a straight-backed chair beside the unlit fireplace, wearing a blue dress with a tight bodice and fur collar. Long braids of blond hair were woven around her head like a crown, glowing in the soft light while her face remained obscured by shadow.

"Your name is Agnetha?" the highborn woman asked.

"Yes, Mistress," Bergrún replied. She stood in the middle of the room, her hands clasped in front, and her gaze lowered.

"An unusual name. You don't hail from Fårosünd?"

"No, Mistress. I grew up in Lindvik in Götaland."

"That's where you learned healing? Edda told me about your astonishing care for poor Stina."

"Yes, Mistress. I apprenticed with the local healer."

"Apprenticed? How old are you?" Toril had risen from her seat and begun circling Bergrún.

"Twenty winters, Mistress. I worked for three years with the healer."

"Do you know runes and letters?"

"Very little. Apologies, Mistress."

"No need to apologize. And no need to call me 'Mistress' all the time when we're alone. My name is Toril, and I'm grateful for what you've done. Stina is dear to me."

"Yes, Mistress... I mean, yes."

"How is she?"

"Still weak and sad. But very grateful for your help," Bergrún rushed to amend. "We both are very grateful. We never expected a highborn mistress like yourself to..." Toril raised her hand, and Bergrún fell silent at once.

"I share her grief for the loss of her mother. I was very young when my mother died, but not a day goes by without..." the jarl's daughter let her voice trail off. She stood less than an arm's length away. "Stina will remain under my father's roof, and I'll take care of her. That's the least I can do."

"That is very gracious of you, Mistress Toril. Thank you!" Bergrún bobbed a clumsy curtsy.

"You've done much more for her, and I thank you, Agnetha. I wish I could ask you to do the same for my father. His cough does not get better. And with healer Gunhild gone..."

"Of course, Mistress. I do as you command."

"If only it were that easy. My cousin Rikard claimed you, and he seems very protective of his... thrall." Toril had turned her back on Bergrún and walked to the window.

"I'm sure he'll agree. He must be worried about his uncle."

"Do you know my cousin that well?" Toril asked. "Powerful men plot their own destinies. If my father were to die... Rikard was very angry with me when Olver took you and Stina to safety. He accused me of mistreating his property." She turned and looked Bergrún straight in the eyes. "If I could be sure about his intentions, if I could know what he thinks. I love my cousin like a brother, and I want to trust him. I need to know if I can," she pleaded.

To suppress a knowing smile, Bergrún forced her eyes wide and let her mouth drop open.

Is that an actual tear on her cheek? the witch thought. *Impressive!*

The trial had demonstrated this woman's wit and determination. Now, Bergrún couldn't help but admire the skill of a fellow manipulator. Lowering her gaze and shuffling her feet, she took a brief pause before stammering her response.

"Mistress Toril, I don't know what to say. I don't think Master Rikard... He seems like a kindhearted man. On Fårosünd, he fought to protect me."

"Yes, I heard about the duel. He killed a fellow warrior in cold blood to get what he wanted. And now, he carries the banner of Leif Rødskæg, demonstrating his legacy. Perhaps his destiny? I just don't know him anymore," Toril lamented.

"Mistress Toril, I'll do anything."

"I think you should go now. Perhaps, if you ask to care for my father, he will let you leave the house. But be careful. Don't anger him; don't tell Rikard of my fears. I want to trust him; I need to trust him. Please, help me understand if I can trust him."

"Of course, Mistress Toril. I owe you my life. Whatever I can, I'll gladly do."

CHAPTER SEVEN

Revelations

Bergrún stepped out of the longhouse. The sun had crested the horizon, climbing a pale blue sky. A gentler breeze had replaced last night's wild gusts of wind, herding gray clouds eastward. The witch inhaled the cool air, savoring the rare moment of serenity. Only a handful of villagers milled around, rushing toward their daily chores with downcast expressions. No one spared her a glance.

"Ahem," one of Edda's twins coughed. "Must go," he mumbled, averting his gaze. She couldn't place his age. He wore an oversized tunic, making him appear small, and his hair was cropped short. But a pronounced knot bobbed in his throat as he swallowed.

"Your name is Frick, isn't it?" the witch asked in a friendly tone mirroring her raised spirits. In place of a response, the youth started walking, leading her along a gravel path toward the Svensen house. The two-story building stood beyond the village boundaries on a sloping meadow overlooking the bay. Ornamental carvings of beasts and sea creatures surrounded the windows and adorned the roof. Framing the house on either side, two fieldstone chimneys emitted a welcoming scent of wood smoke.

According to healer Gunhild's tales, Rikard's late father had been Hamarrfjord's most successful raider, often returning with rich bounty and exotic slaves. Everybody expected him to succeed or challenge his brother for leadership until a ferocious autumn storm sank Sven's ship, taking all souls with it.

Entering the courtyard, she spotted the master of the manor splitting wood like a common laborer. He'd taken his shirt off and stood with his back to her. Resisting Frick's prodding, the witch remained in the doorway, admiring the shifting of lean muscles under the sweat-covered skin.

He's an unusual young man, she thought. *Quite different from what I expected.*

With a sigh, she tore her eyes away and followed Edda's boy to her new position. For a time, she would do as she was told and keep her head down.

It's the chance I've been waiting for. I'm just not sure about the not-making-any-trouble part, she conceded with a wry smile.

Despite her best efforts, it took Bergrún over a week to get her chance to be alone with Rikard. The young master spent his days between the sparring yard and the great hall, often staying until late at night. Since he hadn't given his permission, the witch was not allowed to leave the house. She cleaned dishes, carded wool, and slept in a crowded dormitory, relegated to absorbing the gossip of her fellow servants. She hadn't even explored the house's upper floors and didn't know where the young Viking's bedroom lay. Whenever she raised her gaze from her tasks, Bergrún spotted Frick or his identical brother watching her.

Edda must not agree with her mistress's assignment, the witch thought.

Still, her luck changed when a giggling maid named Rissa told her about Master Rikard's fondness for soaking in a nearby hot pool. Bergrún had mixed a chamomile paste to treat the girl's aching tooth, and her new friend became a veritable fount of information.

"He goes there at twilight," Rissa explained. "I've watched him undress from behind the willow bushes," she confessed, blushing. "I didn't mean to, of course. Sometimes, I return late from the sheep pen…"

"He's quite good-looking," Bergrún agreed.

"Yes! And kind-hearted, too. He treats us well, doesn't even bother the maids," she added in a tone that carried the slightest hint of disappointment.

"Say, aren't the feed sacks for the sheep too heavy for you? I'm almost done kneading the bread dough, and neither Frick nor Frock is in sight. Why don't we walk past those willow bushes?"

"Edda must really not like you to have her spiders trail you like shadows."

"Spiders?" Bergrún laughed.

"That's what we call the boys. They're thin and gangly. They don't speak, keep to dark corners, and like creeping up on you, especially when you bathe. Edda holds their leashes tight, not allowing them to mingle. But I've spotted them watching the women by the river, their hands in their trousers."

"They're growing boys," Bergrún chuckled. "Nature has its way."

"They're creeps!" Rissa insisted. "Let's go then. The weather is nice. Who knows how long until the first snow? And I could use the help."

* * *

AS EVENING FELL, Bergrún hiked up the narrow path toward the hot pools Rissa had shown her earlier. The witch carried a basket with food, a soft blanket, and a hooded lantern. Ale sloshed in the ceramic pitcher with every step, threatening to soak the plate of cold mutton and the loaf of freshly baked bread. She had evaded the prying eyes of the spider twins since both of them spent their evening confined to the outhouse.

They must have eaten something spoiled, the witch mused.

Careful to mask her footsteps on the crystalline rocks, Bergrún headed toward a series of pools that lay like pearls on a string nestled in a glen. The rising steam shimmered in the sun's fading light, and the sea breeze wafted a light sulfurous odor her way. Straining to peer through the fog, the witch detected a head poking out of one of the lower basins. As she grew nearer, the figure turned. Rikard's usually wavy blond hair hung in wet strands, obscuring half his face.

"Who goes there?" he called.

"I brought ale and supper, Master Rikard," Bergrún replied.

"Oh, it's you. How did you find me?"

"Your favorite spots are well known," she replied. "Especially among the maidens who like to peek through the bushes." She placed the basket on the ground and laid the blanket beside it.

Bergrún had tied her long hair into a bun. Stepping around to the pool's shallow end, she loosened her rough-spun cape and folded it neatly onto a large stone. Underneath, she wore a gray linen dress, exposing her slender neck and pale shoulders.

"What are you doing?" he asked as she started to unfasten her bodice.

"I only have the one dress," she replied, her gaze fixed on her fingers. "If it gets wet, I'm in for a cold night."

Untying the last knot, she slipped her arms out, pushed the fabric down past her hips, and stepped free without letting her dress fall to the ground. She'd turned her back to Rikard and, bending over, placed the garment on top of her cape. Then she straightened, faced the speechless young man, and entered the pool. The water felt wonderful in the chill evening air. A layer of sediment covered the smooth rocks, making them slippery, and she raised her arms to the side for balance.

"I never had a chance to thank you," she whispered. "You spared me on Fårosünd, arranged my stay with the healer, and confronted your cousin Toril on my behalf." The water had reached her navel.

"You've treated me with respect, never demanding a warrior's right." A sigh of contentment escaped her lips as she submerged herself to the neck into the invigorating warmth.

"Bringing you supper and ale is a small way to show my gratitude," she breathed. "A young warrior needs strength. And perhaps, I can provide a massage to relax your muscles after your day on the sparring ground."

Bergrún inched closer. With her dark eyes fixed on his stunned face, the young woman placed her left hand onto his chest when the sharp point of a knife pressed against her ribs.

* * *

"Don't touch me," Rikard snarled. "I haven't forgotten what happened to Thorstein."

Bergrún froze. Her smile vanished like a flower petal ripped away by a blizzard. She let her hand sink, but her eyes remained locked on his.

Here is your reward for saving his life, she thought. *A blade!*

He was just like all the other, small-minded men who saw her as a weak woman until she demonstrated her power. Then, she became a monster. Her blood began to boil.

"You'll find me harder to kill than Sverre, Haddur, or Lyngar," he rasped, a lump forming in his throat. "How many others?"

"Is that what you were doing since the raid, Hero of Hamarrfjord?" she growled. "Hiding from me?" She leaned forward, increasing the pressure against the deadly weapon.

"Shouldn't I? I know how dangerous you are. And you know I know."

"You have no idea how dangerous I am." A flicker of red ignited in her eyes. Raising her right hand above the water, she shouted, "*Springa!*"

With a night-shattering crack, a stone ten paces away exploded, sending shards and debris flying in all directions.

Rikard flinched, his eyes widening in terror as rock splinters hit the pool's surface. He tried to draw back and lower his weapon. Yet quick as a lightning strike, Bergrún snatched his hand, pulling him close to her until the blade's tip pricked her skin.

"What about you, Rikard Thure Svensen?" she hissed. "Master of the practice pit, slayer of Thorstein, aren't you dangerous? Isn't your blade inches from my heart?" Her face hovered less than a handspan from his. Tendrils of the rising steam coiled around her like a nest of vipers. "Ending me is easier than cutting the meat I brought." Her lips pulled into a malicious grin. "What's stopping you? Kill me, and the village will rejoice! You have the power, the weapon, the opening. Do it, now!" she screamed. Her eyes blazed bright red, and her grip tightened, nails digging into his flesh.

He couldn't move; he couldn't breathe. For several tense heartbeats, she held him frozen like a fly in amber. Then, with a guttural groan of frustration, the witch shoved his hand aside. She pushed herself to the pool's other end and disappeared under the black, shimmering surface. A burst of bubbles marked the spot before the water settled into an eerie calm.

Rikard's face had gone pale as the rising moon. Shaking like a pennant in a gale wind, he stared at the ripples spreading in circles. His heartbeat raced, blood thumping in his ears. He should run, call for help, do something. But all strength had seeped from his muscles.

Bergrún's head broke the surface, and she drew in deep breaths. Loosening her topknot, the woman spread her raven-black hair over her shoulders. She leaned back. The cool stone of the pool's rim cradled her head, and her gaze drifted skyward. Only a handful of stars peeked through the swirling clouds. If portents could be gleaned from the constellations, tonight wasn't the night.

"Do you sometimes wish to float on the water like a leaf?" she asked in a dreamy voice. "Away from your roots, not caring where the current will take you?" A sad smile flickered over her lips.

"What?" he croaked, fitting all his fear, anger, and confusion into the single word question. She raised her head and tucked a few strands of hair behind her ears. Then she pulled her legs up, leaned forward, and rested her arms on her knees.

"If I wanted you dead, you would be dead. I dare say the same holds true in reverse." She looked to his submerged right hand, presumably still holding the knife. "The question isn't if someone has the ability to kill. What matters is how they act." Wiping water from her brows, she continued. "Haddur chose to attack Stina and her mother because they hail from Heilladur. I chose to kill Haddur because Stina is my friend."

"Why are you telling me?" he asked, shaking his head, baffled by her shifting mood. "Don't you think I will..."

"Because it makes no difference," she interrupted. "You already know who I am and what I can do. Why pretend?" She closed her eyes and inhaled deep breaths through her nose.

"I want you to know why I did what I did," she said, struggling to keep her voice low and even. "So you understand why I won't harm you, as long as you don't harm me."

"And I should take your word for it?" Rikard scoffed, his voice regaining a bitter edge. "Why should I gamble my life on the lies a... witch tells?" He drew himself up and crossed his arms over his chest, exposing the pointed whale bone he was holding.

"You can't trust anyone's words," she smirked, acknowledging his bluff. "Not mine, not Edda's, and particularly not your dear cousin Toril's sweet lies." Lowering her tone to a conspiratorial whisper, she added, "Trust only that people act for their own goals. The secret of survival is finding others whose goals align with yours."

"Then what's your goal, witch? To seduce me?"

"Sex is a woman's tool," she replied, "rarely her goal."

His eyes widened in disbelief while a flush crept up his neck.

"Surprised?" she asked with a brief chuckle. "Maybe you're too young to know otherwise. And maybe I'm odd, but I care much more about what's between a man's ears than what's between his legs."

* * *

"Why Heilladur? Of all the places in the world..." Rikard asked several hours later. "Why do you dream of sailing there?" He sat at the table by the window, rolling his dinner knife between his fingers. The plate with bread and cold mutton stood untouched on the table.

A fire crackled on the hearth, and several candles illuminated the small room. Bergrún perched on a low stool by the fire, cross-legged. Neither had approached the opulent bed that occupied more than half of the available space. According to Rikard, Edda had arranged the change of furniture after he refused to move out of his childhood bedroom despite grander accommodations being available for the master of the manor.

"I don't know," Bergrún replied. "It sounds nice, the way Stina talks about it, with wildflower meadows on rolling hills, black beaches, ancient forests, and breathtaking waterfalls. And it's far, far away from all the strife and violence in these lands."

The witch and the Viking had stayed in the hot pool for nearly two hours after their initial confrontation, their frosty tempers melting away in the warm water. Bergrún's triple assault of her raw power, her brutal honesty, and her alluring beauty had left Rikard utterly defenseless, caught by his curiosity.

"I despised the narrow-minded fisherfolk of my home," the witch had explained, "with their dull lives and stunted ambitions. They believed they were better than me, better than my family, because we didn't have much." The bitter memories caused her shoulder to tense, and her jaw tightened. "The village children laughed at us, and the elders whispered that we must have offended the gods. I hated the lot of them! When I was sixteen, I couldn't bear the humiliation any longer. I ran away from home."

A long silence followed. Several times, Rikard seemed on the verge of asking her to continue. He leaned closer and, after a deep breath, he whispered, "What happened?"

"I roamed the land until I found an old hag who took me in as her apprentice. I always knew I was special," she declared with rekindled passion. "I had abilities, and I wanted more; I wanted change; I wanted to control my fate and shape my destiny. Alas, my teacher treated me as her servant, never trusting me with the deep truths. So, I... left her and returned home. Nothing had changed!" she growled. "No one respected a girl from a poor family, regardless of what she had learned, or what she could do."

Rikard listened, his lips parted. He watched her face in the candlelight, mesmerized—the stark paleness of her skin and the shadows that haunted her sad eyes.

"I was laughed at, too," he'd explained. "When I questioned the senseless cycle of violence and retribution, the village men called me weak and naïve, as Thorstein did. They said there was too much of my mother in me, and I was a disgrace to my family."

"I wouldn't be alive if you weren't different, Rikard Svensen, Hero of Hamarrfjord," she said, giving him a hesitant smile.

Neither realized the changing weather until the clouds broke, sending an icy downpour over the land. Half-dressed, both ran down to the manor, using capes and blankets to shield against the rain and sleet. Entering the house, a soaked Rikard ushered the bare-legged, mud-caked woman to his room, only pausing when he saw the oversized bed.

Bergrún pushed past him, chuckling, and stoked the dying embers back to life. After adding more logs, she slipped out of her wet dress and wrapped herself in a blanket. Rikard went to his chest and changed his clothes. Blushing, he offered a spare tunic to his female guest. The witch declined, regarding his discomfort with a wicked grin. He fidgeted with the garment before taking his seat by the window, eager to continue the conversation.

"Have you ever been to Heilladur?" he asked after taking a deep draft of the ale straight from the pitcher. "I hear it's strange; the people are strange."

"Because they love nature and don't split each other's heads with crude axes?" she asked. "I've met a few natives of that 'strange' land, and most I like better than my kind Viking hosts on Brótinholm and Hrafney."

The intensity of her gaze caused Rikard to lean in, teetering on the edge of his seat. He offered her the ale. She regarded him, her head tilted. Untangling her long legs, she rose and walked across the room. Her bare feet left wet, glistening footprints. Standing close, she filled her cup, letting the blanket fall open. This time, he didn't avert his gaze.

* * *

THE VILLAGE BELLS pulled Rikard from his stupor. He'd lain awake long after Bergrún had left his room, thoughts and emotions surging through his mind like a mountain stream after the snowmelt. Extracting himself from the tangle of sheets and blankets, the young warrior got to his feet. The room was dark with the window shutters closed. His clothes lay strewn over the floor with one still-wet boot hidden under the bed. Trusting his fingers to guide his actions, the young man dressed in haste. He rushed through the door, still tightening his sword belt, when the bell rang again.

Outside, a purple band on the horizon signaled the imminent sunrise. The air felt crisp, the ever-present salty taste mixing with a faint scent of peat fires from the village. Two farmhands in their early twenties stood outside, carrying pitchforks and waiting for his orders.

"To the harbor," Rikard commanded, leading the way in a hurried jog.

In less time than it takes to gut a fish, the three men had reached the pier. Olver Agnarsen had assembled a host of twenty-odd warriors in full battle gear. Yet the men stood relaxed, shields on their backs and swords sheathed. The commander spoke with two younger soldiers, his back turned to the village.

"What's going on, Olver?" Rikard shouted. "Who sounded the alarm?"

"Envar Finsgúr did," the Shield of Hamarrfjord replied. He stepped forward to greet the new arrival. "He and his brother Eskil had the watch. They spotted an unknown ship approaching."

"Who is it? Fårosünd? Have you sent runners to call the men from the outlying farmsteads?"

"I don't think that's necessary. Look!" Olver waved to his men, and they opened a gap, providing a clear view of the approaching vessel. The angry cries of seagulls filled the air, chased into flight as the boat drew closer.

"A faering?" Rikard asked, shaking his head in surprise. "Your men raise the alarm for a rowboat?"

"Envar spotted lanterns, claiming it was still too dark. He and his brother won't hear the end of their blunder on this side of Ragnarok," Olver chuckled. "Still, after the events of the last weeks, I'm glad the shadow proved to be a fox cub and not a ravenous wolf pack."

Two men seemed to occupy the boat. As they got closer, the rising sun revealed shorn heads and water-drenched gray robes, identifying them as Christian friars. Their ripped cassocks and bloodied faces showed clear signs of violence. Five boat-lengths from the shore, the rower collapsed in exhaustion. His companion called for help in heavily accented Norsk. With a malicious grin, Olver sent the Finsgúr brothers into the freezing sea to pull the men to safety. Seeing their salvation nearing, the monks rejoiced in song.

"If they have enough breath to sing," Eskil Finsgúr grumbled, "couldn't they row the remaining distance?" His brother trudged beside him, cursing the old gods and the new for his rotten luck in being on watch this morning.

With the immediate danger averted, most men dispersed. Rikard and a handful of Vikings led the unexpected guests to the chieftain's lodge as Olver had gone ahead to deliver his report to Jarl Gustav. The great hall felt cold and dark despite servants having lit the fire. Hamarrfjord's chieftain sat in the carved driftwood throne. To his left sat Toril, while Olver stood to his right. A table in the center offered an assortment of bread, cheese, and dried fish. Two maids brought warm blankets for the monks, which the men accepted, and cups with spiced mead, which they politely refused, asking for water instead.

"Welcome to Hamarrfjord's hall," the chieftain called, impatient to end the ceaseless fussing of the servants. "What curious wind blew you to our shores?"

"Hail, great chieftain," the taller monk responded. "We are humble servants of Christ, Son of the Almighty. My name is Brother Eadmund, and this is Brother Aldred. Sadly, he doesn't speak your language well. My apologies."

"Well met," Toril replied. "You are in the presence of Jarl Gustav Haakon Larsen, chieftain of Hamarrfjord and all lands on Hrafney, my father. What ill fate has befallen you, as we can see the signs of hardship?"

"Indeed, fair Mistress, our ship has been beset by raiders from Danheimr."

"From Danheimr?" Jarl Gustav shouted. "This far north? Are you sure?"

"Yes, great chieftain. Most men of our crew were slain, the survivors taken captive. Only Brother Cuthbert, Brother Aldred, and I had been spared. Since the Danske King found the path to Christ, the Son of the Almighty, his men no longer kill monks. But they mocked us and treated us ill. They tied Brother Cuthbert to the mast of their ship to bless their journey east while stranding us in a rowboat out at sea."

"East?" Olver asked. "Did you learn their destination? Could you glimpse their intentions?"

"Oh, much more than that, mighty Viking warrior. The captain boasted of their plans. You see, one warship attacked us, but not far off, we spotted two more. All three vessels were laden with plunder from Inglandia. The vile captain called it a bride-price to woo the Norskar of Trondborg and Starvinger."

"Three ships?" Olver repeated, concerned creases forming between his brows. "How many men did you see, what weapons and equipment?"

"Apologies! We are learned in the Word of God but know little about the cruel art of war," Brother Eadmund replied.

"An alliance between the Danske sea dogs and the treacherous Norskar?" Jarl Gustav bellowed. "There you have it, dear Toril. Your ambitions of a treaty with Åalbrug lie shattered like a longship on a reef. You can't trust the Danskers!" He coughed. Forceful hacks heaved his chest, bending him over. Toril rushed to her father with spiced mead, and he snatched the cup in an angry swipe, spilling half of the contents.

Rikard stood, frozen, shocked by his uncle's words. Seeking his cousin's gaze, he yearned to receive a reassuring denial.

She shook her head, mouthing the words, "Not now!"

Despite more cups of mead, Jarl Gustav's coughing got worse.

"I'll fetch Agnetha," Rikard called. "She can help."

"Stay, Rikard!" Toril's command rang through the hall. "We need to discuss our plans. Edda!" she called.

"Yes, Mistress," the old woman replied. She'd stepped from the shadows as if conjured from thin air.

"Send Stina to the Svensen house. Tell her to bring Agnetha with all haste! Then see to our guests. They could stay in Sverre Borgersen's hut." Turning to the monks, the jarl's daughter added, "Please wait here." Her voice had regained a small measure of composure. "Olver, help me get my father upstairs to his room."

"I can walk, woman!" her father wheezed between hacking coughs. But Olver had already placed the chieftain's arm around his shoulder and pulled him to his feet. Toril rushed to open the door. Taking her father's other arm, she helped him climb the back stairs.

"I guess the audience is over." Rikard shook his head. "What a strange place the world has become," he said to no one in particular. Striding toward the table with the cups of mead that the monks had declined, he drained both in rapid succession.

CHAPTER EIGHT

Treachery

"How's my father?" Toril called as soon as Bergrún descended the stairs from the jarl's chambers. Her words sounded sharp as a whip. Caught up in a heated argument with her cousin Rikard, the fear, stress, and frustration had the young woman's fur bristling at her neck. All she'd ever cared about was the survival of her kin and her clan. Yet, instead of adapting to the changing powers in the world, the men rejected her negotiations with Danheimr.

They call my ideas treason, because I'm a woman!

She'd been pacing in tight circles, clenching and unclenching her fists. Her stiff linen dress swished with every stride, acting as a metronome to the drumbeat of her heart. She wanted to appear regal for the audience, but now wished she had worn her sparring clothes—leather leggings and padded flaxen vest. At least then, she could beat sense into these wool-headed fools.

She needed to hit something. Her back felt taut as a bowstring, and the stabbing headaches behind her temples grew stronger by the minute. Olver stood across the room by the door, barring anyone from intruding. But Toril felt the distance between them.

"Staying out of the family feud," she fumed, remembering his earlier excuse. With her gaze fixed on Bergrún, she refused to acknowledge his presence. *Abandonment!* The thought conjured a bitter taste in her throat. *My father, my cousin, and now my lover! All the men around me are weak!*

"The chieftain is resting, Mistress," Bergrún replied. "I've given him a honey infusion of licorice root and elderflower to soothe the chest ache."

Turning to Rikard, she added, "With your permission, Master, I'd like to search healer Gunhild's hut for any still usable herbs and remedies."

"Of course," Rikard stammered, a flush creeping up his neck. Clearing his throat, he declared, "Someone should go along. I can..."

"I'll go," Olver interjected. He locked eyes with Rikard's for two heartbeats, urging him to make peace, before softening his gaze as he turned to Toril. Then, he pulled the door open, letting a gust of wind flood into the hall.

The weak November sun had disappeared behind a thick veil of clouds, and the air carried the scent of snow. Striding beside Bergrún, Hamarrfjord's shield seemed coiled with tension. With hard lines etched between his brows, he fixed his gaze on the path ten strides ahead. The sound of cracking his knuckles accompanied the crunch of his boots on the frozen ground as he walked. Long moments passed.

"Can you heal him?" he finally asked. He looked at her, his eyes narrowed, and the witch was surprised to detect concern on his face.

"I'll do what I can," she replied. As her breath misted in the frigid air, she wondered how much to tell him.

* * *

WHEN ENTERING THE jarl's chambers an hour earlier, Bergrún had found the aging chieftain standing by the open window, his shoulders hunched. He inhaled a wheezing breath that sounded like bellows laboring to ignite a dying fire.

"My lord," she'd greeted, curtsying. He ignored her despite the door guard's announcement. Long moments passed. "Ahem, Jarl Gustav, my lord," she repeated. "Your daughter sent me. I'm well trained in the healing arts, and I..."

"I know who you are," he replied, his lungs rattling like seashells washing over a rocky shore. "Heard all about your remarkable deeds." The warrior turned; his pale blue eyes bore into hers. Deep shadows lent his gaunt face a sinister expression. "You cared for old Gunhild's daughter, defended her in the forest." He raised a cup of steaming mead to his lips, his eyes never leaving her face.

"Aye, my lord," she replied, averting her gaze too late for a servant of her station.

"You can't heal me," he said, keeping his voice low. "I'm dying. I knew it long before that Heilladur hag dulled my pain with her powdered mushrooms... ever since my brother's wife died." He'd put the cup down and lowered himself into the chair by the fire.

"Lovely Astrid," he continued, a grimace twisting his lips. "She blamed me for Sven's death, you know? Said I'd pushed him too far, sending my brother on raids too late in the season, as if Sven wasn't his own man. He would have raided Asgard if he only knew the course. Sit," Gustav Larsen ordered, pointing to a chair nearby. Bergrún did as she was told.

"Astrid died during Fårosünd's raid less than a season's cycle ago. We fought them off, but Rikard's mother paid a bitter price, as did his sister. And so many more. With her last breath, Astrid cursed me," he rasped, his words dissolving into a hacking cough. "She prophesied my death. My lungs are turning black; the disease eats me from the inside."

"I'm sorry, my lord, I don't..." Bergrún whispered.

"Don't know why I'm telling you? Because my time is short," he hissed. "And my blades are too dull to sever the wicked Norns' thread. But yours! I hear wondrous tales." He laughed, cold and rough like the rasp of steel on steel. Bergrún's eyes widened in surprise. "Amazing, how you wormed your way into my dear daughter's confidence as well as my nephew's bed."

Leaning forward, his face hardened. The lines around his mouth deepened, and his voice became the snarl of a gray wolf.

"I need these foolish children to grow up fast! If someone stands in their way, I need them removed. Be my ears and my knife, and no one will question what really happened that night in the forest."

* * *

LOST IN THOUGHT, the witch followed Olver through the village without taking in her surroundings. Her eyes were on him, trying to peer behind the facade of the loyal guard captain.

"His body's humors appear imbalanced," she explained, hoping to glimpse some of the shield's thoughts. "I've lessened the pain, but I require more ingredients to treat the cause of his ailment."

"Perhaps our chieftain should invite the monks," Olver muttered. "One more god on his side couldn't hurt. Though I don't know what use their Christ could be." He gave a harsh laugh devoid of any humor. "What god lets himself be captured and killed?"

"Monks?" Bergrún asked.

"Yes, two refugees. Arrived by rowboat this morning, looking worse than drowned rats. Our chieftain welcomed them. Now, they entertain the village wives with their fanciful tales. Over there," he nodded towards a man not twenty paces away. "That's one of them, Brother Aldric, if I recall correctly."

As if hearing his name called, the man turned, giving the witch a clear look at his face. She stumbled, her foot catching on an uneven stone, and she nearly lost her balance.

"Forgive my ignorance," she began, trying to keep her voice even and her face impassive. "I know of herbs but little of gods."

* * *

All morning, excitement had surged through the village of Hamarrfjord. While Olver had impressed on the monks in no uncertain terms to keep the details of their misfortune secret, their arrival had sent rumors swirling like gulls around a fisherman's catch. Small groups of villagers huddled in the muddy square around the well, their voices hushed. Others gathered near the bathhouse, cloaked in the steam rising into the crisp autumn air. Even the rhythmic clang of the grain mill seemed to falter as the miller paused to listen to the whispers.

Toril stood by the longhouse's open window, deep in thought, her knuckles white as her hands gripped the rough windowsill. Her gaze sought the horizon beyond the fjord visible between the rooftops, yet her eyes had lost focus. The forceful voice of her father pulled her from her contemplation. She turned from the window and walked with measured steps to the back of the room, eschewing the carved wooden seat next to the chieftain.

"The situation is dire," Jarl Gustav declared, sitting upright in a hard-backed chair. The midday bell hadn't yet rung, but his voice had regained some of its old strength, thanks to Bergrún's potent remedies. Color had returned to his cheeks, though still gaunt. His piercing eyes swept the room. "We cannot allow the Danske longboats to reach the shores of Norskvegn. King Olaf already dominates the south. In the northwest, Fårosünd regroups. They will strike back after Harold's ill-conceived raid. If we lose the east, too, we're trapped like fish in a net. Ah, Olver, sit!" he added as his shield entered the small audience chamber.

Gustav Larsen had called on his most trusted advisors to discuss the troubling tidings the monks had delivered. Rikard, who still hadn't resolved his disagreement with his cousin, found himself among warriors almost two decades his senior. He sought Toril's gaze as she moved with practiced grace, filling horns of ale for the men, yet he couldn't read her expression.

"But isn't Harold forming an alliance with Starvinger to bring Norskvegn to our side?" Bjørn Johansen asked. The seasoned raider turned blacksmith had a deep, resonating voice that still carried much weight in the jarl's council.

"And how likely is that fool to succeed?" Olver muttered under his breath. "I wouldn't trust Harold Svensen to piss straight."

"We must send our swiftest ships," the chieftain argued, his voice echoing in the chamber. "Olver, you and Bjørn will take the sea serpents to hunt the Danske raiders. Set sail before the moon tide. Travel light, a dozen karls as fighting force plus six thralls each to pull the oars."

"They'll outnumber us by three to one, Chieftain," Bjørn interjected, his voice gruff, his hand resting on the pommel of his axe.

"Then send these southern dogs to Hel with flaming arrows," Jarl Gustav growled. "No boarding, no plunder! Show this vermin who rules the seas!"

"My chieftain," Olver started, his voice calm but firm, "Even dispatching only half a krigsband, I fear for Hamarrfjord's defenses. With Harold and his men gone... We might be weeks at sea."

"My daughter has already sent ravens to Starvinger, commanding Harold to intercept the Danskers," Jarl Gustav explained. "Pray their black wings cut swiftly through the swirling winds. In the meantime, Gunnar and Rikard will muster the tradesmen and youths. Their strong hands can hold swords and spears as well as hammers and plows. Rely on Edda," he added, turning to Rikard, "to select trusted thralls."

Rikard jumped, hearing his name called. Pressing his lips together, he gave his uncle a curt nod. Jarl Gustav stood, causing the men to rise, their chairs scraping against the wooden floor.

"By Odin's one eye," he growled. "It's time for battle! For blood and glory!"

"For kin and jarl!" the men replied in unison, slamming their right fists against their chests before leaving the room one by one, their footsteps heavy on the wooden beams.

"Rikard, stay behind," Jarl Gustav said, his voice lowered. "I need a word."

* * *

TORIL WAITED FOR the men to leave the longhouse before grabbing Olver by the arm. Bjørn and Gunnar were the last, their footfalls growing fainter.

"Come over here!" she whispered, dragging her consort into the space behind the stairs.

"I must see to the ships," he protested. "Less than six hours to moon tide."

"You're not the only seafarer in this village," she hissed, her eyes flashing with anger. "Your men know how to bend a rope and hoist a sail. It's more important for you to know what *I need you to do!*"

Straining her neck, she glanced around, her gaze sweeping the dimly lit hall for any eavesdroppers. The fire in the central hearth crackled, casting dancing shadows, but no one else stood near. Dropping her voice to a whisper, she continued with urgency.

"You cannot sink those ships! We need the plunder, and we need answers." She tightened her grip on his arm, nails biting into fabric and skin. "My contacts have never spoken of an alliance with Norskvegn. We need to know where this came from. Is King Olaf double-crossing us, or are his sons trying to stake their claims?"

"You heard the jarl," he said, his voice low yet firm. "His orders are clear!"

"And how long do you think my father will walk this earth?" Her voice rose in pitch. "Without gold, you're nothing. You have no family, no legacy. And without knowledge, I'm nothing. I'm a woman. We'll be pushed aside by the likes of Rikard!"

"The jarl looked hale," he argued, softening his voice. "He wouldn't disown you, Toril. You're his daughter."

"You think?" she sneered, her lips curling in disdain. "So he's parlaying with dear Rikard about the Yuletide festivities right now?" Toril pointed her hand toward the upper floor where Rikard presumably received the jarlship on a silver platter. "Don't be a bigger fool than you are!" she spat, passion coloring her cheeks. "I haven't risked my neck negotiating with my father's favorite 'enemies' just to see a green boy tossing our clan's future into the sea."

"Even if your cousin holds your father's favor," he said in an attempt to insert reason. "No need to rush with unlaced boots into battle. The chieftain looked better, mayhaps…"

"A draught of black henbane and valerian root may stir the dead for a time," she cut in, venom in her voice. "The truth remains, he's dying. Face it, Olver! He admitted it himself. Edda told me of his counsel with the cunning Agnetha." She glared at him, her gaze reducing the tall, broad-shouldered warrior to a stripling being scolded for stealing sweet bread.

"What do you want me to do?" he asked, his voice resigned, his shoulders slumping. "We don't have the men to seize all three ships."

"Then don't. Let my dear cousin Harold clean up the mess. I need one ship's commander and its cargo."

"The jarl won't abide disobedience!" he protested.

"Who knows how long until my father feasts in Odin's hall. His health might fail tonight or tomorrow. We must be ready!" Her voice wavered, and a shadow of sadness flickered across her face, revealing the girl beneath the steely resolve.

Olver's mouth stood open, yet no words came. He sought her eyes, trying to read her expression, but she'd lowered her gaze. With a sigh of frustration, the young woman leaned against the wooden boards. A hidden door swung open, and she stumbled backward. Olver grabbed her arm, pulling her upright.

"Ow!" she complained, rubbing her arm and looking around the small chamber. An oil lamp hung from a ceiling hook, illuminating the tiny space. Dusty urns and barrels lined the back wall, while a table with various herbs and powders occupied the center.

"What's this?" Toril hissed, spotting the door in the opposite wall standing ajar. A sliver of darkness was visible beyond, and a cold draft seeped in, creeping over the floor. "Someone was here!"

"Yes," Olver admitted. "I brought Agnetha here to mix her remedies and potions for your father."

"You're telling me now?" she shrieked. "You dim-witted oaf! She overheard us! Find her, you lackbrained fool!" She shoved and kicked him with a berserker's ferocity, her blows raining with surprising force on every inch she could reach. "Find that wench!"

* * *

Twilight began to settle as Rikard strode toward the harbor. A light breeze wafted dense fog inland. He'd endured a long day, and the evening would bring little relief. Jarl Gustav had summoned him to the longhouse for a formal supper with the monks, during which the discussion would return to Danheimr's threat and Hamarrfjord's response. Yet, before suffering through another tense argument between his uncle and his cousin, the young Viking wanted to see the departing warriors off, wishing them the gods' favor on their voyage.

Deep in thought, he'd entered an alley between two rows of crafter workshops. A figure jumped from the roof, landing two strides away in the middle of the path. Wrapped in a gray cloak with the hood raised, the figure rushed him before he could draw his dagger. A cold hand clamped over his mouth, pushing him backward. He smacked against the wooden boards with a dull thud. Letting go of his pinned dagger, Rikard's free hand seized the attacker's arm. His hand circled the wrist with ease.

"It's me," Bergrún whispered, her breath warm against his ear. "Don't shout! I'll let go." Her arm fell limp, and she stepped back.

"Hela's tits, woman," he gasped, his heart hammering against his ribs. "What are you playing at? You scared me half to death!"

"Keep your voice down!" she growled, low and menacing, like a great white bear. "In here!" Snatching his hand, she pulled him into the gap between a storehouse and the smithy. The intensity radiating from her stopped him from struggling, and despite being half a head taller, he let her drag him along.

"Explain!" he commanded after she lowered her hood. Her face looked pale and drawn in the dim light.

"There's a plot, Rikard. You're in danger; we all are." Her head swiveled left and right like a deer catching a wolf's scent, her eyes straining to detect any movement in the deepening shadows. The night was quiet except for their accelerated breathing echoing in the confined space.

"Two conspirators," she said. "I overheard their conversation this afternoon. Then, I had to hide. But the Danheimr ships, something terrible is going to happen."

Bergrún rushed to explain in great detail everything she'd learned about the traitors' plans. "They're going to poison everyone attending the feast tonight," she concluded, "to create chaos before seizing power. I've been looking for you since I found out, but I had to hide from Edda and her spiders."

Rikard's jaw tightened. "Come with me to the harbor," he urged. "We must stop Olver's ship from setting sail."

"That'll tip them off, and they'll deny everything. Who'll believe a thrall, Rikard? My word means nothing against theirs."

"And who will believe me?" he asked. "What proof do I have?"

"Take this." She pushed a lumpy, cloth-wrapped bundle into his arms, the fabric rough and damp. "That's the proof, but you must present it at the right moment. Wait until everyone gathers and pays attention." Her hand tightened around his arm, and red sparks flickered in her eyes. "I'll be with Stina. Call me when needed, but be careful. Don't trust anyone."

"Why?" he asked after a long pause. His posture shifted, the initial shock giving way to concern. He'd been leaning in, hanging on her every word, until deeper and deeper creases appeared on his forehead. His shoulders tensed.

"Because I can bear witness, tell everybody how I overheard them plotting."

"That's not what I'm asking," he declared, emphasizing every syllable. "Why are you telling me all this, Agnetha? What's it to you?" His voice became as hard as steel. He stepped back, crossed his arms, and straightened his back.

"I'm in danger as well, Rikard. Everybody in Hamarrfjord is."

"Don't make me laugh!" he scoffed. "You survived the raid on Fårosünd and the attack on healer Gunhild. Can you even be harmed?"

"Of course, I can, fool! Remember me collapsing in Fårosünd? You want to waste more time discussing magic or save your village?"

"I'm saving my village by questioning you. Didn't you shout at me just last night to not trust anyone's words? What's your goal, Witch? Why do you care for your captors?"

She looked at him, her head tilted, and her lips pulled into a crooked, almost smile.

"Don't tell me you've fallen in love with me, Agnetha!" His voice jumped in pitch as color flushed his cheeks. "I don't believe in fairytales anymore!"

"Of course, I haven't fallen for you, dullard!" A bark of laughter escaped her lips. "I'm your servant, not your betrothed. Don't flatter yourself."

"Then why? I don't see the humor!" he insisted, his flush deepening.

"You're growing up," she said, nodding. "That's good; Someone needs to."

His glare hardened. His hand felt for the dagger on his belt. The witch regarded him with a mixture of incredulity and admiration for two more heartbeats before relenting.

"Because I hope you're different, Rikard Svensen," she said in a soft voice, meeting the Viking's stern gaze. "Because you object to the strong preying on the weak. Because you could lead your people into a future of wildflower meadows on rolling hills, where everyone is given a chance, regardless of birth. And because I want to come along!" She looked into his eyes. Hers were deep and dark, yet full of fire. She touched his hand, and her skin burned like a fever. He didn't recoil.

"If I'd lied," Bergrún whispered, stepping closer, "you'll look like a fool. Direct the Jarl's wrath upon me. But if I'd told the truth, and you ignored my warning... Will you ever be able to forgive yourself?"

For a heartbeat, time froze, and the world stopped spinning. Then Rikard nodded once, turned on his heel, and marched toward the longhouse.

CHAPTER NINE

Heroes

RIKARD'S FINGERTIPS TINGLED as he ascended the steps to the great hall. He wore a stiff-collared, dark-blue tunic, the fringes adorned with golden embroidery. A leather belt studded with iron discs cinched the knee-length garment. The young warrior carried no visible weapons, though he concealed two daggers within his high leather boots.

He'd arrived early. Servants bustled about, setting out mead and meat and lighting the torches along the walls. Toril stood by the fireplace, conversing with one of the monks. Alerted by his footsteps, she glanced in his direction but averted her gaze upon recognizing him. Her father had not yet joined the feast.

Stina approached, curtsied, and offered Rikard a cup of wine. He thanked her with a smile. After draining the contents in one gulp, he handed her the cup, shaking his head to dispel the sour taste. He wasn't fond of grape wine, preferring the sweetness of mead. Finally, Jarl Gustav descended the stairs, wearing a warrior's leather cuirass and a battle skirt over a white tunic. He took his seat at the center of the table and invited Rikard to sit to his right, a seat usually reserved for the Shield of Hamarrfjord. The young Viking sought his cousin's gaze, trying to read her emotions, but Toril wore a mask of noble serenity.

While the men took their seats, the jarl's daughter carried a silver pitcher to the kettle of mead warming over the fire. A table with herbs stood nearby. With her back to the room, she added spoonfuls of spices, such as clover, cinnamon, and ginger, to the pitcher before Stina ladled the simmering honey wine on top.

"Allow me to bless your drink, mighty chieftain," Brother Eadmond called, rising to his feet, "so the Lord's favor shall rest on you and your kin, and the light of Christ, Son of the Almighty, shall guide your path in these times of darkness and strife."

"Bless away!" Jarl Gustav grumbled, tearing his gaze from Toril's lengthy preparation. The monk took the pitcher from Toril. A muscle twitched on her cheek as she took her seat next to her father.

"May the blessings of the True God descend upon this mead," the monk intoned, raising the pitcher toward his hosts, "and fortify your bodies and spirits." Turning to the hearth, he continued, "May this brew, purified by fire, shield you from all harm, both seen and unseen." He turned to the right, where shields and weapons decorated the wall. "May this drink bring forth the vigor and renowned strength of the noble tribe of Hrafney." Finally, he placed the pitcher on the floor between him and the door, making the sign of the cross over it. "In the name of the Father, the Son, and the Holy Spirit, I consecrate this mead, that it may bring peace."

"And may the pitcher reach the table before we all die of old age," the jarl growled.

"Forgive me, uncle," Rikard interjected, "but we cannot rush the blessings of a god who sent us such selfless and humble messengers when dangers and treachery may lurk all around us." His gaze swept the room, settling on his cousin. Rising to his feet, he lifted his ornate cup and approached the monk. "Brother Eadmund, can we ever thank you enough for your timely warning? And Brother Aldred, too. A place is set at the table, but I don't see him. I hope nothing ill has befallen our dear guest."

"Your kindness touches my heart, young warrior," the monk replied, bowing his head with a benevolent smile. "Brother Aldred is in good health, though he abstains from sustenance in praise of the Lord for our safe passage. He sends his sincere apologies for missing supper. I'll be joining him in his prayers tomorrow."

"Oh, excellent!" Rikard exclaimed, taking the pitcher from the monk's hands. "So you can toast to my uncle's health tonight." He filled his cup. "Here you go, the first draught, for the bearer of such important tidings."

"Oh no, young Viking lord," the monk protested, shaking his head. "I will join you for bread at the table, but I've taken a solemn vow preventing me from tasting your delicious mead."

"Admirable," Rikard nodded. "So many new customs you bring. Still, *our* custom is to drink to the chieftain's health. Surely, your god sees the difference between honoring our host and indulging horn after horn to dull your senses. Now take the cup and drink before my uncle grows impatient."

"I cannot, my apologies," the monk replied, stepping backward and raising his hands.

"And I insist, my apologies." Rikard seized the retreating man's hand and forced the cup on him.

"What's going on?" Jarl Gustav bellowed.

"More than we thought, dear Uncle." Rikard pulled an empty vial from the monk's sleeve. "Belladonna," he said after sniffing. "I'm not a healer, but I would like the monk"—he spat the word—"to demonstrate his blessing first."

"Then have him drink," Jarl Gustav roared. His face flushed crimson, his eyes blazing with fury. He slammed his fist on the table, the sound echoing through the hall. Brother Eadmond tore himself from Rikard's grip and rushed to the door. But two warriors blocked his way. They shoved the struggling man to his knees, pulled his head back, and pried his mouth open.

Rikard pinched the monk's nose and poured the mead down his throat. The imposter struggled, gasped for air, and spluttered, but couldn't prevent swallowing half the pitcher's contents. The guards released him and stepped back, drawing their weapons.

"It matters not," he groaned as his stomach heaved. "You are doomed; you're all doomed!" He sank to all fours. "The fires are lit. Our mighty ships will come before sunrise. Your sailors chase shadows," he rasped, clutching his throat. "They'll return to ruin and ashes!"

"You'd planned to light signal fires once our warriors had left, right?" Rikard asked, not expecting an answer. "Was that Brother Aldred's task? I'm afraid my thrall delayed him." Rikard turned to the head table. "This afternoon, Agnetha overheard two conspirators plotting treason," he declared.

Toril's face lost all color. She pushed back from the table and balled her hands into fists, but couldn't prevent them from shaking. Her father's hand went to his bejeweled battle axe leaning against his chair.

"This false monk," Rikard pointed to the man who struggled to draw breath, "and his 'brother' are no Christian friars; they're Stígur Asmundsen's grunts."

"What?" Toril's shout of surprise cut through the angry murmurs filling the hall. She'd jumped to her feet, cold sweat glistening on her forehead.

"They believed us fooled because neither Greger nor Ivar," he pointed again to the suffocating man, "ever left Brótinholm before. But my Agnetha spent time in Fårosünd's hall and recognized them. She had so many questions requiring painful answers. In the end, her need to learn the hidden truth was so profound that the good brother Aldred couldn't help himself. He lent her a hand."

Rikard pulled the bundle Bergrún had given him from his satchel and tossed it on the floor. Landing with a dull thud and the clinking of metal, the package slid over the rough wooden floor. Its contents spilled from the wrapping, and inches from the dying false monk lay the severed hand of his co-conspirator, surrounded by a dozen silver coins from the Inglandia campaign, many bearing the Lion and the Thistle, the seal of the High King of the Britons.

* * *

STÍGUR ASMUNDSEN TOWERED at the bow of the *Dragon's Tooth*, Fårosünd's grandest warship. With one foot on the railing, he looked out over the black waves toward a speck of deeper darkness on the horizon. His hands twisted the end of a rope until the tortured fibers groaned. He wore light leather armor, and the muscles in his thick arms flexed beneath a sleeveless tunic. A double-bladed axe hung on his belt, and he carried a battle-scarred shield slung over his shoulder. Sensing the approach of another man, Fårosünd's chieftain turned.

"Still no signal, sisterbrother?"

"Patience, my chieftain," Hannu Gundulfsen replied. "A good ale requires a moon's span to ripen. Our plan is of Loki's making, but even the trickster needs to bide his time." The younger warrior wore black from head to toe without any visible weapons. His wiry frame created a stark contrast to that of a war leader.

"The plan may be," his chieftain replied, "but Greger... He's an idiot! I always wondered if his mother had lain with a troll."

"How fortunate, then, that our 'Brother Aldred' does not speak the Norsk tongue. All he needs to do is strike flint against steel. I'm sure even a troll could do that."

"Still, I should've sent you."

"Me? Alas, the mighty warrior Hannu Gundulfsen is too famous across the worlds." Chuckling, he pulled a concealed throwing knife from under his sleeve. "I'd have given it all away. We have hours yet until dawn. And a bloody dawn it shall be!" The younger warrior's tone grew more serious, and he let his gaze wander to the east. "That, my chieftain, I promise you!"

Both men stood in silence, listening to the voices of drowned sailors drifting on the wind. Swift-moving clouds covered the sky, obscuring the moonlight while revealing fleeting patches of stars. The rigging creaked in time with the swaying ship while the sail lay furled and covered to hide her from prying eyes.

"Fire, ho!" The shout from the crow's nest ripped through the silence. "Two scales starboard, fire, ho!"

"By Odin, men!" Stígur Asmundsen bellowed. "To the oars and row! Pull for the souls of your wives. Pull for the blood of your daughters. Bring us in for vengeance and glory!"

Drums started beating, and wood groaned as the oars cut into the sea with angry chops. To their left, the rhythmic sound echoed as the *Stormbringer's* crew fell into lockstep. Slicing through the waves like an axe through an apple, both longships gained speed, closing the distance to the island ahead.

"Fire, ho!" the boy in the crow's nest shouted again. "Second fire, a scale to port of the first."

"See, my chieftain," Hannu said, a smirk twisting his lips. "The confirmation! Their warriors have left. Fools! We'll have to make do with their bairns and womenfolk."

"On that island, sisterbrother, there are no men, women, or children. Just enemies," Stígur Asmundsen spat. "We'll take no prisoners! We're wolves tonight, Fenrir's brood. Let them feel our teeth!"

"As you command, my chieftain. Pity, though, for old Jarl Gustav's daughter. I hear she's a beauty. But then, she must already be in Hela's embrace, the poison strangling her throat." Hannu let out a low, mirthless chuckle.

"Enough of women-talk! Enough of plans and poisons!" The chieftain turned and grabbed the younger man by the arm, his hand squeezing. "Time for bloodwork!" he hissed, his eyes blazing. "Ready the men!"

* * *

RIKARD CROUCHED BEHIND a group of boulders, a dozen men by his side. The air hung heavy with the scent of brine and seaweed, and a chill wind whipped his hair around his face. His heart pounded against his ribs. Wiping his sweaty hands on his tunic, he looked down toward the bay and the dark waves beyond.

Half an hour had passed since Jarl Gustav ordered the fires lit—half an hour during which the faint sound of drums grew steadily louder. His combat masters had warned about the moments before a battle when doubt erodes confidence and strength seeps into the ground with every idle heartbeat.

Following their advice, the young warrior checked and rechecked his armor and weapons, tightening straps and honing edges.

"Not long now," he encouraged, his voice low. The splashing of oars sounded in rhythm with the drums. "Stay firm, shields up, ranks tight, and shout to the heavens," Rikard instructed. The man beside him nodded. Some were youths in training, others crafters and farmers, outfitted with spears and shields. Positioned at the top of the gravel field cutting through the cliffs, his contingent served as both a decoy and the last line of defense.

The trap had been Rikard's plan. He'd placed the fires to lure the enemy onto a battlefield of his choosing. Once the invaders landed their ships, they would have to ascend through a narrow ravine. Toril had a score of archers, mostly women, hidden on one rise, while Edda led a group of thralls with farm tools to the other side. Some older warriors stood with the archers to repel any men climbing the cliffs. Hamarrfjord's remaining fighters, led by the jarl himself, waited with the thralls to flank the Fårosünd Vikings once the trap had been sprung.

The ships came into sight. Two longboats, packed to the brim with warriors, flew toward the shore, swift as diving razorbills. That meant at least four score of men, matching the assembled defenders in numbers. But those men were killers all.

"We have the high ground," Rikard called, seeing his fear reflected in his men's eyes. "On my command, form a wall of shields, spears leveled. We'll hold them down, repel their advance, and give our longbows easy targets."

The first ship ran aground. The wooden hull scraped against the rocks. The drums fell silent. The second ship beached further up the coast. Splashes followed in rapid succession as men jumped into the surf. One more moment of quiet hovered between heartbeats. Then, the blood-curdling shouts of Viking raiders rushing up the incline signaled the battle's beginning.

* * *

"LOOSE!" TORIL SHOUTED. The horde of hostile Vikings had spread out below, the narrow ravine impeding formations. Their advanced runners had already come within twenty paces of the top. Others remained at the bottom while the main body clogged a choke point halfway up.

Arrows rose high into the air. A second volley followed, and a third, before the first wave hit its targets. Men stumbled, screaming in pain. Ripping shields from their backs, they turned to face the onslaught of deadly projectiles.

"Forward!" Toril ordered. "Pick targets at will. Stop their ascent!" Her archers emerged from concealment, stepping to the edge of the cliff. Arrows streaked through the night in broken patterns. The hunters took deliberate aim, choosing their prey with precision.

A rumble from the opposite hill caught Toril's attention. Edda's thralls had tipped stones and logs over the rim. The objects rolled down the hill, picking up speed, and created a gravel avalanche that slammed into the backs of the overwhelmed invaders.

Toril had been skeptical about Rikard's plan, doubting what a handful of shovels and pickaxes could achieve. Yet the effect proved devastating to their enemies. The earth shook under her feet as large chunks of the cliff broke off. Countless boulders thundered over the steep slope, providing a deep and menacing counterpoint to the high-pitched screams of dying men.

This isn't the work of thralls with shovels, Toril realized. *This is something else... too easy, too unexpected, too unnatural.* She narrowed her eyes, squinting across the gorge, but couldn't make out any details in the darkness.

Below, some raiders turned, scrambling back to their longships. Desperate to escape the trap, they found Olver's vessels barring the bay.

Prior to attending the feast, Rikard had sprinted to the harbor, arriving moments before the Shield of Hamarrfjord set sail. Despite Olver's initial skepticism, Rikard convinced him of the monks' treachery, the Danheimr ruse, and the impending attack. Her consort agreed to stay close and cut off the invaders' retreat.

Who'd have thought my cousin so cunning and persuasive? Toril pondered with a tinge of bitterness. *He's grown from a novice to a player to a challenger in such a short time. I'd better watch out!*

On the killing field, flaming arrows arced through the night, finding targets in men, wood, and cloth alike. Some Fårosünd Vikings returned fire. Two archers from Toril's ranks had fallen. Yet, the resistance grew feeble. Over two-thirds of the raiders had already been killed or wounded when the Jarl, with a mighty roar befitting a much younger man, led his men into battle.

* * *

"Retreat!" Hannu Gundulfsen shouted. "We must retreat." Bending over, he leaned on an axe next to his chieftain amidst a field of death. Only five other warriors still stood upright. Covered in blood and gore, many sported arrow wounds.

"To where?" Stígur Asmundsen raised his axe—heavy, though not yet bloodied. "The burning ships? The deadly slopes? Or the Hel-sent archers?"

"We need cover," Hannu replied, his gaze sweeping the devastation.

The chieftain followed his gaze. Warriors he'd known from childhood lay crushed, slain by inhuman foes. Deadly arrows kept raining down. Fires blazed on the water, consuming his fleeing men. Death everywhere.

"No," he snarled. Fixing his dead sister's husband, the brother he never had, with a glare of cold fury, he declared, "I won't hide! I won't flee! I won't surrender!" His voice rose, thunder becoming a hurricane.

"Onward!" chieftain Stígur bellowed. "Onward to Odin's halls! Let us take as many with us as we can." He dropped his shield, hefted his axe, and started toward the row of spearmen ahead.

"To Odin's halls!" the remaining men shouted. And they, too, rushed the deadly shield wall atop the ravine.

* * *

RIKARD STOOD AT the center of the line, shoulder to shoulder, shield to shield. Like watching a puppet play from the children's row in the hall, he'd seen his plan unfold. The scent of blood and smoke choked the air. Cries of men mixed with the grumble of rocks as bones cracked like twigs. Arrows thumped into flesh far more often than scraping on rocks.

The young warrior, son to a hero, nephew to the chieftain, had squeezed his shield and spear so tight he'd lost the feeling in his fingers. Beyond that, he hadn't done anything. He just stood and watched.

"It's over," the boy to his left exclaimed. "The battle's over. We won!"

More chatter started among the men. Words repeated, "We won! We won!" growing in strength. Rikard closed his eyes and sent a silent prayer to Odin. His muscles relaxed, and the grip on his weapons loosened until the boy next to him screamed.

Like demons stepping from a sulfur vent's deadly veil, figures emerged. Rikard's eyes widened in horror. Bleeding from countless wounds, these inhuman fiends attacked, throwing themselves against the line. Axes cracked shields, shoving men to the floor like reeds. Deadly thrusts followed, silencing the cries of alarm.

In less than two heartbeats, the line had shattered. Some youths dropped their weapons, turned, and ran. They fell before reaching safety.

Others sliced and hacked with their swords, hitting friend and foe alike.

Dodging a vicious blow, Rikard dropped his useless spear and parried the onslaught with his shield in both hands. The attacker's axe got lodged, and the berserker ripped the shield from Rikard's numb fingers.

He toppled sideways. An opening appeared, and the young Viking lunged. His dagger pierced the man's jugular. Blood sprayed like a geyser. Rikard let go of his knife and pulled his sword. He stood alone, facing two demons, while from below, a third figure approached, clothed all in black.

* * *

"FIRE!" TORIL YELLED. "They're getting through!" She had seized two women from the line of archers and shoved them to face the ravine's lip.

"But, Mistress," the younger woman complained. "We'll hit our men."

"Our *men* have fled like sheep!" Toril waved her hand toward the village. "Taking cover with your babes. And both shall perish ere the night is out if you don't shoot!"

"One warrior is still fighting," the other woman argued. Toril grabbed the woman by her throat. Viper-quick, a knife was in her hand. The tip hovered an inch from the shocked woman's eyeball.

"Kill every last one of them!" the jarl's daughter snarled, her eyes wide, her teeth bared. "Or, so Fenrir help me, I'll gut you where you stand!"

* * *

BERGRÚN STUMBLED DOWN the slope. Her vision swam, her ears rang, and a legion of giants pounded their hammers inside her skull. She'd done it again, overextended herself. She'd deployed her powers recklessly. Now came the reckoning. She needed to replenish her life force before she fell unconscious.

"No time," she wheezed, placing one foot in front of the other on the uneven ground.

Wouldn't it be to the Norns' taste if my own avalanche swallowed my black soul? The thought cut through the swirling haze like a crone's cackle at a funeral.

"Not yet!" she hissed, shaking her fist toward the heavens. Rikard was in danger. His shield brothers had fled like pigeons, finding a fox among them. Bergrún had to get closer. She stumbled and fell to her knees. Her cry of pain was a miserable croak, missing the strength of her deflated lungs.

Rikard, she thought. *Must get to Rikard! That stupid boy with his honest blue eyes...* Her mind started to wander. *When has he become more to me than a chess piece?*

Desperate, she squeezed her eyes shut, casting out with a deeper sense. She searched the rubble for the flickering ember of life. *There!* A groan to her left, a hand sticking out from under a rock, the fingers still twitching. Bergrún crawled like a beast and snatched the hand in both of hers. She drew in a deep breath, pulling the last vestiges of life from his broken body. As his fingers went limp, a wave of pure bliss washed over her, causing a guttural moan to escape her lips.

* * *

RIKARD PARRIED ONE raider's sword stroke and dodged a second man's axe blow. The larger attacker lost his balance, falling to his knees as the axe blade sliced into the ground. Rikard pivoted, his senses sharp, his movements precise. He punched the sword wielder in the face. Then, he stepped in to kill his toppled comrade. A sharp sting pierced his left arm. Rikard stared in confusion. A throwing knife stuck in his flesh, blood staining his tunic.

He staggered backward, eyes widening in shock. There was no pain, not yet, he knew. Retreating two steps to level ground, he widened his stance. He swung his sword with grim determination, seeing all three enemies closing in.

This is how Ragnarök must feel, he thought, looking at the gruesome specters advancing toward him. *When Hel's doors are flung open, demons like these will walk the world.*

The larger man had freed his axe and ordered the others to spread out. All three charged him as one. Their battle screams shook the night as arrows began to rain down.

* * *

BERGRÚN'S MUSCLES TWITCHED, her whole body vibrating. She needed, as always, several heartbeats to rise again. Starting to walk, she jogged, ran, and finally sprinted as the energy surged through her veins. Twenty paces from Rikard's desperate fight, the witch snatched a fallen spear from a dead Viking's grasp without breaking stride. She threw, sending her curses along with it. The weapon soared true, hitting a sword-wielding warrior. The broad iron tip split his head open, exiting bloodied between his eyes.

* * *

ATOP THE HILL, an arrow had struck Rikard in the foot. His large opponent took one through the shoulder. Neither quit the fight. They circled each other like wolves from rival packs, probing the space in between with lunges and feints. The young Viking felt his strength draining with every drop of blood spilling from the knife wound. And more deadly blades flew past, thrown by the black-clad warrior. To Rikard's relief, someone had eliminated the third aggressor. He hoped for reinforcement, yet only arrows were sent his way.

Rikard ducked, avoiding another vicious blow. He'd lost his sword. Raising his gaze, his eyes fixed on a gleaming knife streaking toward his face. He couldn't move. Like in a dream, the world slowed. His arms and legs felt as though they were stuck in honey. The blade neared with mesmerizing grace, promising the ultimate gift to mankind—oblivion. Then it veered off course, clipping his ear, and the spell was broken.

Looking around in confusion, the young Viking spotted Agnetha slicing the black-clad warrior's throat open from one ear to the other. She jumped to her feet, her eyes glowing red, and her movements defied the bounds of reality. She kicked an axe into her hand and rushed the last standing invader.

"Hello, Stígur," she snarled with the ferocity of a rabid badger. Stígur's eyes narrowed before widening in recognition.

"You!" Fårosünd's chieftain staggered, struggling to raise his axe.

She took two steps, jumped, and kicked. Her foot hit the stunned chieftain on his cheek, sending the large man flying sideways. He crashed to the floor with a thud.

"Like for like!" she hissed. He rolled, trying to reach his fallen weapon. Swift as a deer, she sprang. One foot landed on his outstretched arm, shattering bones. The other foot found a soft spot between his legs. He howled in pain. She twisted with a dancer's grace, raising her axe for a deadly blow. Then, an arrow pierced her chest.

Bergrún fell to her knees, coughing blood. Her hands fumbled at her chest, trying to dislodge the arrow. She couldn't manage. Sinking onto her haunches, she planted her hands on the ground to steady her swaying body. Her breath came in ragged gasps, accompanied by a sickly, wet gurgle.

Stígur pushed himself to all fours. He struggled to pull a dagger from his boot with his mangled hand. Wheezing, he crawled toward Bergrún.

"No!" Rikard shouted. His vision blurred. The blood loss made him lightheaded. He was unarmed, every muscle hurt, and his weariness threatened to overwhelm him. It didn't matter. He limped forward and threw himself onto the larger man's back, dropping him to the ground. Rikard pulled the invader's head by the hair. With cries of agony and frustration, he smashed Stígur's face against the rocks. Over and over, he bashed the fallen man's skull against the gravel. Then he let go, took a large stone in his hand, and hit his foe on the back of the head.

"Rikard," Bergrún wheezed. She lay on her stomach, her legs struggling for purchase. The arrow had broken off, and her hand stretched toward him.

"Hand..." she rasped.

Rikard rolled off Stígur's corpse and seized her hand, tears in his eyes.

"His hand," she coughed. He looked confused, his jaw dropping. "Do it," she begged, a breath away from death.

Rikard yanked Stígur's hand toward her, and she snatched it with surprising speed. Then, her head fell limp. She didn't move; she didn't breathe.

The young Viking knelt beside her, the gravel biting into his knees. Blood slicked his hands, his tunic, and the very stones beneath him. His gaze rested on her, lying so still, her face pale against the dark earth.

The sun hadn't yet risen. The sky just faded from black to indigo, tinged with the glow of dying fires. A wave of sorrow, thick and suffocating, washed over him. He would be dead, never seeing another sunrise. They all would be if it hadn't been for her. She saved her captors, warned her enemies, rescued the useless owner of her bondage, and paid the ultimate price.

He reached a shaking hand, trying to wipe a strand of her raven-black hair from her face. His fingers touched her cold skin as tears welled in his eyes. Then she gasped, her body shuddering. A soft-glowing aura enveloped her. The light pulsed like a heartbeat before vanishing into her skin.

Succession

"HERE HE IS!" Toril skipped from stone to stone toward the water's edge. "The Hero of Hamarrfjord!" She'd lost her shoes, a rosy flush colored her cheeks, and her golden braids had come undone.

Rikard turned. He sat on a bone-white driftwood tree, his boots scuffing the wet sand. He'd been looking out over the ocean. The tiny beach hid in a cove not far from the village. The eroding cliff, topped with prickly thorn bushes, made it the perfect place to be alone with one's thoughts. To get away. To hide.

"Not you, too," he groaned. "Isn't there a limit on how many cheers I have to endure merely for surviving a battle?"

"Endure?" she laughed. "Aren't 'enjoy, savor, and relish' the words you're looking for?" She sat beside him, pushing him to make space with a nudge and a pout like in their childhood days. "Here!" She offered him the wineskin she carried.

"Thanks, but I had more than enough for a day."

"Ah, but this is the oak-matured sack mead from Father's private store. Remember when you and your friend Claas stole a jug?" she asked, grinning. "You got so drunk that we had to put you in the sheep pen to sober up. How long ago was that?"

"Just two summers," he grumbled. "It feels like a lifetime."

"Right... Sometimes, I forget how fast you've grown." She ruffled his hair, having to raise her arm higher than expected. He scowled. But then, he broke into a grin despite himself before taking a long pull from the wineskin. The mead was warm and rich like summer sunshine.

"So why are you here, all alone, hiding, when the whole village is celebrating you?" she asked.

"Because I wanted to be here, all alone, hiding, when the whole village is celebrating me," he replied, his gaze on the horizon. "I didn't do anything! Agnetha uncovered the treachery, you organized the archers, Edda directed the thralls, our chieftain led the men into battle, and Olver sank the fleeing raiders. And what did I do? I let seven men die." His voice turned bitter, and his hands squeezed the wineskin. "I had the smallest force, the easiest task, and I lost the most men."

While the battle had been won with Stígur Asmundsen's death, the horror didn't end there. Twenty-one villagers had lost their lives defending their home. On the square in front of the longhouse, their bodies had lain on a funeral pyre, shoulder to shoulder, ignoring rank or riches. Their spirits rose with the acrid smoke to the heavens, seeking welcome in Odin's halls.

Though Jarl Gustav, his arm in a sling and his weathered face bruised, offered Rikard the honor of lighting the pyre, the young warrior declined. He insisted that Toril and Olver performed the sacred task, as her archers and his ships had won the day. Together, the couple strode forth, igniting the oil-soaked wood.

The bitter smoke burned Rikard's eyes, and tears welled in their corners. His mother and sister had lain on such a pyre less than a year ago. The same raiders from Fårosünd had killed them. With the rising sun, Fårosünd was no more. More than eighty of their warriors lay dead. Rikard felt no satisfaction. His kin would never rise again, regardless of how many foes he slew. Every kill was just one more blood debt the Norns would collect in due time, with heavy interest.

"The men fighting and dying beside you," Toril said in a somber tone, her hand on Rikard's knee, "I'm not saying don't mourn their passing. But Rikard, look how many lives you saved." He tilted his head. The rising sun crested the horizon, the warm glow reflecting on Toril's face. Tears glistened in her eyes, yet a fire burned within. Her hand squeezed his leg.

"Your plan led us to victory," she insisted. "Your thrall, the enigmatic Agnetha, wouldn't have brought you the news if you hadn't spared her on Fårosünd. The Norns weave their pattern in ways we might not understand. But what thread they use—strong or weak—makes all the difference. And the Norns chose you, blessed you!"

He lowered his gaze, dragging his feet back and forth over the wet sand, leaving deep furrows. Then he nodded, taking another draught of the mead.

Both fell silent, listening to the wind and the restless waves washing over the beach. She let go of his knee and pulled her cloak tight against the chill.

"Thank you, Toril," he finally said. "I'll sit here a little longer before going to sleep. It's been a long two days."

"I understand, but there's more. I didn't come here to just talk about the battle. The strife we endured..." she whispered. "Dear cousin, I want to be friends again. You care for the people, for all the people. And so do I. I need you by my side; I want to be on yours! Like in the old days." She gave him a sad little smile. "We banded together to battle your brother. Harold never saw us coming. Let us work together again, strive, fight, win together!" Her voice rose, passion coloring every syllable. "For the future of *our* people."

"You speak of your father's prophecy?" he asked.

"Yes! The prophecy."

"You think it means you and me, not you and Olver?"

"*With warrior's strength to seize her goal...* I don't think this line refers to only one man," she replied. "Wouldn't more strength be even better?"

"And the rest of it?" he asked. "The black sin, the marring of heart and soul... Aren't you concerned? What does it all mean?"

"Of course, I am. But then, I've never met a soothsayer who didn't speak in riddles. I'm not even sure if I believe in prophecies sealing our fate in amber, fixed and unmoving. But the signs don't bode well," she implored. "We cannot stand alone against the gathering storm. Whether the Danskers, the Norskar, or the Gauls... We need allies."

"That's why you wish for Danheimr's rule over us?" Color rose in his cheeks.

"I don't wish it..."

"The false monks carried several Danheimr coins," he argued. "Who says King Olaf hadn't arranged for one troublesome clan to eliminate another?"

"Rikard," she pleaded. "I don't know the answers. They could've brought them to prove Danheimr warships attacked them."

"I've never heard of raiders giving their victims coins," he scoffed.

"All I know is we are mired in the past. Our houses, our crafts, our society... We are leagues behind the larger nations to the south." She looked at him, her eyes shining. "We can either march to our doom alone or sail into the future as part of a mighty fleet. That's what the prophecy means by raising a *queen without a crown.*"

* * *

THE SUN STOOD high in the sky as Rikard slipped into the yard behind his house. His hands and knees were dirty, stained reddish-brown with clay from climbing the muddied cliffs. He stayed at the beach long after Toril left, his thoughts churning like the turbulent sea. When his tiredness threatened to overwhelm him, he left, skirting the village. He couldn't face any more cheers, nor was he eager to walk past the pyre's ashen remains.

Dropping his soiled clothes by the rain barrel, he dunked his head. The icy water sent shivers down his body while also freezing the onset of headaches. He scrubbed his knees and elbows, washing off the sticky muck as best he could. Bare-chested and clothed only in his thin undergarments, Rikard climbed the stairs to his bedroom. He sank onto his bed and fell asleep in a heartbeat. Cold hands rolled him over, freeing the furs underneath, and wrapped him like a babe in a cradle.

It was dark when Rikard woke. His ears strained to identify the noise that had woken him. Yet the house remained silent. The window shutters were closed, and only a faint red glow emanated from the fireplace. He struggled to sit upright. His head swam; every muscle hurt. Someone had buried him under a pile of blankets. Massaging the bridge of his nose, he took deep breaths. His mouth felt dry, and last night's mead caused his stomach to churn. Freeing his legs, he planted his bare feet on the cold floorboards.

The creak sounded again. Rikard snapped his gaze to the right. His skull throbbed after the sudden turn. He stared into the darkness. Someone or something hid in the shadows between the fireplace and the window. Then a flame ignited, a candle catching fire, and the light revealed a pale face framed by long, black hair.

"Have you slept well, Master Rikard?" Bergrún asked.

"Agnetha?" Rikard gasped. "By Odin's remaining eye! You could've frightened me to death. What are you doing here?"

"I watched you sleep. Did you have bad dreams? You tossed and rolled, almost falling out of bed. Did you reenact the battle?"

"I don't remember... Why aren't you in your bed? Your injury... I gave instructions to let you rest in the other room. Did Edda kick you out?"

"Edda wouldn't dare defy the wishes of Hamarrfjord's Hero," Bergrún chuckled. "No, I got bored; too soft a bed for just me by myself."

"And you prefer a creaking chair?" he asked. "Excuse me one moment." He moved to the chamberpot in the corner and hesitated, considering his company. "Would you mind?" he stammered.

She got to her feet and walked to the window, opening the shutters. The sun hadn't yet risen; only a purple band ringed the horizon. A draft of icy air entered. Rikard relieved himself, cringing at the noisy splatter filling the silence.

"I apologize," he croaked, turning his head toward the window. Then he jerked in surprise, almost missing the pot. She stood naked, her long black hair spilling over her shoulders, reaching almost to the middle of her back. Her pale skin shimmered in the faint light.

"Mind yourself, Master Rikard!" she huffed. "I have to clean up after you."

Blushing deep red to the roots of his hair, Rikard pulled his underpants up and stood rooted to the floor, lowering his gaze. She walked past him, picked up the pot, and dumped the contents out of the window.

"I could've done that," he stammered.

"Emptying a chamberpot is not a task befitting the Hero of Hamarr-fjord," she mused.

"Stop it, please," he groaned. Then he raised his gaze. The young woman stood in front of the window, backlit by the dawn's orange tint. Her posture was relaxed, one knee bent inward, one hand resting on her narrow hip as if she were posing for a sculptor. A jagged wound, dark red and swollen, marred her smooth skin between her breasts, corrupting her beauty like a charred tree in a wildflower meadow. Yet the wound looked weeks old, not mere hours.

"Aren't you cold?" he rasped, clearing a lump from his throat. "The air is freezing."

"Terribly," she replied, not moving. Her lips pulled into a crooked smile.

"Please..." He pointed to the fur-covered bed. "I'll take the chair."

"But this is your chamber, Master Rikard. Surely, the bed is large enough for both of us." She closed the window, leaving the room in the flickering light of a single candle, and slipped under the covers.

* * *

"Do you want to talk about it?" he asked some time later. She lay beside him, her head nestled on his shoulder, letting her nails slide over his wiry chest.

"Men," she laughed, "always need to relive their battle prowess. Must I praise your glory?"

"Not about that," he choked. "I mean the raid... Your wound... And after..."

"Oh, that," she muttered, offering no further explanation. Silence fell.

"I thought you were dead!" he whispered. "I thought I'd lost you."

"I almost was," she whispered. "I felt Hela's cold embrace, saw the fires of damned souls burning ahead..."

"But how? I was hurt, dizzy, and bleeding, yet I swear to Odin I saw a glow enveloping you. And after..." He remembered Bergrún sitting up on the killing field, wiping the blood from her lips and instructing him to cut the arrowhead out of her chest. Then, she'd stumbled down the ravine to look for injured foes, relieving them of their suffering. He'd been swept away by the victorious warriors and hadn't seen her again until this morning.

"Rikard," she said, raising her head. "I'll never hurt you, I promise. I like you very much." Propping herself up on her elbow, she let her right hand rest over his heart, blinking rapidly. Her lips twitched. The lie had come too easily, the words flowed too naturally. Her heart raced and her skin tingled. What was going on?

"Can you trust me," she whispered, swallowing the lump in her throat, "even if I don't share all my secrets? If I told you now, I'm afraid it'll break you, break us... I'll explain another time," she rushed on as he opened his mouth to speak, "I promise. Please, don't press me at this moment for the whole, ugly truth." She looked at him, her eyes wide, unguarded, and a sheen of moisture reflected the faint red glow of the rekindled embers."

"Agnetha," he rasped, lost in her gaze. "You saved me, thrice!" He rolled on his side and placed his left hand gently under her chin. "I don't know how and why I've won your loyalty. I can't deserve what you've given me. But what I do know, deep in my heart, is that you are a brave person, an honest person, a good person. And I do trust you!" He pulled her close, and they kissed.

* * *

"So, why did you do it?" she asked hours later. The sun had risen halfway into the sky, and Edda's boys had entered the room twice, serving breakfast and adding logs to the fire. Rikard made no effort to hide Bergrún in his bed, sending the already swirling rumors into a gossip hurricane. He didn't mind. He felt happy and content, forgetting for a few blissful moments the battles past and those yet to come.

"What do you mean?" he replied, pulled from his own train of thought. There were many things he'd done lately that warranted the question *Why?*, inviting a mysterious thrall into his bed being the first and foremost among them. Anxiety rekindled.

"The Fårosünd raiders," she clarified. "Why did you insist on a sea burial of your foes? Why not throw their bodies into a ditch, or leave them where they'd fallen for the crows and foxes?"

"Well..." He coughed, not expecting the conversation to turn that direction. "They came to avenge their dead. The Fårosünd warriors felt honor-bound, owing us *blóðhefnd* because we raided their village a moon's span ago. We killed their women and children. But we also felt honor-bound to avenge our dead, my mother and sister among them. A vicious cycle, once fueled by violence, keeps spinning." His voice had gained strength, passion coloring his cheeks. "Yet, none of the dead will ever rise again. Only new souls perish, new blood is spilled, and new scars mar the living."

"I can't offer my open hand to bloodthirsty raiders crawling onto our shores," he said after a pause. "I'm not a monk of the White Christ, believing forgiveness is the highest of virtues. I was raised a warrior. I am my father's son and Jarl Gustav's nephew. But I can show respect to the dead—men bound by their upbringing as much as I am, dying for what they'd believed in. Once a man is dead, he isn't an enemy any longer."

"You are a strange man, Rikard Thure Svensen." Bergrún's eyes held his gaze captive, her nails digging into his skin.

"You think me a fool?"

"Perhaps," she mused. "But a *fool* I could like, a *fool* I can live with. Watch out, mighty warrior, you might end up making the world a better place."

A knock sounded at the door before he could respond.

"Master Rikard," one of Edda's twins called. "The chieftain has sent for you. He called a council in the longhouse, requesting your presence with haste."

"Hop along then, fool," she laughed before pulling him into a kiss.

"I'm coming," he replied, his voice muffled.

"The jarl asked for Mistress Agnetha to come along. She is to bring her potions, respectfully."

"*Mistress* Agnetha?" Rikard chuckled, surprised.

"I could get used to it." She grinned. "Go ahead, Hero of Hamarrfjord. I need to dress, but my clothes are in the other room." She jumped out of the bed and wrapped herself in the blanket from the chair. Then she paused and looked into his eyes. "You're a good man, Rikard Svensen," she said, her tone fervent. "Give your counsel, decide our future, but beware: The world swallows good men for breakfast." With that, she left, pushing past the flabbergasted boy standing outside the room.

* * *

RIKARD HASTENED UP the stairs to the great hall, his fingers fumbling with the fastenings of his tunic. The day was fair, the sun bright against a pale blue sky. A mild breeze blew inland, though winter's cruel breath could not be far off. Very few people milled around, their movements moody and sluggish. The village was quiet, heavy with the lethargy of the victory feast.

Entering the hall, Rikard found it empty. No fire burned on the hearth. Looking around in bewilderment, he spotted the Finsgúr brothers standing guard in front of the small chamber to the side, arrayed in full battle gear.

"In here, Master Rikard," Envar called in a carrying whisper. The young Viking approached, and Eskil knocked, opening the door without waiting for a response. Rikard entered.

Jarl Gustav sat behind a table on a straight-backed chair. No fire was lit. No meat nor mead provided. Three chairs stood across in a tight arc. Toril sat in the middle, opposite her father, her face a mask of cool serenity. Olver sat to her left, his sword, shield, and axe left by the door. Picking up on the cue, Rikard unbuckled his sword belt and, dropping it next to Olver's weapons, he took the remaining seat. He looked expectant around the room. No one spoke, and Rikard's anxiety flared. They had to wait for him. Was there anger in the chieftain's glare, disapproval in Toril's tight lips? He couldn't read Olver's expression at all.

"Nothing of what's spoken under my roof leaves these halls without my consent," Jarl Gustav finally declared. His voice was deep and gravelly, having regained much of its strength. His pale blue eyes swept the room, fixing each in turn for several heartbeats. "You are the future of Hamarrfjord, our hope to weather the storms to come, and steer our clan into bountiful seas." He paused, letting his words sink in, before asking, "How could this happen?"

The silence that followed pressed on Rikard's ears. No one dared so much as to move a muscle. The jarl steepled his fingers to await their confessions.

"Toril!" His words cracked the silence like a whip. "Where is your clever tongue? Do you have any explanation?"

"Father," she replied, her voice low and steady. Rikard envied her composure. "We knew our enemies weren't vanquished but biding their time to strike again. We owe Rikard and his thrall, Agnetha, a debt for their timely warning and the victory his plan brought. If they hadn't..."

The chieftain raised his hand, cutting her off. His gaze turned to Rikard, boring into the young Viking with raw, unrelenting power. Rikard swallowed, his mouth dry.

"My Chieftain," he croaked, eschewing a more familiar address. "The victory does not belong to me. Olver's ships and Toril's archers... Our strength lies in the arms of our warriors. We fought..."

"Is that so, Olver?" Gustav Larsen interrupted. "Are our warriors superior to the Gaulish hordes, the Norsk mountain clans, or the Danske sea dogs?"

"Our men are fierce warriors, my Chieftain, as are our women. Our blades are keen, our shields broad. We pride ourselves on following the Thundergod's example to fight as long as a single drop of blood flows through our veins. Yet we are few." The tall Viking took a deep breath before continuing. "Too few to stand against united foes. If Toril hadn't organized the thralls, we might have lost the day ."

"So," the jarl growled. "Each of you points their blade's tip at someone else. Will no one claim the 'glory' for yesterday's bloody massacre?"

"Father!" Toril protested as Olver interjected, "My chieftain."

"I do, Uncle." Rikard forced his words through gritted teeth. A vein in his temple pulsed, and his muscles twitched with the tension. "The plan was mine, the guilt is mine. The blood of our kin clings to my hands, and mine alone."

Silence.

Jarl Gustav placed his hands flat on the table and leaned forward. His chair creaked under his shifting weight.

"You mistake me, Nephew," he said. His voice had lost the razor-sharp edge. "I'm not looking for a scapegoat." He turned to Olver. "I'm not talking of a desperate defeat." His eyes rested on his daughter. "There is no blame. I have naught but gratitude to share." He leaned back, and his thin lips drew into an almost smile as he regarded the three stunned figures across from him, staring back with eyes wide and mouths gaping open.

"We won a bloody battle against a superior force with little preparation," he said with pride. "We slew four foes for every soul lost. Farmhands, thralls, and young maidens taken away from their dolls, they fought and killed and won. Why would you think I blame any of you?"

"My chieftain..." Olver started, but the jarl stopped him with a raised hand.

"I brought you here," the aging warrior explained, "to make you see who won the battle. I need you to understand who's responsible for our victory. By confronting your deeds and those of others, I forced you to realize the truth, to speak it out loud."

Jarl Gustav paused again, letting the room vibrate with tension. Rikard sat frozen like a hare in a snake's glare. His heart hammered against his ribs, threatening to burst from his chest. Cold sweat trickled down his neck, and he squeezed his fists so tight his knuckles cracked. Toril's rapid breathing kept the rhythm with the creaking floorboards under Olver's twitching leg.

"The three of you together, and only together, you ensured our survival." Jarl Gustav Haakon Larsen stood and drew his dagger. The blade gleamed in the sunlight entering the window. "Hear my words and mark them well." His voice boomed in the small chamber. "My time is short, and our future is fraught with peril. So I decree that upon my death, the rule of our clan shall rest on your shoulders. Olver, I charge you with our defense. You rule supreme in questions of weapons, tactics, troops, and fleet. May Thor be on your side."

"Toril, my daughter," the chieftain continued, "I charge you with the domestic rule of our clan. Your word is law in questions of labor, customs, trade, and justicia. May Freya guide you, and us all, into a prosperous future."

"And you, Rikard," the warrior declared. "I charge you with truce-weavings and ally-bonding. You represent our clan on missions abroad. Bring us the strength to maintain our identity as the world tree changes and new horizons come into view. May Loki's wisdom, luck, and cunning help you on your journeys."

The chieftain stood tall, his jaw set, and his shoulders squared, reminding everyone of the bear-like strength he held when younger. Sliding his knife across the palm of his left hand, he let his blood drip onto a parchment on the table.

"These are my words, my commands, my law. Hear and obey, by Odin! For blood and glory!" he bellowed.

"For kin and jarl!" the three stunned future leaders replied in unison.

PART TWO

BLOOD-RED SUNRISE

*"I held a world in my hand,
and however I shook it,
however the pieces fell,
in whatever new patterns,
nothing changed."*

– Jorg Ancrath[1]

---

[1] Mark Lawrence (2012): King of Thorns, Book two of The Broken Empire series

CHAPTER ELEVEN

Return

B ERGRÚN STROLLED OVER the flowering meadow, down the hill past Rikard's house, her arms full of sweet-smelling violets. The sun shone bright from a blue sky, and birdsong filled the spring air. Less than a fortnight had passed since the last snows melted. Yet the mild breeze from the south relegated the wet winter and its long, cold nights to distant memory. She wore a new dress, deep blue with a white linen kirtle and intricate embroidery along the hemline. Her raven-black hair flowed in a tight braid down her back almost to her hips, and a handful of shy freckles accentuated her pale skin on her nose and cheeks. She hummed a tune, her high spirits evident to all the world.

Entering the longhouse, she marched past the guard, who greeted her with a nod, toward the tiny room below the stairs where she stored her herbs and prepared her potions. Stina descended from the upper floor, wiping her mouth and looking ill. Sweat glistened on her face, and her slender hands grabbed the railing in a vise-like hold.

"Stina," Bergrún called in alarm. "What is wrong?"

"Oh, Agnetha," the young woman replied, her voice faint. "Nothing. It'll pass. I'm just feeling a bit queasy."

"Come in here," Bergrún ordered. She kicked the door to her workshop open. Then, cramming the flowers into one arm, she reached her free hand toward her friend.

"The flowers are beautiful," Stina panted, reaching level ground. "Did Master Rikard..."

"What? No! Those are for the jarl."

"Why did you gather flowers for the jarl?" Stina asked, flabbergasted.

"Not flowers, tea. I'll brew an infusion. It helps with his chest pain. Get in here and sit down, I'll make you some tea as well." Bergrún planted her friend on the single, wobbly stool and took a pewter pitcher from a shelf. She returned to the hall to fill it with simmering water from the fireplace.

Back in the room, she crumpled chamomile blossoms into a clay jug, added sage and nettle, and poured steaming water on top. A delicious aroma filled the tiny space—floral, woody, and sweet.

"We'll have to wait for the tea to steep," she explained. "In the meantime, I'll prepare the infusion for our chieftain, and you tell me what has befallen you." The witch plucked the petals from the flowers and dropped them into a mortar for grinding.

"It's nothing," Stina said. "I told you." Lifting one flower to her nose, she sighed, relishing the blossom's sweet scent. "I think I'm with child again," she whispered, blushing.

"What?" Bergrún shrieked. "Who? When? I thought you were safe under this roof. Who was it? Tell me!" she growled.

"It's not like that," Stina protested. Her blush deepened, and she lowered her gaze. "It's the Shield's. You know, Master Olver's..."

The mortar exploded with a crack like a thunderclap. Splinters pelted the walls and fist-sized chunks thumped onto the floor. A whirlwind rose, rustling the drying herbs. Hooks clanged, pots shook, and the warped window shutters rattled.

"I went with him willingly," Stina shouted in alarm. "Please, Agnetha, calm down!" She jumped to her feet, seizing her friend by the wrists. "Please, it is well... Everything is well! He was gentle and kind. We talked at first, and he held me."

Bergrún took deep, steadying breaths. Her arms shook. Yet, the red glow in her eyes, pulsing with every heartbeat, grew fainter and went out. She relaxed her hands, dropping the pulp of crushed flowers to the floor. Refraining from wiping her sticky hands on her new dress, she pulled a strip of cloth from under her kirtle.

"If the jarl's daughter finds out," she hissed.

"But Mistress Toril arranged it all," Stina protested. "She came to me, offering the honor."

"SHE OFFERED THE HONOR?" Bergrún bellowed, reigniting the glow of molten lava in her eyes. The walls shook, the table rattled.

"Please, Agnetha!" Stina cried, raising her hands to her ears. "Please, don't ruin it!" Tears spilled from her frightened eyes.

That stopped Bergrún. She raised her hands, palms out, in a gesture of peace. Taking two steps back, she slid to the floor, pulled her knees up, and buried her face in her hands. No one moved, no one spoke. Finally, Stina sat beside her, sickness and tea forgotten.

"He made me his *elja*," the young woman explained, "his pillow wife. That is a great honor! No one in the village can touch me as long as he claims me. And my son... If it pleases Shield Olver, my son will be a freeman in his houschold. What more can I ask for?"

"And Toril arranged it?" Bergrún muttered, the sound muffled by her hands.

"Mistress Toril has so many duties, with the Althing and her father being ill. She suffers headaches at night and cramps on the full moon."

Bergrún raised her gaze and looked at her friend, astounded by the other woman's naïveté.

"A warrior... strong and handsome, you know..." Stina continued. "Well, all men have needs. Not unlike Master Rikard," she added with a sheepish grin.

"What about Rikard?" Bergrún asked, suspicious.

"He is said to have needs..."

"Who says?"

"Oh, come now, Agnetha. The whole village gossips about the two of you."

"I'm his thrall!" Bergrún protested.

"Aye, his thrall, in a queen's garb. Prancing through the village with the guards bowing their heads and the maids curtsying. I can see the ill fate that has befallen you." Bergrún scowled.

"It must be the rage then, about your disobedience, that brings the redness to poor Master Rikard's face whenever you promenade past him." Bergrún's scowl deepened.

"Oh, don't be coy! The only question left unanswered among us mortals is why you aren't yet with child," Stina giggled. "It can't be from lack of trying." She looked at Bergrún with heartfelt joy, and the witch, against all efforts, had to smile along. Yet, like the hopes for spring snuffed out by a snowstorm in April, her smile faded and her expression hardened.

"I can't bear children," she said in a low voice, almost inaudible. Stina's green eyes grew wide, and the witch averted her gaze. "I suffered... an injury when I... left the old healer in my home," she whispered. "I wasn't well for a long time. And after..."

"Oh, Agnetha…" Stina placed her arm around her friend. "I'm so sorry."

"Forgive my intrusion," the jarl's daughter interrupted, entering the room. "I just wondered if my father's tea was ready."

"Mistress Toril," Stina stammered, rising to her feet. "Forgive us. It's my fault. I delayed Agnetha with my trifles."

"Oh, nothing to forgive," Toril replied, her smile not reaching her eyes. "I'm sure there was much to discuss. Mayhaps advice on womanly matters? If I could ask you kindly to bring this tea to my father, as I, too, would hear good Agnetha's counsel," she added in a conspiratorial whisper.

Stina curtsied, seized the jug of chamomile tea, and rushed from the room without a backward glance. Bergrún had also risen to her feet. She straightened her dress, pulled her braid over one shoulder, and stood with her hands clasped, her eyes meeting Toril's gaze.

"How is dear Rikard?" Toril asked. "The Althing gathers in two days. I hope the anticipation doesn't give him sleepless nights. His opinions carry much weight among our people."

"I wouldn't know of his concerns, Mistress," Bergrún replied, her voice low and even. "The affairs of mighty Viking leaders are not mine to know." Her gaze wandered to the door, still open since Stina's departure.

"But if you'd asked, when he is… relaxed, he might share his thoughts even with a thrall like you."

"I wouldn't know how to explain such an unusual request, Mistress. If he suspected prying intent, it might provoke his anger."

"Such delicate things spring flowers are," Toril mused, picking up a violet and twirling the stem between her fingers. "They seem full of life and zest, yet a sudden frost crushes them in a heartbeat. I'm glad you met with dear Stina," the jarl's daughter continued. "You saw how happy, safe, and well she is under my roof."

"You may find flowers delicate," the witch replied. "Yet many carry potent toxins. And some will sting the careless picker."

"I wouldn't know of poisons." Toril gave a short laugh, harsh and mirthless. "That's not my forte. But men who fall on the battlefield when touched by a bare hand, such an interesting story Edda told me. You think it would entertain dear Rikard?"

"Some men might find a ghost story entertaining, while others prefer the sagas of intrigue. I heard one myself, not long ago, right here, outside this very room."

"Yet Rikard doesn't know of it?" Toril growled.

"As you said, Mistress. Master Rikard has many concerns. Why bother him with a tale older than last winter unless... a need arises anew?"

"Well then!" Toril huffed, smoothing the creases in her dress with unnecessary force. "We'll keep our stories, for now. And I must find out for myself what my dear cousin intends to do. Go back to your flowers, Agnetha. But beware the vines that creep in the shadows. They bind and strangle as easily as they bloom." The jarl's daughter fixed Bergrún with her glare, willing the other woman to avert her gaze first, when the village bell rang.

* * *

"WHAT HAVE YOU seen?" Hamarrfjord's shield asked the guard who had raised the alarm. "Not another rowboat, I hope!" He added, yet the tension in his voice strangled his attempted humor.

"No, my Shield. I spotted three sails on the horizon. Hard to tell against the sun, but one looks striped, red and blue, like the *Wave Dancer's.*"

"So, Hamarrfjord's lost son returns. Keep watch, man. Have the warriors form a double line, and don't sound the all-clear until you see the whites in the sailor's eyes. I'll inform the chieftain." He turned and took two steps before facing Toril.

"Who is it?" she asked.

"Looks like your dear cousin is coming home. That should make things interesting two days from now."

"First Agnetha and now Harold... If I had one moment's pause, I'm certain I shall hear Loki's laughter drifting on the wind."

"Why? What did Rikard's thrall do?" he asked, furrowing his brows.

"She thinks she can play the game," Toril replied, her gaze on the horizon. "We might need to do something about her."

"Shall I see to it?"

"Not now, sweetling. The mysterious Agnetha might know how to play, but I know how to win. Let's first see what flotsam the waves toss onto our beach. Does my father know?"

"I was on my way to the longhouse."

"Let me deal with our chieftain. It smells like rain, and my dress is new."

* * *

HAROLD SVENSEN STOOD at the bow of his longship, inhaling deep breaths as the smell of seaweed and damp earth grew stronger in the air. Ahead lay Hrafney, his home of craggy shores, sandy beaches, rolling hills, and windswept wooden huts. Njord's mighty breath had faltered, cut off by the island's shadow. The mainsail fluttered listlessly in the leeward eddies. He'd ordered to leave it hoisted, wanting its bright pattern to herald his return. Wood creaked and oars groaned as the men laboured to close the distance.

"She hasn't changed," Einar Finsgúr declared, his gaze on the nearing island. "Some specks of color, yet still as dreary as a pile of seagulls' droppings. Smells the same, too." The wiry warrior stood beside Harold, his hand resting on an unusually long sword that used to belong to a Gaulish knight. Being the same height as his war leader, the salt-and-pepper-haired Viking weighed at least two stone less. Although he was several years older, he'd been Harold's friend, mentor, and brother-in-arms since the latter's childhood. Hailing from Norskvegn, Einar spoke the local dialect and proved a great help to Harold's mission to Starvinger.

"What would you know of beauty?" Harold retorted. "I've seen only sheer walls of rock in your fabled land of the fjords. Yet the men I've met had soft spines. I'll take gentle hills and men as hard as flint any day, my friend."

"Looks like the village noticed our return." Einar pointed to a gathering crowd. "If it's not too much to ask, my captain, could you refrain from getting us banished again? At least until I had a night with Abby's thrall and her two sisters," he chuckled.

"Oh, this welcome will be different. We did as my uncle asked."

"I'm not sure I remember the jarl telling us to slaughter a village. Weren't we supposed to find him allies?"

"Details, my friend, details. No anger can survive the gleam of gold. It's how my father got away with anything. We'll do just fine, trust me!"

"Your word in Odin's ears. Let me see if I can get this scum to row faster. I feel an itch in my sword hand, never a good sign."

"Unless we're on a raid." Harold grinned.

"You don't intend to...?"

"No, no, relax. Just an observation."

An hour later, the *Wave Dancer's* narrow hull glided past the storm breakers. The two other ships had fallen behind, their captains unwilling to match the relentless drumbeat Einar had ordered. A sizable crowd had gathered on the pier. Harold spotted Olver and Toril but couldn't find his uncle or brother. *Would there be trouble again?* He'd projected a confidence he didn't fully possess.

"Too late to mourn spilled ale," he muttered under his breath, "when your axe broke the pitcher."

Like after his return from the Fårosünd raid, Harold jumped onto the pier before his men moored the longboat. Yet he intended to take a more amiable approach.

"Hail, Olver, Shield of Hamarrfjord," he called, his voice booming. "How fares our chieftain and our home? I have returned with both bounty and tidings of great value."

"Hail, Harold, son of Sven," Olver replied, somewhat taken aback by his rival's greeting. "Odin's blessing on your return. Much has come to pass, and much more is coming about. Will you allow me to lead an honor guard? Our chieftain awaits you at the longhouse."

"No need for that, Olver!" Jarl Gustav's deep and gravelly voice parted the crowd. Leaning one hand on Rikard's shoulder, Hamarrfjord's aging chieftain stepped toward the new arrival. He held his head high and his back straight.

"Uncle," Harold greeted, sinking to one knee. "I've spent the winter in the south as you commanded, where much change stirs in the wind. I've failed to capture more sheep, nor have I brought bales of clothes," he added with a wry smile, making light of his confrontation with Jarl Gustav after his last raid. "Instead, I bring a new ship, swift as a jaeger, with a crew of three dozen. Also, a score of thralls, some of enchanting beauty and finest Danheimr breeding. And I present to you this..."

With a wave of his hand, four men carried two iron-bound chests of dark wood, placing them to either side of Harold. He rose to his feet.

"Gifts I bring, for the men!" He opened the larger chest full of shining weapons. "And for the women!" Einar lifted the lid of the smaller chest, revealing cups, pitchers, plates, and goblets, interspersed with coins and jewelry, everything gleaming golden in the afternoon sun.

* * *

RIKARD HADN'T BEEN able to find a quiet moment with his brother until late into the welcome feast. After the arrival, the jarl ordered a lavish gathering in the hall. Celebrating Harold's bountiful return put additional burdens on Rikard and Toril. Their thralls were already strained to their limits, preparing for the Althing in two days. Dozens of outlying landowners would arrive. Now, Rikard needed to authorize furniture and provisions to be brought into the hall for the feast. He organized the kitchen maids to prepare the food and assigned space to house the foreign warriors Harold had brought along.

When Rikard finally sat down next to his brother at the high table, Harold was already deep in his cups. The seafarer had spent the afternoon reporting on his journey to his uncle.

"And talking always makes me thirstier," he chuckled, "than a month at sea with spoiled water."

"You'll take back the house and everything within, of course," Rikard offered. "I haven't moved into your room. I just..."

"No, by Hela's tits," Harold protested. "You're the master of the house. I just need a room, any room really. Won't be for long."

"What do you mean?" Rikard asked, alarmed. "You haven't been banished again, have you?"

"No, all is fine between ol' Gustav and me. But this stuff—running a house, ordering thralls about, counting plates? That's not men's work. I mean," he whispered so loud the whole hall could hear if anyone had been listening. "You're good at it. And it's needed, I guess. Just not..."

"Men's work," Rikard replied, dejected.

"That's not what I mean. It's not for me, I should say. The sea, she's calling me. I'll stay a while. I haven't slept in a nice bed for many months. And if my bed is as large as I remember, I'm not intending to sleep much in it either. If you know what I mean," he grinned, clapping his brother on the shoulder.

"But where will you go?" Rikard asked.

"Where there's plunder and women and mead," Harold laughed. "They don't even have proper mead in Starvinger, you know? Curse the Norskar!" Rikard wanted to press further, but Jarl Gustav raised his voice.

"Harold," the chieftain called. "Long has been your journey, and many happenings you reported. Tell the hall of the Norskar treachery! Let us hear how far King Olaf's greedy grasp reaches."

Harold stood, drained his horn of mead, and let his gaze sweep across the flushed faces looking up at him. The murmurs died down, and a mighty belch from Envar broke into the excited silence.

"Well said, sisterbrother," Harold shouted over the howling laughter that followed. "We lived and worked in Starvinger for months. And day by day, the deep division among the fickle Norskar became more palpable, like the smell of a mackerel left in the sun." The hall jeered. "Some men," he spat the word. "They've lost their honor. They're merchants, bowing and scraping to coin alone. Others," he shouted over boos and curses, "they see themselves as kin to Danheimr, yearning for foreign rule."

More shouts filled the hall; men stamped their feet and banged their cups on the table.

"Death to Danheimr!" somebody called.

"We found our welcome running dry like a leaking wineskin. We defended their shore, built their ships, and taught them to fight—as much as you can teach a pig to dance," he laughed, causing the hall to erupt in renewed jeers. "So my trusted Envar and I... we thought we were owed a little compensation. The ships prepared, the cargo loaded, a trap was set, well hidden under thick foliage of smiles. In a hall, large as this, but cold and bare... No hearth to warm old bones, no wenches to warm old desires..." Another round of raucous laughter followed.

"We shared a dinner when the mayor ordered us seized," Harold bellowed, anger flaring in his eyes. "That's what they call a jarl in these Thorforsaken lands. Knives came out, first gleaming silver and then glistening red. Throats lay cut, and ringed fingers. Sadly," he chuckled, "for the mayor and his ilk, that is, we'd bought ourselves the loyalty of every man still walking upright in that village. And so we left, stoking the fire a little before we went." The men hammered their fists onto the table, calling, "Harold, Harold!"

"On our way home," Harold shouted over the din, "as Odin wills it, we met a Danheimr knarr, laden with things we needed and they don't need any longer. So no," he concluded in a voice only the men sitting next to him could hear, as the tumult in the hall grew deafening. "Starvinger won't be our new ally."

Rikard offered Harold his cup, and smiling, his brother accepted, draining it in one gulp. Jarl Gustav stood, and the hall grew quieter. Rikard had seized a pitcher from a passing thrall and filled the cups around him. His eyes gleamed with pride and adoration.

"You are your father's son, Harold! A battle axe is not the tool to braid a flower wreath. I'm glad you escaped treachery, and I'm grateful for the rich bounty you brought. What the future might hold... We'll talk more on the morrow, when all karls and outlying farm owners shall gather. Tonight, we celebrate you and your men. To Hamarrfjord's great raider! Hail, Harold Fisk Svensen!"

"Hail, Harold Svensen!" the men echoed several times, with cups refilled and drained.

* * *

Hours later, Rikard walked on unsteady feet along the cliffs, hoping the salty air would clear his mind. His ears still rang with the noise and laughter. Yet the feeling of warmth from partaking in an epic saga by listening to his brother's adventures had been marred by the rising queasiness from overindulgence.

A figure approached, dressed in black, startling Rikard. He fumbled to draw his dagger, stumbling close to the cliff's edge. Before he could pull the weapon free, a hand shot out, clamped onto his arm, and yanked him away from the precipice.

"Careful, Rikard," a low voice warned.

He blinked, recognizing the face under the hood. "Agnetha?" he asked, the whisper far too loud. "What in the gods' names are you doing out here?"

"Watching," she replied. "Last time, a ship's arrival didn't turn out the way we thought. I saw a figure skulking. That made me suspicious."

"Why would you find me walking alone after nightfall suspish... sushpics... unusual? Don't you prowl around every night?"

"I like the dark; it suits me. But I can move unseen at night, without arousing scrutiny."

"Like thieves and murderers," he stammered, his tongue struggling to obey his mind.

"Many seek the cover of night," she said, her voice a low growl. "Some scurry like rats in the shadows. I'm more like an owl, watching without being seen, moving without being heard."

"And striking without warning?" Rikard's voice rose as he sought her eyes hidden in the shadow of her cloak. "Killing without being caught?"

"What brought this on?" she asked, surprise coloring her voice.

"The tide," he retorted. "My brother's ship pulled a body from the water near our shore. It was that farm owner from the east end, claiming that his thralls were better behaved. A few nights ago, in the ale house, he'd boasted about strangling a girl in front of her mother to make an example." Bergrún remained silent, a statue in the dark.

"Men like that appall me!" Rikard spat, his voice dripping with disgust. "But I can't go around and kill those whom I dislike. We have laws!"

"I know, *you* can't!" she hissed. "Your law protects monsters like him."

"Agnetha..."

"Didn't you see the thralls your brother brought?" She took a step closer. "Maidens, barely bloomed, bruised and bloodied, and hurt deeper than you can imagine. Did you look away, Rikard? Didn't he offer you the first pick?"

"Will I then wash up on our shores next?" he shot back, his growing anger clearing his mind.

"There is a better way, Rikard. We talked about it. Escape this cycle of violence while your heart is still pure," she begged. "Sail with me to Heillaður, to new lands, a new beginning! At the Althing, the chieftain will announce your role. Yours, Toril's, and Olver's..."

"How do you know?" he barked.

"All the walls have ears," she replied, taking deep breaths to remain calm.

"Are you spying on me?" His face turned into the ugly mask of drunken rage.

"I'm watching people who could harm you. Remember the monks?"

"Remember your place!" he shouted. "The jarl's plans are not meant for a thrall's ears!"

"Remember my place?" She recoiled as if he'd slapped her. Then, her eyes flashed red like irate fireflies, and the ground beneath their feet began to rumble and shake. "Perhaps I will!" she growled, cold as a winter storm. "Next time, I remember my place when the belladonna strangles your throat, or a raider's axe splits your skull."

"I cannot be led by the nose like an ox," Rikard squealed, stepping backward, his eyes wide, his face draining of all color. "A woman shouldn't control a man's actions. You shouldn't mingle."

She rushed him. Her pale hand jabbed forward. Grabbing the stunned Viking by the collar, she pulled him from the brink and tossed him into the dirt at her feet. He squeaked like a mouse.

"I fear the ale is talking now," she snarled, venom dripping from every syllable. "Your brother's return has reawakened your childish notions of honorable strength and male domination. I let it go, this once!" She bent down, her face hovering inches from his. "Sober up!" she spat, spittle flying from her lips. "Grow up! And maybe have a chat with brave, strong, honorable Olver on the virtues of being dragged around by his nose, or by the balls in his case!"

With that, she turned and disappeared into the darkness.

Althing

THE DAY'S HECTIC activities had left Rikard exhausted. His head hurt. The insistent throbbing behind his eyes intensified with every passing hour, demanding painful recompense for last night's countless cups. His stomach churned like eels in a bucket.

Earlier, he fled the village, trying to outrun the growing anxiety about this evening's gathering. The young man had sought solace atop the cliffs, but found only bitter fragments of a half-remembered confrontation. Disheartened, he'd trudged back, entered the longhouse, and took his seat at the high table with an air of inevitable doom.

After enduring long hours, his time came. He rose to his feet. His mouth felt dry. Reaching for the ale with a sweaty hand, his eyes swept over the audience. Few men returned his gaze, their hardened glares ranging from rejection to hostility. His cup was empty, its contents spilled across the table in a dark puddle glistening in the firelight. Rikard swallowed hard, straining to clear the lump from his throat.

A discordant buzz filled the vast room, a sound like a swarm of angry bees trapped inside a wooden box. The aroma of too many unwashed bodies in damp clothes mingled with the smell of spilled drink and greasy food. The hall's massive door stood open, letting splatters of heavy rain enter with gusts of bitterly needed air. Torches flickered in their sconces along the walls. Yet their faint light cast more shadows than illumination. Here and there, the polished metal of a knife's blade reflected the gleam.

Earlier that afternoon, Jarl Gustav had welcomed the karls and farm owners from across the island to the Althing, the first general assembly in many years. He demonstrated the wealth and hospitality of Hamarrfjord with food and drink in abundance, lifting the mood despite the relentless April rain. Yet with each report on the state of affairs, the merriment dimmed, mirroring the darkening skies outside.

Many men had called for war and bloodshed on the news of Danheimr's growing threat. They waved their horns of ale in the air while others stamped their feet in agreement. But these spirited outcries died like candle flames in a blizzard when the jarl spoke about his failing health. He had looked ill throughout the feast, drank little, and spoke with a rasping voice. Only the most oblivious spectator could have missed his condition. Still, never in recorded history had an acting chieftain admitted weakness.

Gustav Larsen's open acknowledgment of his impending death quieted the room like a knife to the heart. For long moments, no one moved, no one spoke. Rikard felt the suffocating silence pressing onto his ears as if an avalanche had buried the hall and everyone within. Yet in hindsight, he preferred the quiet over the storm of outrage that broke loose with Jarl Gustav's decree about his daughter's domestic rule.

"A woman to lead us?" cried one warrior. "This is madness!"

"The chieftain's hall is no place for a skirt!" shouted another to a chorus of boos and whistling.

"Odin has one seeing eye," jeered a drunken Viking at the front. "Is our jarl blind on both?" Men tossed their horns of ale to the floor. Everyone shouted at the top of their lungs. "Ruin... Witchcraft... Strength... To war, to war!"

"QUIET!" Shield Olver roared, hammering a pewter pitcher onto the head table with such force that plates bounced and candles toppled. With a wave of his hand, he ordered his guards to break up a fight that had erupted.

When his actions had little effect, Jarl Gustav rose. Seated on a dais, he towered over the assembled crowd. The chieftain seized his bejeweled war axe and, with a mighty roar, buried the blade into the table. Wood cracked, and boards splintered. The table sagged in the middle, held together by a mere handful of stubborn fibers.

"You want strength?" the chieftain bellowed, quieting the hall. "You challenge me? Who wants his skull crushed first? Who needs his head removed?" His chest heaved with labored breaths. He squeezed the handle of his axe until his knuckles shone white.

"My daughter's rule saved your women and children," he boomed, his voice echoing from the walls. "My nephew's cunning won the battle, when the old ways had led us into new graves."

Releasing his axe, the chieftain marched to the man who had questioned the leader's blindness. Lifting the challenger by the collar, Jarl Gustav growled. "Doubt my foresight again, and I'll plug your eyes out with a spoon and piss into your skull." He shoved the man backward. The startled Viking tripped over his seat and crashed to the floor, taking the men on either side with him.

Gustav Larsen bent over, steadying himself against a pillar of darkened wood. Toril jumped to her feet, eager to rush to her father's aid, but Olver seized her by the arm, shaking his head. She glared daggers at him, yet stayed where she stood.

The chieftain's rattled breathing filled the sudden silence. Spilled ale dripped into puddles on the floor, and the fire on the hearth crackled. Nothing else dared to move. After long heartbeats, the chieftain straightened. He grabbed a horn of ale from the hand of a frozen warrior and drained it in one gulp.

"Rikard," Jarl Gustav commanded, his voice hoarse and brittle. "Tell the Althing about the destination of your first voyage." Then, he trudged back to the mangled head table and lowered himself into his carved driftwood chair.

* * *

"INGLANDIA?" TORIL EXCLAIMED, her voice like the crack of a whip. She paced in tight circles between the window and the fireplace. Her spacious bedchamber felt too small to contain her restless energy. "Has my cousin lost his mind?" Her furious glare fixed on Edda, who stood by the door.

Hours had bled into the night since the Althing dissolved into chaos after Rikard's speech. The men had stormed from the longhouse. A disgruntled, confused, and agitated tide swept into the village, seeking to drown their unease in the dregs of ale and mead. They'd left the great hall in a state of disarray, mirroring their inner turmoil. Benches lay overturned, food and drink coated the floor, and the stench of discontent lingered. Olver and his guards had departed with them, leaving Toril to tend to her ailing father before finally retreating to her own room.

"What in Loki's twisted mind has driven my cousin? Inglandia?" Toril turned to the door, her arms crossed in a tight knot. Deep creases furrowed between her brows. The fire's flickering light painted sinister shadows onto her face, making her look gaunt and aged by a decade.

"You've talked with him?" Edda ventured, "About the prophecy, Mistress?" Her tone was low, her words calm.

"Of course, I did!" Toril huffed. "I told you. I made him understand..."

"Then perhaps, your understanding of the prophecy and his differ."

"Obviously! But why Inglandia? I never thought." She resumed her pacing.

"To break 'customs old,' Mistress," Edda recited. "You thought the prophecy calls for an alliance with Danheimr, our ancient enemies. But Rikard..."

"He seeks to ally with superstitious *fools*, who wear deer antlers and dance naked in the moonlight to appease nature spirits," Toril exclaimed. "What strength lies in gathering around standing stones to sacrifice sheep?"

"Master Rikard has always been, shall we say, different," Edda replied. "He worships his brother's heroic deeds and yet yearns for the gentler touch of his late mother. You've hoped his nature might be to our advantage."

"I don't need you to rub salt into the bleeding cut," Toril retorted. "Especially one I inflicted on myself. Why don't you tell me what we'll do about it?"

She inhaled deep breaths but failed to cool her temper.

"My contacts expect an answer. For Hela's sake, how can I tell them that we are rejecting their generous terms in exchange for wood witches and magic swords."

Toril stomped to the fireplace and sank into the fur-covered chair, rubbing her temples while Edda poured her tea.

"But there you uncovered the truth, Mistress," the older woman explained, handing a cup to her mistress. "The straight arrow often hits the mark. Someone compels young Master Rikard to ally with wood witches."

"Agnetha," Toril snarled. "But you assured me she hails from Heilladur?"

"I had suspicions, Mistress. I couldn't be sure. But whether our mysterious thrall hails from Inglandia instead, or she feels a kinship... It's clear she holds sway over Master Rikard."

"So much for your grand idea of using her!" Toril scoffed. "Didn't your spiders watch her every move? Or has she bewitched your sons with her heathen ways?"

"She certainly has a talent for deception and disguise. As I told you before, the plan to use her was very risky."

"Mind your words, thrall!" Toril slammed her tea onto the table, breaking the cup. "I gain little from you shifting the blame onto me. But you!" she growled. "Continue and you'll lose everything!"

"Forgive me, Mistress," Edda replied, lowering her gaze. "My hopes of winning her over were misplaced. I'm afraid I need to correct this error."

"And how?" Toril jeered. "Will you tell my cousin to invite a different thrall into his bed?"

"He'll have to, eventually... Once dear Agnetha is no longer with us."

"INGLANDIA?" EINAR FINSGÚR snorted, lowering his mead horn onto the wobbly table with a clatter. "I must say, a lot has changed since we sailed to Starvinger."

He sprawled across from Olver Agnarsen at the back of the Mighty Crab tavern with his boots propped on a vacant chair. The salt-and-pepper-haired Viking puffed with content on an ivory pipe filled with Byzantine tobacco. His companion sat as rigid as a carved stone, his drink untouched. The Shield's gray eyes darted around the room. Every sudden movement, every twitch in the shadows, snagged his attention, while his strong hands tortured a pair of leather gloves.

"By Thor's hairy balls, Olver, be at ease," Einar urged. "Anyone still upright at this hour is too deep in his cups to cause real trouble."

In the wake of the Althing's tumultuous end, a throng of men had sought refuge in the drafty tavern by the harbor. There, they attempted to wash away the gathering's bitter aftertaste with the cheapest ale under Odin's sun, according to the proprietor's boasting. The drink, while having much in common with the brackish harbor water, managed to erase the agitation, horn by horn.

Though many still fumed over Toril's appointment, Jarl Gustav's forceful display and the efficient persuasion by Shield Olver's guards had steered the conversations onto safer shores. In carrying whispers, the men engaged in the collective mockery of the Svensen boy's hilarious idea to ally with the odd folk from the Brittonic Isles.

"What will your master make of it?" Olver asked, his voice low so as not to be overheard.

"My master?" Einar replied. "You do know my wife Ally has been dead a year and more."

"Don't play games with me," Olver growled, his arms crossed.

"Ah," the older man sighed. "You mean Harold?"

"Who else?"

"Well, see. There was my confusion. Harold is my friend, my captain, and my brother-in-arms. He is not my master!" Einar's tone grew cold.

"Your friend, then," Olver relented, having no intention to clash with the renowned fighter hiding behind the mask of a carefree jester. "What will Harold make of it?"

"I suggest you ask him."

"I'm asking you. Harold and I... we don't talk often."

"I imagine not. Conversations starting with 'You stole my wife and my inheritance' must inevitably become awkward."

"I didn't steal anything!" Olver retorted, color flushing his cheeks. "Toril chose me, as did our chieftain."

"It's not my place to judge. Yet often, the axe bites deepest where the wood is rotten."

"This was a mistake," Olver snarled, rising.

"Sit!" Einar commanded. "Speak openly for once in your life. And mayhaps, I'll return the favor."

"Will Harold seek to usurp Rikard's position?"

"I assume he's talking to his uncle right now about the future of Hamarrfjord's leadership. And I assume our chieftain will tell him to quit yapping and be gone."

"What then?"

"Harold will sulk, and drink, and curse, and whore—maybe all four at the same time."

"Will he challenge Rikard? Will you help him overthrow our chieftain?"

"Hela's tits, Olver. Now you're too open. Have you no respect for proper backstabbing rules? I can't tell you how we're going to murder everybody."

"You might find that harder than you think!" The shield jumped to his feet again, drawing steel.

"You're hopeless," Einar sighed. "That's why I never trained you. You're just no fun!" The older man took his feet off the chair and rose, his empty hands raised, palms out. "My friend Harold is a Viking warrior of the old way. Maybe he is Leif Rødskæg incarnate. Maybe he just wishes so."

"What does that have to do with anything?" Olver asked.

"Everything!" Einar replied with passion. "You've slunk around dear Toril's scheming for too long, poisoned by Edda's spiders, denouncing everyone. You see ominous shadows even in the bright midday sun." The wiry fighter glared at the younger, taller, and broader warrior.

"Harold loves his brother, and he loves his uncle," Einar continued. "He'd die for them a thousand times. And he loves Toril, despite her *choice*. He even respects you, though he would never admit such a thing," the older Viking snickered.

"When Harold seeks a goal, he is fierce, reckless, and direct. He is ambitious, make no mistake. But when his chieftain commands him to eat sheep dung, he'll grab the largest spoon, and then he gets on with it. That, my dear Olver, is the difference between my friend and our chieftain's guard dog, who hides his insecurity behind rank and title. Your unquestioning obedience to the jarl's devious daughter has robbed you of trust, honor, and brotherhood."

Einar shook his head. A tinge of sadness pulled at his lips before he slipped past the frozen figure of Hamarrfjord's Shield.

* * *

"Inglandia?" Harold asked, taking a seat next to the fireplace, across from his uncle. "Was that your idea or my cousin Toril's cunning plan?"

He'd been halfway to a tavern with Einar when he stopped and turned. His gaze drifted toward the cliffs beyond the village, seeking the outline of his father's house. Should he go to his brother? Rikard had seemed a different man upon Harold's return—all grown up, wise, and respected. A true hero, if Harold believed half of what the villagers gossiped about the battle against Fårosünd. He'd even felt a tinge of resentment at his little brother's rising fame. Still, the bonds of blood ran deep through the valleys of memory, carved by shared adventures. And tonight, shoved into a corner by their uncle's harebrained gambit, Rikard had made an utter fool of himself.

Who would ally with men who wear skirts and eat sheep bladders stuffed with blood-drenched grains?

Harold could picture himself having his way with a wood nymph or with the fabled beauty the young High King of the Britons had recently wed. Those rewards might be worth a raid.

But allies? What foolishness!

Already intoxicated, Harold had decided to forgo an extended night of bottomless horns for brotherly care when a runner hailed him.

"Master Harold," the winded messenger boy huffed. "Our chieftain wishes to speak with you."

"Now?" Harold asked, incredulous.

"Yes, Master Harold, immediately, if it pleases you."

It didn't please him in the least, but Einar, who'd overheard the conversation, pushed him to follow.

"Go!" the wiry warrior laughed. "If it's honor and praise our chieftain heaps upon you, meet me later in the Mighty Crab. But if he banishes us again, don't go looking for me until the next moon. I need a bed and a wench and a period of rest befitting my age!"

Sitting in the chieftain's chamber, Harold still didn't know which of Einar's predictions would come true. So instead of waiting, he took the initiative.

"Are you saying, Uncle, that my brother has come up with this insanity on his own?"

"Yes, he has," Jarl Gustav replied.

"So sorry to hear. He's still young. Will you banish him now, like you did to me?" A tinge of anger colored his voice. Then he wiped his hand over his face and continued in a calm tone. "However you choose, I'm yours to command, ready to take his place if you wish it."

"Of course, I won't! Despite the amusement of sending you on missions of diplomacy, Rikard has earned my trust. He has proven more loyal and resourceful than any of the experienced warriors in my council."

"But this? Uncle, forgive me, this breaks all customs and traditions."

"Exactly! And that's why he has my trust."

"You can't be serious. Are you quite well, Uncle?"

"Perhaps, if I throw you out the window, you'll grasp my resolve?" the chieftain growled.

"But..."

"Enough!" Gustav Larsen barked. "It is late, and I'm tired of being contradicted. This is my decision. It's not up for discussion."

"Then why call me here?" Harold cracked his knuckles. "If you have no need of me, I'll join the men drinking to forget this evening."

"Because I have need of you! Now quit sulking and listen!"

"You're not sending *me* away again, will you?" Harold's eyes narrowed.

"Indeed, I will. But not the way you think."

"No?" he barked. "Which way will it be? Like Lyngar, as a thrall, bound and gagged?" Harold rose to his feet, his fingers sliding toward the dagger on his belt.

"As chieftain of your own lands. Now sit and listen, you idiot, before you stab yourself in the foot!"

Harold sank back onto his seat, the wicker chair groaning under his weight. He looked dumbfounded, his eyes wide, his mouth hanging open, as if his uncle had hit him over the head.

"You are your father's son. I want to give you the chance I wish I'd given my brother." Jarl Gustav fixed his nephew with a penetrating stare. "This island is too small for you and Toril. It's too small for you and Olver. For Hela's sake, it's even too small for you and Rikard." He leaned forward, the shifting weight causing the chair to creak. "Either you'll be unhappy for the rest of your life," the chieftain explained, his voice grumbling like rocks rolling in the surf, "or you'll ruin everything by starting a war of kin on kin." He took a long draught of spiced mead. Harold sat motionless, his stony face giving nothing away.

"Our clan is threatened by forces to the south and the east," Jarl Gustav continued. "To keep our way of life, our identity, and the honor of Vikings still true to Odin, we need to seize our fate and shape our destiny with our own hands. Finding allies is half the battle. Spreading ourselves onto new horizons completes the haul."

He leaned back and fixed his nephew with shrewd eyes, seeing the hunger rising in the younger Viking's gaze.

"Find a new home for our people," the chieftain commanded. "Conquer the remains of Brótinholm or sail north to Heilladur. I'll offer you all the support we can muster and eternal bonds of kinship. You've squabbled with your cousin Toril all your life. Often, you've been bested. Rule your own lands, and you'll always receive welcome and succor in our halls. What say you, Harold the Conqueror?"

* * *

"INGLANDIA?!" BERGRÚN WAILED, her arms clamped tight around her chest to keep her body from shaking. "How could he do this? After I gave him everything. He would be dead, everybody in this thrice-devil-cursed village would be! And the world would be better for it. Yet, what do I get in return? Stinking, rain-drenched, swamp-riddled, backward Inglandia!"

She hadn't talked to her lover since Harold's unexpected return. After the confrontation atop the cliffs, Bergrún had avoided Rikard. She completed her assigned chores, yet disappeared each time mere moments before he arrived. At night, she shared the narrow bed in Stina's small chamber.

Still, her thoughts kept returning to their argument. Had she overreacted? Rikard had been drunk. He might not remember a single word he'd said. He was still young and inexperienced. Weren't the horns of ale to blame for his sudden arrogance? As much as Bergrún felt she was owed an apology, she knew she wouldn't receive one. Would her pride get in the way of reconciliation? Or worse, would her pride be the boot to crush her blossoming plans?

Despite her frustration, she'd looked out for him, watching the currents in the village churn like rapids. Toril's attempts to pull her cousin into her web of intrigue grew more desperate by the day, while Harold's heroic return renewed the men's appetite for conquest. Jarl Gustav was to blame! His unfathomable decision had heaped enormous pressure onto Rikard's skinny shoulders. Seeing him this afternoon, alone atop the cliffs, his shoulders hunched and his face pale, Bergrún decided to forgive him. She would visit him after the Althing, intending to rob him of his sleep that night, regardless of how exhausted he felt.

But his speech changed everything. Like an icy hailstorm in April, his words washed away the cozy dreams hatched under the blankets during long winter nights.

"Inglandia!" Several pitchers had exploded in a burst of shards, spraying the stale ale onto the surprised bystanders. Bergrún stormed from the hall. Her friend found her in their room, hiding under the blankets among a jumble of toppled furniture and broken pottery. A vase with flowers lay tossed into the cold fireplace.

Throughout the night, Stina perched beside Bergrún, her knees pulled up tight. Dawn couldn't be far off, and the young woman struggled to stay awake. She wanted to lend her friend strength. Yet at the same time, she felt anxious, seeing Bergrún's eyes glow deep red. Waves of fury and disappointment emanated from the witch's shivering frame.

"Inglandia might not be so bad," Stina ventured, forcing a smile. "The Inglans aren't as bloodthirsty as the Vikings, I hear. And they don't practice enthrallment. We would be free."

"We aren't free anywhere, Stina," Bergrún sighed, deflated. "We're women! Men don't respect us, don't respect our opinions. Oh, they swoon when their passions surge, buzzing like honeybees around wildflower blossoms when they want us to spread our legs. But spreading our influence, spreading our thoughts and ambitions, even green boys like Rikard know how to deny us our place."

"If you talked to him..." Stina suggested. "As you said, he's still young and inexperienced. After you've explained, he might see you for who you are."

"Oh, yes!" Bergrún's cackle sounded bitter and mirthless. "If we talked now, he would see me for what I am, believe me. Such an encounter, he'd never forget, regardless of how ever short he lived!"

"Agnetha, please," Stina begged as a tremor spread through the floorboards. The window shutters rattled. "You're scaring me. You can't mean to harm Master Rikard."

Bergrún took deep breaths, straining to cool the rage forever seething inside her. She rested her shaking hand on Stina's bare foot.

"Forgive me, Stina," she whispered. "I didn't mean to frighten you. You deserve a better friend. And no," she added after another series of calming breaths, "I'm not going to harm Rikard, ever! That stupid, stupid boy has a hold on my heart." The witch raised her gaze, seeking Stina's honest eyes.

"When I ran away from home," she muttered, resigned, "barely sixteen winters old, I promised myself never again. I knew for every moment of bliss, the Norns would collect double in pain and humiliation. Still, they tricked me. Against all better judgment, they tricked me into falling for him. What pathetic creatures we are!" She hid her face in her hands, tears spilling from between her fingers. Stina wrapped her arms around her friend, steadying her trembling body.

"Listen to me, Agnetha," she whispered after a long silence. "I know Rikard promised to sail with you to Heilladur. Knew it long before tonight. I'd overheard Edda telling Mistress Toril." Bergrún raised her gaze. Her onyx eyes seemed to swallow the light as they met Stina's.

"You've done so much for me, Agnetha. Don't ruin your happiness on my behalf. Go to him! Talk to Rikard, and sail with him into a better future. Why do you care where the wind will blow you? Inglandia, Götaland, the frozen North, or the deserts of Afrique... as long as you're together, nothing else matters!"

"I can't," Bergrún croaked.

"Why? What is Heilladur to you?"

"Everything!" The air rushed from the witch's lungs as if she had held her breath for months. "Don't you know by now? Don't you see? My looks, my powers, our kinship... Stina, I've never been to Götaland. I am what these southern pigs think of when they talk about our beautiful island." She stood, turned, and took her friend by the hands, pulling the stunned girl to her feet. "I'm the witch they fear, a daughter of Earth's raw energy and the spirits that rule the world! Edda must've suspected. I remember her smirk when she introduced me to your mother. Can you forgive me for lying to you all these months? Please! I couldn't live with myself if you hated me." Stina looked dumbfounded, her lips parted, her eyes wide.

"I've even lied about my name," the witch confessed, her voice breaking. "I didn't want to give these superstitious brutes more reasons to hate us. Please, Stina..." Her grip tightened, afraid of losing her last anchor holding her back against a deadly whirlpool. "My parents named me Bergrún, Bergrún Lilith Gullveigardóttir," she whispered. "I was born in Svartvik, a tiny fishing village on the West coast of Heilladur. All these years, I carried a pouch

with black sand from home with me. It gives me strength and purpose."
She closed her eyes and swayed as her slender body shivered.

"My home is Heillaður!" She declared, her voice shaking. "It always was and always will be... And I want to go home!"

CHAPTER THIRTEEN

Honor

R IKARD MARCHED THROUGH the village. His eyes on the ground, he pulled his cloak tight. He felt frozen to the bone, wet, and miserable. Pounding headaches threatened to crack his skull open, and his intestines writhed in agony. Sour bile burned his stomach. Never in his young life had he slept so poorly. Deep shadows ringed his eyes, and his hands shivered. Too much turmoil, too much pressure, too much drink, and too much loneliness—he would've loved nothing better than to hide under his blankets until Ragnarok. But the stench of vomit clung to his sheets, driving him out into the bleak and joyless world. He hated the pitying expressions on his household staff's faces. They spoke in soft voices as if he were dying.

I'm not dying, he thought, *better if I were. But no, I'm just an idiot!*

One overeager maid even hinted at her willingness to fill the vacant space in his bed. He glared with such venom that she dropped her stack of linens and started weeping as she gathered the sheets with clumsy hands. His empty stomach contracted in another spasm, and he ran for the outhouse. Escaping the sickening smell of fried eggs and freshly-baked bread, he stomped down the winding path to the village.

Here, things got worse. People glared at him with every possible emotion except for pity. Mutters grew in intensity as he passed. No one seemed to mind him overhearing their nasty whispers. Icy rain splashed into his face, blown sideways by the furious wind.

Even the wind is angry!

At least locating Shield Olver required little effort; four guards surrounded the stable. No one else lingered nearby, thank Odin for the horrible April weather. But Rikard felt their eyes on him, from open windows, from gaping doors, and from under the eaves—judging, accusing, damning.

Stepping inside the stable, he spotted two men lying on the hard-packed earth. They embraced each other, almost like lovers. But the dark patches of deeper brown, where blood had soaked into the soil, told a different story. A circle of footprints, cleared of straw, completed the picture of a deadly fight. Rikard didn't know the men. They'd traveled here to attend the ill-fated Althing, yet would never return to their remote farmsteads or hamlets.

"Ah, Rikard," Olver greeted. The tall Viking knelt on the floor, inspecting the dagger that had severed one man's spine. "I would hear your counsel. What shall we do with these bodies? Shall we give them to the sea? By Thor," he exclaimed, looking at the younger man. "Are you quite well? You look paler than Death's twin brother."

"How kind, Olver," Rikard rasped, attempting a smile. "I'm well enough, as one should be on such a delightful spring day. Did you know the deceased?" he asked. "Did your guards witness any strife?"

"Both men were sheep farmers from Eastend. They might be cousins. Well, everybody in Eastend is," he chuckled. "I heard they were on friendly terms. But who knows what old grudges are washed to the surface by floods of ale."

"So, no clear cause?"

"There was some trouble with a serving maid last night. Toril *told* me about it this morning. You know how she gets, especially after what happened to Stina. She won't abide men who roughhandle the serving girls. But no telling if these two were involved."

"We should give them to the sea. We'll never get a pyre lit in this weather. Are there any close kin?"

"Not sure yet. But Holger Claassen, my watchleader, knew one man from childhood. The shorter one." Olver pointed to the body, still clenching the killing dagger in his right hand. "Said he was a strange lad, always wielding his weapons left-handed. Holger won't be thrilled to set sail in this weather, but he'll do it."

"My thanks, Olver... for calling on me, for holding to our chieftain's plan."

"Rikard, I know how you..."

"Got to go," Rikard said, cutting him off. "Need to speak to someone else."

* * *

After inquiring in the longhouse, Rikard found Bergrún at the village well, filling two buckets. She wore her old brown dress under a rain-soaked overcoat of rough-spun flax. Her bare legs were mud-caked up to the knees, and her long, sodden hair hid her face behind an unkempt curtain.

His squelching footsteps alerted her to his approach. Yet she continued filling the buckets without favoring him with so much as a glance.

"I haven't seen you in days," he called from several strides away. His throat was dry, and his tone carried a sharper edge than he'd intended.

"Much to do, Master Rikard," she replied in a perfectly subservient tone. Nevertheless, her detached coldness stopped him dead in his tracks.

"This island is small, this village tiny. How come I never see you?"

"You must've looked in the wrong places, Master Rikard." Lifting the two buckets, she turned. "I, for one, saw you yesterday at the Althing. I saw you—perhaps for the first time—for who you truly are."

She started walking past him. He seized her arm, holding on with desperate force. His eyes blinked rapidly, but an angry redness crept up his cheeks.

"You're hurting me," she said, her voice a low growl. "You *really* don't want to do this!"

He recoiled as if he'd touched glowing coals, and she marched on.

"Agnetha, please," he begged. All strength had fled from his voice. She turned. He stood there, twisting his hands, his skinny shoulders sagging. Gone was the Hero of Hamarrfjord. In its place stood Rikard, a desperate youth, a rain-drenched boy in an image of misery.

She let the buckets drop into the mud and crossed her arms.

"I need to talk. Please!"

"What's there to talk about, Master Rikard?" she asked, her voice harsh and unrelenting.

"About yesterday, the night of the Althing," he rushed to explain. She narrowed her eyes. "It's hard for me to talk about it," he mumbled.

"From where you stand, I imagine it must be." She regarded him with her head tilted, one hand placed on her hip. Yet, some of the bitter lines on her face softened.

"The events have gained momentum," he whispered, fidgeting with his sodden tunic. "Like an avalanche, they destroy everything in their path. We need to stop them!" He forced himself to look into her eyes. "Agnetha, I need to..."

"Go on," she coaxed when it seemed the well of his words had run dry.

He bit his lip. A hundred things fought for release: the conflict with Toril, his uncle's suffocating expectations, the dream of Inglandia, and how much her casual executions terrified him. But beneath the turmoil, stronger than anything, was his desire to apologize and to finally tell her what she meant to him. He opened his mouth to say it all.

"I need to know where you went after the Althing," he blurted.

"What?" she shrieked, stretching the one-word question into a discordant tune that rose through three octaves. Startled birds rose from the marshes.

"Last night," he called with forced bravado. "Where did you go after the Althing? What did you do? What happened?"

"You dare to ask me," she roared, her words like rolling thunder, "what happened *after* the Althing?" The earth began to tremble under their feet.

"The men who died last night," he shouted as a whirlwind rose, gushing splatters of mud and rain into his face. "We talked about it before. You cannot do this! I won't allow it!"

"You won't allow it," she cackled. A bolt of lightning flashed across the sinister clouds. "Stop me then, Hero of Hamarrfjord!"

Anger boiled in his veins, matching the blazing fury in her eyes. Anger about his inability to reach her, about her refusal to hear him, about the unfairness of this world.

This isn't going the way I'd planned, he realized too late. But his helplessness and frustration shoved him into a corner, and like a beast caught in a trap, he lashed out.

"We talked about it," he shouted in a desperate attempt to rescue this conversation.

"We talked about many things," the witch hissed. She took a step toward him, and the world around them fell into a dead silence.

"None of those seems to mean anything to you, truce-weaver." She took another step. Her gaze twisted his guts.

"Silly things whispered between pillows, they don't mean anything to real men." And another step closer. His body shook from a chill that had little to do with the cold.

"Promises, professions of gratefulness, vows of eternal bonds, they are just whispers in the wind," she snarled, spittle flying from her lips.

She stood less than an arm's length away, her brows pulled together like thunderclouds. A muscle twitched in her cheek.

"Foolish maidens," she whispered, more menacing than anything she'd said before, "with their minds too weak and their hearts too irrational, they can't understand that honor and honesty only count between *men*."

She rammed her index finger against his chest, and the cold spread into Rikard's bones, stealing the air from his lungs.

He tried to get away, but she'd pinned him against the well's wall.

"Go find your allies, honorable envoy, and better luck next time," she taunted. "So far, you've lost the only one who mattered." She whirled on the spot and stomped away, muddy water splattering with every footfall.

"Wait, Agnetha!" he croaked. "I wasn't done talking." He tried to follow.

"Yes, you were," she replied with regained indifference. With a wave of her hand, a blast of concentrated air hit him in the stomach, lifted him off his feet, and threw him six feet backward into the sludge.

* * *

DAZED, RIKARD PICKED himself up from the ground. His ribs hurt. Mud stuck everywhere, on his hands, in his boots, sliding down the back of his tunic. He tried to wipe his face and only managed to spread the muck further. The puddles of muddy water had drenched his clothes to his undergarments in heartbeats, raising gooseflesh. He shivered from head to toe, feeling nausea rising. The world spun. He needed to go home, to get out of his wet clothes, and to lie down before he lost consciousness. But one thought had grabbed hold of his mind, dominating all others.

Has anyone seen what happened? Has anyone witnessed Agnetha's spell?

What if the villagers came for her to burn her at the stake? He couldn't let that happen. He wouldn't! Whatever she'd done, whoever she was, he wouldn't let anyone harm her. But, if he were too late? What if they cornered her? What if she had to defend herself, alone, against an angry mob?

By Odin's remaining eye, in her wrath and destructive rage, we all might perish.

Her immense power, so casual, her fierce resolve, so unrestrained, her burning fury, so primal, Rikard had underestimated the witch's true nature, again, despite everything he'd witnessed. She could unmake the entire village, burn it to the bedrock. He should be terrified for his home, for his kin. But the memory of her on the battlefield, with an arrow in her chest, blocked all other concerns. The sound of her labored gasp, the feel of her hand going limp in his... In that frozen moment, the world reordered itself around a single, undeniable truth. The pillars of his world—kin, jarl, honor, truth—they all dissolved into meaningless words. Only Agnetha mattered. The ravaging fire in his chest that had no name, now he knew it to be love. And the revelation hit him like a tidal wave, forcing him to his knees. Tears streaked over his muddy cheeks, and, raising his gaze to the heavens, he prayed.

"Oh, gods, old and new, have pity on us. Let it pass that no one has seen!"

* * *

AFTER SQUATTING IN the mud for long minutes to catch his breath, Rikard dragged himself back to the village square, determined to find Agnetha. He would talk to her. He didn't know what to say. He didn't know if she would listen. He only knew he would try.

He'd decided to look in the longhouse first, where she prepared the healing potions for the chieftain. But before he could climb the stairs, he heard his name called.

"Rikard Svensen!" an agitated voice called. Rikard turned and saw an unfamiliar outlander approaching. He looked old, his face gaunt and worn. His eyes were red, puffy, and bloodshot. Deep lines formed harsh angles on his face, allowing little doubt about the man's mood. "You! Rikard Svensen," he repeated. "I blame you for my brother's death!"

"What?" stammered Rikard, stumbling a step backward. His muddled brain could not comprehend the ridiculous accusation.

"My brother, Kael, lies dead in that stable!" the man shouted.

"Your brother, Kael? Ah, he's one of the men. There was a fight last night, I'm sorry. I had nothing to do with it."

"Aye, a fight you say, with cousin Killian. Kael never fights! Nor does Killian. Now, they're dead, both of them. Dead and cold. And it's your fault, Rikard Svensen."

"How can it be *my* fault? I've never met your brother in my life, nor his cousin Killian."

"But you lured them here, to their deaths!"

"Don't spout nonsense, man!" Rikard's voice rose in lockstep with his temper. "I went nowhere near the stable!" The hammering headaches had resurfaced, providing the agonizing drumbeat for the chorus of his aching ribs, his cramping muscles, and his churning stomach.

"Mayhaps, not near the stable, no. But you lured them here into this cursed village... where there's witches lurking in the shadows! Because you *are* a witch lover. Said so yourself, yesterday."

"I said what?" Rikard barked, turning toward the man. His blood started to boil, and his fists shook.

The man glared back. His eyes were pale green and misaligned. Rikard took a deep breath, rubbing the bridge of his nose.

"That's absurd. You don't know what you're saying," he muttered. "It was an alehouse brawl, nothing more. I'm sorry for your loss." He turned to go, but the man seized him by the arm.

"Brother Kael died because you fornicate with witches!" The man spoke in a nasal, high-pitched whine. "Witches from Inglandia... You brought them evil into this land. And now my brother's blood stains the soil!"

"You're drunk and confused." Rikard wrenched his arm free. He was nearing his limit. "Take your old wives' tales to the Shield if you must. I'm in no mood for this."

He shoved the man aside, intending to clear a path. But he used too much force. The man stumbled off the stairs, tripped, and fell. Rikard groaned in frustration. Raising his palms in a gesture of apology, he stepped off the porch. He bent down, offering to help his accuser rise.

The fallen man scrambled to his feet, swift as a rat discovered under a woodpile. He hawked up phlegm, rushed Rikard, and spat into the younger Viking's face. A thick gobbet of goo, yellow and disgusting, clung to Rikard's nose before oozing down his cheek. For two heartbeats, he stood frozen in utter disbelief. Then, something inside him snapped.

Rikard lunged.

His fist connected with the man's chin. Again. And again. The man fell. Rikard jumped on his chest. His fists flew. Bones crunched. Blood sprayed. The man grunted, then he whimpered. Rikard didn't stop. He couldn't stop. He wouldn't. Rage had seized him, fueled by the hurt and rejection. His fear and humiliation, his tiredness and his bruised body—every ounce of his misery stoked the blinding frenzy.

To hurt!

To break someone the way he felt broken. To retaliate, and more. The man stopped resisting. He cowered. It didn't save him. Rikard's fists rained down on him, a true berserker out for vengeance.

Strong arms grabbed Rikard from behind, hauling him away from his glorious revenge.

"Enough!" Olver Agnarsen barked. His command cut through the red haze. He pulled Rikard to his feet. The young Viking didn't resist. Blinking rapidly, he gazed with horror at his beaten foe.

What have I done?

The older man lay on the ground, blood spattered all over his face. Fresh streams of crimson spilled from his split lips and broken nose. Both eyes had swollen shut. His skin looked raw, almost inhuman, like a hunk of mutton the butcher had tenderized with a mallet. His mouth gaped open. He dragged in labored breaths, displaying missing teeth. Two of Olver's guards pulled him upright. He winced, holding his ribs, and spat blood.

An eerie calm blanketed the scene, like the eye of the hurricane after the violent frenzy. Only Rikard's gasping breaths marked the passage of time, echoed by the beaten man's wheezing.

"This won't stand," the outlander croaked. "I demand blood pay!" Raising his hideous gaze to Rikard, he screamed, "Holmgang! For my honor." His leer widened into a devil's grin, showing bloody gums. "Tomorrow, at noon!" he shrieked, madness straining his voice. "Cousin Kieran will crush you, boy. Holmgang! Tomorrow! To the death!"

Rikard stood frozen, his chest heaving. The word "holmgang" sliced like a butcher's cleaver through the swirling fog in his mind. He'd heard of Viking duels in stories. These were ancient, barbaric rituals. It couldn't happen. The jarl wouldn't allow it. Olver wouldn't. Rikard stepped free of the shield's loosened grip and turned his head.

"He has the right," Olver declared, his face grim. "You've given him cause. Best, I'll get you home for now. Bjorn, see to the man," he ordered before taking Rikard by the arm.

The runes were cast. A stone plummeted into Rikard's stomach. Nausea rose at the thought of more blood being spilled before sunset tomorrow—and that time, it could well be his.

* * *

"There you are," Stina exclaimed, rushing into the tiny room behind the stairs. She pulled a rain-drenched cloak from her shoulders and bent over, one hand on her knee, the other clutching a stitch.

Bergrún stood behind her table, grinding herbs with so much ferocity one could almost hear the granite mortar plead for mercy. She hadn't changed, still wearing her sodden dress. Muddy footprints covered the wooden floor, interspersed with puddles of dirty water. Her hair clung matted to her head, with a constant stream of water dripping from its windswept tassels. Yet her disheveled attire paled in comparison to her expression. Her face looked carved from iron wood with a broad axe and little finesse. Her onyx eyes lay in shadow, but an angry red fire pulsed in their depths.

"Have you heard?" Stina wheezed between gasping for air. "I've just been to Master Rikard's manor. It's horrible! You must do something. Stop it!"

Bergrún didn't reply. She kept pounding the herbs. Pulses of noxious energy emanated from her, filling the tiny space with a bristling hum and causing the warped wooden boards to vibrate.

"Please, Agnetha... I mean, please, Bergrún. Do something!" Stina pleaded.

"What?" the witch snarled. The light of the oil lamp flared up with her scorching exhale, and the mortar cracked. "*Skitr!*" she hissed. "Soon, there won't be any more left on this God-forsaken island."

"Who cares about stupid bowls of stone? It's Master Rikard you should care about!"

"These are more valuable," Bergrún grumbled, scraping the ground herbs into a small urn. Stina took a seat on the wobbly bench and pulled her friend to sit beside her. The witch showed only token resistance.

"Rikard has been challenged to a deadly duel," Stina rushed to explain. "He'll face his opponent tomorrow at noon. Hiding behind your herbs won't change that. What are you going to do?"

"Nothing!" she spat. "From what I've heard, his challenger is old and beaten up. The Hero of Hamarrfjord shouldn't have a problem breaking him. He's good at breaking things, you know?"

"So you've heard?"

"Of course I have. This village is the size of an anthill. Above this flimsy wooden ceiling resides the queen, and busy soldier ants have scuttled up and down these stairs all morning. A deaf crone with only one eye would've known by now."

"Then you must know that the old man won't fight against Master Rikard."

"Stop calling him *Master* Rikard. He's a stupid boy, nothing else."

"Be that as it may, he will be facing the challenger's cousin, who stands close to seven feet tall and weighs thirty-five stone or more."

"He's not seven feet tall!" Bergrún scoffed. "You must know by now that all men exaggerate size."

"Still, he's huge. He'll crush Rikard like a... well, like an ant."

"Then go and tell *dear* Rikard to pick a champion of his own. His brother Harold can fight!"

"Harold offered," Stina replied. "Even Shield Olver offered to fight in Rikard's stead, can you believe it?"

"Of course I can. All men are stupid."

"But Rikard refused. He said it's a question of honor."

"See?" Bergrún spread her hands, and her eyebrows rose. "Stupid! All men, and apparently also all boys!"

"Bergrún, please! You can't allow this to happen."

"Watch me!" The witch sprang to her feet and paced the tiny room, clenching and unclenching her fists.

"But..."

"Because Rikard forbade me," she explained, cutting off Stina's objection.

"He told me in no uncertain terms, *'We talked about it before. You cannot do this! I won't allow it!'*" she recited, mocking his words in the voice of an infant.

"Since when do you listen to anyone telling you what you can and cannot do?" Stina asked with undisguised adoration.

"You're right," Bergrún sighed, sitting back down next to her friend. "I shouldn't have listened to his words, his lies. Where was your wise counsel earlier?"

"That's not what I'm saying!" Stina's words gained strength. "And you know it, too."

"What do you want me to do, Stina?" Bergrún asked, deflated.

"Can't you, you know, turn cousin monsterman into a frog or something?"

The witch barked a laugh, a silly sound, her mood swinging like a loose sail in a storm.

"You people amaze me," she said, shaking her head. "Calling my kind evil demons, devils' whores, unholy fiends. And then, you urge me to curse a man's life with the casualty of asking for a glass of water."

"So, you can?" Stina asked, fascinated.

"Of course not! My power comes from nature. What you ask for... That is unnatural!"

"Then what will you do?"

"Nothing! As I told you. I won't tarnish Master Rikard's honor with my wicked ways. He is Odin's chosen," Bergrún mocked. "Thor's strength flows through his mighty arms. Loki's wisdom and cunning have guided him from victory to victory. He doesn't need me!" She rose again and walked to the door. With her back to Stina, the witch whispered. "And neither do I need him." A traitorous tear spilled over her cheek.

Stina got to her feet and approached. She took Bergrún's shaking hand. There they stood, together, in silence, until the witch's breathing quieted and her muscles relaxed.

"I'm not wise," Stina whispered. "I'm neither learned nor have I traveled far. I've only left my home once, when I was fourteen, and fate's bitter wind blew me here. You could say I'm still a child, ignorant and naïve. I truly know little, but I know if someone lies, especially if she lies to herself!" She squeezed Bergrún's hand and walked from the room, leaving her coat and a bewildered witch behind.

CHAPTER FOURTEEN

TREMORS

DRUMS BOOMED AND pipes blared. The discordant sound echoed through the valley. Three dozen Vikings marched toward the village in a tight formation. With their painted broad shields gleaming in the midday sun, the column of warriors wound its way down the narrow path like an enormous, many-legged insect. Up front, tied to a long pole, flew the ancient banner of Leif Rødskæg, the snarling wolf's head prominent against the faded red background.

A hush fell over the packed village square. All eyes turned toward the approaching warriors. Nearly every soul in Hamarrfjord had gathered in front of the longhouse, including the farmers from Eastend who'd come for the Althing. They stood in distinct clusters, displaying their allegiance for the upcoming fight.

The smallest group huddled around the towering figure of Kieran Peddersen, cousin to the man Rikard had beaten the day before. Their agitation grew, and hands drifted toward sword hilts as their eyes scanned the crowd for treachery.

Across stood a larger group of thralls and women. Bergrún was at the forefront in a black dress, her long hair whipping in the wind. She'd tied a strip of red cloth around her right arm, like many others, demonstrating her loyalty to Rikard of House Rødskæg, the Hero of Hamarrfjord.

Yet the largest group, dominated by older men, stood in between. They came for the spectacle, having no love for the sheep-herding folk from Eastend nor for the foolish Svensen boy and his ridiculous idea for an alliance with Inglandia. This group faced the longhouse's porch with crossed arms, mirroring Jarl Gustav's grim expression. Their rigid posture spoke volumes about their displeasure toward their chieftain's recent decisions.

Since sunrise, thralls had carted wagonloads of black sand from a beach over a mile away. They heaped the sand into the center of the mud-soaked village square, forming a raised circle twelve strides across that represented a symbolic island. Two men would step on, yet only one would leave alive as the traditions of a holmgang required; the term literally meaning "going to the island."

The earth seemed to tremble under the marching feet. All week leading up to the Althing, short tremors had shaken the volcanic island. Just the day before, a new fissure had opened above the valley with the hot pools, sending sulfurous steam into the air. As the wind turned, it wafted the acrid smell toward the village, adding dark portents to Harold Svensen's return, Jarl Gustav's sickness, and the deadly fight ahead.

The *krigsband* had reached the square. Rikard's brother Harold led the men, carrying the banner. He'd assembled the crews of his ships, including the men who'd followed him from Starvinger. Each Viking had painted his face for battle—stripes of red and black crossed eyes and cheeks in diagonal lines. The sunlight reflected on iron-studded leather armor and gleaming weapons. A murmur rose among the gathered crowd as even the seasoned veterans of Hamarrfjord had seldom witnessed such a show of force in bright daylight.

With a final flurry, the drum beats cut off, and the column parted. Rikard stepped into the open. He lowered his hood and let his cloak slide off his shoulders, eliciting a collective gasp.

The young Viking had shaved his head. He stood bare-chested. Half of his face and body were painted black, the other half white, giving his striking blue eyes an otherworldly intensity. He wore a leather battle skirt over knee-length breeches. His feet were bare except for a strange bracelet of raven feathers and black pearls around one ankle. He, too, had tied a strip of red cloth around his right arm, providing a stark contrast against the blackened skin. The dramatic war paint gave the wiry warrior a spectral appearance.

Rikard stepped onto the island of black sand, his head held high, his stance upright, and his shoulders pulled back. He turned to his uncle, Jarl Gustav Haakon Larsen.

"I have been challenged," he called, his voice clear and strong, "and here I stand." He placed his right fist over his heart and gave his chieftain a curt nod. Then he turned to the group of outlanders. "You've disputed my honor. I've come to prove you wrong!"

He stood there, unmoving, his gaze fixed on his challenger. The village seemed to hold its breath. Tension grew like the charge in a thundercloud as the seconds ticked with glacial slowness. The outlanders fidgeted, their eyes moving between the strange boy and their towering champion.

"By our laws, I claim the right to choose the weapons," Rikard declared, causing renewed murmurs to erupt. "No broad shield, no battle axe," he called as the muttering grew louder. "No sword, no spear, no chest armor." He needed to raise his voice over the agitated chatter. "I demand Odin's judgment the old way, with buckler, hatchet, and dagger, nothing more. Choose!" he bellowed.

Three thralls stepped forth, each holding one set of weapons.

"Your antics are quite amusing, boy!" Kieran Peddersen called, his voice deep like the growl of a bear. "But they won't save you. You asked for Odin's judgment. It'll be Hela who shall embrace you all too soon!"

He tore his chest armor off, snapping the leather straps. Ripping his gray tunic open, he revealed a broad chest and muscular arms. Thick, reddish hair extended from his chin to his navel, and a scar ran down the inside of his left arm from the shoulder to the elbow. He stomped toward Rikard's thralls and snatched the first set of weapons without giving them more than a perfunctory glance.

"Let's get this over with!" he barked, marching toward his opponent.

"Hold!" Olver Agnarsen called. He stood to the right of Jarl Gustav. "We must observe the proper rites! To follow the old ways, that's the only way!" he shouted over cries of alarm mingling with excitement. Turning to the man whom Rikard had beaten, Hamarrfjord's Shield asked, "Kaleb Olfredsen, you've brought forth the question of honor. Does your challenge yet stand?"

"Aye," he hissed, his voice muffled by his broken nose. "I demand blood pay!"

"And does Kieran Peddersen act as your chosen champion?"

"That he does! As Odin wills it, he'll collect what's due."

"Will you be satisfied with first blood?" Olver asked.

"Nay! The boy wasn't when he beat me."

"But will you allow the challenged man to yield?"

"Nay, I say! I demand the old way! That's the only way," he cackled.

"Then to the death, it is." Olver declared. "Send forth four men to hold shields, Kaleb Olfredsen. And you, too, Harold Svensen, as will I. A dozen men shall form a wall around the island, ensuring two shall enter, yet only one shall leave. May Odin guide the righteous fighter to victory. For blood and honor," he shouted.

"For kin and jarl!" came the villager's thundering response.

* * *

Rikard placed his feet with deliberate care, his bare soles registering every small pebble among the coarse sand. His breath came slow and even. He couldn't fathom where he took the strength to stand upright. He hadn't slept last night and hadn't eaten since the Althing two days ago. Yet his mind was clear, his hands steady.

His eyes found her at the front of the crowd, a statue of black stone with a flash of red.

Is this the last time I'll ever see her? The thought stabbed into his mind, and the world narrowed to that single, unbearable possibility.

He glanced down at the bracelet on his ankle—*her* bracelet, as Stina had said. A warmth radiated from it, a defiant pulse against the cold sand. *Survive this!* It seemed to command, deep and subconscious, like an instinct. *Win this!*

His left hand squeezed the handle of his buckler. The round shield, made of beaten copper, measured two handspans in diameter. With his right hand, he held the hatchet. Everything else faded—the crowd, the drums, the fear. His focus narrowed to the fight ahead, on the huge, angry warrior across. Only the Gods knew what came after.

Then, it began. Olver had recited a prayer to initiate the fight. Ere the last word was spoken, Kieran rushed Rikard. The large man swung his hatchet in vicious strokes. The deadly weapon looked tiny in his huge hands. Rikard dodged the first blow and blocked the second. The brutal force sent him tumbling sideways.

Instead of fighting the momentum, he moved with it. Falling onto his shoulders, he rolled and jumped upright mere heartbeats later. Kieran came again. This time, he anticipated Rikard's movement. He punched with his shield, knocking the wind from the younger man's lungs.

Rikard tumbled backward against the wall of shields, bruising his spine on an iron boss. Someone shoved him forward. He fell to his knees and ducked in time to evade a decapitating blow. Lying on his side, he kicked, scoring a hit to the taller man's midriff. The counterstrike slowed Kieran's next attack, but nothing more.

The young Viking jumped to his feet and went on the offensive, executing a rapid series of axe blows. Left, right, high, low—each and every stroke Kieran blocked with his buckler. The sound of ringing metal filled the air in an ear-piercing staccato.

Kieran moved with the swiftness of a weasel despite his size, and Rikard felt his arm tiring. He stepped back, gasping for air. That provided his opponent with an opening. The larger man swung his hatchet in a hammer blow, hitting the inside of Rikard's shield. The blunt impact ripped the buckler out of the tiring Viking's sweaty hands. In a high arc, the metal disc sailed across the island, landing in front of two men. They started pushing and shoving each other. One seemed intent on kicking the shield back to Rikard while the other struggled to pull it away.

Rikard grew desperate. He couldn't defend himself without a shield. Avoiding the next blow, he dived, sliding between Kieran's legs. In a stroke of luck, he managed to cut his opponent's left calf above the ankle. Kieran howled in pain, twisted, and fell, ramming his knee into Rikard's stomach. A rib cracked, and agony seared through his body. Rikard couldn't breathe, couldn't move. Kieran was on him, the other knee pinning his weapon hand to the ground. The attacker's gleaming hatchet descended, blocked in the last moment by Rikard's left arm. Snarling like a rabid badger, the large man pressed his weight against the weapon, the blade inching inexorably toward the young Viking's throat.

Kieran bared his teeth in a devilish grin. Rikard's vision narrowed. He couldn't draw air into his lungs. He gasped like a fish on dry land. The deadly blade pressed into his skin, drawing blood. He couldn't get free. He couldn't stop the vile axe from splitting his throat like a ripe plum. He would die.

Then the earth shook.

This quake felt different—much closer, much longer, and much more violent. Stone slabs slid off roofs. Doors and window shutters rattled, breaking off their hinges. A crack in the ground opened, extending from the longhouse to the stable. On one side, the ground rose, and the stable collapsed like a house of cards.

The villagers screamed in fear. Some fell, taking their neighbors with them like dominoes. Stina grabbed Bergrún's arm, holding on for dear life. The witch stood rigid with her eyes closed, muttering under her breath.

Kieran looked around, his eyes widening. The sand beneath him vibrated. The grains jumped like raindrops on metal plates. Then, the soil drained like bathwater from a barrel. Confused, the outlander released the pressure on his weapon, and Rikard managed a glancing, backhand blow to his opponent's face. That shifted the larger man's weight, freeing Rikard's right arm.

The desperate young warrior swung with all his remaining strength. He needed to knock Kieran's suffocating weight off his tortured body. His vision swam. He aimed his numb fist to strike the face, and the spiked end of his hatchet hit his opponent's temple with a sickening crunch. It cracked the skull, penetrating two inches. One eye burst. Kieran's face grew slack. He teetered for several heartbeats. Then he keeled over like a felled oak, burying Rikard under his dead body.

* * *

The wild panic among the spectators evaporated as the tremors subsided. The villagers picked themselves up and looked around. One by one, they fell silent, looking at the sunken island. No movement, no sound of battle. Olver Agnarsen was the first to break the paralysis. He rushed from the porch and shoved the stunned shield bearers aside. Jumping onto the island, he saw a deep depression in the middle. Both men lay there, unmoving. He hesitated, disheartened until Harold and Einar shouldered past him. Together, the three men rolled Kieran off Rikard, realizing that one man was dead, while the other still clung to life.

Fifteen strides away, Bergrún dropped to her knees, gasping for air. Her heartbeat raced, her head pounded, and every muscle in her body burned. She felt her hands and feet grow numb. Cold sweat covered her skin from head to toe. A deafening ringing filled her ears. Nausea rose, and the young woman vomited, her slender body heaving in vicious spasms. She was on the brink, again. The familiar agony that followed each overextension of her powers had seized her trembling body. Like carrion feeders descending on a starving animal, it threatened to rip her apart, only tenfold amplified this time.

No one paid her any attention, not even Stina. The red-haired woman had rushed forward to gain a better view. Crawling on all fours, the witch inched toward an elderly woman who huddled in the dirt, massaging her foot. She must have twisted her ankle during the earthquake. Bergrún reached her shaking hand, touching the exposed calf. The woman turned. Her look of surprise softened with concern for Rikard's favored thrall. She extended a helping hand, her lips pulling into a reassuring smile.

Bergrún squeezed, and the woman crumpled like an empty flour sack. The witch drew in a deep breath, basking in the blissful influx of life-giving energy. A soft glow enveloped her body, almost invisible in the bright, midday sun.

* * *

Harold lifted his bruised and bloodied brother to his feet. He wrapped

Leif Rødskæg's wolf-head banner around the young man's shaking shoulders. The village square erupted in cheers. Jarl Gustav rose from his seat and bellowed a wordless war cry to the heavens, raising his bejeweled battle axe. Only the outlander contingent remained subdued until angry mutters rose like a swarm of bees. Two of the chieftain's guards had seized the challenger and dragged him before the jarl.

"Kaleb Olfredsen," Gustav Larsen roared, quieting the onlookers. "Odin has rejected your vile challenge. You've stained the honor of my nephew—the Hero of Hamarrfjord, my envoy abroad, and trusted advisor. You, like everyone else who cackled like toothless crones behind his back, you are a disgrace to our clan. I hereby strip you of your standing as a freeman. Your possessions, your wife, your children, and everything you own, belong to Odin's chosen champion, Rikard Thure Svensen, from this moment forth."

"Make me his thrall, great chieftain," the irate man spat. "And I slit his throat in the night. He is a witchfriend, a lunatic. Everyone in your noble clan knows!" He struggled to get free, but the guards held him tight. "Step down from your mighty hall and go to the alehouses. Listen, great chieftain," Kaleb challenged, red-faced. "Then you'll discover who has strayed from Odin's path. You and your ilk are ruled by dark forces, by womenfolk and witches!" He hawked up phlegm and spat on the ground.

"You won't be Rikard's thrall," Olver whispered. He'd moved close. "You demanded the old way, remember, to the death. That's the only way," Hamarrfjord's Shield shouted, before slitting Kaleb Olfredsen's throat.

* * *

"He's setting sail three days from tomorrow, Mistress," Edda reported, closing the door to Toril's bedroom. Night had fallen, but the raucous din from the great hall still echoed throughout the longhouse. Toril had joined the celebrations of her cousin's victorious fight earlier, hugging the young man in a tearful embrace. But then, she'd excused herself, claiming headaches from the anxiety.

"You did a man's bloody work today," she'd shouted into his ear. "You deserve a warrior's feast, with meat and mead and other delights. That's no place for a proper woman like me."

Now she stood in her darkened room, brooding, while the howling of drunken men below caused her temples to ache in earnest.

"Neither his brother's counsel," Edda continued, "nor his fresh injuries could deter Master Rikard from seeing his plan through."

"He's becoming his brother," the jarl's daughter huffed, "willful and unbending. A dozen times or more, we've talked about the prophecy; how our fates are interwoven. And still he refuses Danheimr's protection." She took a deep pull of the oak-matured sack mead Edda had brought her. "It's that thrall, the nefarious Agnetha! She's to blame for my dear cousin growing from a sweet dandelion into a constant thorn in my side. You promised to deal with her!" Toril turned on Edda with thunder in her eyes. "I need that creeping vine torn from Rikard's bed, before she strangles the last bonds of kinship between us."

"Sadly, the circumstances have changed, Mistress. Pulling this weed has become much harder. And it might not yield any sweeter-smelling flowers."

"Stop talking in riddles, woman!" the jarl's daughter snarled. "You boasted of sending her into Hela's embrace. Where's the willing henchman you mentioned?" She walked to the window and looked at the night sky. The moon hung low, its disc almost at its fullest.

"I did. But that was before today's fight," Edda explained, "when Agnetha was still Rikard's thrall."

"What's this?" Toril whirled around, spilling the mead over her dress.

"Your cousin declared her a free woman before your father and the gathered hall. He granted her all of Kaleb Olfredsen's possessions."

"That serpent-tongued wench," Toril spat. "She has addled his brains with her wicked wiles!"

"She certainly has, but not recently." Edda started to wipe her mistress's dress. Toril shooed her away. "There's been tension between the lovers since before the Althing. As it turns out, dear Agnetha wasn't behind the Inglandia idiocy, quite the contrary. She's withheld her bodily delights for several nights. And this afternoon, their 'conversation' shook Master Rikard's manor harder than the *jarðsquake*."

"Not *her* plan? Then whose?"

"Definitely not. She stormed from his room, shouting about broken promises, cursing his notions of honor and duty. Seems like Master Rikard convinced himself of his folly. Neither we nor she could steer him as we liked."

"That's troubling," Toril sighed. She dropped onto her bed, and Edda refilled her cup. "If he's brewed the foul ale himself, there's nothing we can do to stop him drinking. The Hero of Hamarrfjord," she hissed, "Odin's chosen, my father's trusted advisor—he's untouchable. He's not simply dragging us down with him. He's walking off a cliff with his head held high! And my father marches along. What can we do?" Toril shrieked.

"We need to take a more direct course of action."

"Like what? Another challenge? Instigating this one was nearly impossible and barely delayed him. With Loki's luck, he'll turn another duel into another victory!"

Toril started pacing again.

"We can't be seen!" she muttered. "Anything pointing our way will mean a bitter end. We'll share Kaleb Olfredsen's fate, if we're lucky."

"He's setting sail soon," Edda replied. "The journey is long. Who knows what dangers lurk beyond our shores?"

"Yes, but you neither control the wind nor the waves. We can't leave anything to chance anymore. My contacts grow impatient. If we don't deliver soon, they will seize with force what they desire."

"But on a ship, at sea for many weeks, we could control the food and water."

"Poison?"

"If half the crew grew ill and perished from spoiled water?" Edda ventured. "Happens all the time. How unlucky that brave Master Rikard was among the afflicted."

"Watch your tongue, woman!" Toril hissed, spittle flying from her lips. "You're talking about my cousin, my blood!" She stalked up to her thrall, and her face, carved from stone, hovered inches from the older woman's. Toril's eyes glared daggers.

"I only wish to serve, Mistress," Edda replied, her tone low and even. She retreated one step and bowed her head in deference.

"I should hand you over to my father. Nay, I should strangle you myself for thinking of such a vile act. How dare you?" Toril barked. "What madness has come over you?" Her chest heaved, drawing in agitated breaths. She whirled on the spot and stomped to the window, staring out at the indifferent moon. Her hands looked ghostly in the pale light, and the chill night air stung her moist cheeks. The cold seeped into her bones, freezing her soul. Toril squeezed her eyes shut. "How will you do it?" she whispered, her voice quavering.

"My sons, Mistress. Master Rikard has no reason to distrust them. They often prepare the food. And they're of an age when they wish to prove themselves, to see the world. Young Rikard will understand such familiar desires."

"You are a despicable crone, Edda Ingmarsdotter!" Toril slammed her fists on the windowsill. "You disgust me! Leave! I cannot bear to look at your hideous face any longer. I wish never to see you or your devils' spawn again!"

"Of course, Mistress. My apologies. I only wish to serve."

"Out!" Toril barked, furious tears glistening on her cheeks.

Edda opened the door to leave.

"Don't make him suffer in agony, Edda," the jarl's daughter said, fighting the sobs welling up in her chest. "I owe him that much. He's my blood, my Ricki... Please," she begged. "Promise me he won't suffer long!"

CHAPTER FIFTEEN

Departures

ON THE MORNING of Rikard's departure to Inglandia, Harold Svensen lay on his bed, panting. Sweat glistened on his bare chest. The rising sun shone through the window, infusing each droplet with the sparkle of a diamond. The warrior strained to sit upright, reaching to grab his horn of ale, but the effort proved too much. Sinking back into the tangled sheets, he closed his eyes. A sigh of contentment escaped his lips.

"By Freya's bountiful womb, woman," he gasped. "You've left me more spent than an assault on my enemies' shield wall." A gentle breeze washed over his skin, dousing the steaming heat. He let his muscles fall limp. His heartbeat slowed, and his breath quieted.

Feeling a slight burning sensation on his shoulder, Harold touched his arm. His hand came away bloody. "By all the devils that tempt the flesh of men, did you bite me, woman?"

"I might have scratched you, Master, lost in the heat of my passion," his companion replied. Her melodic voice sounded lighthearted, but with a discernible hint of mischief. "I do apologize," she amended. Yet, her eyes conveyed the opposite.

"Thor knows," he grinned, "it's not the first time I've been bloodied in combat. Still, none of the injuries I've endured have been as pleasurable."

"Truly, Master," she whispered, playing with a strand of her raven-black hair. "You bear so many scars." Her deep, dark eyes enthralled him before she turned away. "And some... Oh, in places I wouldn't suspect. Like the scar on your thigh?"

The young woman stood with her back to him, wiping her pale skin with a wet cloth. Her shining hair flowed over her shoulders. He'd never watched a woman wash, but found the spectacle enticing. She moved with the fluid grace of a great cat stalking her prey—hypnotic, alluring, lethal. Placing one delicate foot onto a low, wooden stool, she let the soaped sponge glide along her slender leg. His blood rose.

"Aye," he chuckled, clearing his throat. "That was a close shave with a longsword. Had my opponent aimed a little higher, we might've spent the night reading religious texts instead of the fierce battle you fought."

"I hope I haven't overexerted you, Master." She turned, resting one hand on her narrow hip. A coy smile played on her lips. She stood relaxed, one knee bent inward, as if she were posing for a sculptor. "Forgive me for saying so, but I've noticed some silver streaking your fearsome beard and temples."

"Hah," he laughed. "Don't fear, vixen! There's strength in abundance in these bones. My blood boils hot as ever, and my appetite only grows with each conquest." His eyes devoured her body. "The harder the fight, the more grueling the victory, the greater the warrior's glory." He stretched, his back arching under the thin sheets.

"So I see, Master," she gasped, her eyes widening. "Has my loose tongue sealed my fate?" She crawled onto the bed. "Shall I be bound to your desires indefinitely? Without food or rest?" Her voice grew low and husky. With a sharp tug, she pulled the blanket from between them, exposing his excitement.

"What dire fate," she moaned, inching forward. "What a miserable existence!" She pinned him to the bed, her cold hands seizing his chest. Nails bit into skin. "What monster you are, Harold Svensen," she growled, leaning close. Her teeth snatched his lower lip. "Have mercy, fierce Viking, have mercy," she chanted, her words matching the rhythm of her oscillating hips.

"I fear... I'm the one who's bound," he moaned as shudders ran through his body. "Trapped by a succubus's insatiable hunger, I shall surely wither and die! But sadly, another time." Harold seized her arms and pushed her away, his large hands gentle, reluctant, but relentless. "We need to spare each other for a few hours," he lamented, straining to maintain his resolve under her ravenous gaze. "I need to see my brother off," he coughed, "before he embarks on his adventure to Inglandia."

At the mention of his brother, her face became a bitter mask of stone. A visceral growl escaped her clenched lips; her body grew rigid, a sinister red glow igniting in her eyes. Her nails dug deeper into his flesh. Harold shivered as waves of cold fury washed over his skin, chilling his bones.

He lay there, gasping, his mind struggling to comprehend the sudden change, until a forceful knock sounded at the door. No one moved, no one spoke. After a short pause, the door swung open without invitation. Rikard stepped in, dressed for travel.

"I know you're not alone, brother," he called with an embarrassed laugh. "My apologies. But I wish to say my farewell here. It's best I maintain the image of the steadfast hero for a little longer. And a tearful goodbye at the pier might..." His gaze met Bergrún's, and he froze mid-sentence.

* * *

HOURS HAD PASSED since Bergrún fled the angry shouts and frenzied activities preceding Rikard's departure. She'd rushed up the hill, past the former healer's hut. Fighting her way through the forest's thick underbrush, she sought refuge at the island's western shore. The constant wind rustled the bare branches, drowning the aggravated noises from the village.

She sat at the cliff's edge, her feet dangling over the sixty-foot drop to the jagged rocks below. The angry surf washed over them, and the wind carried the spray up and over the edge. Despite seeming indestructible, the boulders would succumb to the ocean's relentless assault, worn down by failure after failure of blocking the pitiless waves from fraying the land.

Rikard's ship had disappeared behind the cloud-ringed horizon a long time ago. The icy wind ripped through the witch's threadbare cloak. Her body shivered. Still, she couldn't find the strength to move, not even to pull her thin garment tight. All her resolve, the single-minded determination that had dominated her thoughts for years, her essence and her spirit— they'd disappeared with the tiny wooden vessel fighting its course against the wind into the west.

She hadn't spoken a single word to Rikard before his departure. What could she have said? He'd seen her doing exactly what she was doing—punishing him for abandoning her dream. Her calculated actions served the single purpose of enticing the next Viking leader. One who would aid her glorious return home to Heilladur. As soon as Rikard decided to sail to Inglandia, he was of no use to her any longer.

But then, she'd watched in silence the heated confrontation between the brothers. Never had she expected to cause such an agonizing rift between Harold and Rikard. Being an only child, she'd never been so close to anyone. Hearing the brothers shout unforgivable insults twisted her black heart. The bitter words echoed long after Rikard stormed from the room. She shuddered at the thought that they might never have a chance to take them back.

The witch didn't mind Harold calling her a whore. That's how she had acted; that's what she was—the devil's whore. Yet, the blow Rikard landed on his brother's chin hurt her like a stab to the heart. Despite her vindictive betrayal, despite his hurt, dismay, and revulsion, the young man had defended her *honor*.

What cruel irony! What immeasurable debt had he heaped on her soul with his parting deed of chivalry?

Bergrún's plans lay in ruins, broken like the rocks below. Rikard was gone, and Harold would never sail for Heilladur. Or if he did, he wouldn't take her along. She'd witnessed his humiliation, being struck by the little brother who'd eclipsed his fame. Men like him had killed for less.

Another year wasted, another clan alienated, another field scorched. Soon, there wouldn't be a Viking tribe left in the known world that hadn't measured and rejected Bergrún Lilith Gullveigardóttir.

What now? Her gaze, seeking the horizon, blurred by the pooling moisture. *Is there a reason to go on? Should I join the rocks below?* If she disappeared, and the curse with her, wouldn't the world be a better place? *Is the fall truly the end?*

Didn't the harsh and unyielding stone break into soft sand? Might it not end up on a moonlit bay, where it shaped itself in graceful fluidity around the bodies of young lovers experiencing their first closeness under the stars? Bergrún wouldn't mind such a fate. Nature wasn't cruel! Nature wasn't wasteful. If something stuck out in the wrong shape, at the wrong place, or at the wrong time, nature encouraged growth, change, and adaptation.

She raised her gaze to the sky. The dying sun had set the clouds on fire. The orange glow, promising warmth and refuge, invited her in. She lowered her hands and grabbed the edge. Straightening her spine, Bergrún relaxed her shoulders. She would see the miracle for herself, seeking rebirth, embracing the change. Whatever became of her, it couldn't be worse than what she was!

The witch smiled. The wind had quieted. No, it hadn't, but she no longer felt its cold judgment. She recalled Rikard's face, his gentle hands, his hesitant lips, his honest eyes. For a little while, he'd allowed her to bask in the unwavering hope that radiated off him. Whispering a prayer for him to find a worthier companion in the years to come, she slid her trembling body forward. The witch allowed a single tear to roll over her cheek.

* * *

SOMEONE CALLED HER name: "Bergrún!" again and again. The piercing scream shattered the quiet like a crossbow bolt ripping through a wineskin.

Who dares to intrude? the witch thought, her temper rising.

She channeled the wind, weaving a shield of air. The shimmering barrier expanded in all directions. Pushing rocks and roots away, it grew into a sphere of twelve paces in diameter. Bergrún had never mastered the manipulation of air to the extent of her control over the earth. All her life, she'd felt an inseparable connection to the land, especially her homeland, of which she carried a tiny piece in a leather pouch. But her emotional upheaval unleashed a recklessness that forced her will onto all the elements.

As her protective wall solidified, the witch heard fragments of hysterical screams. Words like "Toril", "poison", "Edda", "ship", "danger", and "help" drifted past her ears. She didn't care. She just wanted it all to end. She didn't feel the slightest curiosity about who'd come to mar her final moments. Taking a deep breath, she leaned forward. She needed to dissolve her protective shield to allow her to fall. The last thing she heard was the only thing that retained meaning.

"Rikard will die!" the panicked voice cried.

The witch sprang to her feet. She rushed toward a small figure cowering among raspberry bushes. It was Stina, her dress torn, her face and hands crisscrossed with angry scratches. Her cloak billowed in the wind twenty paces back, snagged in a thicket. Stina's face shone ghostly white. Her lips trembled and tears streamed over her cheeks.

Bergrún raised her hands, palms up in a calming gesture. She reached her friend with the slow, deliberate steps one would use to approach a spooked horse. Stina's words were lost to heaving sobs. She shied away, fear etched into her face. The witch extended her hand, pulling her onto the patch of withered grass between the forest and the rocky cliff.

Long moments passed before the distraught woman could form coherent sentences. Stina had been tending to Toril's infant son, carrying him up and down the longhouse's hallways to ease his indigestion. Passing by her mistress's room, she'd heard raised voices. Not wanting to be spotted eavesdropping, she turned and was about to leave when the names "Agnetha" and "Rikard" caught her attention.

"Edda suggested killing Rikard," she explained, her voice shaking with renewed sobs. "She plans for her sons... Oh Gods! She'll have them poison him... To poison half the crew on their voyage to Inglandia."

"Are you sure?" Bergrún demanded, seizing her friend by the shoulders.

"I heard her words clear as the village bells," Stina wailed. "And Mistress Toril... She scolded her. Calling her a despicable crone."

"Toril intervened? That's good, very good. Edda wouldn't dare go against her mistress's wishes. We have time yet. I'll deal with the spider-whisperer."

"You don't understand," Stina howled. She looked at Bergrún, and her eyes conveyed the terrifying truth before her words did. "It was an act!" she stammered. "Mistress Toril acted her outrage. In the end... In the end, she agreed! She ordered Edda to do it... 'Promise me he won't suffer long!' she said. That's when I ran."

Bergrún let go of Stina's shoulders, and the distraught woman collapsed into a heap. The witch stood dumbstruck, unable to move, unable to speak. Toril's final words rang in her ears, but their meaning refused to fit into Bergrún's mind. She knew Toril to be a conniving snake. And the Norns knew, she herself wasn't a stranger to murderous plans. But she'd seen the jarl's daughter laugh with her cousin. She'd felt their deep bonds of affection.

To order him killed by poison... Bergrún shook her head in disbelief. *To cloak the monstrous command in a mummer's farce?*

Rage boiled like molten lava, filling cracks, breaking barriers, until exploding in a primordial scream of denial. A mighty tremor shook the ground, and the outcrop of rock, on which she had sat earlier, broke off with a sharp crack that echoed across the churning water. With a grinding moan, a chunk of stone the size of a roundhouse lurched free from the cliff face. It plummeted downward, breaking apart with a low rumble that intensified into a deafening roar until the heavy boulders crashed into the waves. In a series of thunderous booms, colossal plumes of sea spray erupted skyward.

"Come along!" the witch hissed, pulling Stina to her feet. "There's yet a chance if Harold's ship is as fast as he claims."

"But Bergrún, how? The entire village gossips about the fight between the Svensen brothers. There're vile rumors, some involving you..." she stammered.

"Leave that to me! The rumors are true." The witch marched inland, dragging the younger woman along. "I'm a despicable person, a habitual liar, a horrible friend, but most of all, I'm a black witch. It's time for the world to see me for who I am, starting with Rikard's older brother."

* * *

BERGRÚN STORMED INTO the Svensen house. She rushed up the stairs, taking two steps at a time. Clasping Stina's wrist in a vice, she dragged her friend along. Stina struggled to keep up, looking harrowed and frightened. Her dress was torn, and twigs and leaves stuck in her wavy, auburn hair.

Reaching the landing, the witch spotted an unknown Viking warrior guarding the door to Harold's chamber. Without breaking stride, she punched a concentrated blast of air into his face, ramming his head against a wooden beam with an echoing thump. He crumpled to the floor.

The witch blasted the door off the hinges and marched in. The room was dark. No trace of this morning's fevered passion remained. Harold stood over Rissa, the often giggling maid, who had shared the secret of Rikard's bathing spot with Bergrún months ago. She was sobbing, her face swollen. Harold had been hurting her. With a wordless cry, the witch hurled him off his feet. He flew across the room, smacking against the fireplace.

"Help Rissa downstairs, Stina," Bergrún said, her body shaking with barely restrained fury. Her eyes blazed like glowing coals. "Give her a draught from the blue flask in my room. The blue flask! That'll dull her pain for now. I'll see to her later, once I'm done with *him*!"

Stina pulled her cloak off and wrapped the other woman's half-naked body in the tattered cloth. She started toward the door only to come face-to-face with a group of angry Vikings barging their way into the room.

"What's going on?" Einar Finsgúr shouted. Bergrún had seized Harold by the shirt collar and pulled the large man to his feet.

"Tell your men to ready the ships!" she growled, shaking him like a rag doll. "We need to follow your brother. He's in danger!"

Overcoming his stunned surprise, he pulled himself free. Anger blazed in his eyes.

"Who do you think you are, woman?" he spat, swinging for a savage back-hand blow. She raised her index finger, and his hand smacked into an invisible barrier. Bones cracked with a sickening sound, followed by his inhuman howls of pain.

"Tell your men to ready the ships!" she repeated. Einar drew his dagger and charged. Stina and Rissa jumped backward until they stood pinned against the wall. With a feral snarl, the witch stepped between them and the Viking, spreading her fingers. Einar tripped. Stumbling to the floor, he smacked his face against the bedframe. Blood spurted from his split lip. He rolled over, moaning, and spat out his two front teeth.

"Enough!" The witch shouted. Her voice echoed in the cramped room, causing everyone to cover their ears. She pulled an amulet from under her dress. Two tiny vials set into a silver disc held liquids. One was dark red, and the other yellowish-white.

Bergrún touched the red vial with her index finger. Harold clutched his chest and collapsed to the floor, writhing in agony. As she lifted her finger, his spasms subsided. He lay there, panting. Taking a step toward him, she touched the other vial. He howled in pain, holding his groin as if a horse had kicked him between the legs. The witch bared her teeth, turning toward the warriors standing dumbfounded in the doorframe. All four men recoiled.

She lifted her finger. Harold's body grew slack. He pushed himself onto all fours and vomited, soiling the floor in a wide circle around him.

"Tell your men to ready the ships!" she repeated, every word like a crack of the whip. The walls shook. Dust and straw rained from the thatched roof.

"Do as she says," he wheezed, his chest heaving. His body shuddered like an infant left in the snow.

"You'll tell no one!" Bergrún added in a whisper like an arctic blizzard. "Try me for an inch, and I'll rip the beating hearts from your chest."

She took a step closer. The men had helped Einar back onto his feet. As one, the five mighty warriors retreated from the witch's slender figure.

"You cannot flee, you cannot hide. I'll find you wherever you are!" Her eyes blazed red like Hel's eternal lakes of fire. "You'll hear me coming in the night. Listen to the cries of agony. I'll break you one by one, starting with him." She jerked her head toward Harold. He'd collapsed into his pool of sick.

"Ready the ships!" she screamed. A whirlwind rose, blowing dust into the men's faces, and they scarpered from the room head over heels.

CHAPTER SIXTEEN

Bloodmoon

THE SHARP CLAP of wood on wood woke Toril. She blinked, confused, trying to detangle the dull impressions of the waking world from the haunting images of her unsettling dreams. Faint moonlight entered through a half-open window, and a chill clung to the air. The jarl's daughter pulled her furs up, covering her bare shoulders. She felt tired beyond words. She always slept poorly during the full moon as her cycle aligned in perfect synchronization with the waxing and waning of Sól's brother. But these days, dark thoughts kept her tossing for long hours before they chased her into the realm of nightmares.

She lay alone, half of her bed empty, and the thought bothered her. A month ago, she'd all but ordered Olver to seek another woman's bed with a resolve bordering on indifference. During the day, her *clever* brain dictated every single step, overruled emotional objections, and squashed childish longing. But during the dark, sleepless hours, her resolution wavered. Her trembling hand searched for the muscular body of her consort. How she wished to nestle in his arms, like a fawn seeking safety in the embrace of a mighty bear. Listening to his breathing, hearing him chuckle at her wit, feeling his heartbeat quicken when she touched him, there was no better remedy for troubled dreams. Was it a sign of weakness to long for someone to hold her? Couldn't she be strong, determined, and independent and still be Olver's loving wife? Though even without the Stina diversion, she might have sent him away tonight, as his musky smell irritated Toril when she bled.

Mired in confused thoughts, she'd just sunk back into slumber when the wood clapped again. With a groan of frustration, the young woman fought herself free of the sheets. She placed her bare feet on the floor, sensing the rough grain of the cold boards. Her head swam, and her mouth felt dry. She rose. A pitcher of small ale stood on a table in the far corner, next to the chamber pot.

Most of the room lay in darkness. The embers had died long ago. But her stride was sure, her aim perfect. Since early childhood, Toril had practiced navigating her bedchamber with closed eyes. She could get up, relieve herself, and even dress in total darkness without making a sound. Olver never woke up when she stirred. And this night, he definitely wouldn't; he wasn't there.

With a goblet of ale in hand, Toril turned to the window. One shutter stood open, swaying in the wind like a badly secured boom of a longship. Had Edda neglected to fasten the hook, or had the wood swollen, preventing her from securing the latch? As old and dry as the window frame was, it warped in the spring's moist air as if its juices still flowed within. Toril watched the faint moonlight entering, detecting an unusual redness. Intrigued, she walked across the room, her gaze mesmerized by the ruby gleam.

Her foot caught. She tripped, stumbled, and fell to the floor. The goblet hit the floor with a reverberating clang. Spilling the ale, it rolled under the bed. Toril's shoulder hit the frame, and a spike of pain jolted her body as her knee landed on her wooden clogs. Cursing through gritted teeth, she rubbed her leg, fighting the childish tears that welled in her eyes.

As the stabbing pain faded into a dull throbbing, she turned and spotted her undoing. A hemp sack the size of a small dog lay two strides away. She'd kicked it during her fall, and it had rolled toward the open window. Crawling without putting weight on her smarting knee, the young woman approached. The sack was tied, and wetness had seeped through the rough fibers in places. After trying in vain to untie the knot, she seized her dagger, which always hung on a wall peg next to the window. Toril cut the rope and upended the sack. A large, lumpy object fell to the floor with a sickening thud.

She screamed.

The shrill cry shattered the quiet like a hammer blow to winter ice. Over and over, she screamed. The sound reverberated, bursting forth into every corner of the longhouse, before the echo of creaking doors and agitated footsteps answered.

* * *

Moments later, Olver rushed into the room, his sword drawn. Two armed men followed close behind. The warriors' gazes peered into the darkness of the bedchamber. Toril cowered in the far corner, weeping. She'd pulled her arms around her knees, and her body swayed like autumn leaves in a gale wind. No one else seemed to be in the room, and the men hadn't spotted anyone leaving.

"Toril, what happened?" Olver asked in a whisper. Then, his gaze found the severed head of Edda Ingmarsdotter lying near the window. Her dead eyes stared in his direction, accusing.

"Holger," he barked. "To the jarl! Protect our chieftain. Tell him what happened. Envar, gather all the men you can rouse. Search the longhouse and the grounds. Find whoever did this!" Hamarrfjord's Shield growled. "Move!" he roared.

"No!" Toril croaked, straining to breathe strength into her words.

"Toril, dearest," Olver replied, softening his voice. "We need to find out who did this."

"I know who," Toril whimpered. "And if you find her, we'll all die!"

"But..."

"Please," she begged. "Send Holger to my father, but have him report that I had a bad dream. The moon... I suffered a nightmare because of the moon."

"By Hela's dead embrace," Envar Finsgúr rasped, staggering away from the window. "Look at the moon!"

"What are you babbling about?" Olver barked. He shoved Envar against the wall, having no patience left for superstitious stargazing.

"It's red... as blood," Envar stammered.

"What is?"

"The full moon, my Shield," Holger explained. "It hovers over the treetops, tinged crimson, as if someone had cut a god's throat."

* * *

OLVER HAD LIFTED Toril in his arms. He cradled her to his chest like a child before placing her onto the bed. She didn't speak, didn't react. The other two men had left, closing the door before marching to their assigned tasks with the strictest orders to keep the gruesome find secret. Having propped up his beloved with pillows, he buried her bare legs and soiled nightshirt under the blankets. Then he filled a fresh cup with ale.

"Drink," Olver encouraged, his voice low and calm. "It'll help with the shock." She obliged mechanically. "That's good," he whispered. "Now, tell me: Who did this?" He pulled a stool over and sat beside the bed, holding her ice-cold hand in his.

She didn't answer. Her face could've been a waxen mask. Her eyes, wide with fear, stared unseeing. Her fingers trembled, and her head swayed forth and back in a steady rhythm.

"Please, Rilly," he said in a soothing voice, using her childhood pet name. "Tell me! I need to know how to protect you, how to protect us!"

He squeezed her hand. A shudder ran through her body.

"Agnetha!" she mouthed, her voice cold and lifeless. "Agnetha did this. She must've learned of our plan... She killed Edda!" Toril shrieked, hysteria rising. "And now, she's coming for me. She wanted me to know that she knows." The frightened woman's words came in a rush, her breathing erratic. "Oh, Gods! She wanted me to know what she'll do to me. I'm going to die! All of us... We're going to die!"

"Toril, listen!" Olver jumped onto the bed and held the shaking woman by the shoulders. Her muscles jerked so violently that the bed vibrated, its carved legs rattling on the uneven floorboards. "Listen to me," he begged, holding her ashen face in his calloused hands. "She's not coming for us."

"SHE IS!" Toril screamed.

"You've got to listen to me, dearest. Agnetha is gone! She left an hour ago on Harold's ship. She's gone!"

"Gone?" she repeated, her voice rising through three octaves. Her eyes were wide as barn doors, and her nostrils flared.

"Yes! Gone! We're safe!"

"Gone!" she sobbed before dissolving into incoherent weeping, melting into him. He held her, his strong arms around her slender frame.

* * *

ONLY A HANDFUL of minutes had passed before a forceful knock broke the tense silence. The door swung open without Olver's invitation. Holger Claassen entered, leaving the entrance wide. Behind him, two men stood in the hallway. These warriors, who'd come with Harold from Norskvegn, wore shields and spears and grim expressions.

"What's the meaning of this?" Olver snarled, turning his head. He sat on the bed with his back to the door, facing Toril. The awkward position robbed him of the opportunity to tower over the uninvited intruder.

"Forgive me, Shield Olver," Holger replied, his voice grave and his eyes downcast. "Jarl Gustav asked for your presence... immediately."

"Tell my chieftain I'll be with him soon. His daughter is in great distress. I need to care for her. Has Envar reported to you? Has he found any traces?"

"Forgive me, I haven't spoken to Envar since we parted. I rushed to the Jarl's chambers as you commanded. And our chieftain..."

"Speak, man!" Olver barked.

"He ordered me to escort you to him... immediately."

"Escort me?" Olver jumped off the bed and rushed toward the intruder. "I don't appreciate your manners, Watchleader!" The warriors in the hallway stiffened, readying their spears. "Who are these?" Olver growled. "Where are the chieftain's guards?"

Holger raised his hand, ordering his escort to stand down. Yet he didn't flinch away from his irate commander.

"These are the chieftain's guards," he explained. "Sworn to him in the presence of his nephew, Harold. They mean you no harm."

"Mean me no harm? What nonsense do you speak?" Olver bellowed.

"Please, Shield Olver, I'm acting on our Jarl's orders. I urge you to come with me... immediately."

"Impossible! I can't leave Toril alone in her state. You know what happened."

"But I do not. I don't know anything anymore. Everything is upside down. But our chieftain asked to see his daughter as well... immediately. I apologize!"

"I need to change," Toril hissed. "Get out and close the door!"

The sudden confrontation had pushed all other thoughts and fears aside, causing the detached, rational, and imperious jarl's daughter to resurface.

"Forgive me, Mistress..." Holger started, but the look his commander gave him froze his tongue. He retreated, and Olver slammed the door in his face.

"What was that about?" he asked, turning.

"Nothing good." She rushed to her chest, pulled her soiled nightshirt off, and threw it with disdain into a corner. Then, she dressed in leggings, leather boots, a tight-fitting tunic, and a studded leather belt.

"You're dressing for the sparring pit?" he asked, astounded, as she hid a dagger in her boot and tied her willful hair into a messy topknot.

"For war!" she whispered, testing her freedom of movement in the unusual clothes. "You've seen the moon? 'Once full moon bleeds and sky turns red,'" she recited. "It has begun, Olver. The prophecy, you and me." She rushed him, pulled his head by the hair down to her face, and kissed him. "Thank you, Olver, for protecting scared little Rilly earlier. Now it's time for Toril Ingrið Gustavsdotter to protect you!"

"What do you mean?"

Another knock on the door.

"We need to go... immediately!" Holger Claassen called, with no hint of apology left in his demand. Toril pulled the door open, pushed past the stunned watchleader, and marched to her father's chambers.

Jarl Gustav Larsen wasn't waiting in his small audience chamber; instead, he lay on his bed, propped up against the headboard. He looked aged by a decade since she last saw him. Two more men from Harold's ilk stood beside him, armed for war with shields and spears.

"Father," Toril greeted without giving the men so much as a glance. "You've asked to see me. I hope you're well."

Before he could answer, Olver's irate voice carried from the hallway.

"You can have my sword when you pull it from your stinking guts," he shouted. "Get out of my way, you spineless *maðkur!*"

"Olver," Jarl Gustav rasped, his voice brittle like stockfish left in the open too long. "Come. Let him pass," he said to his guards. "He's my Shield."

The tall warrior entered, went to one knee, and bowed his head.

"My Chieftain, you called?"

"Sit! Both of you," the ailing Viking commanded. They did as asked. Holger stepped into the room behind them, followed by his new companions.

"I assume you know why I called you, daughter, at this unholy hour?"

"You've heard of Edda's death," she ventured without hesitation.

"I did," Jarl Gustav replied. Olver turned, giving his watchleader an angry glare. "Not from your man, Olver. Holger is loyal. His lips were sealed until he learned that I already knew."

"Then who told you, Father? Envar Finsgúr?"

"Agnetha did," he declared, causing Toril to recoil as if he'd turned into a sea serpent. "I had a visit from two young women last night. A rare occasion these days. And this time, it wasn't as pleasurable as it might sound."

"Whhhhooo?" Toril stuttered.

"Agnetha, Stina, and Harold. And shortly after came these fine men who you now see surrounding me."

"What hold does she have over you?" The young woman jumped to her feet, eager to rush to her father as a dutiful daughter should, but one of the guards barred her way. "What foul magic is this?" she cried.

"The most powerful," Gustav Larsen replied. Sadness flickered across his face, aging him by another decade. "The truth, my daughter, the truth." He pulled a dead raven from under his blanket and tossed it before her feet. A parchment was attached to one leg. A metal ring encircled the other, bearing the ram's head—the seal of King Olaf of Danheimr.

* * *

"Exile!" Toril repeated in a stunned whisper, shaking her head. She'd suffered ill dreams for weeks. Yet none of her nightmares came close to the cruel reality of her existence. "My father has sent me into exile." The infuriated woman paced in her bedroom like a caged beast, followed at every step by the hostile glare of an armed guard from Starvinger.

"Exile!" A muffled scream escaped her trembling lips. She grabbed the window frame for support. Everything she had worked for, everything she had endured—all her plans, her dreams, her destiny, and the very prophecy she'd believed in since childhood—gone, like she would be before the midday sun. Agnetha had outplayed her. She must've learned of Edda's plan to kill Rikard at sea.

That stupid old hag had been right, Toril thought, sinking onto her bed. *Someone had listened that night. Stina!*

Shy, innocent, demure, and freckled Stina had been the knife for vicious Agnetha to butcher Toril's future like a squealing pig.

The jarl's daughter had been given one hour to pack her belongings before leaving her home forever—a mercy. She would be dead by now if she weren't who she was. Yet all her pleading, arguing, and begging hadn't softened her father's resolve. How could she argue about wicked witchcraft, cunning plots, and fanciful tales when the damning evidence, written in her own hand, lay in the open, attached to a dead bird.

This is the moment I feared. The brutal end. The journey without return.

Minutes passed in tense silence until the guard coughed. She turned to look at him, her head heavy as a millstone. Lowering her gaze, she gave a resigned nod and pushed herself to her feet.

Toril closed her eyes. Taking two steps, she swayed, her arms raised for balance. Then, she clutched her chest and stumbled forward. Her hand seized hold of her bedpost, and she bent over, her breath coming in ragged gasps. Her grip tightened, her knuckles shining white.

Still, the sudden attack seemed to overwhelm her defenses, forcing the young woman to her knees. With her free hand, she tried to pull her tunic open. The stiff collar was strangling her. She choked, her hold slackened, and she fell onto her hands.

"Water," she croaked. "Please, water."

Her sole jailer walked to the washstand and filled a cup from the pitcher. She coughed, a dry rasp like seashells sliding over rocks. A fleck of spittle escaped her lips.

The guard bent down, holding the cup close yet still out of reach. She raised her left hand, grabbing his wrist on the second try. Clutching his arm with desperation, she pulled him down to kneel beside her.

Quick as a lightning strike, Toril's right hand shot upward, stabbing her hidden dagger through the hollow of his lower jaw. The eight-inch blade buried itself to the hilt in his skull. He jerked once. Then he collapsed onto the floor like a sack of grain, only with less noise.

* * *

"Exile," Olver repeated in a defeated voice. He stood in the great hall, stripped of all weapons. Across from him stood Holger, his foremost brother-in-arms, his trusted watchleader, and now the usurper of his position as Shield of Hamarrfjord.

Holger had sent one of his new guards to the harbor to ready a faering, a small, single-masted boat for the condemned couple's journey into exile. He left the two other guards with the ailing chieftain. He'd taken Olver's weapons on the Jarl's orders, sending them to the harbor to be placed into the vessel. Until their departure, Olver was to remain under guard and not to leave the longhouse.

"I'm sorry, my Shield," he muttered. "Our chieftain's word is law. I had no choice... You know that, right?"

Olver didn't reply.

"At least no foreigners guard you," Holger pleaded. "I owe you that much."

"Of course," Olver replied, nodding his head in acknowledgement. "We have our honor. We keep to the old ways. We serve... For kin and jarl!" He placed his hand on Holger's left shoulder, squeezing the arm in a masculine show of emotion.

"For blood and glory!" Holger replied, raising his right fist to his heart. He held his former commander's gaze for two heartbeats, looking up at the taller warrior. Then, he lowered his head in respect.

Olver slapped his opponent's cheek with all the force he could muster, slamming the stunned watchleader's head against the central pillar. A sickening, hollow thud echoed through the empty hall. Bones cracked, and blood spurted from a cut on the man's brow. With his other hand, Olver pulled his former comrade's dagger. In one fluid motion, he slit Holger's throat. Everything was over in the blink of an eye. Holding his victim by the shirt collar, he let the body sink to the floor.

"That's why I'm the Shield of Hamarrfjord," Olver whispered into the dying man's ear, "and not you, Holger Claassen. You're too slow, too weak, and too dead."

* * *

Toril eased the door open a tiny gap. She winced as the hinges groaned, the sound magnified in the empty hallway. She couldn't see anyone. The longhouse lay quiet. Slipping from her room on bare feet, she tiptoed across the landing toward the storage room at the other end. Her heart hammered in her chest; she feared the sound alone would give her away.

Once she passed the stairs, she heard two men talking in the hall below. She couldn't hear what was said. Then, a sudden slap froze her blood, followed by a dull thud and a pained groan. She hid, pressing herself against the wall, her dagger at the ready. The veins in her temples pulsed, and a faint ringing filled her ears. Clapping her left hand over her lips, she fought to remain quiet. Her right hand squeezed the dagger's hilt. Sweat trickled down her spine.

Agonizing heartbeats passed in tense silence. Her breathing quickened, and her fingertips tingled as footsteps came up the stairs, slow, measured, careful, and quiet—the gait of a seasoned warrior. She coiled, ready for the attack. Surprise was her best ally, coupled with speed and dexterity.

I have one chance, Toril realized. *Only one chance!*

The footsteps halted shy of the landing. Someone was standing around the corner, waiting.

For what? Toril thought. *Has he spotted me? Has he heard me? What shall I do?*

Wild ideas ran through her mind, one more futile than the other. She had to attack; she had to eliminate the threat. She would do it on three.

One... Two...

"Almost, Rilly," Olver chuckled, his voice barely above a whisper. "Almost!"

She gave a strangled squeal and jumped into the open, her knife at the ready, bracing for any trickery. It was her consort, with a wicked grin and a bloody dagger.

"Olver!" she exclaimed in a strangled sigh. Relief flooded her, so potent it was dizzying. Then her face fell. "How?" she growled, narrowing her eyes.

His blade pointed toward the floor beside her. Following his gesture, her gaze fixed on her shadow.

"Stupid!" she hissed before pulling him into a kiss. They stood entwined until he broke free. Toril gasped as if she'd surfaced after a dive from the island's cliffs. "In here!" she commanded, wheezing, before pulling him into the storage room.

"What happened to your guard?" he asked after closing the door with care.

"My dagger. And Holger?"

"His dagger."

"That leaves three. Two are in my father's room. Where's the last?"

"At the docks, preparing the boat," Olver explained. "He'll be back soon. Let me deal with the others first."

"With a dagger against two, armed for war?" she asked.

"Won't be two for long!" he growled.

"And then what? Will you kill my father?"

He recoiled.

"We can talk to him," Olver ventured. "Explain…"

"Explain what exactly?" She stepped close, her eyes boring into his. "That I had a good reason to order the death of his nephew? That I was doing the best for our clan by inviting Danheimr? That overthrowing his rule is my way of showing loyalty to my father?" She shook her head, and he paled at her words, feeling at a loss. "The time for talking is over. Its irrevocable end came this morning."

"Then, I'll do it," he declared. "I'll make it quick."

"No, you can't. He's your hero, your mentor, your commander—your chieftain. I won't have that stain fall onto your honor."

"There is no other way!" He threw up his arms in frustration.

"Yes, there is. I'll do it!"

Silence.

"Toril, you can't… Your own father!"

"It's the prophecy," she replied, turning away to hide the traitorous moisture blurring her eyes. "I have to absorb the black sin, even if it mars my heart and soul."

"Oh, Rilly, no!" He stepped close and held her shoulders. A shudder ran through her body.

"It'll be a mercy," she whispered, her voice cracking. "You saw him an hour ago. He's in pain." She turned. Her lips quivered. A tear spilled over her cheek. But her jaw was set, her chin raised, her gaze firm. "Edda prepared everything. He won't feel pain, she promised. We have to do it now!"

She pulled from his embrace.

"Gather the men true to you!" she commanded with forced strength. "Weed out the traitors."

He nodded, his expression grim, and turned to go.

"Lock the main door before you go and roll the barrels of whale oil into the great hall. Once I have... once I'm done, I'll give our chieftain a worthy funeral pyre."

He nodded again, unable to meet her gaze, and left, leaving the door open.

Toril climbed to the top of the shelf and squeezed into the tiny attic above the jarl's apartment. A head-sized limestone dangled from a rope above a large wooden tub, filling the tight space. To the sides, four clay urns stood crammed under the roof beams. Each urn was the size of a toddling bairn. Seal skin covered the openings. Edda's boys had carried them down from the sulfurous springs in the mountains.

Toril sliced through the lids and struggled to pour the liquid into the tub. Acrid fumes rose, burning her eyes despite her squeezing them shut. She held her breath, working with fury. When her air threatened to run out, she left the last urn untouched and crawled backward.

She lay on the shelf, back in the storage room, panting. Muttered conversation from the jarl's chambers reached her ears. She waited, her nerves stretched like bowstrings. No sounds of alarm.

Untying the rope's other end, she lowered the limestone into the acid. Immediately, the liquid frothed and bubbled like a witch's cauldron, filling the tiny space in heartbeats with dense fog. Fitting a wooden board over the tight opening, she sealed the passage into the attic, forcing the deadly gas to sink through the crack into the chamber below.

Sprinting past her father's room, she heard coughing and banging. The oaken door shook, yet Olver had wedged a bench from the hall below between it and the opposite wall, blocking the escape. Toril reached the stairs. She stumbled in her haste to escape the noxious fumes and fell, rolling down the stairs. Pain exploded all over her body. Slamming her teeth together, she rushed on.

Two large barrels stood in front of the room under the stairs. The determined woman pushed them over. Oil spilled over the floor with uncanny smoothness, seeking cracks, splitting around chair legs, transforming bumps and fallen plates into islands before sloshing over them. Eager tendrils reached the hearth. They pooled against the border stones until a spark landed in the shimmering lake. With a whoosh, the oil ignited. Hungry flames climbed the walls and pillars. They devoured chairs, tables, shields, and weapons. The blaze gushed through the hall, reaching all the way to the hidden back door through which the young woman had escaped mere heartbeats ago.

CHAPTER SEVENTEEN

Sacrifice

FOUR MEN HUDDLED at the stern of the *Wave Dancer*, pulling their cloaks tight against the constant wind blowing from the west. Snorri Gundlofsen stood at the helm, leaning his weight against the rudder and shouting commands for the frequent tacking required when beating windward. His brother Frode tried to keep the course with a wooden disk marking the constellations, yet the thickening cloud cover and a rising fog made his efforts futile. To the side, observing the proceedings with grim faces, stood Einar Finsgúr and the ship's commander, Harold Svensen. Harold's right arm lay in a sling, strapped tight to a wooden splint. His gaze flickered back and forth between the helmsman and the hooded figures of two women, sitting close together at the bow.

"This is a pointless endeavor," Einar muttered, repeating his strong objection for the tenth time. His tongue flicked like a snake's, feeling the space where his front teeth had been hours before. "Not even Odin's remaining eye could find your brother's longship in weather like this."

"What would you have me do?" Harold growled. "You've been there. You've seen her. If you have any doubts about our options, inspect your reflection in a looking glass."

"She's taken us by surprise. Now we're at sea. All we need is a lucky shot, and we'll feed her to the kraken. There are thirty men, and just one witch!"

"No," Harold declared, shaking his head. "There are thirty lambs, and one dire wolf with her cub. We'll be slaughtered ere the sun rises."

"But, Harold," Einar protested, "you can't allow a witch to control our fate. We're men, warriors, Vikings!"

"I'll do it," Snorri suggested. "I'm good with a bow. At less than twenty strides, I'll hit the black in the iris of her eye—if her irises weren't entirely black, that is."

"Enough," Harold growled, his tone leaving no room for argument. "All she wants is to find Rikard. Then we'll return, and I'll be Jarl. I'm not prodding a sleeping bear just to test its claws. Call a tack," he commanded. "We're heading too far south."

"I feared Olver Agnarsen would become jarl under a woman's skirt. But this..." Snorri grumbled.

"Watch your tongue or lose it!" Harold hissed. "I still have one working arm and, despite my unusual restraint, my fingers itch to kill someone."

* * *

"I DON'T LIKE the angry stares," Stina whispered. "Everybody hates us. They'll murder us as soon as we fall asleep." She sat on a coil of rope, her arms around her knees, yawning. The stress of the last days had taken a lot out of the young woman, and her head drooped with increasing regularity.

"Go to sleep," Bergrún encouraged. "I'll keep watch. Harold won't dare to suffer another humiliation. I've handed him the jarlship, but he won't keep it if his men see him as a weakling."

"But some men have already seen, and the rumors are spreading."

"Einar will remain loyal because that's his best chance for a seat at the table. If he calls a challenge, the hunt is on. And there are fiercer wolves in the pack yearning for power. As long as rumors remain rumors, he'll keep his friend at the top."

"He might be loyal. But everyone sees the lead wolf's broken paw. How long until the unrest in the pack turns into bared teeth and snapping jaws?"

"You're right," Bergrún sighed. "I'll have to do something about that."

"What can you do?" Stina asked.

"Giving dear Harold more teeth," the witch grinned. She stood, lowered her hood, and marched through the ranks of resting thralls, toward the group of grim men at the stern.

* * *

THE WIND HAD grown stronger as the hours passed, but didn't change direction. Einar ordered the mainsail struck, and the thralls pulled the oars for a while. But eventually, he let them rest. The fog had thickened. Nothing could be gained from taxing the men to their limits if they rowed the wrong way.

He was about to suggest a quick nap when the men around him stiffened. Turning, he spotted the witch approaching.

"Have we slowed?" she asked, her tone imperious, carrying far in the relative calm. She stood with her hands on her hips, facing the four tall Vikings.

"We have indeed, Mistress Agnetha. A most astute observation." Einar spread his hands in a gesture of helplessness, his voice dripping with a mock deference. "Our crude eyes are no match for the settling gloom. Could you point the way with your... particular guidance?"

Harold's noisy breath left no doubt about his thoughts on Einar's actions. Bergrún, on the other hand, chuckled, delighted by a verbal sparring match.

"I can indeed," she replied, pulling an object the size of an apple from under her cloak. "Are you familiar with this?"

A dial with a circle of golden markers was visible under a crystal dome. The dial tilted and turned in an effort to stay level and pointed in a constant direction.

"A Byzantine loadstar finder," Einar exclaimed in awe. "Where did you get this? It's priceless. Villages have burned for lesser treasures."

"It belonged to Stígur Asmundsen, may he rot in Hela's embrace! Jarl Gustav was so kind as to lend it in order to rescue his nephew."

"What is it?" Harold asked, his tone gruff. He'd followed the exchange with narrowed eyes, edging away from Bergrún. Yet, at Einar's appraisal of the object's value, a muscle in his cheek started twitching.

"It points north, however you twist and turn it."

"More magic?" Snorri snarled.

"Of a kind," Einar explained. "A tiny loadstone on the needle keeps it pointing to the heart of Jötunheimr."

"How does that help us now?" Harold asked. "Rikard is off chasing the fairies of Inglandia, not the ice giants in the north."

With her other hand, Bergrún pulled a tiny vial of blood from under her cloak. Harold stiffened, his eyes widening in undisguised panic.

"Not yours," the witch mused, "Rikard's." Raising her hand, she muttered, *"Brottu í sundur!"*

The crystal dome of the compass shattered into a million tiny shards. She blew, and they disappeared like snowflakes in the midday sun. The men gasped. The witch chuckled. She pulled the vial's stopper with her teeth and poured one drop onto the needle. Immediately, it changed direction, pointing into the wind.

"There, Master Einar, is your direction. Even eyes as crude as yours should be able to hold the course now." Placing the device into Einar's trembling hand, she turned to go.

"Black witchcraft!" Snorri snarled. "Devil's work by devils' whores." He lunged, attempting to seize the compass. Einar dodged, and Harold stepped in while Frode struggled to hold his brother back. "Let me go!" the restrained man hissed. "We must toss it into the sea! Else, this evil curse will damn our souls." He twisted and struggled until Harold's blade touched his throat.

Bergrún regarded the confrontation with amusement, her head tilted. She locked gazes with Snorri. He glared daggers. As her lips moved, muttering words too low to hear, his stare went blank for a few heartbeats. Then his face contorted in rage, his gray eyes burning with madness. She flexed her fingers, pulling on his mind. In a sudden outburst, he jerked free, turned, and slapped Harold's knife hand away.

"It's all your fault, Harold Svensen!" Snorri screamed like a rabid animal. "You're the root of everything wrong in Hamarrfjord, where witches and womenfolk rule."

"Hold your vile tongue!" Einar barked. "A day pulling the oars will teach you respect!"

"Respect?" Snorri shrieked, shoving Einar aside. "Our chieftain is weak, and our captain"—he spat the word—"is of his blood. Look at this spineless *maðkur*! Letting a scrawny waif order him around like her pet hound. She sent us on this fool's mission to rescue our captain's worthless brother. Witch-lover!" he screamed at Harold. "Devil's thrals, both of you, sharing her bed!"

He hawked up phlegm and spat into his leader's face. Harold rammed his dagger into Snorri's throat, ripping it free in a twisting slice. Blood gushed from the wound like a spring flood. Frode rushed to his brother in shock as the dying man sank to his knees.

"Let's not waste more than we must," Bergrún declared in a calm voice. She knelt across from Snorri. Placing her hands on his neck, she let the blood run through her fingers. The witch inhaled a deep breath. He jerked once, and his lifeless body fell to the deck. A soft glow enveloped her, pulsing with every heartbeat, before it vanished. With blood all over her hands and dress, Bergrún stood, facing the remaining men.

"Keep a direct course, helmsman!" she commanded. "Hoist the mainsail and watch her fly. Dear Snorri has found a better way to speed our journey than slaving at the oars." With that, she turned and marched forward, intent on bending the wind.

* * *

"SAIL, HO!" THE shout sounded from the crow's nest one hour after sunrise, causing a communal groan of relief from the exhausted oarsmen. "Two scales to port. Sail, ho!"

The *Wave Dancer* had flown across the water for a day and a night with an uncanny speed, slicing through the choppy waves on a straight course west by southwest. Yet the favorable wind had faltered with the rising sun. Bergrún lay huddled in a heap at the bow, her head in Stina's lap. Her chest rose and fell with strained wheezing. She massaged her temples to dull the headache throbbing in time with the groan of oars. Stina cradled her friend, stroking the raven-black hair. She fixed anyone who dared to glance in their direction with the fierce glare of a she-wolf guarding her cub.

Heavy footfalls drew near, and Bergrún lifted her head. Two figures stepped close, looming over the women. Their shadows stretched long in the early morning's light. The witch pushed herself into a sitting position. A wave of dizziness washed over her, and she raised a shaking hand to shield her eyes from the sun.

Her other hand closed around the enchanted amulet containing Harold's blood and seed. Bergrún had pushed these men to the brink with her blatant display of magic; any perceived weakness might provoke a knife in the back.

"*Angist!*" she muttered. The younger man gasped, clutching his chest, and his companion seized his arm, holding him upright.

"That was uncalled for," Einar hissed through the gap in his teeth.

"On the contrary, helmsman," Bergrún replied. "After I've dedicated my energy to bringing us close, a reminder of our *common* goal seemed more than appropriate." She unfolded her legs and rose to her feet, glad for Einar's challenge, unlocking her defensive reserves. "Have the men row double-time. We can't waste a second."

"They're exhausted," Einar protested, but Harold seized him by the arm.

"Beat them if you must," the leader commanded. "Our guest is right. Let's get this done and over with without delay!"

An hour later, Harold's longboat had closed the distance, coming within four hundred yards of the sighted vessel. Rikard's ship, the *Vindsbrúð*, drifted listlessly on the choppy waves. Several sheets had come loose, letting the mainsail flap in the wind like a banner. No one seemed to man the rudder.

"Something is amiss," Einar ventured. "See there?" He pointed to the ship's bow, where a group of men stood. They huddled behind a wall of shields. The tips of spears and blades of axes gleamed in the sunlight. Some of them waved and shouted, but the wind dragged their voices out to the open sea.

"Bring us in close, Einar, but keep three ship's lengths clear until we know what happened."

"Get me on board, now!" Bergrún hissed. "You know as well as I what's happened on that ship."

"We'll do it my way or not at all!" Harold growled. He turned to the witch, squaring his shoulders. "If my men fear death going near that cursed ship," he explained, "they'll lose all respect for the whip, the sword, or your foul magic." He took a step closer. "Then you'll stand alone—one scrawny woman against a score of battle-hardened men. It's your choice," he jeered, almost daring her.

The two locked gazes. A crimson light ignited in Bergrún's irises, meeting Harold's icy glare of barely restrained hatred. The tension caused the air to sizzle with raw energy. The watching men fell silent and ducked their heads between their shoulders, fearing the imminent lightning strike.

"Lower the faering!" Bergrún growled. She straightened her spine and flexed her fingers. No one moved. "Load the provisions, and have four of your strongest men row Stina and me across."

"As you wish," Harold replied, a smile touching his lips. He inclined his head a fraction without breaking eye contact. "Einar! See to it!"

The small rowboat reached the *Vindsbrúð* twenty minutes later.

"By Odin!" One of the surviving crew called. "Take us away, I beg you. A terrible illness has befallen the crew. Everyone is dying, except for the five of us."

"Lower the ropes to hoist the provisions," Bergrún commanded. "We're coming aboard."

"You don't understand," the speaker screamed. "We have to get off. Hold the faering steady," he called to the oarsmen. "We'll jump." He swung one leg over the railing. The witch hit his face with a blast of air, sending him tumbling backward.

"Lower the ropes!" she repeated, adding a magical boom to her voice.

The terrified men aboard the *Vindsbrúð* did as told, and Stina clambered up first. The petite woman sprang onto the deck. She pulled two daggers from her belt and crouched, securing a foothold for Bergrún's ascent. Between the magic spell and Stina's unexpected posture, the men cowered behind their shields. The witch spared them no thought. She rushed aft to where several bodies lay under a sail canvas.

Rikard lay among them. With his cheeks sunken and his skin ashen, he looked like a corpse. Bergrún sank to her knees. Ripping his tunic open, she touched his chest. His heart beat, faint and erratic yet discernible. Her trembling hands felt the fever burning him up in a futile fight against the poison. She wiped moisture from her eyes and looked around, her desperate determination keeping her from collapsing.

Two more men clung to life, drawing labored breaths through cracked lips. The other three were gone. Leaving her right hand resting on Rikard's chest, the witch seized the throat of a dying sailor with her left. Her nails bit into the man's clammy skin. She chanted, her voice hoarse and the tune discordant. Pulling the last ounce of life force from the sailor's poison-ravaged body, she channeled the energy into Rikard. The world around her vanished. From far away, she heard Stina shouting, "Hoist the provisions!"

The witch repeated the transfusion with the second sailor. Despite her fatigue, she kept no energy for herself. Relief washed over her as Rikard's pulse grew stronger. Yet on every breath, the witch smelled the vile toxin's corruption. She'd bought him some time, perhaps hours, but not enough to heal him.

Drained and disheartened, she pushed herself to her feet. The crates of provisions and barrels of freshwater lay dumped onto the deck. Stina directed the *Vindsbrúð's* remaining crew to secure the cargo while the rowboat returned to the *Wave Dancer* in haste. Harold's men hadn't allowed anyone to leave Rikard's cursed ship.

"Where are the twins?" Bergrún rasped, her voice unsteady. The men looked at her with confusion. No one spoke. "The twins," Bergrún barked with an unnatural echo. "Where are they?"

"There ain't no twins aboard, Mistress," a gray-haired sailor replied.

"She's looking for that boy," a second man interjected. He held his nose, blood seeping through his fingers. He must've been the man whom she'd knocked over earlier.

"How should I know?" the first speaker argued.

"He's one of Edda's brats. She has two boys."

"So? I don't care!"

"You know a lot about that old hag," a third man mocked. "Are those brats yours, Jarro?"

"Enough!" Bergrún bellowed. A tremor spread from her feet, rattling the ship's planks. The men fell silent. "Where is the boy?"

"Below deck, Mistress," Jarro replied. He lowered his hand, displaying a broken nose. "His name is Frock. He's hiding. Must be frightened, seeing everyone getting sick."

"Oh, he's frightened, no doubt!" the witch snarled. "Fetch him!"

"Aye, Mistress." Jarro and the other two men went below.

Bergrún swayed, seizing a rope for balance. Stina caught her and steered her friend to sit on a crate. Loud banging sounded from below, interspersed with deep groans and high-pitched screams, as if the men hunted a feral bobcat instead of a gangly youth of thirteen summers. When they emerged, holding the struggling youth between them, all three sported fresh bruises. Jarro's nose had resumed bleeding like a spigot, and gray-haired Osmund's lip had been split.

They pushed Frock onto the deck, tying his hands behind the main mast. He'd grown half a foot since Bergrún saw him last up close. The witch rose and blocked the sun. He squinted until his eyes adjusted. Then he shuddered in recognition, and all the fight left his body.

"Hello, Frock," she said in a voice soft as a freshly filled grave. "I see that you recognize me. That's good. It'll make our conversation much simpler."

He squeezed his lips into a thin line, unable to stop them from quivering.

"Your mother ordered you to poison the crew," Bergrún continued, shaking her head. Venom dripped from every syllable. "That wasn't very nice. Whatever came over her? She must've lost her head." She knelt, pulling a small dagger from her belt. The curved blade sparkled in the sunlight. Raising the tip, she let it hover an inch from Frock's left eyeball. "What poison did you use?" she whispered. Her left hand rested on his knee.

"I won't tell you, witch!" he spat. "You'll kill me anyhow!"

"You think death is the worst I can do?" She closed her eyes, shaking her head again. Her lips pulled into a sad smile. "*Springa!*" she breathed. With a sickening crack, his kneecap exploded. The boy howled in agony.

"You look surprised," she asked, raising her voice over his screams. "You're not a child anymore. Boys your age have gone to battle. What did you think would happen after you poisoned all these men?" He writhed and whimpered. "What poison did you use?" she roared, pressing down on his broken knee. The men covered their ears. In the distance, a flock of seabirds took flight.

"Bog's bane!" he howled. "You can't stop it, fiend!" he cried. "They'll die. They'll all die."

She recoiled, shock shattering the facade of the emotionless inquisitor.

"GO TO HELL!" he screamed, twisting in agony.

Fast as a striking viper, her hand jabbed forth. Her knife pierced his heart, cutting his cries short. His body relaxed as the pain left him, and he slumped forward as much as the ropes permitted.

The witch stood. The spray of his blood had drenched her dress. The men stared in disbelief at the demon in their midst. Then, they dropped whatever they held and jumped into the sea. Bergrún managed to trip one man with magic. In a rush, she was on him, leeching the life from his fallen body. The others were gone. Some immediately sank, weighted down by armor and weapons. Others tried to swim. They, too, would drown.

What a waste, the witch thought. Harold's vessel had left long ago. The favorable wind stretched its sail on the journey east, toward Hamarrfjord.

* * *

STINA KNELT BESIDE Bergrún, her hands on the arm and shoulder of the swaying witch. The young woman had helped her companion prepare for the ritual of blood transfer. She'd heated the daggers to a red glow, scrubbed the wrists of both lovers with scalding water, and made the incisions. Bergrún sank into a trance, chanting, while Stina bound their arms together. The urgency of the actions had helped her ignore the brutal images that refused to fade from her mind.

She knew, on some rational level, that Frock had done a vile deed. He was the villain, the deadly weapon executing his mother's despicable plan. Still, after watching Bergrún—*her friend*—torture and murder the youth with such brutal detachment, something fundamental inside Stina had broken. She'd known her companion to be ruthless. But she'd never understood her until today.

She would see the entire world burn, Stina realized, *if it helped her achieve her goal.* Looking at her hands on Bergrún's shoulders, she wondered, *Am I holding her up, or holding her away?*

Hypocrite, Stina scolded herself. *You didn't question her powers when she saved you over and over again—after your beating, in the forest, and at the longhouse.*

Still, this felt different. Was it because Frock was still a boy?

A boy who murdered half of the crew, Stina reminded herself. Yet the thought did little to soothe the cold knot in her stomach.

The boards creaked as the ship rose and fell in the ceaseless ocean swell. Stina lowered her gaze, starting to feel drowsy, when a shifting shadow caught her attention. Without conscious thought, the young woman turned and lunged, tackling the attacker a mere eyeblink before his deadly weapon found Bergrún's throat. The blade sliced into the witch's shoulder, tearing skin and flesh to the bone. She moaned, rocking from the impact, but didn't surface from her trance.

Stina landed on top of the attacker, recognizing him. Frick, Frock's twin brother, had lost his weapon in the fall. His hands grabbed Stina's throat, squeezing. She punched and kicked, scratching him with all she had. They were of similar height and weight, two scrawny alley cats fighting over a discarded fishbone. He cursed and spat, squeezing harder. Her nails cut into his hand. He didn't relent. When her vision started blurring, she pushed her face close to his and bit his nose. He screamed and bucked, throwing her off.

She jumped to her feet, spitting the chunk of cartilage to the floor. He snatched a fallen battle axe, raising the heavy weapon. Stina grabbed a wooden bucket and smashed it against his chest, knocking the air from his lungs. He toppled backward. Without hesitation, the young woman lunged, slamming her fist into his groin. He squealed like a piglet marked for slaughter. She raised her arm again, but Frick grabbed hold of her hair. He yanked her sideways, and she hit her head on a strut. Stars burst behind her eyelids.

Frick was on her, punching her face and chest. His blood-smeared face contorted into a mask of demonic rage. Trying to push him off, Stina jabbed with her free hand. Her right thumb poked into his left eye. He screamed, and she managed to get free.

Both fighters rolled apart. They scrambled to their feet in unison, panting, bleeding, and mad with fury. Frick looked around. With the devil's luck, he found a sword and shield leaning against the railing. Hefting the weapon with apparent familiarity, he charged.

Stina pulled a hatchet from a chopping block. Intended for splitting wood, her tool was no battle axe. Still, she was swift on her feet. She dodged Frick's predictable lunges and retaliated with swift blows to his shield. The girl might not have weighed more than a wet cat, but her slender arms were all sinewy muscles from grinding herbs and churning butter.

Her onslaught forced him to retreat. He stumbled over a coil of rope, toppling backward, and his shield smacked him in the mouth. Yet as he fell, his flailing legs kicked Stina, sweeping her feet out from under her. With a yelp of surprise, she landed atop him.

Her hatchet buried itself between his brows. At the same time, his sword impaled her. He jerked, and she coughed up blood. Their bodies convulsed in a macabre dance until their limbs stopped twitching. Both youths lay still, and an eerie silence fell over the creaking ship, swaying with the relentless waves.

CHAPTER EIGHTEEN

TRUTHS

RIKARD CRAWLED FROM the tent, his head dizzy. The bright sunlight hurt his eyes. His mouth felt parched, and he reached for the sheets, steadying himself against the relentless ocean swells. The breeze carried the spray of seawater, and he shivered like a spring lamb in a hailstorm. Yet inside him, an unnatural furnace burned, searing his guts and blazing into angry flames with each sudden movement. He'd never felt anything like it.

Squinting, he looked around. The sun had crested the horizon behind a low ring of clouds, painting the sky a blood-red hue, streaked with orange. Weapons and dead bodies lay strewn across the deck. His nostrils flared, detecting the metallic scent of blood, and an unprovoked anger rose, coursing like liquid fire through his veins. *What was going on?*

As his eyes adjusted to the brightness, he spotted movement. A figure huddled at the bow, rocking with every labored breath. The face lay hidden behind a veil of black hair. The clothes were torn, and blood oozed from a cut on the shoulder. Cradling a motionless body in her arms, the figure's pale hand stroked over the auburn locks and freckled cheeks of a young woman.

He staggered closer, not trusting his senses. Raising his arms to the sides for balance, Rikard placed each step with care to avoid tripping over uncoiled rope, fallen shields, and lifeless limbs. A stronger wave hit the boat as he reached midships. He toppled, falling to his knees, and cried out in pain. The figure ahead lifted her gaze. Her burning red eyes fixed him. Her face was ashen-pale, and her thin lips quivered as tears spilled down her cheeks.

"Agnetha? What happened?" he stuttered. "Did the world end?"

"No," she rasped. "The world does not end for the likes of us!" She sat upright, straightening her rigid spine like the blade of a folding knife, and her movement tilted the dead woman's face toward him.

"Stina!" he exclaimed. "Is she...?"

Bergrún recoiled upon hearing her friend's name. A shiver spread through her body, extending outward and rattling the wooden planks. The wind picked up, snapping the ropes and flapping the loose sail canvas. Then, as suddenly as it had started, all fell still. Bergrún sagged.

"Stina is free at last," she whispered, her voice cracking. "Free of cruel men who hurt her, free of conniving mistresses who misused her, and free of a friend"—the witch spat the word—"who only scared her." Her jaw tightened. "If there's any shred of justness left in this world, she's in a better place—a place of light and warmth that never needs suffer the touch of my shadow."

"What? No! Agnetha, please... Nothing makes sense! My head throbs, my stomach burns. I can't decipher your words." His voice grew more forceful, matching the rising turmoil within. "How come you're here?" he asked, and after a handful of deep breaths that failed to squelch the fire within, he shouted, "And why?"

Rikard winced at the sound of his own voice. Squeezing his eyes shut, he fought nausea.

"Why indeed," she muttered, shaking her head. "Because your dear cousin arranged for you to be killed. Because I broke your brother's arm and then his pride before securing him the jarlship. Or because your mission is doomed since Danheimr is already on the move. Take your pick!" Her voice had lost all inflection as she bombarded him with the dire news. "All these reasons are true, yet none matter compared to my petty cause."

"Which is?" he replied without comprehending a single word.

"Because I hurt you, Rikard Svensen," she lowered her gaze, hiding her face behind the curtain of her raven-black hair. "After all the vile deeds I've done in my cursed existence—the lives I ended, the dreams I shattered, the souls I scarred—hurting you is the one thing I regret most."

He didn't move to close the distance. Rooted to the spot by the weight of her unfathomable confessions, he remained kneeling. His eyes had lost focus, and his body swayed from side to side to counterbalance the ship's rolling motion.

She didn't move to close the distance, either. She remained sitting, pinned to the deck by the dead weight of her only friend's lifeless body. The crushing guilt for Stina's sacrifice drove tears into her onyx eyes, and her fists clenched and unclenched in time with the beating of her black heart.

Above, the sun had disappeared behind a thick layer of bulging clouds. Averting its gaze, it blanketed the fate of the two sole survivors in a mantle of celestial indifference.

* * *

THE DRIZZLING RAIN had grown into a downpour by the time Bergrún had enshrined Stina's body in a sailcloth. Before pulling the shroud over the young woman's face, the witch reached a shaking hand around her own neck. She pulled a leather band over her head. A small drawstring pouch hung in place of a pendant.

"A piece of home," she whispered. With fumbling fingers, she tied the bag filled with black sand from Heilladur around Stina's neck. The witch had carried this token of her home for almost a decade since she went into exile. It'd been a talisman, a reminder of her past, and the manifestation of her dream to one day return and make everything right.

"You need it more than I!" she said to her only friend. Tears streamed unchecked down her cheeks, useless and irrelevant in the heavy rain. Bergrún kissed Stina on the forehead and pulled the cloth closed, hiding her angelic face with cruel finality. The witch swayed, and a pain burned in her veins like Hel's fires. Steam rose from her exposed skin.

"Is that what you want?" she screamed into the wind, raising her head to the heavens. "Is this a pattern to your liking?" The ferocity of the icy rain only managed to stoke her fury. "Why her? Why not me? Are you afraid? Cowards! Curse you, Norns! Curse your foul weaving! My thread isn't cut. By all the devils, I swear I'll come for you, to strangle your scrawny necks! One day, you wait!"

Lightning flashed in the clouds, and the icy gusts grew into a whirlwind. Twelve-foot waves hit the ship, sending the mighty longboat tipping and rolling. It rose and fell, tilting close to capsizing, helpless like a fallen leaf in a mountain stream. Yet it weathered the storm.

Rikard climbed up from below decks, carrying a handful of ballast rocks. When she turned her gaze on him, the demonic fire in her eyes stopped him dead in his tracks. He dropped his load.

After several tense heartbeats, the red glow faded, and she nodded. He placed the rocks into a fold of the cloth at Stina's feet, and together, they lifted the shroud, lowering the body over the railing as far as their arms reached. Rikard let go first, and Stina's feet hit the water.

"*Vertu blessuð*," Bergrún whispered. Then, she too let go, surrendering her friend into the embrace of the endless ocean—the watery grave for countless seafarers, yet also the eternal womb from which all life is born anew.

* * *

IN THE AFTERNOON, the rain let up. After Stina's sea burial, Rikard had sought shelter under the tent cloth while Bergrún stayed in the open. She'd dumped the dead bodies and useless weapons overboard, neither speaking nor exchanging so much as a glance with him. Instead, she'd stared into the distance, seeking answers beyond the invisible horizon, giving him the clear sense that she wanted to be alone.

As soon as the clouds broke, he stepped forth, offering the drenched woman a spare tunic and cloak. She nodded once, slipped free of her ripped and sodden dress, and pulled the dry garments over her shivering body. The cut on her shoulder had closed. The angry line looked days old, and the heavy rain had washed the blood off.

Sporadic sunbeams pierced the holes between the thinning clouds, and the wind had quieted to a steady breeze. Rikard rolled two empty kegs onto the deck as seats and shoved the box with fresh provisions between those, as if he were setting a table for two in the longhouse. Opening the lid, he found crispbread, cheese, and a wineskin. He placed the food onto the crate and waited for Bergrún to take her seat. She eyed him with apprehension.

"You eat!" she commanded. "I've neutralized the poison, but your body is weak. You need your strength to heal and to control the..." She stopped, grinding her teeth. Then she jumped to her feet again, turning her back to him. "You need your strength!" she declared. Her tone was firm, yet a little too rushed. She was hiding something.

"I eat when you eat," he replied. Bergrún turned, her arms crossed, and pinpricks of red sparked in her eyes.

"You think I'd poison you!" she snarled. "After everything I went through saving your life?" The wooden planks started vibrating. The cheese bounced, and the crispbread slid off the makeshift table.

"Of course not!" he shot back, his own anger flaring in response to hers. "I'm not a fool!"

She snorted a laugh.

"But look at you! You're hurt. You need your strength as much as I do. If you're here to save me, then I'll allow it if you save yourself as well. Sit and eat." His voice carried a fire she hadn't seen before, and his eyes bore into hers, matching the witch's intensity without the ruby glow.

"You'll allow it," she laughed in a raucous bark. "Well, I never thought. This shall be interesting."

She dropped onto the barrel across from him, grabbed the cheese, and bit into it like an apple. Then, she tossed it back onto the crate, daring him. He did likewise. They glared at each other, sizing each other up. But soon, both struggled to chew and swallow the oversized portion of the dry and crumbly mass. Rikard and Bergrún reached for the wineskin at the same moment. Their hands touched. A jolt of electricity sparked, and they recoiled in unison, breaking into reluctant smiles with hamster cheeks. Bergrún stood first, spitting the gooey mass into the sea. Moments later, Rikard did likewise.

"Will you tell me why?" he asked half an hour later, after they had eaten in silence.

"I told you. Stina overheard Toril plotting your death. I needed to convince Harold…"

"Not that," he interrupted. "I'll hear the whole story from the beginning. But not now. Can Toril's treachery wait for a little while longer?"

"What do you mean, can it wait?"

"Is anyone else chasing after us today? Must we hurry to prevent another disaster tomorrow?"

"We're as safe here as mice traversing the great hall in daylight. There's no cat in sight. Doesn't mean we should take a nap halfway across."

"Good enough for me," he replied, leaning forward. "Before I worry about cats, I'd like to understand why to cross the great hall in the first place. Why did you do it?" His words carried the bitter tone of an accusation, and his blue eyes fixed on her with a burning intensity. Her breath caught.

"You mean Harold… that morning?" she asked, reading the confirmation in his hardening glare. He leaned back, crossed his arms, and squared his jaw. A vein pulsed in his temple.

"I was angry," Bergrún started. "I was disappointed, I was hurt, and I was vengeful." She'd lowered her eyes, fiddling with the end of her leather belt. "And I was stupid," she amended, raising her gaze again.

His face became a mask of jagged stone, with hurt and disappointment visible through the cracks. At that moment, he looked aged by a decade, like someone forced to carry the burden of a much older man.

"I'm not who you think I am," she finally confessed.

"Of course not," he spat. "I thought you my friend, my confidant. Oh, stupid me, I thought you my lover!" His cheeks flushed deep red, and his eyes blinked rapidly.

The muscles in his arms twitched, and he clamped them tight around his chest. She saw into the chasm of pain and betrayal under his forced bravado, so deep and ragged as only the first rejected love can carve into a young human's soul.

"Rikard," she said in a broken whisper. She couldn't find the air to give her voice strength. "I betrayed you much earlier and much deeper than you think. Since we first met, I planned to use you like a tool. The naïve young warrior from a mighty house, elevated to a local hero, and besotted by my wiles—I couldn't have wished for more. You were the perfect steed on which I could ride home to Heilladur in glory. And then came your Inglandia folly. First, an idea, then a plan, and finally, when everybody around you called you a lunatic, it became your fixation. I had no use for you any longer."

He stared, dumbfounded by her brutal honesty. The relentless hammer blows had cracked his armor like eggshells, leaving him naked in a deadly assault. Like a child who'd tripped and fallen when running down the stairs, the overwhelming shock stemmed the flood of cries for a handful of heartbeats. Yet the cry would come, and with it the end.

"When you left, everything changed," she continued, not giving him a chance to react. "You took something with you that I didn't believe I still possessed, until it was gone. Call it the last vestiges of my human soul." Her words pattered like raindrops against a tent canvas, gaining in frequency and ferocity as darker clouds moved in. She had to get it all out before the storm broke. "I felt a loss like I had never endured before. I wanted to end my life," she declared in a factual manner without a hint of melodrama.

His mouth dropped open, his hands sinking into his lap.

"I was about to jump from the cliffs when Stina's voice stopped me with the only words that still held any meaning: 'Rikard will die!' I threatened your brother, killed Edda, conspired against Toril, haggled with the Jarl, bent the wind, and murdered a child. I even gave you my blood, everything just for the chance to lay the entire, unvarnished truth at your feet. Will you allow me that much before you must do what you must do?"

* * *

BERGRÚN TALKED UNTIL long past the sun had gone to sleep and the moonlight painted the sea with a glint of ghostly silver. Rikard had agreed to let her speak, reserving the right to cut her lies short as soon as he grew tired of them. But the witch had him ensnared in her tale of tragedy, magic, ambition, and vengeance after only two sentences.

"What you must understand, Rikard Svensen, is that you are a good person and I'm not. You are the total opposite of me, yet, at the same time, you're the person I wanted to be if I could start over. I can't. I'm a black witch. I need to kill humans to stay alive. And I chose that fate willingly."

Both sat wrapped in blankets against the creeping chill. A fire burned in a brazier between them, and they had started out sitting as far apart as the deck allowed. But as the night wore on, they crept closer to the warmth. Rikard hung on Bergrún's every word with gruesome fascination, bound by the allure of her terrifying tale.

"My real name is Bergrún, Bergrún Lilith Gullveigardóttir. I've never been to Götaland. I was born thirty years ago in Svartvik, a tiny fishing village on the West coast of Heilladur."

"Thirty years ago?" he asked, astounded. She raised her finger, and he fell silent.

"Everything else I told you about my childhood and upbringing was true. But I left out some important details. Yes, the villagers shunned my parents because of their disfigurement and the lowly tasks they could perform. My father mended nets, and my mother cleaned the pig sties. But I didn't make it easy for anyone to be my friend. My burning passion for justice rubbed many influential villagers the wrong way. I had my pride, my stubbornness, and my dreams, yet not much more.

"When I was sixteen, I was a skinny waif—even more than I am now." She gave a mirthless laugh. "I looked famished, and my chest wasn't bigger than an eleven-year-old boy's. There was a young man," she sighed. "The son of the smith. He was a year or two my senior, but tall, broad-shouldered, and handsome. The village girls asked me if I fancied him. 'Of course,' I said, we all did. For anyone else, admitting a shared yearning may have opened the door to true camaraderie. For me, it opened the abyss of humiliation and set me on the path into darkness."

She paused, taking a long draught from the wineskin. Rikard slid closer, nudging the brazier aside. He wanted to read her expressions, unobstructed by the dancing flames between them.

"They played a vile trick on me," she whispered after wiping her lips. With her eyes downcast, she fidgeted with the stopper. "They told me sweet lies, that he'd inquired after me, the shy girl with the raven-black hair. They suggested that I wait by the waterfall where he often went for a refreshing bath. If I were in the water, unclothed, well, nature would run its course from then on. I was stupid, and gullible, and lonely, and infatuated. So I did as my 'good friends' suggested. I left my shabby dress on the rocks by the pool and stepped into the chill waters. The day hadn't been too warm. After several minutes, I started fearing he wouldn't come. I grew cold. Shivering, I left the pool to find my clothes missing. I looked around, searching for any trace. Had a fox or a badger seized the unexpected treasure to soften their den? Standing there, at a loss for what to do, with gooseflesh all over my body, I heard male voices. A group of woodsmen, large hairy brutes, marched into the clearing, eager to wash the day's sweat off their dirt-caked hides. They spotted me. Whooping in delight, they made rude insinuations and spread out as if to catch me. I ran, sprinting through the underbrush like a deer chased by bears, their bellowing laughter ringing in my ears."

Rikard's hands clenched into white-knuckled fists. He looked at her, his face a mask of shock and disbelief. The earlier anger lay forgotten, tossed aside by the sheer magnitude of Bergrún's story. For long moments, they remained quiet, listening to the harmonies of the gentle breeze, the rolling ocean, and the creaking ship.

"What happened then, Agnet... I mean, Bergrún?" he ventured, trying out the unfamiliar name. She looked at him. He looked much younger now, so eager, so naïve.

"My happily ever after," she scoffed with disdain. She closed her eyes and massaged her temples before continuing. "I hid in the forest. After night-fall, I snuck near an outlying farm and stole some clothes—a pair of torn pants and a sweat-stained tunic, a careless farmhand had left out to dry. I also stole some eggs and barely escaped with my life as the farmsteader let the dogs loose.

"I roamed the land, not daring to slink home like a beaten dog to cruel rumors and vicious snickers. I stole more food and better-fitting clothes: boots and a knife. I even found a fishing rod. But I had no patience, can you imagine that?" She gave a short, bitter laugh.

"After weeks, I found what I was looking for. Or what I was meant to find, curse the Norns. The healer I told you about, the old crone I apprenticed with, she lived in a hut deep in a forest of gnarled trees and thorn thickets."

"Was she a witch?" Rikard guessed.

"Aye, a witch. But not your run-of-the-mill wart-curing herb woman. She was a black witch. One of only five in the entire known world. One of Death's true daughters, powerful, bitter, and stupid!"

"Why stupid?" he asked, caught in her tale like a squirrel in a lynx's claws.

"Because she lived in a hovel, a rung below a pig's wallow, feasting on tubers and slimy mushrooms, and letting her powers waste away." Bergrún's body tensed, her agitation emanating in waves. "Of course," she spat, "it took me years to figure her out." Her lips formed a feral grin, and the fire in her eyes rekindled. "Three years of my youth stolen away with meaningless chores and cold nights in a smelly, earthen burrow every self-respecting groundhog would eschew."

A long silence fell. Several times, Rikard was about to prompt her. He was captivated, burning to hear the fullness of her tale. But he feared spoiling the moment. The unsettling truce between them balanced on a knife's edge. It'd be better to let her continue at her own pace.

"One night, I'd had enough. I'd grown impatient. The old hag often called me willful and disobedient. Dear Ingvild Bramsdóttir, she was forever going on about the foibles of youth and how I was prone to rash actions because of my raging emotions. As it turns out, she was right. When I couldn't take her abuse any longer, I knifed her in her sleep."

Rikard recoiled, appalled by her despicable act, but more by her cavalier retelling.

"Oh, the torrent of pain when her black curse took me," the witch said, shuddering from the memory. "You can't imagine. The fire you feel inside you... That's just a dying candle compared to a bubbling pool of molten lava. I writhed all night, unable to scream. But then, the sun rose over a glorious new world." She looked at him, a sinister smile on her lips.

His face had lost all color, and he pulled back, his eyes wide as millstones.

"Don't look at me with your innocent shock and moral disdain. You've known me, you've seen me. How did your uncle phrase it: 'A battle axe is not the tool to braid a flower wreath.' I seized my chance for a better life, rejecting the bleak fate the Norns had placed upon me."

"You're right, I'm shocked," he rasped, clearing a lump from his throat. His voice sounded shaken. "Your tale is shocking. You might think that I'm innocent and naïve for feeling that way, but you feel it too." He raised his gaze. Seeking her eyes, he struggled to remain steadfast under the furious onslaught of her demonic glare. "You've lived a shocking life," he whispered. "But, Bergrún, more than anything, it is sad. I'm so..."

"Don't you dare, Rikard Thure Svensen!" she screamed, jumping to her feet. "Don't you dare pity me! That's what THEY want! That's what the whole world always did to me: Grimarr Snortsbane, Stígur cursed Asmundsen, Toril Cunningsdotter, and her spiders. Your uncle, your brother, your stinking village—everybody thinks themselves stronger, smarter, and so much better than pitiful little Bergrún. But you won't!" she shrieked. "Do you hear me? YOU WON'T!"

She whirled around and rushed forward. Ripping a battle axe from the leather straps that had tied it to the railing, she took a running leap and swung. The gleaming blade soared in a graceful arc, severing in a single blow the swan's neck that decorated the ship's bow. She let go. Wooden ornament and mighty weapon sailed into the darkness before splashing into the pitch-black sea. Bergrún sank to her knees, keeled over, and started weeping.

He stood, frozen like a statue, useless like the decapitated carving of a bird. He should go to her. She needed him.

Maybe not me, he thought. *But she needs someone!*

She would kill him if he touched her. She was a killer. He'd known it long before her admission. She was the most dangerous creature he'd ever encountered, comparable only to the dragons and sea serpents of ancient sagas.

Her unrestrained power had appalled and attracted him since the raid on Fårosünd. Since their first fateful meeting, the mutual saving of lives had formed an irrevocable bond between them. She was a stunning woman, even in her demonic rage. Her slender body was a mystery, vulnerable like the wings of a butterfly, yet enticing like a water nymph. Their lovemaking had been moments of pure bliss, always teetering on the brink of fatal disaster. But her soul, her beautiful yet damaged soul, had drawn him in since he'd first looked into her onyx eyes, like the fish she claimed never to have caught.

Rikard closed the distance, taking careful steps. He knelt beside her and took her in his arms, holding her tight. His breath came in uneven gasps, and his body trembled, vibrating in harmony with hers.

CHAPTER NINETEEN

Headwind

As the ship lost all forward momentum, Rikard let his tired hands slide off the rudder. He stepped back, shook his head, and muttered curses into the unrelenting wind. A large wave hit the hull, jamming the rudder sideways, and the well-worn steering bar slammed against his hip. With a cry of frustration, he kicked a nearby wooden bucket, sending it tumbling down the stairs to the main deck.

Bergrún abandoned her attempt to furl the mainsail. Leaving half of the sailcloth flapping in the gusting wind, she slid down a tie line and landed on the balls of her feet. She strolled aft, to where her companion leaned against the railing, massaging his aching foot.

"I guess that didn't work," she shouted, still several strides away.

"You'd think so?" he grumbled. "What gave you the impression?"

Over the last couple of days, the two remaining souls aboard the *Vindsbrúð* had tried everything possible to steer the vessel onto a western course despite the constant wind blowing and sometimes gusting from the opposite direction. But their efforts proved no match for the indifferent sea and a ship that demanded more hands and more experience than they possessed.

"What now, master helmsman?" Bergrún asked.

"Now is the time when you admit you could've magicked us to Aberdeenium all along, right? You were just holding back to spare my pride, what with my renowned nautical skills."

"Perhaps, I could," she mused, giving him a wicked grin. "But I'd have to kill you. And even then, such a feat might be a stretch. My curse is like a ravaging fire, always demanding fuel in exchange for magic."

Rikard flinched at her mention of killing, though he knew she was joking. Between their failed attempts to tame the ship, they'd talked. Her words painted a chilling picture of her curse, that insatiable fire burning within her. He looked from her pale face to his own calloused hands.

"And you always feel its hunger?"

"Always," she said, dropping the humor. The witch had expected Rikard to attack her after the brutal confession of her deceit. She'd given him plenty of reasons to hate her, not least her admission of being a black witch—a demon that lives off the life energy of humans. Yet he'd surprised her, showing her compassion and understanding.

"Sometimes, when the curse is satiated, I can smother the fire for a while," she explained. "But it always smolders, ready to be stoked when needed. Once the blazes rage, though, eager for fuel, I can't stop them. I can only choose where the inferno spreads." She looked into his eyes, trying to read his thoughts. Was there a flicker of revulsion? Still, he didn't shy away. So she continued. "The more I fight it, the more I have to pay for it later. Every cell in my body screams for me to give in."

"Then why do you fight?" he whispered. "Surely, the world can't punish you any further."

"Why?" she laughed without a hint of mirth. "Ask yourself! Why didn't you kill me during the raid? Why haven't you taken any girl by force? The world wouldn't punish you either. You had the 'warrior's right,'" she spat.

Rikard's jaw tightened.

"I don't care for arcane traditions. Those are excuses for cruelty. Maybe the world doesn't care. But I do!" He stood straight, and his eyes blazed with fervor.

"Would you believe me that I care too?" the witch whispered, lowering her gaze. "I don't want to be the fire that consumes the world."

* * *

Hours later, the longboat drifted rudderless on the choppy waves. The clouds had thickened, adding a constant curtain of rain to the ocean spray riding on the wind. Lacking any promising plan of action, Rikard and Bergrún had sought shelter under the tent canvas. They'd shared crispbread and mead. Bergrún sat with her legs crossed, her head resting against the pole. She kept her eyes closed and listened to the drumbeat of raindrops. Rikard fidgeted with a strand of rope, his gaze darting from his fingers to the horizon and back. Finally, he threw the rope down in frustration. "I can't remain still," he snapped. "My head feels all wrong. My skin burns, and my guts churn like writhing snakes."

"I feared as much," Bergrún whispered, opening her eyes. "I gave you my blood. Tendrils of my unholy fire must now burn in you."

"So, I'm a witch now?" he asked in an accusing tone. "Like you?"

"You're alive, that is certain. Everything else... I don't know." She straightened up. A muscle twitched on his cheek. His eyes were wide with anxiety, yet the dim light stole the color from his striking blue irises. In a slow and deliberate movement, she placed her hand on his, stopping his fidgeting.

"You're not a witch. You have neither a cat nor a broom; not even a cauldron." When her attempted humor failed to lift his mood, she continued in a soothing tone. "You're not cursed, believe me. You'll never have to kill to quell an insatiable hunger."

"But I feel different," he insisted, his voice rising. "This... restlessness. This anger. Maybe it is the demonic hunger! Isn't this how you feel?"

"My curse is singular. It can neither be split nor shared. As long as I carry the fire in me," she said, tapping her chest, "no one else can. So no, you are not like me."

"But..."

"But you might be tainted," she acquiesced. "So I'll have to share my blood with you from time to time to prevent the fire from charring your soul."

"So, I'm stuck with you?" he asked, his voice sounding flat. But his shoulders sank, releasing tension.

"Hardly," she chuckled. "You're free to ally yourself with any black witch there is. I, however, am stuck with you!"

"How is that?"

"Because I came to save you, dullard, remember?" She held his gaze without blinking.

His brows were furrowed, and his eyes held an inscrutable expression. Then, a slow breath escaped his lips, and with it, some of the hard lines on his boyish face softened.

"In that case, we're stuck with each other," Rikard ventured. "Where do we go from here?" He raised his head, seeking the patch of gray sky visible beyond the ship's bow.

A restless silence settled, punctuated by the raindrops drumming on the canvas, until he stretched out his right hand, finding hers. She felt a tingle where their fingers touched.

"Seems like Abberdeenium is out of reach," he sighed in answer to his own question. "Even if the wind changed, we've been blown off course too far to find it. Not that it matters," he added with a snort. "It's just a couple of mud huts around a half-built godhouse."

"Then why all the rush to get there?"

"To meet the local chieftain and make an alliance. The people call him Duck Something."

"I think you mean Duke," she laughed. "And wasn't this your grand plan, an alliance with Inglandia? What changed your mind, besides the non-co-operative wind?"

"Pebbles!" he grumbled, his mouth twisting into a bitter line.

"Pebbles?"

"I'd planned to bring gifts to impress the duke, gold and weapons," he explained. "There are three ornate chests below deck."

"And?"

"And cunning Toril sent me off with a rich cargo of pebbles. I only realized her ruse an hour ago, looking for a pair of boots." He placed his fist into his palm, cracking his knuckles. "My resourceful cousin," he hissed, "she never intended to part with a small fortune if I were to die at sea anyhow."

"That double-headed snake!" Bergrún cursed. "I should've known! I could have brought..."

"Doesn't matter now," he sighed, reaching for her hand. "We'll never reach Aberdeenium in this wind."

The silence that followed stretched on for so long that it became uncomfortable. She watched him, trying to decipher the inscrutable mask his face had become. His gaze drifted from their intertwined hands to some distant point on the horizon. His thumb stroked over her knuckles, yet the muscles in his jaw worked, as if he were chewing on unspoken words. Several times, he seemed to draw himself up, ready for action, only to fall back into statuesque stillness.

Then, his focus snapped back to her, and his eyes shone with intensity. He stood in one swift motion, pulling Bergrún to her feet before she could react. "The rain is letting up," he said, leaving no room for debate. "Help me set the sail."

"To go home and confront Toril?" she asked, following him into the rigging.

"No," he shouted over the wind, loosening the mainsail. "My uncle will have dealt with his daughter by now. We're sailing south."

"South? To where?" Bergrún asked, pulling on a rope as he untangled another. He didn't answer. Instead, he slid back down to the deck below.

She followed. Rikard began tightening the sheets, and Bergrún seized his arm, the question burning in her eyes.

"My brother is on his way to Hamarrfjord," Rikard explained, not looking at her. "You arranged for him to be the next jarl. So there is no place for me. I won't go back to being mighty warrior Harold's little brother. Not after..." he grumbled.

She let go and stepped back. Her cheeks blushed, and she looked away.

"Unless you long for Chieftain Harold's embrace..." he asked, unable to hide the bitterness beneath his forced smile.

"Of course not, dullard," she growled, punching his arm.

"Then we sail south, towards Éira. I hear it's green and beautiful, with wildflower meadows on rolling hills." He paused for one heartbeat before declaring, "And I decided, we should go there. To start over, you know, me and... you." His cheeks blushed, but he held her gaze.

"You've decided?" the witch asked. "How kind of you to let me know." Her tone became a low growl. But her eyes didn't glow red. Instead, something sparkled within their depths.

"Well," he ventured, emboldened. "With the whole being-stuck-with-each-other thing... Do you have a better idea?" His lips pulled into a sheepish grin.

"I'm still contemplating the killing-you-for-magic option."

"Somehow," he whispered. "I don't believe you do." He stepped closer, placing his hands on her shoulders. She narrowed her eyes, baring her teeth. In response, his smile widened and his eyes twinkled. He still looked young and somewhat innocent. But there was a new determination in his posture, a confidence that hadn't been there before.

He leaned in as if to kiss her.

She punched him in the stomach.

For a second, his bravado faltered, and he froze, his eyes widening.

"Coward," she growled before seizing him by the front of his tunic and pulling him into a kiss of burning passion.

* * *

THE NEXT MORNING dawned gray. Bergrún had woken early. She wandered to the railing, looking out over the endless ocean. Having wrapped her bare skin into Rikard's fur coat, she pulled it tight against the morning chill and inhaled his scent. Rikard lay sprawled-eagled under the tent canvas, still sleeping. They'd shared closeness throughout the night without intimacy. Bergrún had felt a hesitancy in Rikard, a struggle to let go despite his apparent yearning.

Who could fault him? He'd seen her in his brother's bed—an image that cemented her betrayal. Could they mend what had been broken that day?

The witch looked south, squinting, imagining distant lands of rolling hills. The *Vindsbrúð* seemed to sail toward Éira of its own accord—the rudder tied, the wind steady. Was there a chance of reaching a new horizon? If she held very still and didn't interfere, would she be able to slip out from under the Norns' malicious pattern onto a shore of wildflower meadows? She looked back north and found her answer. Two sails, striped black and yellow in the colors of Danheimr, crested the horizon.

Bergrún roused Rikard, and both dressed in haste. Neither believed the hunters appeared by happenstance, nor did they need to speculate about the consequences of being caught. While the pursuit was still hours away, the swift warships were gaining.

Rikard began tossing everything unnecessary overboard, starting with the pebble-filled chests. Bergrún trimmed the mainsail and added smaller lateen sails fore and aft. The *Vindsbrúð's* hull groaned as the ship gained speed, and the distance to the Danskers grew. Rikard adjusted the course westward, sacrificing some speed for a chance to hide among the rocky islands guarding the channel into the Inglan Sea.

"We'll make it!" he insisted. "There's no way these southern sea dogs will catch a Hamarrfjord longship." Bergrún smiled, appreciating his silly bravado as an attempt to make her feel better.

"There!" She pointed to shadows off the starboard bow. "Are those the Iarntann Islands?"

"Yes!" he shouted, raising his fists. "We're almost there." He gazed across the open sea toward a row of jagged peaks rising from the waters like the spine of a dragon. "I'll swing her out to catch more wind before we tuck inland."

Rikard threw his full weight against the steering oar. The massive timber fought him like a living beast, shuddering as the rudder bit into the churning water. The witch rushed to help him. Together, they turned the *Vindsbrúð* into the heart of the stiffening wind.

The world tilted at a dizzying angle. The starboard rail dropped so low it threatened to kiss the foaming wavetops. Every timber in the hull groaned. The entire ship protested in a symphony of deep rumbling, high-pitched shrieks, and the sharp cracking of tension. The mast leaned like a spruce in a gale wind, letting out a low guttural moan that seemed to resonate from the vessel's very bones. Then, as the bow sliced past its apex, the wind caught, filling the sail with a deafening boom, and the ship came alive.

No longer fighting, the *Vindsbrúð* heeled over and launched forward. Its prow carved a trench through the waves. Twin curtains of icy spray erupted from the bow, glittering like shards of ice. The timbers changed their tune, shifting from a groan of strain to a hum of power. The *Vindsbrúð* lived up to her name, enveloping Bergrún and Rikard in the thrill of flight over the churning sea. They looked at each other, breathless, their eyes twinkling. A smile tugged on Bergrún's lips, and she leaned closer, when his face fell.

"*Skitr!*"

"What?" She turned, and her heart plummeted. Two more sails, one to the east and one to the south, closed the trap. "We have to go west. Between the islands. Turn her around!"

"We won't make it," Rikard explained, his voice flat, his face losing all color. "If I yank her too hard, the mainsail will stall our momentum. We don't have the men to douse it in time." He looked around as if searching for hitherto unseen sailors. With a resigned expression, he amended, "If I turn her too slow, they'll have us."

"Do it!" Bergrún urged, squeezing his hand. "There's no way these southern sea dogs will catch a Hamarrfjord longship!"

He gave her a fleeting smile before pulling on the rudder. Closing his eyes, he gritted his teeth and pulled with everything he had. But the turn was slow, the wind still holding them hostage. Frustrated, he was about to call for help when he spotted Bergrún standing rigid, her hand outstretched toward the mast. A low hum vibrated through the deck, and the air felt charged with energy.

"*Rífa!*" the witch shouted, and the rigging lines burst apart with a deafening thunderclap, sending the yard crashing to the deck. The railings on either side splintered. Bergrún opened her eyes, reaching one arm out to steady herself.

"There," she croaked. "Mainsail struck, helmsman."

* * *

FOR THE NEXT hour, sweat and seawater blurred their vision as they battled the ship in tandem. While tacking the smaller lateen sails proved possible with only one pair of hands, Bergrún needed to sprint fore and aft in an endless obstacle race against the wind. The broken yard proved a constant menace, and ropes and debris blocked her path. At every turn, the ship lurched like a drunken sailor who'd spent a month's wages in the alehouse.

Rikard's muscles screamed for mercy. The damaged ship fought him harder than a boulder rolling down a hill. With the weight of the main yard gone, the *Vindsbrúð* was sluggish to respond, threatening to stall in the wind each time he pulled on the rudder. Again and again, he threw his body against the steering oar, forcing the ship into its tightest possible turn. The unsecured yard careened across the slick deck, forcing Bergrún to leap aside as it splintered the railing where she'd stood.

While the islands ahead grew larger, so did the pursuing ships. One of the Danske vessels broke away from its partner, closing the distance. Its oars dug into the water like a centipede's legs, giving it a burst of speed. Soon, the angry shouts of the hostile warriors carried on the wind, harsh, guttural commands that made the hair on Rikard's neck stand up.

Bergrún sought Rikard's gaze. They didn't speak; neither had breath left for words. In desperation, they doubled their effort to the tune of the creaking hull and the hiss of lines sliding through block and tackle. Every now and then, the witch cursed when a line burned her palm or she stabbed her toe on a strut. Rikard admired her tenacity, and hope rekindled. Might they achieve the impossible and outmaneuver an entire war fleet? Then, he saw the whirlpools.

"What's happening over there?" Bergrún called, pointing. He didn't need to look to know what she was seeing.

"Whirlpools," he replied as the weight of a boulder settled in his stomach. "The tide is rushing in. We won't make it." He let go of the rudder. "No ship can sail between the islands when the tide rushes in."

"Why?"

"WHY?" he screamed, raising his hand to the sky. "Because the current will shove us onto a reef, smash us against the cliffs, or just pull us under. We can't steer with a current that strong."

"You steer in strong winds!" she pressed. "How is that different?"

"It is different!" he shouted in frustration. "The sails harness the wind. But no ship has sails underwater!"

"And why not?" she growled, low and threatening.

"Because you can't... No one has... Because it's impossible!"

"Like cutting the rigging with a word?" the witch asked. "Like healing you from an incurable poison?" She took a step closer. "That kind of impossible?"

He looked at her, open-mouthed.

"Listen to me, Rikard Svensen!" she shouted. "Those Danske ships aren't here by accident, and they're definitely not here to attend our wedding. I don't know how they managed it, but I smell dear Toril's hand in this. I haven't come all the way to give up now! Stina hasn't died for us to give up now!" the witch bellowed. "We'll get away from these sea dogs, or we'll die trying!"

She drew in labored breaths. Her eyes blazed red like the dying sun. Rikard almost expected to see sparks flying from her nostrils. He squeezed his eyes shut but stood his ground as waves of white-hot fury washed over him. The feeling was so intense that he feared his skin would blister and burn. Wave after wave twisted his guts. The deck planks vibrated under his feet. Then, the effects of her fury subsided, collapsing inward. Reluctantly, he opened his eyes, afraid of what he would see. He was unharmed.

Across the deck, Bergrún slumped against the hull. Sobs racked her chest, and tears spilled over her cheeks. Her hands clamped onto the railing, the knuckles shining white, and her whole body trembled in the struggle against the raging emotions.

She's losing, he thought. *After all she's done, she doesn't feel hope anymore.*

He walked across and took her hands. Her skin felt feverish, and her chest rose and fell in a frenetic rhythm. He squeezed, and a shudder ran through her body. She raised her gaze with inhuman effort. Their eyes met, and he gave her a hesitant smile.

"Stones," he whispered.

"What?" Her voice sounded hollow.

"We weigh the sail down with stones. If we position the main yard over the bowsprit, we can lower the sail below the waterline. No one has ever done it," he laughed. "Because it's stupid. But I've done many things others would call stupid. Falling for a witch must top the list. For a beautiful and terrifying, brave and ruthless, deeply troubled and utterly wonderful witch!" And with that, he kissed her.

CHAPTER TWENTY

LANDFALL

RIKARD DUCKED HIS head to crawl under the lean-to shelter, wiping the moisture from his face. His wavy hair lay plastered to his skull, and his patched tunic hung drenched over his lanky frame. The air smelled of moss and wet soil. The improvised roof leaked in countless places.

Despite the sodden atmosphere, the young man whistled a tune. He hooked the line with two good-sized mackerels over an exposed driftwood branch, smiling. Bergrún huddled in a corner, wrapped in all the clothes they had left, still shivering. The skin on her exposed forearms shimmered a faint blue while her lips were deep purple. She shook her head at Rikard's inexplicable good humor.

"Do you think we're in the blessed halls?" he mused while wringing the dripping hem of his tunic. She replied with a stare of utter disbelief. "I mean," he continued, "we could've died without realizing it, and this is the afterlife."

"Absolutely not!" she hissed. "Too wet for Valhalla and too cold for Hel! How in Loki's treacherous name could you call this," she pointed at their waterlogged lair, "the blessed halls?"

"Well," he began, "we have food and shelter..." garnering an angry hiss. "I've roamed the lush landscape for hours," he continued, undeterred. "I've spotted deer and rabbits, caught fish, and found mushrooms. Yet far and wide, I haven't seen a single soul. No sign of settlements anywhere."

"The land is lush because it rains nonstop!" she growled. "If the winters are cold enough, the rain might turn to snow."

"It doesn't rain all the time," he protested. "Earlier today, at the beach, the clouds broke and I felt the sun on my skin." She gave him a withering glare, and he admitted, "For a couple of minutes, at least."

"And you haven't seen people," she continued in her harangue, "because no one in their right mind would live on a windswept cliff that draws *all* the moisture from the ocean breeze."

"Perhaps, we should move on." He looked at her splinted leg, and she ground her teeth following his gaze. "And you might be right," he ventured with a twinkle in his eyes.

"As always?" she prompted when he remained silent too long.

"As quite often," he relented, grinning. "This can't be Valhalla, because I've never heard of a deceased soul breaking her leg after dying."

"Oh, haha! Very funny!" she scoffed.

"But it is," he grinned, trying and failing to suppress his laughter, "when you think about it. We had everything against us: the wind, the whirlpools, the cliffs, and the Danske ships. We bet our lives on a harebrained plan, and with the devil's luck, we literally scraped through a tight spot. We survived the *Vindsbrúð's* violent death on the submerged rocks and crossed the Inglan Sea in a tiny rowboat, living off raw fish and rainwater. And once we set foot onto safe shores, you stepped into a rabbit hole and broke your foot. The Norns must have keeled over laughing, their skeletal frames rattling with hysterical guffaws as they clutched their loom for support."

The witch glared for two more heartbeats before a traitorous twitch, a tiny flicker at the corner of her mouth, cracked her resolve. The absurdity of the hilarious image seized a foothold in her mind, turning the trembling lip into a full-scale rebellion that pulled her mouth into a reluctant curve. The air rushed forth in a strangled snort. And while she tried to disguise the noise as a cough, the dam had cracked. A genuine laugh bubbled up and spilled from her lips. She shook her head, grinning, and warmth rushed through her body for the first time in days.

He joined her, chuckling, and she seized his hand.

"You're such a silly boy!" she wheezed. When she regained control, she added, "Thank you!"

They sat beside each other for a long while, not needing words.

"I wish we could get a fire going." He eventually sighed, looking at the pile of wet wood in front of them. He'd covered it with grass, shielding the twigs from the rain in the vain hope they'd dry up enough to catch a spark. Yet so far, he had been unsuccessful. "I do like mackerels, but every now and then, I'd prefer them roasted over a fire."

"You're not complaining, are you?" she smirked. "Weren't you saying we're in the blessed halls?"

He mumbled something unintelligible, and she poked him in the side.

"Listen, there's something I haven't told you yet," she said. He turned his head, and his brows knitted together. "I'm not sure why I kept it a secret—perhaps because my leg hurt, because my mishap injured my pride, or because I wanted to hate this place after you planted such fantastic expectations in my mind. But there is something to this land, something in the air I haven't felt for a long, long time... Not since I left my home on Heilladur."

"What is it?" he whispered, intrigued.

"Magic!" With a clap, the witch ignited the heap of sodden branches, conjuring a bonfire—bright and warm and oh, so welcomed.

After they'd eaten the delicious fish, charred to a crisp, Rikard hung his wet clothes to dry, and they huddled under the sole blanket, their bare feet stretching toward the crackling logs. Bergrún rested her head on Rikard's shoulder. Her long fingers wandered over his bare chest. His eyes had lost focus, and with his lips parted, he drew in deep, slow breaths.

"I've never thought that I would ever sail this far," he said after a long pause. "They say my great-great-grandfather, Leif Rødskæg, was the first Viking to sail among the Iron Teeth, finding the shores of Éira beyond."

"The one with the wolf's head banner?" Bergrún asked.

"Yes, our first chieftain," he replied, tilting his head toward her. "He found his twin wives on Éira."

"Twin wives?"

"Oh, yes. It's a fascinating tale. When he first came to Éira, he saw a young woman of unrivaled beauty. For days, he stalked her through field and forest until one evening he found her alone by a river. So, he stole her and brought her home to Hamarrfjord."

"Yes, I can see," the witch scoffed. "A fascinating tale. Very romantic."

"Well, not quite yet. See, she was sad..."

"You don't say!" Her nails sank into his skin.

"Yes, yes... but more than that. From time to time, she wept, bemoaning that half of her was missing. Well," he said, "she didn't speak much Norsk, and my great-great-grandfather could handle an axe much better than foreign tongues. Still, since he loved her so much, he returned to Éira to seek what she was missing."

"And?" Bergrún asked, intrigued despite her earlier remarks.

"As the Norns willed it, he found her twin sister. Naturally, my great-

great-grandfather stole her, too. From then on, they lived happily together. He had many children with both sisters."

"So, you're saying, there is an ancient custom to..." she ventured, probing his sense of humor.

"No!" he replied, catching on, and his voice lost some of the jovial tone. "We do not practice marriage with multiple siblings! Not at the same time, that is... Neither with two sisters nor two brothers."

She stiffened, fearing she'd pushed him too far. Ten painful seconds of silence followed until he cleared his throat. "Anyhow, this is different," he whispered, "since we weren't married... yet."

Bergrún's sigh of relief turned into a gasp as she dissected his last word.

In response, he pushed himself up, letting her gently slide off his shoulder. With a sparkle in his eyes, he bent down to kiss her.

* * *

THE TWO REFUGEES spent a week in their damp hideout before Bergrún declared her leg was healed enough for them to move on. She'd grown restless, eager to explore the heart of the island in the hope of finding the source of the ambient magical energy. Rikard had scoured the beaches for flotsam and jetsam, finding a length of rope and a partial sail canvas to serve as a tent. He packed their limited possessions into four makeshift bundles but still hesitated to set out.

"You're sure your leg is strong enough?" he'd asked for the dozenth time, receiving a glare in return.

"Yes, father," she scoffed. "This isn't the first injury I've sustained. You might not believe it, given my delicate disposition, but my life hasn't been all down pillows and sedan chairs."

"I know," he conceded, raising his palms. "But the bone looked broken. How can it mend itself in a week? When my friend Claas broke his arm, it took ages, and even after, the arm was never right again."

"I assume your friend Claas wasn't a witch?"

"Of course not... You mean you can use magic to heal bones?" he asked. "How does that work?"

"I don't know."

"How can you not know?"

"Do you know how your stomach works, your lungs, your heart, or your eyes? They just work. And sometimes, when you do something stupid like eating rotten food or poking a twig into your eye, you learn what not to do."

"I guess, but this sounds so different... a bit unnatural," he said, mumbling the last words. Still, she heard him.

"Flying is unnatural to a fish," she huffed, narrowing her eyes, "but most birds find nothing wrong with it. I guess magic is a lot like logic."

"How is that?" he asked, perking up.

"Most women form a connection to both, while men are clueless, not able to wield either."

"Oh, haha," he scoffed, relieved to see her grin, even if her levity came at his expense. They readied their packs, searching their lair for any items they might have missed.

"I can do more if I have more energy," the witch explained. "I would've been up and running in a day or two if I'd gotten my hands on one of the Danheimr warriors. But even without a soul to harvest, I can channel nature's energy, especially if it is as abundant as on this island."

"Why do you think that is? The abundant energy, I mean." He hoisted the largest pack on his back and strapped one over his shoulder. He was about to take the other two when Bergrún gave him another of her milk-curdling glares. He retreated, spreading his hands in an invitation to do as she pleased. She tied the rolled-up blanket to the top of the remaining bundle and slung the combined pack onto her back.

"Let's go," she commanded. "I'm as eager as you to find the answer to your question."

For the next three days, the couple wandered through endless meadows of waist-high grass. They followed deer trails, seeking shelter at night under stunted trees. The rain had transformed into a constant drizzle. But the wind quieted as the travelers walked farther inland. In early May, the air was mild, so they didn't mind the constant precipitation as much. Rikard tried his luck in hunting game birds with an improvised sling, wishing for a bow and arrows. Bergrún gathered edible roots and plants such as dandelions, wild garlic, and pignuts.

After three weeks in total isolation, Rikard climbed a ridge and spotted the first signs of civilization. Excited, he waved Bergrún to follow. In the vale beyond, a circular village huddled on both banks of a glistening stream. About twenty small houses with weatherworn roofs stood close to each other. Sheep grazed on the opposite slope and a little higher upstream, a stone castle crowned a rocky outcrop. The clouds had thinned, and brilliant shafts of afternoon sun streamed through the gaps, bathing the picturesque scene in a welcoming light.

"Finally!" Rikard exclaimed, eager to descend, but the witch held him back.

"Wait!" Bergrún hissed, grabbing his arm with surprising strength. She tilted her head, sniffing the air. Her gaze swept over the scene. "It's too quiet," she murmured. "No dogs barking, no children shouting."

"We're too far away," he protested.

"No, the wind blows this way. I have a strange feeling. This looks a little too convenient for my taste. Something seems off."

"What do you mean by 'too convenient'?" he asked in utter disbelief. "I don't see a palisade wall or earthen bulwark around the village. These people aren't afraid of raids. That's good. They might welcome travelers with news from the outside world."

"And what news do you bring? We've been cut off more than they are."

"I mean..." he ventured, but Bergrún interrupted him.

"Look there!" She pointed to the castle where a column of dark smoke rose into the sky.

"And?" he asked, growing irritated with her objections.

"I don't think we should rush in unprepared. It's getting late. Why don't we spend the night up here? You can hunt for birds, and then we'll have something to trade."

"If you insist," he replied. "Shall I pitch the tent here?"

"No, let's continue along the ridge. Over there," she pointed toward a cluster of trees. "Let's spend the night under a canopy of hawthorn blossoms."

"Sounds intriguing." He squinted toward the distant grove. "Can you make out what trees those are from two miles away?"

"It's a guess, but we had hawthorns on Heillaður as well, and when they bloom in May, it looks exactly like this."

It took them almost an hour to reach the spot Bergrún had indicated. He gazed in awe at the thousands of tiny white flower petals covering the gnarled trees like a bridal veil. She laughed at his slack-jawed expression and sent him off with a nudge and a kiss to go hunting while she prepared the camp for the night. Her skin tingled, and she wanted to be alone for a moment to let her senses roam and probe the increasingly strong pulses of energy. They must be near a focal point.

Rikard returned from his hunt in high spirits, carrying two plump pheasants over his shoulder. He found Bergrún sitting motionless under the tree with her eyes closed.

"Is everything well?" he asked.

"Yes, wonderful," she replied, giving him a strained smile. "I was thinking about something."

"About what?"

"You caught two birds, amazing!" Untangling her legs, she got to her feet. "Show me your catch."

He held his arms out, one pheasant dangling from each fist.

"Let's take this one to the village tomorrow." She pointed at the larger bird. "We'll trade the pleasant pheasant for supplies, perhaps a bow and arrows. And tonight we feast on his fabulous fellow fowl."

He gave the smaller bird a disappointed glance, taken aback by her unusual chipper tone, but then he acquiesced. While she prepared the food, Rikard bubbled like a mountain creek in spring. He praised the beauty of the land, depicting the exciting opportunities now that they had found other humans. But soon, he realized that his partner wasn't listening. Bergrún seemed distracted and at ill ease.

"Is anything wrong?" he asked again.

"Why? No... I'm just a little distracted."

"By what?" He raised his hands, gesturing to the peaceful surroundings.

"I can't point my finger at it quite yet. Something feels strange."

"Like what?" he insisted with growing unease.

"You wouldn't understand," she replied absentmindedly, realizing her poor choice of words the instant his face fell. "I'm sorry, it has to do with me." But this explanation didn't make things better.

"Never mind," he shrugged. "Let's eat."

They ate in silence. She glanced at him, seeing a shadow falling over his face. When the food was consumed, she stood, gathering the bones, and tossed them down the hill. Passing him, she ruffled his hair in an attempt at affectionate gratitude.

"Eww," he shouted, jerking his head to the side. "Wipe your greasy hands on the grass!"

She believed he'd made a jest, but his voice carried an unusual edge. A deeper silence fell, leaving the words hanging in the air for long minutes until the rustling of the leaves eroded the echo.

Bergrún felt her muscles twitch with nervous energy. Something was nearby, exerting a strong mystical presence. Not knowing bothered her, and she spent little effort on her companion and his needs. After several attempts to draw her out of her preoccupation, trying both verbal and physical advances, the young man gave up. He crawled under the blanket and turned his back to her with a clear air of disappointment.

The witch slept poorly. Strange images invaded her dreams. She didn't recognize any place or event. Instead, she felt sadness and loss mixed with the sense of danger and impending doom. After tossing and turning for hours, she gave up. The clouds had broken, and the pale light of a waning moon blanketed the world in a faint, silver light. Bergrún looked at Rikard, who remained fast asleep. So, seizing her dagger, she left the camp on bare feet, following her gut along a narrow deer trail that led further up the ridge.

Since the wind had died with the setting sun, the witch placed each step with care, sacrificing speed for stealth. Her skin tingled, and the hairs on her neck rose. Someone or something watched her from the darkness. She turned at the faintest sound, peering into the gloom to see if an animal's movement or a more sinister cause had broken the silence. After what felt like an eternity, she reached the hilltop and stepped into a clearing.

The moonlight revealed a strange sight. Large stones formed a perfect circle of twenty strides across. Only a few of the weathered monuments still stood upright. Most lay toppled over, and some had rolled down the hill, leaving deep gouges in the dense shrubbery. At the center, a massive stone table lay cracked in half. Someone had shoved the broken pieces apart to make space to erect a twelve-foot-tall cross. The Christian icon towered over the site, its fresh timbers oozing sap.

Bergrún shivered as renewed feelings of sadness and loss washed over her, stronger this time. The earth under her bare feet seemed to tremble, and she felt the urge to tear the alien object from the hallowed ground like pulling a splinter that had caused a wound to fester.

A sudden noise, louder this time, drew her attention. Footsteps. Someone was coming. Bergrún hid behind a large standing stone, her knife at the ready.

Patience, she instructed herself. *Let's have answers first.* She closed her eyes and held her breath, extending her senses. *Definitely footsteps,* she thought, *one pair of feet, treading carefully but not with skill.*

She crouched, coiled like a spring. As soon as the figure reached the circle, the witch lunged. She kicked high, hitting the opponent's chest and sending the figure to the floor. In a heartbeat, she knelt on top. Seizing the front of the fallen's tunic with her left hand, her knife went straight to the throat. The razor-sharp tip pricked the skin.

"Who are you?" the witch growled. Her silhouette blocked the faint moonlight, leaving the intruder's face in darkness. As her gaze pierced the shadows, she discerned two eyes wide in terror, a messy mob of wavy blond hair, and a familiar mouth agape in a choked, silent scream.

"Rikard?" she gasped.

* * *

The weight lifted off Rikard's chest. Bergrún scrambled back as if his skin had burned her. The dagger fell from her numb fingers, landing on the ground with a dull thud.

He lay there, unable to respond, gasping for air like a fish on dry land. His whole body shivered in the violent aftermath of the adrenaline shock. Pushing himself into a sitting position, Rikard's hand went to his throat where the ghost of her blade still lingered. He could feel a drop of blood clinging to the tiny pinprick of broken skin. His mouth hung open, his lips twitching. His eyes, wide with fear, reflected the pale light of the moon. But soon, the swelling flood of his anger swept his paralysis aside.

"By the devils!" he rasped. "What were you thinking?"

"I heard footsteps," she replied, her voice meek. "All evening, I'd felt eyes on me, watching from the darkness. And then someone drew near."

"Yes, I did!" he retorted, too loudly. "The dullard who worried about you."

"But I didn't know," she pleaded. "These are strange lands, and this place... It feels wrong."

"What did you think I would do, finding you gone?" he shot back, ignoring her argument. "Did you imagine me saying? *Oh well, good riddance! At least now, I can go explore the village whenever I want.*" His voice became an angry snarl, and his arms carved exaggerated circles in the air, punctuating every single word.

"But you were sleeping and I..."

"...had no use for me!" he shouted. "*Oh my,*" he intoned in a girlish voice, "*with all these magic odors wafting in the air...*"

"Stop that!" she barked, feeding off his anger.

"*...and the earth speaking to me,*" he continued in a rude parody. "*What need have I of a half-wit who sleeps like a bairn when exploring can be done?*"

"I don't mind a man sleeping like a bairn," she said with scorn, a red glow igniting in her eyes. "But a boy who sulks like a bairn when I don't play with his sword, that's a different thing."

"So that's it!" he cried out, pain bleeding into his voice. "You're growing tired of me. And instead of being man enough..."

"I'm not a man!" she cut in.

"You know what I mean!" he bellowed. "No need to invent fancy fairy tales! You can say it out loud: Do you miss my brother?"

She staggered as if he had slapped her.

"That was uncalled for!" she hissed. A sudden gust shook the branches, and the earth began to rumble under their feet.

"Oh yes?" he mocked. "I wonder why that came to my mind. He'll be chieftain soon," Rikard jeered. Blinded by the burning anger, he took a step toward her, losing any remaining inhibitions. "I'll bet he'll take you back. You could be his third or maybe fourth whore."

With a night-shattering crack, the stone next to Rikard burst apart in the middle. The upper half crashed to the ground between the warring lovers.

Rikard stumbled back, raising his hands as fist-sized chunks flew within a hair's breadth past his face. One shard sliced through his tunic. He blinked several times, wiping dust from his eyes. But then, his glare hardened, and he drew himself up.

"Missed me!" he spat. Without another word, he turned and stomped back to the camp.

* * *

As soon as dawn's first light tinged the sky, Rikard jumped to his feet, snatched the pheasant, and marched toward the village. For a handful of heartbeats, Bergrún debated whether she should follow.

They hadn't spoken. After the violent confrontation amidst the standing stones and Rikard's abrupt departure, the witch stood petrified for long minutes. The dust of the explosion stung her eyes, her ears rang, and her chest heaved with exhaustion after the devastating spell.

She knew how her curse blinded her, stoking her anger. She knew that once the demonic fury seized her, it would take hours for her to calm down. But at that moment, a terrifying thought had doused her blazing rage with a barrel of bone-chilling meltwater.

I've almost killed Rikard. The witch sank to the ground as her knees gave out. *I've almost killed him twice in one night!*

She wasn't better than the drunken men in her village who used fists to close an argument. She was worse, so much worse. She'd used powers that could shatter mountains to settle a dispute. That wasn't the brutal honesty of a partner; that was the poisonous brutality of a coward.

When she finally made it back to the camp, she saw him lying twenty strides away from their prior sleeping spot. He'd cut the blanket in two and, wrapped in the tatters, pretended to sleep. She'd slumped down by the tree trunk. Leaning her head against the gnarled wood, she closed her eyes, seeking oblivion. But her mind replayed the vicious confrontation with cruel accuracy over and over again.

When she woke from her fitful slumber and saw Rikard rushing toward the village, Bergrún had no idea what to do. She wasn't sure if there was anything she could do to bridge the rift that had been torn open last night. All she knew was that if harm befell Rikard in that unnerving village because of his blinding anger or his tarnished pride, that would be *her* fault. With a groan, she pushed herself to her feet and started after him, a gloomy rain cloud trailing the edge of the thunderstorm.

The witch kept her distance, staying twenty paces behind. When her foot slipped, dislodging a loose rock on the uneven slope, Rikard half turned. But he checked his motion and marched on. To Bergrún, the message was brutally clear: he knew she was there, and he chose not to care.

It took them over two hours to reach the main road as they had to circumvent a patch of marshland, extending far inland from the river's eastern bank. To their left, the rutted trail led to the stone castle. Its sheer walls lay still in the mountain's shadow. To their right, the path led over a stone bridge into a dense forest clinging to the upward slope. Rikard rushed on, neither looking left nor right, and Bergrún hastened to follow.

The world changed as they stepped under the canopy of tall beech trees. The light dimmed, and the smooth trunks stood like sentinels, their twisted branches intertwining like fingers above them. The thick underbrush blocked the view of the river, giving Bergrún the impression of wandering in a cave. Even the wind quieted, becoming a gentle breeze shushing through the tender leaves, and the air was thick with bird song. Despite her tension, the witch could almost taste the rejuvenating energy of spring, creating new life.

They'd walked on the shaded path for several minutes when the noises of an approaching horse cart drew Bergrún's attention. Metal ringed wheels crunched on the packed earth. Hooves clopped, accompanied by the squeaking of poorly greased axles. Soon, a patrol came into sight, rounding a bend. Five armed riders escorted a wheeled cage holding a handful of dirty and famished peasants. Another soldier sat atop the buckboard, and two more walked behind.

Rikard slowed, letting Bergrún catch up.

"*Quis accedit?*" the lead rider called in Latin. His voice carried an angry rasp, and he kicked his horse, closing the distance in a trot.

"*Sumus viatores... Normanni. Quare... Quaerere commercium,*" Rikard replied, struggling to remember the few phrases a Gaulish thrall had taught him as a child. With his free hand, he pulled his tunic straight and tried to brush the dirt from his travel-worn garment.

"What did he say? And what did you reply?" Bergrún asked in a strained whisper. He didn't answer.

"Norsemen?" a second rider jeered in Gaelisk. "I'd believe it if I saw a hairy brute like an oak with a brain the size of an acorn. But you? Isn't your mommy still looking for you, boy!"

Rikard stood at a loss, unable to understand a single word.

"*Non audet Normannus Éiram tangere,*" the leader shouted, "*ex illa sancta victoria Summi Regis Brittonum!*"

"*Nos... Nos solum quaerere...*" Rikard stammered before Bergrún cut in.

"My brother means, we were thralls of Norsemen," she replied in fluent Gaelisk, her voice taking on a lilting melody. "We escaped in a rowboat when the Viking warship sank among the Iarntann Islands. We're looking for work and shelter."

"I'm not used to women addressing me unasked," the leader growled, switching to Gaelisk. He urged his horse forward, and his men put their hands on their weapons. "But since your brother's skull is too thick to speak a civilized tongue, I'll tolerate this insult, for once!"

"Of course, forgive me," she said, unable to smooth the edge that crept into her voice. Bowing her head, she backed off, pulling Rikard along. Her hands shook, yet she grabbed his arm in a vice. He did not fight her, realizing the severe turn the conversation had taken. Both stepped off the road, their gazes fixed on their feet, giving the patrol ample space to pass.

The lead soldier glared for two more heartbeats before kicking his horse into a walk. He'd ridden past Rikard when his second in command spotted the pheasant slung over the young Viking's shoulder.

"Poacher!" the guard called, and all five riders drew their swords.

"Run!" Bergrún shouted. He obeyed, and she followed, her hand still on his arm. They fled the way they'd come. The witch ran with her eyes closed. Muttering under her breath, she projected the image of searing hot flames into the animals. The lead rider's horse reared, whinnying in fright, and threw him off. He landed on his back as the hoof of a fellow soldier's steed crushed his ribs. The remaining three horsemen regained control and gave chase.

Rikard veered right. Spotting a gap in the underbrush, he sought refuge among the trees. Bergrún tripped, and he seized her, holding her upright.

Stumbling along a narrow deer trail, the witch shouted, "*Springa!*" and a heavy tree limb broke free, knocking another pursuer to the ground.

They weaved between the ancient trees, managing to keep ahead of the riders. But too soon, they reached an open meadow, dotted with large, moss-covered boulders.

"Split up!" Rikard commanded, and Bergrún obeyed without hesitation, accepting his superior knowledge in battle situations. She went left, rounding a boulder as one rider had caught up. He struggled to turn his horse, giving her a chance to climb atop the rock. As he drew near, the witch clapped, conjuring a ball of blinding light in mid-air. Disoriented, he fought to rein his steed in, and Bergrún used the confusion to jump onto the horse's back.

Her hand clawed into his hair, her nails gouging his scalp. He threw his elbow back, connecting with the side of her face. She almost fell off, pulling his head to the side. He roared in pain and, letting his sword drop, he seized the pommel to remain in the saddle. Her free hand had slapped his face, her fingers digging into his mouth and stretching his cheek for purchase. In a vicious mental assault, she shattered his soul and pulled his life force from his dying body. His grip slackened, and both fell off the horse. The corpse landed across her chest, knocking the air from her lungs.

* * *

RIKARD HAD SPRINTED right. As the rider closed in, he swung the pheasant, slapping the dead bird against the soldier's face. The man grunted, pulled on the reins, and resumed the chase.

Rikard snatched the dagger from his belt, wishing for his shortsword. He turned and ducked, evading a decapitating blow. The soldier kicked him, and the young Viking fell to the ground. Rolling between the snorting beast's legs, he barely avoided being trampled. When he jumped to his feet on the other side, the soldier was ready. He swung his sword in a chopping motion, and Rikard threw his arm up in a desperate deflection as if he were wearing a shield. The blade glanced off the bone, tearing a deep gash from elbow to wrist.

In the single heartbeat before pain exploded, the wounded Viking stabbed the horse with his dagger. The beast reared, throwing the rider off but also landing a glancing kick against Rikard's head. Both men fell to the ground.

The soldier got to his feet first. He'd lost his sword in the fall. Pulling a dagger from his boot, he advanced on his dazed opponent. Rikard lay on his back, defenseless, cradling his mangled arm. His executioner loomed over him. He raised his weapon for a deadly strike when a crossbow bolt ripped through his chest.

An eerie silence fell over the battlefield. Bergrún must've seized the crossbow from the soldier she'd fought. Dropping the spent weapon, she rushed to Rikard. The sight of his mangled limb froze her in place for one heartbeat. Then, she ripped her tunic open, wrapping the garment tight around his gushing wound. The spray of blood had coated her pale face and bare chest. Wiping her eyes, she seized his breeches, pulling the leather belt free. With deft hands, she tied a tourniquet around his upper arm, stanching the wound.

Then, she turned and glared at her victim's spooked horse. The animal snorted and shook its head before trotting over. The witch heaved Rikard onto its back and jumped behind him. They galloped up the incline, away from the fallen soldiers, as shouts, yells, and the clanging of weapons sounded from the distant road behind.

CHAPTER TWENTY-ONE

GHOSTS

BERGRÚN STEERED THE horse in a slow walk up the incline toward the valley's opposite ridge. Following an overgrown goat path, they entered the low-hanging clouds. At every switchback, she turned to see if any soldiers followed. Not spotting pursuit, the witch sighed in relief until Rikard sagged. He almost toppled off the horse. Hoisting him upright with effort, she urged the beast on, fearing he'd lost too much blood.

Cresting the ridge, Bergrún spotted a mighty oak the size of a chieftain's lodge presiding over a circular wildflower meadow. She pulled on the reins and kicked the horse into a trot. As soon as they reached the tree, the witch jumped off the animal's back and let Rikard slide into her arms. She cradled him like a child, straining under his weight, and he placed a sluggish arm around her shoulder. With gritted teeth, she shuffled toward the enormous trunk and eased him onto a smooth patch between protruding roots. He grunted in pain. She straightened with a groan, stretching her back. Then she knelt beside him and examined his arm. Her makeshift bandage was soaked in blood, creating an ominous contrast to his pale fingers. She hesitated, unsure of what to do next.

The horse snorted. Turning her head, she noticed the bulging saddlebags. Tossing the soldier's possessions to the ground, she found a spare tunic and breeches. With her teeth and nails, she ripped the clothes into strips. Then she returned to Rikard. He'd closed his eyes. Sweat glistened on his skin, and his chest rose and fell with shallow, labored breathing. She unwrapped his arm. The wound looked bad, the ragged cut sliced to the bone. Blocked by her tourniquet, the spray of blood had slowed to a trickle of dark crimson oozing from the wound. But his skin had turned pale and felt cold to the touch.

"Can you move your hand?" she asked. He tried, gritting his teeth, and his fingers contracted an inch before the pain grew too strong and he cried out.

"Good!" She seized his hand in both of hers and straightened his fingers. "Now take a deep breath and relax. Does your arm feel numb?" she asked, prodding the muscles.

"Not enough," he groaned.

"Then take this." She'd picked a one-inch-thick branch from the ground, and after shortening it to a foot in length, she handed him the stick. "Bite down on it. This might hurt."

"What will you do?" he asked, his tone sharp, his eyes sought reassurance.

A myriad of sarcastic retorts shot through her mind: *teaching you a lesson, payback for your stupidity, wondrous witch work,* or *something unholy and unnatural.* Then she rebuked herself. She'd promised never to hurt him, and had broken that promise twice during the last night alone. She was the villain, not he. He was in pain.

"Can you trust me, Rikard?" she whispered. "After what I've done, can you trust me… just one more time?" Her breath caught. "I never meant to harm you." She looked at him, pleading, and he held her gaze. His blue eyes bore into hers of onyx. A muscle twitched on his cheek.

"Do your worst, witch," he rasped. She froze, every muscle locked, save for the frantic flicker in her eyes. Then his right hand slid over the moss-covered rocks, finding hers, and he squeezed. A shudder of relief ran through her body, and a string of tears carved their way through the grime on her blood-smeared cheek.

With a nod, he let go of her hand and placed the stick between his teeth. She bent over him, placing her hands on either side of the gaping wound.

"On three," she croaked. "One… two…"

Fire exploded in his arm. He writhed, tossing his head left and right, but she held him pinned. With her knee on his chest, her hands became the talons of an eagle clutching an eel in its unrelenting grip. The blaze grew into an inferno, searing with white-hot agony. His bones and muscles must surely melt and skin burn to a cinder in this fiery ruination. He bucked, and she moved with him, keeping her perch without crushing his ribs. Strained gurgles escaped his taut lips. With a snap, the stick shattered, and his teeth ground together. The fire engulfed his entire arm, from his fingertips to the muscles of his neck. He spasmed, his nails biting into his palm. Then, in the blink of an eye, everything was over. He sagged, the air escaped his lungs, and he fell unconscious.

* * *

HIS MOAN PULLED Bergrún from her stupor, and she rushed to his side. Night had fallen, and a curtain of rain encircled their sheltered island. Earlier, she'd stretched the soldier's bedroll between the low-hanging branches, creating a slanted roof. The rhythmic drumbeat of water dripping from the tree's canopy created a soothing background, and she'd given in to her exhaustion.

When Rikard stirred, she was wide awake. He lay on his back, his head resting on a pillow of moss, and his left arm placed in a sling. His eyelids fluttered, and a low moan escaped his lips as he woke.

"How are you feeling?" she asked. His eyes rolled, disoriented, and he smacked his lips. "Are you thirsty? Want some water?"

Without waiting for an answer, she put her arm around his shoulder and helped him sit upright. Her other hand seized the waterskin. She pulled the stopper with her teeth and guided the opening to his mouth. He placed his free hand on hers and drank, accepting her assistance.

"That's enough for now. Let's see if it stays inside."

"Yes, mother," he croaked, conjuring a smile on her lips. "What happened?"

"You were injured, remember? You... I mean, we... We went to the village," she stammered. "And there were soldiers."

"I know that," he replied in a dry rasp. "I mean after. You tried something... Did it work?"

"I've tended to your arm," she explained in a soothing voice.

"Tended?" he said, jerking forward. "Not healed?" he rasped as the pain of his sudden movement subsided.

"Almost healed," she said, steadying him. "Look for yourself."

He lowered his gaze and flexed his fingers. Some tension left his shoulders as he saw his hand working.

"I've never done anything like that before," Bergrún confessed. "At least not to someone else," she amended.

"You haven't?" His head snapped around, his voice sharp with alarm. The world wobbled, and his stomach heaved, causing him to squeeze his eyes shut.

"Relax! All is well. It's just that I've never cared for someone enough to heal a battle injury. Usually, when I find someone hurt, I..." She stopped herself. His brow furrowed. "Regardless," she rushed on, "I've healed myself often enough, and I had practice with Stina. Although with her, I had more time."

"So usually, when you find someone injured…" he said, his eyes narrowed.

"But look!" she said, forcing a cheerful tone into her voice. "Your fingers work, right? Show me again."

He squeezed his fingers into a fist, but his gaze remained locked on her, demanding an answer.

"So tell me," he insisted, not letting her get out of this. "What makes me different from a wounded warrior or a horse that has broken its leg?"

"Horses are stronger and more useful," she rambled, fidgeting with a loose thread of his bandage. "Some might even say they're more intelligent." His free hand seized her hand, holding it in an iron grip.

"What am I to you?" he demanded. His voice became a growl of a bear confronting an intruder, the perfect shield to hide the anxiety reflected in his eyes. She sucked in a breath. Her body grew rigid, knowing that this moment would decide their future. And more, her answer would cast the shape of *her* own.

"I've never been with someone," she admitted. "I've used men and seduced them. I've allied with men and even felt kinship with a few, triggered by a shared past or shared goals. But I've always left them, betrayed them, or killed them in the end. Everything I've ever done was for me. I needed to get what I wanted, or I would turn my back and move on."

He remained silent, his face becoming the unreadable mask of an inquisitor, keeping the accused guessing whether any information provided would garner leniency.

"This is new to me," she declared after several frenetic heartbeats. "I'm older than you but not wiser, not in these matters. I have my pride, my anger, my curse, and other countless excuses for being an ass. I don't know how to do this. I'm not sure if I can. All I know right now…" She had to stop as a lump formed in her throat, and she swallowed hard. But then, she straightened her spine, raised her chin, and met his unwavering stare. "I want to try this!"

He tilted his head, and she read his gesture as an encouragement that she might be on the right path but not quite there yet. Resigned, she sighed and gathered her nerves.

"Rikard Thure Svensen, I want to be with you, not because I can use you, fool you, or benefit from you, but because of *you*. I want to share my life with you! And I hope, when I prove myself to you, you'd want to be with me, too."

His face remained inscrutable. Her heart hammered against her ribcage; she feared it would burst from her chest. The seconds flowed with the viscosity of frozen honey. Finally, his lips pulled into a crooked grin.

"See, that wasn't too hard, was it?"

She groaned in relief and punched his shoulder.

"Ouch!" he complained. "I'm an injured warrior."

Her apology turned into a scowl as she realized that his grin hadn't faltered.

He lifted his right arm and, placing it around her shoulder, he pulled her against his chest.

"I've never been with someone either," he whispered. "Can you believe it, with my looks?" He chuckled at his own wit, but the movement caused him pain. He inhaled a slow breath before continuing in a low and measured tone. "This is new to me, too. But that's a weak excuse for being an ass. I need to learn, I need to grow, I need to deal with my anger and my pride. Because... I want to be with you!"

* * *

THEY'D LAIN BESIDE each other until the gray light of dawn woke Rikard. Bergrún hadn't slept. She told herself to keep watch, and the fear of more calamities kept her awake: soldiers with wolfhounds could find them despite the rain. Rikard's wound could fester despite her best efforts. Or he could get up and leave her, realizing, despite his words, that she was too unhinged and dangerous. Her heart beat a frantic rhythm, and the only thing that kept her from screaming was the feel of his hand in hers.

After helping him sit upright, ignoring his protests of being healed enough, they ate the strips of dried mutton from the soldier's rations. Bergrún was eager to discuss the events of the prior day. She wanted to share everything, even if her suspicions were vague and her jumbled ideas hadn't coalesced into a clear picture yet.

No more secrets, she'd promised herself. But more than that, she wanted to hear his opinions and show him she saw him as her equal.

"How come you speak the local tongue so well?" he asked after they'd recounted the previous day's violent confrontation, each filling the gaps in the other's understanding.

"Éiran isn't much different from the language of my home in Heilladur, a little softer perhaps with more melody to the words."

"And you think the soldiers returned from a witch hunt?" he asked, spitting the bitter juice of willow bark to the ground. Bergrún handed him the waterskin, and he took a deep pull before, relenting under her stern gaze, he seized another strip and started chewing.

"You've seen their attitude," she replied, "invoking the holy conquest in the name of the High King of the Britons. They treated me like scum because I'm a woman." Her lips drew into a line, and her eyebrows knitted together.

"I'm not saying those were nice people. But an occupying force has many reasons for taking prisoners, not least as a show of strength. They didn't seem to like Norsemen either," he amended after a short pause.

"But only female prisoners?" she retorted.

"I didn't realize..."

"Well, I did. And together with the defiled stone circle and the ominous black smoke rising from the stronghold, one does not need a soothsayer's gift to glean the truth of it."

"I still don't know," he hedged. "You might be right. But you must admit that you're looking at the world with the eyes of a... I mean, from a very particular perspective."

"Oh, do I?" she scoffed, and a flicker of red sparked in her eyes.

"There's nothing wrong with that," he rushed on, raising his palm. "It's completely natural..."

"You're sure you don't mean *unnatural*?" Her grin became a leer.

"Bergrún, please. Grant me this much. I just want us to look at all the runes before jumping to one reading. We haven't even spoken to the folk living in this land."

"Fine!" she sighed, backing off. She closed her eyes, letting the air rush from her lungs.

"I mean, there are other terrible things one could do with women prisoners."

"Thank you for mentioning that! That makes me like these soldiers so much better," she growled.

"Listen, no one here knows about your... abilities." His voice rose with the last word as if he were asking her approval for his term.

"You're right," she sighed again. "I'm just..." Then an idea struck her like lightning. Her body jolted upright. "Wait a moment! You're not doubting my verdict! You're just arguing because..." She looked at him, her head tilted.

He fidgeted, not meeting her gaze.

"Rikard, look at me," she demanded, her voice carrying calm authority. He raised his gaze with deliberate slowness, his head heavy as a boulder. "I can feel it," she declared, reading him like a book. "In your heart, you agree with me. But you fight what your bones are telling you. Why?" Her eyes bore into him, and after several heartbeats, he wilted. His shoulders slumped, and he threw his hands up as much as the sling around his injured arm permitted.

"You know why!" he wailed. "Where else is there?" His chest heaved from the force of the words. "We're shipwrecked on this rain-drenched island. We have no wealth, no clan, no livestock. If we can't live in a village like that, where do we go?" Deep lines formed between his brows, and his eyes lost focus as he gazed into the distance.

"Rikard," she said, seizing his hand. "We can go back to the coast, or somewhere else, anywhere really!" Her lips pulled into an encouraging smile.

"But you hated it there!" For several heartbeats, no one spoke. Bergrún remained by his side, holding his hand.

"It wasn't all that bad in the *blessed halls*," she whispered. He gave her a reluctant smile. "And the devil knows, I'd sooner be wet than dead."

* * *

As the sun rose higher, Bergrún left to scour the land. They needed food and water, and she wanted to see what had happened to the fallen soldiers. Rikard questioned the wisdom of her plan, fearing for her safety since he was in no shape to come along. A fever had seized hold of his body, causing headaches, and he felt drained.

"Another reason for me to go," she'd insisted. "I need to gather healing herbs. There must be yarrow blossoms somewhere." He kept arguing, but she reassured him that she could take care of herself, closing her statement with a kiss. "Don't run away," she whispered with a smile that trembled at the edges.

The clouds had thickened, but the rain held off until she returned, two hours later. Bergrún carried two waterskins, a crossbow, and two carcasses that once might have been rabbits over her shoulder. When her footfalls caught his attention, she saw the tension leave his shoulders with the breath he hadn't realized he'd been holding.

"Missed me?" she smirked.

"No," he replied, swallowing a lump in his throat. "But I'm thirsty." Her smile broadened at his attempted humor, though his voice sounded weak.

"Then here you go!" She offered one waterskin. "The best water under Odin's sun."

For the next hour, she prepared the food and relayed her observations.

"I went all the way down to the river. No signs of the soldiers or prisoners, no carts, horses, or anything else hinting at a struggle."

"Then where did you find the gear?" he asked, swallowing a mouthful of roasted rabbit.

"I might have crossed paths with a lone rider," she confessed. His mouth dropped open. "Look, these are dangerous lands. We needed weapons, and two horses are better than one."

"Another horse? Where is it?"

"I left it farther up the ridge. I wanted to scout our surroundings, and I didn't want to frighten you."

"Wonderful," he exclaimed in awe.

"I thought it better to approach on foot," she said, stunned by his gratitude.

"No, I mean everything. Two horses, weapons, and gear. Now we can go anywhere we want." He seized her hand and squeezed, causing her heart to flutter like a sparrow's wings.

They decided to return to the hawthorn grove after sunset to reclaim their possessions. They would spend the night there and be off before the sun rose again. The rain had started pouring down, making the trek treacherous. Bergrún set a cautious pace, fearing Rikard's fever would cause him to stumble and fall. But with the buoyancy of a bright future ahead, they crossed the valley without incident, drenched to the bone.

Rikard tied the horses to a tree a little farther away while Bergrún fixed the sailcloth roof and conjured a small fire from wet wood. Since she hadn't found the right herbs to brew a fever tea yet, she ordered an early rest, seeing the toll their short journey had taken on Rikard. He only gave a token resistance. He wanted to talk about their future, but tiredness soon overcame him.

As he slept, Bergrún lay beside him, wide awake despite her exhaustion. From time to time, noises caught her ear—snapping twigs and rustling leaves. She couldn't make anything out in the darkness. Feeling the urge to relieve herself, she pulled on her breeches and boots and seized her dagger for good measure. The rain had stopped, leaving the ground a sodden mire. To assuage her growing unease, she scouted the perimeter of their lair before squatting behind a boulder. The air felt cold and crisp after last night's downpour.

Bergrún debated whether to return to Rikard or use the time before he woke to search for healing herbs. The witch believed she'd spotted a cluster of yarrow blossoms on her prior excursions. She was about to descend the hill when a light caught her attention. Someone was near. The flicker came from the direction of the standing stones. Without a second thought, she took off in a run, weaving between the brambles. Icy water spilled onto her each time she brushed the foliage.

Rounding a bend, she spotted the light again. This time, she saw it clearly. A torch or lantern illuminated a figure wearing a long, white cloak.

The witch doubled her speed. Her soft leather boots flew from stone to stone to avoid the squelching of mud. She moved like a deer, barely making a sound. The path took another turn. She must be near.

Another light appeared, to her left and much closer. Making a snap decision, she cut through the underbrush. Her heart raced, the thump of blood pounding in her ears. She welcomed the simple excitement of a hunt after the emotional turmoil of the past few days.

Squeezing through a narrow gap between two elm trees, she spotted a tiny piece of white cloth that a bramble thicket had snagged. She halted for a moment, letting her eyes penetrate the semi-darkness.

A twig snapped. She whirled around, and there it was, to her right. The light flickered as a figure in white fled down the hill. She ran, augmenting her speed with her magical reserves. She never lost her prey, spotting the light left and then right. Once she overshot, and it was behind her. But try as she might, she didn't seem to get any closer.

And then it happened. To her left, up an incline, one light flickered, incomprehensibly far away, while behind her, another light shone, highlighting the accursed white robe.

"*Skitr!*" the witch hissed, bending over. Her lungs wheezed, her muscles burned. She clutched her side, feeling a stitch like a shard of glass twisting under her ribs. But all these aches paled in comparison to the painful realization that she'd been made a fool. There were more than one of these "ghosts" in the forest, and they'd led Bergrún on a wild goose chase. When her boiling anger threatened to explode and bury all reason under raging lava, another thought stabbed into her mind, freezing her blood in an instant.

Rikard!

She needed to get back. But where was she? The chase had taken so many twists and turns. Squeezing her eyes shut, the witch fought to smother the raging anger inside her. She needed to open her senses to her surroundings. Her body shook, sending tremors into the ground, as her black curse demanded violent destruction. Bergrún fought with everything she had, using the last vestiges of her human soul to shield the rational part of her brain. She needed to get back to Rikard, ensure he was safe, before unleashing her fury on the foolish phantoms who'd enraged her.

There!

She felt the presence of the standing stones, over a mile away. The circle was behind a ridge, but visible to her inner eye like the sun on a clear day. She ran straight, ignoring thorns tearing at her clothes, branches whipping her face, and gnarled roots bruising her feet. She ran. The sun crested the horizon, illuminating the hilltop with the stone circle.

She clawed her way up the incline and veered right, past the shattered table. With a running leap, she cleared the stone column she'd exploded the night before last.

Has all this really happened within two turns of the sun? she wondered.

She was so close. The path wound through the thick underbrush. Left, right, left, then a hairpin turn. Something white caught her eye, seizing her attention for the briefest moment.

She turned her head for an instant, and her foot slipped in the mud, sending her crashing to the ground. Her shoulder hit the ground first, knocking the wind from her lungs. She had no air left to scream when her hip rammed against a skull-sized stone. Her teeth bit into her tongue. Nothing slowed her momentum. Bouncing like a dislodged boulder, she crashed through the brambles and tumbled down the hill.

Every muscle hurt, every bone felt broken. Her vision blurred. She spat mud from her bruised lips. The index finger on her left hand pointed in the wrong direction. With a snarl that vibrated through her body like the tremors of an earthquake, she pushed herself upright. One heartbeat of rest to quell the dizziness. Then she looked up. There stood the cluster of hawthorn trees, gleaming bright white and innocent in the early morning's light.

She snapped the finger back into place and trudged up the hill. Using all her remaining willpower, she placed one foot in front of the other.

"Rikard!" she croaked, but the sound didn't reach farther than her shadow. She had nothing left except the burning desire to see him safe. Ten more paces... Five more paces. She reached the top. And all hope was lost when she spotted a white robe on the ground where she'd left him mere hours ago. The witch stumbled the remaining distance and fell to her knees. She clawed the robe aside, driven by the insane hope that he might hide under it to play a cruel joke on her.

He's gone!

Two deep gouges in the wet soil marked the path where some despicable villain had dragged her lover away. And with him, the fiends had stolen all remaining life from her tormented body.

The horse was gone.

Rikard was gone.

All hope was gone.

The world spun.

Vicious spasms racked her chest; she couldn't breathe. A ringing filled her ears. Her hands clawed into the wet soil, her shaking arms sending tremors outward like ripples in a pond. Inexorably, the world stilled, indifferent, as her muscles seized. Her fingers went numb, her strength failed, and the witch collapsed. All went black.

PART THREE

Ashen-black Sun

"There's a slope down toward evil,
a gentle gradient that can be ignored at each step, unfelt.
It's not until you look back,
see the distant heights where you once lived,
that you understand your journey."

– Jorg Ancrath[1]

---

[1] Mark Lawrence (2013): Emperor of Thorns, Book three of The Broken Empire series

CHAPTER TWENTY-TWO

Judgement

THE CREAKING OF tortured wood ceased as the men pulled the oars in, letting the crippled vessel drift the remaining distance into the harbor. Seagulls rose into the air, their shrill calls countering the wordless groans of the exhausted sailors. Dark clouds obscured the midday sun, promising more rain, and the wind carried the distinct odor of peat fires despite the mild spring temperatures.

This wasn't the homecoming Harold had wished for. The main mast of the *Wave Dancer* lay shattered, and the head of the carved dragon riding at the bow was missing. Torn bits of sailcloth plugged the many holes in the battered hull with limited success. With the danger of sinking before reaching safe shores averted, the tired Viking leader fought to suppress the one thought that festered in the mind of every man aboard: did their misfortune bode ill for the reign of the future Jarl Harold Fisk Svensen?

Days earlier, Harold had had such great hopes for his return. After his humiliation by the black-haired witch, he regarded the sighting of a Danheimr knarr as a potent omen.

A heaven-sent gift, he'd thought, to raise morale and restore his standing as undisputed leader. Immediately, he'd ordered the pursuit, ignoring the wall of menacing clouds amassing in the distance. He'd spat into the rising wind and beaten one man to an inch of his life for daring to question the orders.

He'd known he went too far when the hand of Einar Finsgúr, his closest friend and oldest ally, seized the hilt of his dagger in a death grip. By then, it was too late; the storm had arrived. Waves as tall as watchtowers tossed the ship around like a child's toy. Breakers washed over the deck, sweeping everything they could grasp into the violent sea, men and gear alike. When the hastily rigged mainsail came loose, the mighty mast snapped like a reed, crushing three men where they cowered.

For hours, the storm raged, shoving the helpless vessel ever closer to the ragged islets and submerged rocks of Brótinholm. Harold even considered seeking shelter in the bay of Fårosünd, the seat of their ancient blood enemies, but no man stood a chance to steer his destiny when the elements themselves warred with each other.

When the tempest finally subsided, his proud longship lay in tatters, ruined almost as much as his reputation. He stood midships, numb, a rope tied around his waist, and regarded the utter devastation his folly had wrought.

Einar seized command in all but name, ordering the stunned men into action in a desperate fight to keep the vessel afloat. Half of the remaining crew formed a bucket line, bailing the seawater pouring through the cracks, while the other half manned the oars. They shoved Harold aside like flotsam, working without thinking to save their souls.

With the devil's luck, they survived. As they drifted past the stormbreaker, Harold spotted a large group of soldiers standing arrayed to greet them, dampening his relief. No cheers rose, no mocking insults were shouted. The men carried shields, spears, and battle armor. And while their stance didn't guarantee the inevitability of a bloody confrontation, it carried every promise of violence when the need arose.

The longboat hit the pier at an angle, wood scraping on wood. Four thralls sprang forth, two fore and two aft, to seize the ropes the sailors tossed. They pulled the vessel close, ending the longest crossing from Brótinholm to Hrafney Harold's crew had ever endured.

Harold waited until his ship was moored to the pilings before climbing onto the splintered railing. He let his gaze rake over the assembled men. Some faces he knew, many he didn't, and none looked friendly. With some difficulty, Einar rose beside him. The older man had a crude splint tied to his sword arm. Feeling the tension growing like the charge in a thundercloud, he hawked up phlegm and spat on the pier.

"What welcome is this for a victorious crew?" he barked. "Have you never seen men return from battle? We fought Thor's wrath, Loki's deviltry, and Odin's breath, and we won! Every man who buys me an ale will hear of our glorious adventure. Now spread the word of Hamarrfjord's favorite sons' miraculous survival, such that our jarl might order a feast in our honor!"

"That would be our Jarlress," Toril replied in a clear voice that rang like a midwinter frost. The arrayed soldiers parted, and she stepped forth, Olver on her side. Six crossbowmen followed. They knelt and aimed at Einar and Harold. "By the power vested in me by my late father, as witnessed at the Althing by freemen and thralls alike, I charge you, Harold Fisk Svensen, with oath-breaking, kin-slaying, and *konungsdráp*. Order your men to lay down their weapons and surrender to Odin's judgment. Do it, or we'll end you where you stand."

"YOU!" Harold's defiant shout reverberated through the stunned silence that followed Toril's proclamation. "How dare you charge *me*! After ordering the death of my brother? After conspiring against your father? After offering our land like a discarded bone to the Danheimr dogs... What have you done to my uncle? He knew of your treachery! I was there, remember?"

Olver stiffened, placing his hand on his sword. As one, the men on the pier raised their shields and lowered their spears. The front row shifted half a man's breadth, and the back row moved up, forming an impenetrable wall.

"Yes, you were there, you vile *níðingr*!" Toril called, her serene demeanor unraveling. Her voice caught, and tears brimmed in her furious eyes. "You murdered my father, our beloved jarl... Your own blood!" she screamed. "You murdered him in his bed! And your Starvinger henchmen set fire to the longhouse. They barricaded the door." Her voice grew shrill like the cry of a seagull. "The entire village witnessed the aftermath of your treasonous deed," she wailed.

"You lie, snake-tongue! I did nothing of that sort. You and your lap dog conspired with Danheimr..."

"Do you deny visiting my father in the dead of the night?" she shouted, rage overshadowing her distress. "Were you not the last man to see him alive before your hasty departure? Do you deny bringing the evil witch with you? Servants witnessed you colluding with vile Agnetha," she spat. "You took her to your bed, and her dark magic destroyed half of your father's house."

"What?" he asked, taken aback. "No, that wasn't..."

"Do you deny my words? Under Odin's eye, do you refute my claims?"

"You twist the truth, dear cousin." His words became a growl. "I met with your father to inform him of *your* treachery."

"So you admit barging into my father's chambers on the night of his death. Do you deny dismissing his guards, replacing them with lawless men from Starvinger, foreigners only loyal to you?" An angry murmur rose among the assembled men. "Haven't you boasted in the hall of how eager they were to slaughter their own kin and jarl?"

"You know as well as I that my uncle ordered the guards replaced. He banished you into exile for your treason. And he banished your lap dog along with you. How could he still trust that gutless *ragr*?"

"How could my father trust his faithful shield? How could he trust the man who dedicated his life since boyhood to protect our chieftain? Because of blood oaths, Olver Agnarsen honors and you spit upon!"

"Your thrall, Edda, confessed," he shrieked. "We heard her words. If honor is your concern, then heed me. I rushed after Rikard to save the last honorable Viking under Odin's son!" Spittle flew from his lips.

"Save your brother?" she called, swiping the tears away with the back of her hand. She looked to her men, squared her shoulders, and straightened her dress. "Save the little brother who'd outshone you in my father's favor? Save the man whose bedslave you stole? The brother who hit you across the face in front of the thralls? Don't make me laugh!" she jeered, turning back to face her cousin. "You went after my dear Rikard to kill him. Your pride wouldn't allow it any other way. Everybody, from the Friesen's shores to the Arctic Ice, fears the wrath of Harold Svensen when his wishes are denied."

The murmurs grew louder. Shouts of "Aye" and "kin-slayer" could be heard.

"You spin a web of lies, spider," he growled. "But you won't escape judgment. Your thrall, Edda, confessed to poisoning Rikard on your orders! Agnetha brought the traitor to me."

"Which part of her?" Toril shouted over the rising din. "Because your black-haired witch tortured and killed my faithful servant, throwing her severed head through my window. A deed so vile, even the moon turned red that night." The men gasped. Some made signs to ward off evil, while others shouted more insults.

"But at least now we've heard in your own words." Toril strained to suppress the tremors of disgust in her voice. "You and that fiend worked together. What more proof do you need?" She faced her troops, spreading her arms to invite a response. Their shouts of outrage grew to an uproar.

"You've nothing but a fancy tale of twisted words and outright lies!" he shouted, his voice nearly lost in the din.

Olver banged his spear against his shield, and his men followed suit until the crowd quieted.

"We have the facts, we have witnesses, and we have your confession," Toril declared, calm and composed once more. "By our laws and customs, we judge you guilty."

A deafening silence fell at once.

Looking Harold in the eyes, she added with a quaver in her voice, "For the blood we share, I'll spare your worthless life, Harold Svensen. You and your men are henceforth thralls to work in the mines until Hela takes you. Seize them!" she ordered, turning away.

"You won't take me like this, treacherous snake! I'm of the jarl's blood. By Odin's law, I demand a trial by combat. May Thor's strength favor the hand of the righteous. Name your champion!"

"You dare to claim kinship to the man you killed?" She whirled on him, her voice rose three octaves with rage. "How deep have you sunk, cousin? Have you no soul?"

"Lend me your sword, Einar. I'll prove my honor right here and now."

"No," Toril called in a declaration of finality. "Traitors have no honor, thralls have no rights!" She nodded to the crossbow men. Two soldiers fired, their bolts ripping into Harold's left thigh. He fell screaming, crashing to the pier below.

* * *

As night had fallen, Olver climbed the broad stairs and marched along the upper landing. A door at the end stood ajar, and flickering candlelight seeped through the gap despite the late hour. His hair was wet, and he wiped the moisture from his face, relishing in the nighttime's quiet after the day's unexpected turn.

He'd spotted no soul after entering the large house, despite guardsmen filling every chamber. To keep their forces close, Olver suggested repurposing the servant quarters into barracks for the new troops. Yet his men had the strictest orders not to disturb the mistress of the house.

Reaching the end of the hallway, he pushed the door open. The hinges creaked, and the wood scraped on the floor. Toril didn't react. She sat at a small table, her quill scratching on parchment. Stacks of scrolls cluttered her desk, some dangerously close to the candles that had burned low.

After the longhouse had burned to the ground, Toril had claimed the Svensen manor, built by her late uncle, as the new seat of Hamarrfjord's chieftainess. She'd rearranged some of the chambers into rooms for formal reception and counsel. Yet the largest room, she claimed as her own, removing everything that bore the mark of its former occupant, the alleged traitor Harold Svensen.

Olver stepped behind her and began massaging her stiff muscles. She rolled her head, her neck cracking, and a moan of pleasure escaped her lips.

"You handled yourself well today," he whispered, kneading her shoulders.

"I've grown fond of this room. The view over the bay is breathtaking. I didn't want to relinquish my new abode." Her gaze wandered to the open window. The sea lay dark on a moonless night, yet the air carried its unmistakable aroma of salt and freedom.

"What's all this?" he asked, lifting a scroll from the pile.

"Don't stop!" she chided. "These are my weapons, needing to be sharpened every day and oiled like your mighty sword. Some are reports on the progress in the silver mine, others are plans for the reconstruction of the hall, missives from our allies, and of course, preparations for the arrival of the Danheimr delegation."

"My sword hasn't seen much action lately." His hands tightened, and his voice carried a hint of bitterness. She didn't miss the innuendo.

"How's the village tonight? Everything quiet?"

"Mostly," he sighed after a few heartbeats' pause and resumed kneading her muscles. "I'd reduced the patrols as you suggested. Only men born in and around Hamarrfjord are on watch. The ale houses were packed, but the vast majority of patrons took your side. Letting Harold live was a masterstroke."

"For now, maybe." She stood and walked to the bed, inviting him to sit beside her. "But before long, we'll need to do something about him and Einar. My cousin hasn't risen to fame just because of his bloodline. He might be a bumbling fool in the combat of wits, but he has charisma and strength. Unchecked, he'll gather the thralls in the mine behind him, leading them into a revolt."

"You almost sound admiring."

"Only fools belittle their opponent's strength. We grew up together, and Harold taught me many things. In another life, we might've brought him to our side."

"But you still want me to kill him?" Olver asked, cold and detached.

"You don't like it when I see mettle in our enemies, do you? You like your world black and white, the honorable and the vile."

"Makes it easier to kill someone that way."

"This isn't easy for me, Olver. Nothing is! He is *my* blood. When I was young, there was a time when I fancied him. How can I command my heart to stop beating? All I can do is march on, one step at a time, along the path that follows the clarity of my mind. What has to be done has to be done!" She exhaled in a drawn-out sigh.

"An accident, then?" Olver suggested. "A brawl with another miner?"

"A cave-in creates the fewest suspicions. One poorly secured mine shaft and we rid ourselves of the most dangerous agitators."

"I'll speak to the guards."

"Let a moon pass." She placed her hand into his, their fingers intertwined. "Right now, we have more pressing matters to attend to. Tell me more about the mood in the taverns."

"Only a handful of men voiced discontent about Harold's downfall. One agitator went so far as to call your cousin's treason a necessary cleansing, since our chieftain must have lost his mind when naming you his successor."

"Us," Toril corrected. "My father named us his successors."

Olver gave a noncommittal grunt.

"Anyhow," he continued, "the crowd shouted him down. The resurfaced rumors of Harold's father's plans to dispose of his brother helped."

"Your men resurfaced those rumors?" she asked with an admiring twinkle in her eyes.

"I'm not just a hunk of muscles!"

"I always surmised as much," she mused, starting to unbuckle his belt. "I like my men with a dash of brain on top of their hunk of muscles." She pulled him into a kiss.

* * *

"I HAVE SOMETHING for you," he whispered, several hours later. The orange light of dawn entered through the open window as the sun rose early on the cusp of midsummer.

"More gifts?" she asked with the eagerness of a child unwrapping yuletide presents. She propped herself up, her elbows on his chest and her face inches from his. Her golden hair spilled unbound over her shoulders, and her flushed face looked almost girlish in the early morning's glow. He stretched his arm, his fingers grasping for his discarded tunic. It lay where she'd tossed it, on the floor and out of reach.

"Some help?" he wheezed. Toril jumped on his chest, her knee landing in his lower stomach. Her naked body spilled like a glistening stream over the bed's edge. "Watch it!" he groaned. "I'm not made of stone." He slapped her playfully on her butt. She rose, his tunic in hand, and an expression of indignity on her face.

"How dare you manhandle the noble behind of your chieftainess?" she scolded. "Men have lost their hands for vile acts like that." She sat atop him with only a thin sheet of soft wool between their bare skins.

"Look in the breast pocket," he encouraged with a smile, placing both hands on a narrow waist. "And men have lost their minds over your behind, my Chieftainess."

She pulled forth a small leather pouch. Opening the tie string, she let a large piece of gleaming silver fall into her palm. The intricate brooch depicted two intertwined animals, their eyes set with precious stones.

"A crow and a dog?" she chuckled, yet her eyes beamed with true joy.

"I think it's supposed to be an eagle and a fox. Fitting, don't you think? I found it among the treasures Harold brought from Starvinger."

"I always thought of you as a bear, but a fox works too." She raised her gaze, smiling, yet saw his face losing its softness.

"Wear it, especially after the Danheimr prince arrives." His voice grew somber, and a muscle under his left eye started twitching. "That way, everybody will know who guards your heart."

"Sweetling," she whispered, "you're always close to my heart, my proud eagle." He averted his gaze, and she placed her hand on his cheeks, tilting his face back toward her. "Olver, you and I... That's all that counts!" Her voice cracked, sadness tingeing her determination. "The rest is politics, a public show. We'll always have each other's backs, each other's trust, and each other's hearts."

He grunted, and she seized his face in both of her hands.

"I have to go through with it, you know it," she implored, "for our people, for our future. Our son will be the heir. That was my condition. The Danske prince agreed. And you..." Her eyes bore into him with the ferocity of a she-wolf. "You'll remain my steadfast guardian, my true confidant, my only lover. Sweetling, it hurts me more than I can say. But what has to be done has to be done."

He nodded, and she kissed him, yet the warmth seemed to have already left his lips. A cloud had obscured the rising sun, and the morning felt chill on her skin.

CHAPTER TWENTY-THREE

DRUIDS

RIKARD JUMPED FROM his cot, pushed past the young woman entering his cell, and rushed toward the exit. Too late, the thick oaken door slammed shut, inches from his face, and the iron bolt slid home with an echoing clunk.

"I need to see her!" he bellowed, hammering his fists against the age-stained timbers. "Let me out, you spineless *maðkar!*" His angry voice filled the tiny space, and the young woman recoiled. She pressed her back against the rough stone, her gaze lowered, and tried to make herself small and invisible. The tea spilled from the wooden cup, dripping onto the rushes. He inhaled a deep breath and closed his eyes. Raising his palms, he stepped back.

He'd promised himself to remain calm this time. The woman couldn't open his cell any more than he could. She was trapped with him for the next hour, a deer in the cave of an ill-tempered bear. He was an unkempt stranger from the north whose language she didn't speak. Twice a day, she came to bring food, tend his wound, and empty the bucket. And twice a day, he scared her. But he had to make them understand: It wasn't him these people should be afraid of.

Rikard didn't know how long he'd spent in this underground prison. The hours bled into each other in a feverish dream, while a strange numbness spread across his entire body. But two days ago, he'd spotted Bergrún being carried into an adjacent cell in this damp cave complex. He'd shouted her name, not knowing if she was dead or alive, until his throat burned and his voice failed. He'd banged on the door, but the pain in his arm became unbearable. Every time the guards let the girl enter or leave, he demanded to see Bergrún, alternating between threats and pleading. All to no avail. They held him back with steel-tipped spears and a crossbow trained on his chest.

Seeing his trembling minder standing as far away as the tiny room permitted, he sat on his bed and buried his face in his hands. What could he do? Long moments passed.

"*Tá gach rud go maith*," the young woman whispered, speaking for the first time in his presence. He looked up. She stood in the opposite corner, her body taut as a bowstring. But her eyes had lost some of the fear, and her voice carried a melodic note of comfort. "*Go maith!*" she repeated with a nod toward the door.

"I don't understand." He shrugged, gesturing with open palms.

"Bergrún?" She mouthed the unfamiliar name and pointed to the door and the hallway beyond. "*Tá sí ina codladh.*" Placing her palms together, she tilted her head and rested her cheek on her fingers.

"You mean sleeping? You're sure? Not dead?" He drew his fingers across his throat, shaking his head.

"*Níl sí marbh.*" She waved the idea away with her hands, her brow furrowed. Her green eyes settled on Rikard with a steady weight and depth that belied her youth. "*Codladh! Go maith.*" The gentle cadence of her voice soothed the edges of his fear like a cool breeze on fevered skin. Her lips drew into a hesitant smile, and she edged closer, offering him tea.

"Thank you! I'm Rikard." He pointed to his chest. "Rikard."

"Rikard." She spoke the name in three syllables, tasting it on the tip of her tongue. "*Rikard, is mise Méabh. Méabh,*" she repeated, placing her hand over her heart and bowing her head.

"Under a different moon, I'd be honored to meet you, Maeve." He inclined his head, and she gave him a hesitant smile. Then the door opened.

Both turned to see a dark-haired man with fierce eyebrows enter. He seemed unarmed, but four figures in white cloaks followed, carrying spears. Rikard jumped to his feet, causing the men to lower their weapons.

"I am Theron Briarwood," the leader said without preamble, holding his men back. "I some speak Norsk. You Norsk, no?"

"Yes, I am!" Rikard drew himself up to his full height. He towered at least four fingers over the new arrival.

"*Cé thusa?* Your name?"

"*Rikard is ainm dó,*" Maeve said, causing the leader to turn his head, his brows knitting together.

"She's right. My name is Rikard Thure Svensen. I hail from Hamarrfjord.

What have you done to my...?" He stopped, hesitating for a single heartbeat. Then he took a step toward Theron and repeated in a low voice brimming with pent-up anger, "What have you done to my wife?"

The leader retreated an inch. His gaze became shrewd, and his jaw worked, chewing on the words. A tense silence filled the crowded room.

"She sleeping," he finally replied. "We..." He mimed blowing through a pipe. "Sleeping-poison arrow."

"You shot her, like me?" Rikard asked, rubbing the skin on his neck where he still felt a spot of numbness. "Why?" His question became a growl. His hand drifted to his left hip, where his sword or dagger usually hung.

"We need her, and you make her need us."

"I will what?"

"You make her... help us!" the leader corrected.

Rikard took another step closer. His shoulders tensed. He balled his hands into fists, causing his knuckles to crack. Two feet separated the two men when he felt four speartips against his ribs.

"You want our help?" Rikard pushed forward, forcing the guards to retreat. His nose was inches from the shorter man's face. "Curious way to ask, I'd say. Attacking, poisoning, kidnapping, and imprisoning—those aren't the customs in my land to seek help from an ally!"

"'Tis not your land, this." His opponent stood his ground, his mud-green eyes burning with fierce determination. "'Tis our own land! It is a guest you are, not a prisoner. You healed, no? You had the fever-sickness, and it was our sister who healed, no?" He pointed to Maeve. "It is your life you owe her. So, your wife is to help us free our people! Then you can be going."

"You've no idea who you're dealing with. No one tells my wife what to do or when to go. Now get out of the way and let me see her, or Hela shall have your skin. Do you hear me? Get out of my way!"

In a sudden burst of rage, Rikard shoved his opponent, sending him toppling to the floor. Seeing the guardsmen jerk back in surprise, the Viking twisted, kicking the nearest man against the knee and seizing his spear. In one fluid motion, he brought the butt up, hitting a second guard on the head. The man collapsed, taking his disarmed comrade with him, and both fell onto their leader.

When the other two guards overcame their shock-induced paralysis, they attacked. Rikard dodged one lunge and parried another in a double-handed grip. Pushing the deadly spear tip away, he kicked. His foot connected with one man's groin. The man howled in pain, and another swipe with the spear's butt sent his blood and teeth flying. Only one guard remained upright. He retreated, waving the speartip through the air in erratic patterns. Rikard observed him. The guard held the weapon with both hands too close together, robbing him of strength and control. These weren't warriors. The Viking feinted, letting out a war cry, and his opponent retreated further until his legs hit the bed. He plonked onto the thin straw mattress. Rikard brought his spear around, connecting hard with the pretend guard's fingers. The man shrieked in pain, and his weapon clattered to the floor.

The Viking turned and took a running leap over the pile of limbs blocking the entrance. He'd reached the octagonal hallway when the door on the opposite side exploded.

* * *

MOMENTS EARLIER, BERGRÚN had regained consciousness. She lay on her back in a dimly lit chamber. Blinking, she saw her hand squeezing an unknown woman's throat, her nails biting into the skin. Unbidden, the witch's arm had sprung forth, her curse grasping for salvation with the desperation of a drowning sailor. As Bergrún loosened her grip, the woman collapsed to the ground after the last drop of her life energy had flowed from the husk of her body. For two heartbeats, the witch let the bliss wash over her, basking in the renewal of her magical reserves. Pain vanished, tiredness disappeared, and the red haze lifted.

Her sharpened senses sent a plethora of impressions to her rejuvenated mind. She felt the rough-spun wool on her skin. Her shoulders rested on uneven boards. The air was damp, the smell of wet straw and human waste mixing with the taste of iron and minerals. A nearby commotion reached her ears, muffled through a thick wooden door. She sat upright. Lowering her legs, she felt the fallen body under her bare feet. A tiny oil lamp hung from a wall peg. Her prison cell was a cave where, over millennia, dripping water had covered the ceiling with countless jagged teeth, meeting towers, and turrets on the floor.

A brighter light illuminated the outline of a wooden door. Behind, some men were arguing. Bergrún strained to discern their words. She pushed against the wood. The door didn't budge. She hadn't expected it to. Gathering her energy, she closed her eyes and hummed, preparing her spell. Then she heard the one voice she would always recognize.

"Get out of my way!" Rikard shouted, followed by grunts and yells.

"*Springa!*" Her magic burst forth in an explosion, blowing the door apart like a pile of autumn leaves in a blizzard. The witch rushed through the opening. With her hands outstretched to either side, she stood ready to attack whoever dared to stand between her and her lover.

Rikard stood across the open space, twelve strides away. He held a spear in one hand and murder burned in his eyes. Their gazes found each other. In the blink of an eye, she covered the distance, wrapped him in her arms, and kissed him with the searing heat of molten lava. He lifted her off her feet. For one blessed moment, they twirled on the spot as if they were dancing under the midsummer tree and not in the middle of a violent confrontation in an enemy stronghold.

"I thought I'd..." she gasped when surfacing.

"I know, me too," he rasped, blinking moisture away. "Let's get out of here! This way." He stepped over the pile of timbers cluttering the floor and pulled Bergrún along when a fragile voice from behind called his name.

"*Rikard, táimid ag brath ar do chabhair,*" Maeve pleaded. She stood in the doorway to his cell with tears brimming in her eyes. "*Cabhraigh liom, le do thoil, Rikard! An chlann...*"

Bergrún staggered. "Stina?" she gasped as the deafening echo of her loss pierced her chest like a shard of obsidian. Before she could form another thought, the fallen men shouldered past the woman and rushed forward.

"Behind me!" Rikard shouted, but the witch stood unflinching. She flicked her hands toward the attackers, sending blasts of concentrated air. In rapid succession, she knocked the men to the ground. Yet she didn't press the attack further. Instead, she seized Rikard's arm, holding him back. Her eyes remained fixed on the young woman across from her.

"Who are you?" she asked in Gaelisk, realizing the woman wasn't Stina despite the uncanny resemblance. "What children do you speak of? And how do you know his name?" Her last question carried the undisguised tone of a challenge. The grip on his arm tightened.

"Her name is Maeve Uisce Glan," called a man in accented Norsk from the depths of a hallway to their left. His voice sounded as old as the earth itself, exuding the command of the lead wolf addressing his pack. "She's my ward," the speaker continued, "and she has cared for your man with a healer's touch, not with a woman's wiles, Bergrún, daughter of Gulveig."

In the silence that followed, the five men who'd entered Rikard's cell earlier scrambled to their feet. They formed a line, shoulder to shoulder, with their heads lowered and their hands clasped behind their backs. Maeve took her position next to Theron.

The footsteps grew nearer, accompanied by the swish of a cloak and the clack of an ironwood staff. A tall figure rounded the corner. He wore a floor-length green mantle over a white robe. His hair and beard were braided, the snow-white strands interwoven with straps of dyed leather. He held a gnarled staff in his right hand and carried a lantern in his left. Ten feet from the stunned witch, the man halted and lowered his head in deference.

"Peace be with you, black sister. May the road rise to meet you wherever fate leads." Turning to Rikard, he bowed again. "May you find strength in honor, Rikard, son of Sven, Hero of Hamarrfjord. May the wind always be at your back. I am Garwyn, son of Faelan, druid and keeper of Gleann an Earraigh, your humble servant."

Theron's head snapped up. His face became a mask of disgust at the arch-druid's deference to these barbaric strangers. Fury burned in his eyes, and he hissed something indiscernible.

"*Amach libh!*" the druid barked, whirling his head to the speaker. As suddenly as a lightning bolt across a blue sky, the old man's face lost all serenity, turning into a visage of thunder. His glare sent the men running like sheep in a hailstorm. "*Ní h-é tusa, a Mhéabh,*" he added in a softer voice. The young woman halted in her stride, turned, and bowed in acknowledgment.

"Forgive me," the druid said again in Norsk. "There is much I'm ashamed of. None of the ill-treatment you've received was of my making. I'll have your horses saddled this instant and your bags packed with gear and provisions. Whatever I hold in my possession, it is yours to command, my life included! Spare only this one," he pointed to Maeve, "she has followed her brother's misguided plan, believing I'd ordered the deed."

"I have no use for your life, old man." Bergrún had remained stone-faced. The hairs on her neck stood on end. The energy emanating from the druid roiled her guts, and bile rose in her throat. A familiar fire ignited in her veins as her demons urged her to attack. She would've blasted him off his feet and seized the horses, whether he gave them or not. Only the plea of the young woman, who could've been Stina's twin sister, kept her rooted to the floor.

"What children does she speak of?" Bergrún repeated through gritted teeth, switching to Gaelisk.

For the second time, his serene demeanor faltered; his grip tightened on his staff, making the wood creak, and his lips drew into a thin line.

"I'm not going to eat them," the witch cackled, her laugh sounding like the shattering of icicles. "I'm not that kind of black sister!"

"Forgive me," he replied, bowing his head again. "I've never met one of the five. The sagas speak of... well, unimaginable deeds."

"What was that about?" Rikard asked, unable to follow the conversation.

"A misunderstanding," the druid said in Norsk, "and with it the need for an explanation. Alas, I'll require more time than I'm willing to spend in this dreadful cave. I offer you a place by my fire with mead and meat, and I'll share all I know."

They stood in silence for long heartbeats, sizing each other up. Bergrún probed into the druid's mind, intent on reading his intentions. But she hit a wall, smooth as glass. She pushed further, willing him to yield, when a sudden coldness washed over her, robbing the air from her lungs. She recoiled, shuddering. *Was there a green glimmer in his eyes?*

"What do you say?" she asked Rikard.

"Lead on, old man," the young Viking commanded with anger-fueled authority. He'd placed his free arm around Bergrún's shoulder and pulled her tight. His right hand still clasped the captured spear. "You know who we are. Pray, act that way, else you might end up like that door."

* * *

THEY FOLLOWED THE druid through a labyrinth of tunnels. Maeve went ahead with the lantern, and Bergrún turned back at every other step to see if someone followed since the winding passage seemed to limit the reach of her supernatural senses.

"What do you think he wants?" she asked in a whisper, still marveling at his forceful threat.

"I don't know. I don't trust any of these people."

"No? Not even her?" A flicker of red sparked in her eyes.

"What? No! You heard him, she..." His step faltered.

"We could take her with us, you know?" she teased. "For cold nights when I'm busy elsewhere." Her lips stretched into a wicked grin, yet the red glint didn't fade from her eyes.

"Sure, why not?" he shot back, calling her bluff. "You deal with the druid, and I tie her to my saddle. Would be nice to have someone who doesn't order me around all the time, or, at least, not in a way that I understand."

"Just asking," she chuckled as her irises returned to the deep, mystifying onyx. "I'd say we hear him out. We can always change our minds later and leave... with or without her."

Eventually, they climbed a long staircase and reached the interior of a rustic lodge through a trapdoor. Bundles of dried herbs hung from the rafters, and woven tapestries covered the mud walls, sporting intricate patterns of knots and mystical beasts. The air was thick with the scent of beeswax, old parchment, and moss. On one side, a rough-hewn shelf overflowed with clay pots, rolled-up scrolls, and bowls of polished river stones, while on the other side, a massive oaken table stood cluttered with arcane tools and the skulls of small animals.

Maeve rushed to add more logs to the fireplace, and the druid offered them the best seats by the hearth. Bergrún ignored his gesture and pulled the outer door open, gazing into the downpour. It was daytime, but the heavy clouds prevented her from judging the hour. Her eyes roamed the surroundings until she spotted a massive oak standing on the ridge, less than five hundred paces away. She turned to the druid and saw the crinkles around the corners of his eyes deepening.

"Yes," he said. "You camped right in front of my doorstep after your quarrel with the Inglan soldiers."

"You seem to know a lot, old man." The witch's brows furrowed. "Makes me wonder about your professed ignorance of our 'ill-treatment.'"

"I knew of you since before you arrived in our valley," he replied without the hint of an apology. "And I knew who you were since you destroyed one of our runestones. But knowing doesn't equal doing."

"How?" Rikard asked from behind, his hand searching for the still missing blade on his belt.

"I'm the archdruid. I have my sources."

"Spies, you mean?" Bergrún challenged. "I felt people nearby."

"Some of my people watched you. You must understand, we're an occupied nation. Our way of life is threatened. Other tidings, the birds whispered in my ear."

"Like messages carried by ravens?" Rikard asked.

"That too. Will you not sit? I promised to share what I know, but we might as well be comfortable."

"Make it quick!" Bergrún growled, taking the seat nearest to the door. "I neither care for you nor yours. That girl's plea sparked my interest, but sparks die swiftly."

"The Inglan invaders sell our people into slavery," the druid explained without further preamble. "They hunt anyone with the *Fuil na Draíochta*, the blood of magic, to break our resistance and fulfill the tribute to Danheimr."

"What tribute?" Rikard asked. "Has Inglandia fallen to Danheimr?"

"In a manner of speaking. The Inglans call it a Treaty of Kings under the White Christ, but everybody knows where the power lies. If Danheimr wasn't so busy conquering the northern isles, they might not have bothered with this charade."

"Which islands?" Rikard sat bolt upright, his grip threatened to crush the armrest of his wicker chair.

"They took what remained of Brótinholm by force, and I'm afraid your home on Hrafney will fall into their hands by marriage."

"Marriage? To whom? My brother rules in Hamarrfjord."

"How would you know?" Bergrún interrupted. Her voice had gone cold as ice. "Spies and lucky hideouts are one thing. But I doubt King Olaf of Danheimr sends you letters."

"No, he doesn't write to me," the druid chuckled despite the red glow in the witch's eyes. "However, the commander of Dunscaith Castle receives regular missives."

"That's the fortress up the valley?" Rikard asked. "You have a spy there."

"The court scribe," the archdruid replied. "In their conquest, the Inglans took advantage of old feuds between the tribes of Éira. They recruited clans from the north to do their dirty work. We used the Inglan ignorance to infiltrate their ranks."

"So, who do you think will marry whom?" Bergrún pressed.

"Prince Filip, King Olaf's third son, will wed the local chieftainess. I believe her name is Torina Gustavsdotter."

"Impossible!" Rikard shouted, jumping to his feet.

"That cunning snake," Bergrún hissed. With a sudden gust, the door flew open, and the window shutters rattled. "Her name is Toril, and I thought her finished!"

Rikard went to close the door. Then he paced the room before seizing a cup with mead and draining it in one gulp. He refilled the cup, raising it toward Bergrún. She declined. Shrugging his shoulders, he drank.

"So your spies told you about Danheimr," he stated, glaring at the druid. "That doesn't explain how you know us."

"A fair point," Bergrún agreed. "This smells a little too convenient. Mayhaps, your ties to Danheimr are even closer? Mayhaps more guests will join this party soon, with sharpened steel?"

"The Inglans killed my son," the druid explained in a somber tone. His face looked aged by a decade. "They abducted my daughter and my grandchildren. If they leave the island, our magic dies."

"Sad," Bergrún scoffed without an ounce of pity. "But then you had a reason to 'invite' us into this lovely cave."

"We spoke about seeking your help after your impressive display at the standing stones. When you escaped the patrol of soldiers, I waited for the right moment to approach you, but..."

"But?"

"Theron is my foster son," the old man explained. "He and Morwen grew up together. After Morwen's death, Theron sought to prove himself and show the clan that he could be their next leader. Only,..."

"Only, he doesn't have the *Fuil na Draíochta*?" Rikard ventured. "I know a little about trying to carry someone else's battle axe."

"He's always been too ambitious. I didn't tell him who you were, not exactly. A witch and a capable Viking warrior, that much was obvious, but a Black Sister from Heilladur and the Hero of Hamarrfjord... Your deeds are known among those who can read the signs," the druid declared when both looked at him with disbelief on their faces. "If Theron had only known, he wouldn't have dared."

* * *

BERGRÚN AND RIKARD spent the night under the oak tree despite the persistent rain. The witch had refused to stay in the druid's hut, declaring that she'd kill anyone who came within a hundred paces. Rikard had tied a canvas under the branches, and they huddled together as they had in their lean-to shelter by the sea.

"We could leave in the morning," he whispered, playing with a strand of her hair. "This isn't our fight. We owe those people nothing but an arrow through the chest." She remained quiet for a long time, making him wonder if she'd fallen asleep.

"I could've let the children in Fårosünd die, let them fall to your brethren's blades." Her voice was low and even like the rustle of leaves. "That wasn't my fight either."

"So why didn't you?"

"And you?" she asked, ignoring his question. "You wept after killing that girl. You spared me. Why?"

"I understand the virtue of mercy. I just don't know why you'd risk your life for our jailors." A shiver ran through her body, and he softened his tone. "I mean, refusing to kill someone is different from a futile attack on a heavily defended fortress." He propped himself onto his elbow and looked into her face. "Especially to rescue someone you don't even know."

"You challenged Thorstein before you knew me." The reflected firelight danced in her dark eyes, distorted by the pooling moisture.

"I was a child then, a green boy with foolish dreams of honor. But you? You've seen the world."

"Aye, I've seen the world in all its cruelty," she scoffed. "And so will these innocent children." Her face hardened. "They didn't choose where to be born or to whom. The Norns have placed them in the path of an avalanche, delighting in their misfortune. I can't..." She swallowed the lump in her throat. "I can't stand these hideous crones!" she snarled with sudden venom. "If I have the power to break their loom, I will!"

"No, that's not it," Rikard whispered. He placed his hand on her cheek, wiping a tear away with his thumb. "That might be a part, but not the whole truth. Tell me, please."

"Can't you feel how wrong this is?" Her voice trembled. "Their dreams and ambitions being crushed by metal-studded boots, their future snuffed out like a candle in a cruel wind... They have a gift; they belong to this land! Will we avert our gaze when an unnatural frost destroys the last blossoms of beauty in this world?"

"Are we still talking about the druid's grandchildren?"

"Don't you want to go home and avenge your brother?" she blurted. "Don't you want to bring Toril down after what she's done to you? Where's your sense of duty? Doesn't your honor demand revenge?" Her voice grew bitter, and she swiped his hand away. Just before she averted her face, he spotted fresh tears spilling down her cheeks.

"My honor has done nothing but drive us apart," he said in a low voice, letting his hand rest lightly on her shoulder. "My sense of duty has almost gotten us killed more than once. I don't need to prove to the world who I am. All I want... All I need is to build a life with you. I'm sorry, Rúnie. Please, I want to understand why saving these children is so important to you."

She whirled round, and her eyes blazed red.

"Never call me Rúnie again! I'm not that pitiful waif anymore."

"Grúnie then?" He held her close, and his lips pulled into a hesitant smile. She punched his shoulder, but the corners of her mouth twitched upward.

"Never! Ever! Again!" she hissed, half laughing and half crying.

"I won't," he whispered, "if you tell me."

She lowered her gaze, but he placed his hand under her chin, lifting her face with inexorable gentleness. His striking blue irises fixed on hers, and the flames painted rainbows on the whites of his eyes. He didn't blink until she relented.

"I can't have children," she whispered, her words raw and broken. Her shoulders sagged and her chest deflated as the air fled from her lungs. "I haven't bled since the curse took me. I'm a monster now, not a woman."

He took her face in both of his hands and bent close until their noses almost touched.

"We'll rescue these children, Bergrún. I promise," he said with tenderness and fervor coloring his voice. "The Inglans have no idea what is coming for them!" With that, he kissed her.

CHAPTER TWENTY-FOUR

Rebellion

Soft footfalls woke Bergrún from an uneasy sleep. She jerked upright, her hand outstretched, only to spot Maeve twenty paces away. The young woman froze mid-stride, holding her arms wide, palms up, in a gesture of peace. She wore a green smock, eschewing her traditional white dress for the unpleasant memories. Twin braids encircled her head, letting her wavy auburn hair spill down her back. Bergrún's face relaxed, and she called a greeting, lowering her fist.

"*Maidin mhaith*," the younger woman replied with an unsure smile. "You come to speak with the druid?" she asked, straining to pronounce the unfamiliar Norsk words.

"We will," the witch replied in Gaelisk, "let me rouse this layabout, and we will be in the hut shortly."

"What's going on?" Rikard asked, rubbing the sleep from his eyes. "Who're you talking to?"

"Your little friend," Bergrún chuckled. He pushed himself upright. The blanket slid off his bare chest, and Maeve lowered her gaze, blushing. Bewildered, his head swiveled back and forth between the two women until his companion explained the situation.

"The druid asked to see us. He'll have an answer to my suggestion."

"What suggestion?"

"Well, more of a demand. If they want our help to free their children, they'll have to be forthcoming. No more spies, no more secrets. There was a bit more. We'll talk about it later."

"When did you discuss this?" he asked in surprise.

"Come to speak?" Maeve repeated. Not understanding their words, she appeared unsure of what to do.

"You speak Norsk? Wonderful!" he said with a smile. "So brave of you to come here after your brother's…"

"I told her she had to learn," Bergrún laughed, "to give you orders you'll understand."

"Oh, haha!" Turning to Maeve, he added, "*Táimid.*"

She smiled and turned, allowing him to dress.

Moments later, the three entered the druid's hut. Besides Garwyn and Theron, who looked as angry as ever, four more people crowded the place, two men and two women. The druid rose, bowed his head, and offered them seats.

"The council usually meets below," he explained, "in a large circular cavern. But given our recent misunderstanding, I found it more prudent to stay above ground." Bergrún ignored his pleasantries and sat on the stool closest to the door. Rikard walked beside her. Seeing that the chair next to the druid was reserved for Maeve, he waited until the younger woman had taken her place.

"We really should take her along," Bergrún chuckled under her breath. "If she can teach you manners." He mumbled something indistinct, not looking at her, and everyone waited for the druid to speak.

"Let me give the introductions," the old man said. "You've already met my wards, Maeve and Theron." The young man's face grew even more hostile. He ground his teeth and cracked his knuckles. The druid ignored him and pointed to a middle-aged couple to his left. "These are Ronan MacGregger and Fiadh Nic Chonaill, our best trackers." She was reed-thin with short-cropped hair and a weather-worn face. He was short and stocky. His red beard sprouted unkempt from rosy cheeks. "To my right are Cormac ÓBrian and Saoirse Gobha. Cormac was once a guard for the old clan chieftain, and Saoirse is the village's smith." Both stood nearly a head taller than any other man in the room, with broad shoulders formed by hard labor. They wore matching sleeveless tunics displaying their muscled arms. "Since not everybody speaks the Norsk tongue well, may I ask you, Bergrún, daughter of Gulveig, to translate for your husband? I shall relay the words of Rikard, son of Sven, to my peers."

Both Bergrún and Rikard jolted on hearing the term "husband." He sat up straighter, puffing his chest out, until her elbow connected with his ribs.

"You didn't tell me, *husband,*" she whispered too low for anyone else to hear.

"They must have misunderstood," he mouthed. "You heard the druid, most don't speak Norsk."

"You're not getting out of this that easily. We'll discuss it later," she said in a low growl, seeing the druid's benevolent smile widening into a mischievous grin. Then she stood, addressing the room in Gaelisk.

"I'm Bergrún of Heillaður, black sister and Death's true daughter. Ill fate and unwarranted violence brought me here. I do not trust any of you, and to some I bear a debt of pain." Her eyes shifted to Theron, and he shuddered under her gaze. "Only the kindness of a few and the voice of the land, its fragrant magic sweetening the air, made me spare you long enough to consider your plight. Your children are innocent pawns in the invader's vile attempt to eradicate your people. I will not stand for this. My husband and I... We'll risk our lives to save your children. Your actions alone determine whether they'll still have parents to return to." She sat and let her words sink in. A dead silence fell, and Rikard, seeing the faces of shock all around, didn't need the translation to understand the witch's words.

"What is our opponents' strength? How many prisoners do they hold?" Rikard spoke slowly, letting the druid translate. "We need details to form a plan: armament, disposition, recent actions, and future intentions. We're looking for the weakest link in their shield wall."

"What think you, Northman?" Theron spat. "They're catching to sell our people. What more need knowing? Blow open the gate, and our men will murder these *ainniseoirs*!"

"Your men? Like those in the cell?" Rikard asked. "The spearmen I laid low in heartbeats. If your plan is suicide, you don't need us."

"Not needing you, you true!" Theron sprang to his feet. "Only *cailleach*, if she is who says."

"Sit down!" the druid barked, his voice ricocheting from the walls. Theron remained standing in defiance for three heartbeats. His chest rose and fell in agitation before he caved to everyone's furious gaze. He sat down, leaned back, and crossed his arms. The chair creaked under his weight.

"But he's right," Bergrún mused in a soft voice dripping with scorn. Her grin widened as the red glow ignited in her eyes. "You heard my words, yet few've seen proof. That won't do. *Springa!*" Theron's chair exploded, and he crashed onto his back as splinters of wood flew in all directions.

Maeve rushed to help her brother, but he ignored her offered hand. He scrambled to his feet and brushed his clothes off, not meeting anyone's eyes. His face flushed red like a beetroot. Tension built in the air until he wilted under the druid's glare.

"I... sorry," he muttered, squeezing the words through clenched lips. "Was not insult, was question." His eyes on the floor, he stepped back until his back hit the rough timbers.

"Was not punishment," the witch replied in a crude imitation of his broken Norsk. "Was answer!"

"Who can tell me about the garrison in Dunscaith Castle?" Rikard asked into the deafening silence.

"We believe they're down to twenty men-at-arms," Cormac explained. "Many are Éiran traitors from the north. Only the leaders are Inglans."

"In addition, the castle holds another score of laborers—jailors, carpenters, smiths, kitchen maids, and stable hands," Saoirse said. "They hold over forty of our people in their dungeons, if everyone is still alive. One third each men, women, and bairns."

"The oppressors are scared," Fiadh added. Her voice was rough as gravel. Her jaw was in constant motion, and she spat black spittle into a bowl by her feet. "Patrols went missing. The attack on the last prisoner transport. We caught two messengers heading for Dúnmuir, begging for reinforcement."

"That's the harbor town two days to the west," Ronan explained. "Fresh troops arrive there before marching inland."

"What happened to the messengers?" Rikard asked. In response, Fiadh pulled a dagger from her boot, letting her thumb glide over the gleaming edge. Bergrún gave her an approving nod.

"Where are their things? Their horses, uniforms, missives?" Rikard leaned forward, steepling his fingers.

"We steal not from the dead, Northman," Theron growled. "They're Éirans. Souls be with *The Morrígan* until born new." Everybody turned to him in exasperation.

"Touching," Bergrún mocked. "So if I kill you now, there's no harm done, and we're rid of your presence. The thought grows ever more appealing."

"Why do you need their horses and uniforms?" the druid asked in Norsk, intending to de-escalate.

"Because we'll need to send for reinforcement," Rikard replied. "That's our best way to enter the castle."

"How?" Cormac asked in Norsk after hearing the druid's translation.

"Oh, that's devilish!" Bergrún chuckled, beaming at Rikard. Turning to the room, she explained, "We'll overwhelm the new troops with poison and arrows. Then we'll dress up like Inglans, and march right in through the opened gate. I knew there was a reason I kept you around," she added in Norsk, punching Rikard's shoulder with a bone-chilling grin.

WHEN THE COUNCIL ended, two hours later, Bergrún suggested splitting up for the rest of the day. She wanted to ride out with Ronan and Fiadh to learn the lay of the land. In the meantime, Rikard should band together with Cormac to inspect the available weapons and assess the fighters' abilities.

"Just point, shrug, and grunt," she laughed when he mentioned the language barrier. "That's all warriors do anyhow." She kissed him and swooped away, a borrowed green cloak billowing in the wind as she galloped along the ridge.

"You see spears?" Cormac asked after receiving instructions from the druid.

"I guess." Rikard gestured with an open palm. "Lead on." When Cormac hesitated, the Viking nodded, adding, "*Táim.*"

They descended the stairs into the caves below. Cormac set a brisk pace, and Rikard struggled to keep up. He stumbled several times in the semi-darkness. As soon as they reached the octagonal hallway with the cells, Rikard slowed, narrowing his eyes. He couldn't imagine a reason for renewed treachery, yet the hair on his arms stood on end and his breathing quickened.

"*Tá gach rud go maith,*" Cormac said, and Rikard recognized the phrase Maeve had used, though the warrior's deep voice made it sound less friendly. The Éiran opened a cell door and lit the lamps within. Rikard didn't follow immediately. His eyes roamed over the dark tunnel entrances, and his hand gripped his dagger. When Cormac returned to the hallway with a spear and a crossbow, he held the weapons out to Rikard. Both looked new and well-maintained.

"Inglan?" Rikard asked, receiving a nod. Feeling reassured, he followed the man into the cell. About two dozen spears stood arrayed against the wall. Five more crossbows and a sizable pile of bolts lay on the cot next to a collection of daggers. Those looked different. The blades flowed in a gentle curve, measuring a handspan in length. Leather strips wrapped the yew-wood hilts in intricate knots. The pattern extended onto the blade with delicate etchings. "Éiran?" he asked, receiving a nod and a smile this time. The Viking took one dagger, weighing it in his hand, when Maeve's scream echoed from the cave walls.

Rikard rushed out into the hallway. A leg shot forth, tripping him. Pain jolted through his body as his knee hit a protrusion on the uneven floor. His cry of agony was cut short by a kick to his ribs. He rolled to his side and saw two masked men shove the door to the cell shut, locking Cormac in. Another kick hit near his kidneys. He arched his back and rolled forth, seizing one man's leg. Blinded by pain, he struck upwards. His fist connected with his tormentor's groin. The man squealed in pain and fell.

Rikard rolled onto him and snapped his elbow back, crushing his larynx. But the victory was short-lived as a club smashed against his ribcage. Something cracked. Rikard convulsed in agony but managed to bring his foot up. He brushed his attacker's face with enough momentum to distract, but too little force to incapacitate. In the following tiny respite, the Viking pushed himself to all fours. One opponent was down, struggling to breathe and growing more desperate with each heartbeat. Three men stood in a semi-circle, one holding his bleeding nose. Farther back, a fourth man stood, smaller than the others. He held Maeve by the hair, a blade to her exposed throat.

The trio advanced, two striking with their clubs at the same time. Rikard pulled his head out of harm's way in the nick of time, blocking the second blow with his recently healed arm. He howled in anguish until a foot hit his chin. His head snapped back, stars bursting behind his eyelids.

Rikard lay on his side, curled into a ball, as kicks and blows rained down on him. Something hit the back of his head, and he lost consciousness. Yet he came to, only moments later, and he wished he hadn't. More blows, more pain. Somebody stepped on his hand, shattering the bones in his fingers.

With the crack of splintering timber, the door holding Cormac flew open. It smacked against one aggressor's shoulder, sending him tumbling. The Éiran warrior jumped forth and speared a second masked man through the chest. He twisted the blade before pulling it free, and swinging the butt around, he downed the third thug.

"*Cad atá á dhéanamh agat?*" shouted the fourth man. Despite the excruciating agony, Rikard immediately recognized Theron's voice. Bile rose in his throat, and he bellowed in defiance, channeling his pain into a wordless condemnation. The sound bounced back from the walls, ringing his ears. As the echo faded, Rikard's strength gave out, and blessed oblivion took him.

* * *

Bergrún returned as dusk fell. When she heard what had happened, she rushed to the cell holding the two surviving henchmen of Theron's treachery. Without breaking stride, she summoned blasts of concentrated air, punching the men guarding the door in the face. Their heads hit the stone walls with a sickening crack, and their boneless bodies slid to the ground.

The witch wrenched the door wide. Like an uncaged beast, she attacked the miserable creatures within, draining their lives and exploding their skulls. Dragging the corpses into the open, she demanded that every man, woman, and child present in the cave complex walk by the gruesome spectacle.

The macabre procession had packed the tunnels with trembling bodies, leaving a circle only large enough for the witch and her victims. The wailing of children mixed with the stench of fear. Bergrún stood rigid, regal like the Queen of Hel, her gaze never leaving the druid's twitching face. When the tension grew unbearable, she strode forth, seized the druid by his robe, and forced her dagger into his hands.

"Pluck out your eyes, old man," she ordered in Gaelisk for everyone to hear. Her voice boomed in the tight space. "They do not work!" Waves of menace emanated from her, stealing the air from everyone's lungs. "You haven't seen the treachery among your own. Or mayhaps you have, and you didn't mind." Spittle flew from her lips. Her hissing voice dripped with undiluted venom. "You're blind already since you never saw me for who I am. Do it!" she screamed, mad with rage. "Or I'll kill any living soul in this valley, leaving you for last!"

He looked paper-thin. The aura of wisdom evaporated under her demonic fury, leaving a feeble husk of a man facing a power he couldn't match. He raised the knife with a shaking hand. His other hand went to his eye, pulling the lids wide.

"NO!" Maeve shrieked, stumbling forward. "Not him! Punish me. It was... it was my fault. All my fault!" She gasped for air as violent shudders racked her body. Bergrún's cold hand clawed around the druid's fingers, holding the knife an inch from the druid's eye. "Theron... he came to me, asking for Rikard," Maeve stammered. "Said he wanted... wanted to apologize. About trust... allies. But he just, he..." Her voice cracked. "HE LIED!" she wailed, falling to her knees.

The witch whirled around, her face contorted. Her eyes blazed red like bonfires, glaring with enough ferocity to sear a hole into creation. With an ear-piercing scream, she wrenched the dagger from the druid's grasp, shattering the frail bones in his fingers. He howled, and she tossed the knife to the ground.

The villagers edged away from Maeve, leaving the young woman exposed in the witch's deadly path. Bergrún's hands spasmed, forming claws. Blood dripped from her fingernails. The very ground under her feet rumbled.

She let out another milk-curdling scream. The excruciating sound reverberated in the narrow halls, leaving a ringing silence in its wake. Then she whirled on the spot and cut through the throng of people like a hot knife through butter, marching along the hallway toward the stairs and the hut beyond, where Rikard lay.

The cave walls cracked, groaned, and trembled as she passed. A whirlwind rose, picking up dust and blowing out all torches, leaving the shocked Éirans behind in utter darkness.

CHAPTER TWENTY-FIVE

Homebound

THAT NIGHT, DUNSCAITH Castle burned. The fires started in the stables, hours after midnight. In a sudden flash, the straw exploded into a wall of flame. The blazes engulfed the large structure in heartbeats. Beasts and men cried out in torment as the firestorm consumed their flesh. As the castle woke to their bloodcurdling screams, the guards rushed to save what could not be saved.

One watchleader sprinted up the stairs to the keep's upper floor. Yet, instead of delivering his report, he found the fortress's commander dead on the floor. A dagger protruded from his forehead. The commander's elkhounds lay decapitated near the hearth. Pools of blood spread everywhere, coating the floorboards. In the far corner, the bedslave cowered. Almost nonsensical, she raved about a devil with glowing eyes, a demonic cackle like shattering icicles, and an unnatural chill that froze the air in her lungs.

The captain called for more guards. He was giving the orders to search the castle when, behind him, someone shouted words in a strange tongue. With a sharp clap, the bed ignited. A whirlwind rose, fanning the hungry flames. In the blink of an eye, the fire spread from the down pillows to the opulent hangings. The men rushed to the exit, but the door slammed shut. The bolt slid home, locking them inside as the room filled with suffocating smoke.

Below, in the courtyard, all available hands formed a bucket line. Despite their effort, the stable collapsed. Plumes of sparks burst into the night air, and the men fought to keep the inferno from spreading. Smoke burned in their lungs, and the searing heat forced them to retreat.

That's when the earth shook; a crack opened in the ground. Widening into a fissure, it cut across the courtyard and up the walls. The mighty inner keep trembled. Building blocks the size of pigs broke free, raining down death and destruction, and blocking the entrance.

A large section of the courtyard's pavement gave way as the well collapsed inward, leaving a sinkhole the size of a roundhouse. When the tremors subsided and the dust settled, an eerie silence fell over the castle. The men halted the frantic actions, letting the useless buckets slip from their numb hands. They looked around in disbelief. The blaze had reduced the stable to a heap of ash and smoldering timbers, while all around, new fires ignited. Dark smoke rose from the chapel, and flames shot out of the keep's upper windows.

Somebody pointed to the ramparts, where a shadow moved. A figure climbed from the keep's roof, illuminated by the dancing flames. Two guardsmen with torches blocked the specter's path, firelight reflecting on steel helmets. Twenty strides separated the watchmen and the shadow when an invisible force hit them, lifting them off their feet. Their screams pierced the night as they toppled over the low barbican and plummeted to their death below.

The terror continued throughout the night. Wooden stairs burst apart as soldiers attempted to ascend. A crossbow bolt from nowhere found the sergeant organizing the archers. The steepled roofs of the four corner watchtowers ignited one by one, blazing like beacons summoning the *Morrígan's* black wings. When the exhausted men sought refuge in the cavernous kitchen, they found the water cisterns cracked, the remnants of their contents glistening on the tiled floor. Some resorted to ale, only to writhe in agony like snakes on hot coals minutes later, clutching their stomachs.

Less than a dozen men still stood upright when the sun rose, painting the sky orange. Covered in soot and sweat, they looked at each other, frightened like sheep caught in a blizzard. The words demons and witchcraft clung to every survivor's lips. The large wooden cross above the gatehouse started to tilt, the wood groaning and snapping. As it broke free, they gave in to their fear. Pushing and shoving, they threw the mighty gate open and lowered the drawbridge. They ran for their lives, hellbent on escaping from this cursed place. The first men had crossed the moat, reaching the road beyond, when a line of spears greeted them. Crossbow bolts tore through chests. Cormac ÓBrian led the charge, and the druid's men slaughtered the fleeing invaders to the last soul.

* * *

As the liberators entered the castle ruin to free their loved ones and ransack the place for anything valuable, Bergrún left through the sewer grate in the kitchen, the same way she'd entered hours earlier. The day grew mild under a blue sky dotted with puffy white clouds as the witch steered her horse in a slow walk. She felt lightheaded and tired beyond belief. Her skin itched as the sun dried the layer of filth, soot, blood, and gore covering her from head to toe. Her stomach churned, her guts rumbling as the fiery beast inside her settled down into an uneasy slumber, sated by the slew of violence and destruction she'd wrought.

She reached the druid's hut without remembering the journey. The bright light stung her eyes. Her head throbbed, threatening to explode. Seeing the door standing wide open to let the warm summer breeze enter, the witch dismounted a dozen paces away. She approached with care, her soft leather boots silent on the dewy grass. Maeve's lilting voice sounded through the opening. The young woman laughed in good humor about Rikard's clumsy attempts to speak Éiran.

Bergrún froze midstride. A jagged shard of loneliness pierced her chest. She stumbled, grasping the windowsill for support. Her heart jolted into a frantic beat, and she gasped like a fish on dry land as iron bands constricted her chest. Her hand convulsed, crushing a chunk of the weather-worn wood. The crack alerted the occupants, and their voices fell silent. Bergrún clamped her free hand onto her mouth, retreating two steps. She couldn't be seen, covered in the stink of death. When Rikard spoke again, moments later, she couldn't discern his words; too loud was the ringing in her ears. She had to leave; she had to hide—to crawl under a rock like a horrid spider shunning daylight.

Those two are made for each other, she acknowledged. *They're human.*

Maeve was young, beautiful, and brave, despite her years, like a fierce mother bear defending her cub. She would help Rikard to grow into the man he was destined to become.

He was strong and handsome, idealistic and sometimes naïve, but fearless, loyal, and stalwart, like a shepherd braving a wolf pack in a thunderstorm to shelter and protect his own. He would build Maeve a home, safe from the icy winds, with laughter and tenderness to warm the hearth.

The witch had no place in a future like that. Her vile deeds had already left deep scars on both of their bodies and souls. Everyone who associates with a black sister must pay a bitter price.

She averted her gaze, blinking the treacherous moisture away. Her eyes roamed the surroundings. Seeking a place to rest, she spotted a sight that suited her better. A body hung by the neck from an exposed branch of the mighty oak. Even with the face covered by a burlap sack, the witch had a pretty good idea who that was. Fiadh and Ronan had lived up to their reputation and tracked down the traitor Theron. They'd given him a much kinder treatment than she would've had in store.

Wiping her face, she marched along the ridge, intent on sleeping in the shade with her back against the gnarled trunk of the oak. There she would find the company befitting her nature.

* * *

A DAY LATER, Bergrún rode into the village. She wore men's clothing—a faded linen shirt and a pair of black woolen pants, having discarded her soiled dress after the assault on the castle. She'd tied a rolled-up travel cloak to her saddle. Earlier in the day, she'd asked Maeve for a spare dress, not wanting to meet Rikard with blood and gore all over her garment. The young woman jolted in fright as the witch approached her. Yet after hearing the request, she was only too eager to help. Maeve brought all the clothes she could carry from the tiny loft above the druid's chamber. Bergrún was unwilling to dress in white. So, she ended up wearing Theron's boyhood clothes.

The druid had vacated his hut and moved into the brewmaster's house in the village as long as Rikard and Bergrún were his "guests." Reaching the square with ivy-covered huts, the witch tied her horse to a hitch in front of the smithy and marched in without knocking. Seeing who'd arrived, the brewmaster swallowed his shout of indignation. He showed the way to the back room where the archdruid resided. It was early afternoon, and the old man sat in an armchair, dozing.

"I need a swift ship," she called in a commanding voice, not bothering with a greeting. "Find me a small crew, loyal men who do not ask questions, and secure provisions for a journey north."

"Ah, Bergrún, daughter of Gulveig," he stammered, jerking awake. "My greetings to you. How can I be of assistance?"

She took a deliberate step closer, her shadow falling over him.

"By providing a ship as I asked for," she snapped back. "Don't fake ignorance; your senses can't be that dull. I have little time and less patience!"

"Of course, of course. I have contacts in Dúnmuir. But the seaport is filled with Inglan soldiers and northern Éiran traitors. Filled to the gills, you might say." He chuckled at his own wit.

She stepped closer, her face hardening; a red flicker in her eyes ignited.

"Securing a ship that has permission to leave the harbor won't be easy," he amended, swallowing under her unrelenting gaze. "How fares your husband?" His voice rose in pitch, and he rang his wrinkled hands. "Do Maeve's administrations alleviate his pain? He should be well enough to travel in two weeks' time."

The witch closed the remaining distance, placed her hands with deliberate precision onto the armrests, and loomed over him.

"Stop playing your games, old man!" she growled. Her face was so close that his eyes had to dart left and right to focus on hers. "You know exactly what wonders your ward's 'administrations' do to his vigor. Did you think I wouldn't notice the ants scurrying between the village and the hill? I need a fast ship, and you'll provide it in three days. I don't care if you sell your rotten soul to make it happen. I'd think," she whispered, her voice dripping with menace, "you'd be interested to see me go."

"Of course," he stammered. "Three days. It shall be done." She lingered above him for several tense heartbeats before straightening up. "Send Saoirse with daily reports, and have Cormac pick the crew. Not a word to anyone else, especially to Maeve and Rikard. Have I made myself clear?" He nodded frantically.

The witch turned. As she walked to the door, she spotted his staff leaning against the wall. Her left hand reached for it of its own accord. As her long fingers enclosed the gnarled wood, the witch felt energy rushing through her grip. Like holding her hand under an ale barrel's spigot, she could sense the power but couldn't hold on to it. For one heartbeat, anger rose, and she considered snapping his mark of station in two.

"It comes from the oak on the ridge," the druid said in an effort to remain calm. "Like in your old sagas, we hold trees sacred as they bind the worlds together—the future and the past."

She turned, and her glare squashed the glimmer of his returning serenity, the lofty air of wisdom and mystery that had irked her from the beginning. Her grip tightened, and the wood groaned.

"In that case, you'd better make sure my future is your past, old man." With that, she left the room.

* * *

"Bergrún!" Rikard called, stepping from the hut. His left arm lay in a sling, and his right leaned on a staff. Bandages wrapped his bare chest, and he dragged his right leg behind. Three days had passed since his brutal beating, leaving his entire body a single purple bruise. He winced with every step, but the pain from his wounds paled in comparison to the agony of seeing her walk past without stepping in.

She turned, and her lips trembled seeing him like this. Saoirse walked by her side. The two women had been in deep conversation when he called.

"We can do as you asked," the smith said in Gaelisk. "I'll work on it tonight and show you in the morning." To Rikard, she shouted in Norsk, "Greetings, brave Viking!" Yet her attempt to speak his language did not garner the desired result. His face fell, and he averted his gaze, suspecting mockery in her words. She shrugged and rushed on, eager to give the two heroes the privacy they deserved.

Bergrún closed the distance, forcing a smile onto her lips. An arm's length away, she halted, her hands spread, unsure where to touch him.

"Should you be walking around?" she asked. Her chipper tone sounded off. "Here, let me steer your ship, captain." She took the staff and, folding his arm into hers, guided him back to the hut.

"Where've you been?" he asked. "Haven't seen you in days. Not after that night…" He trailed off, wanting to know more but not daring to ask outright.

"I've been here and in the village. There's a lot to do."

"Like what?"

"We're strengthening the defenses for these people. Tidings of the assault on the castle will spread. The invaders might be back in force any day now."

"Defenses for these people? They're not our people. We did more than they deserve! You did, I mean… I was useless." His voice trailed off, ending in a sigh of frustration.

"Rikard," she mouthed, halting in her stride. He looked her in the eyes and saw turmoil and sadness staring back at him. Her lips trembled, and her grip on his arm tightened. "You don't see me because you sleep all the time, dullard," she whispered before forcing her lips into a brittle smile that didn't reach her eyes. "I'm there, with you, at night, when you're in the land of dreams. Let's get you inside." She pulled him along, her eyes on the open door.

"Will you tell me what happened? No one around here speaks Norsk. Maeve is trying, but she only knows a few words."

"She's fabulous, isn't she?" Bergrún replied, returning to her uncanny chipper tone. "She's a healer and a fine cook. She's very well respected. If she were male, she'd be the next druid."

"That's not the point," he huffed. "I was asking about the... Hold on! You're not jealous, are you?"

"Jealous? Me?" she laughed. "Why, no!" Her voice cracked, and she had to swallow the lump in her throat.

This time, he stopped walking. He pulled her around.

"You're a terrible liar, Bergrún Lilith Gullveigardóttir! Sometimes, at least. I mean, back then, before we knew each other... That sneaky Agnetha, she fooled me right and good."

"I'm not jealous, Rikard. I'm happy that you are in such good hands. You suffered my inept healing less than a fortnight ago." She gave a mirthless snort. Resting her gaze on his injured left arm, she shook her head. "She is a silversmith, while I can barely shoe a horse. I'm a broad axe, good at splitting things apart, while her delicate touch can sew you together. I never want to inflict pain like that again," she whispered. "Never ever again!"

"Please, Bergrún, don't!" he rasped as his sluggish mind caught on. "There is no Maeve and I! You're all I need. You're all I want!" He seized her hand, and she lowered her gaze, squeezing his fingers all the same.

"Let's get you inside. It feels like rain is upon us."

* * *

THE NEXT MORNING, when Bergrún left him with a kiss and a fleeting smile, he counted the minutes until Maeve arrived. As soon as she'd opened the door, he pushed himself to his feet and hobbled across the cluttered room.

"Maeve, finally! I need to see the druid," he called. "I need to speak to Garwyn, now!"

"Morning blessed, Rikard," she replied, her tongue still stumbling over the unfamiliar Norsk words.

"Yes, a blessed morning to you, too! Can you take me to him?" he urged.

"Take?" she repeated, looking bewildered. "You want take?" She pointed to the kettle near the hearth.

"No, I don't want tea. I want to..." He bit his tongue, forcing the tension from his shoulders. Rikard stepped closer, took Maeve by both hands, and gave her a reassuring smile. "*Tá gach... rud go... go maith,*" he said, searching for each syllable. A genuine smile brightened her face. "But," he continued, tapping his own chest. "I need to talk"—he brought his hand to his mouth, miming speech—"to Garwyn." He pointed toward the door.

"*Ar mhaith leat labhairt le Garwyn?*"

"Aye," he nodded. "Now! *Anois!*"

"*Tusa agus Bergrún?*"

"No! Only me, Rikard!"

She tilted her head, making sure she'd understood him. When his eyes bore into hers, conveying urgency and determination, she nodded, turned, and slipped out the door.

Rikard seized his walking staff and shuffled back and forth in tight circles to burn off his restless energy. Maeve came back quicker than expected. She was alone and beckoned him to step outside. He did as she asked and found her holding a horse by its lead.

"*Tá an draoi sa sráidbhaile,*" she said, pointing to the village.

He had difficulties getting into the saddle. His bruised ribs ached, and he couldn't pull with his left arm. When he finally managed, he grunted in pain. She jumped on the horse behind him, took the reins, and steered the animal in a slow walk down the switchbacks.

They reached the village almost an hour later. His face had lost all color. He clenched his jaw, inhaling rapid, shallow breaths. When his feet stood on firm ground, he bent over and vomited. Maeve cried out in alarm, and the brewmaster rushed from his house.

"*Cabhraigh leis dul isteach!*" Maeve called. The broad-shouldered man pulled Rikard's good arm over his shoulder and half-dragged and half-carried him inside. He placed him in the armchair, and Maeve filled a cup with water. Rikard thanked her with a nod and drank. Squeezing his eyes shut, he let his bruised body relax.

"Where's Garwyn?" he finally wheezed.

"You sitting, I going," replied Maeve. "*Tá gach rud go maith.*"

Many minutes passed until the druid entered. Rikard had somewhat recovered from his ordeal, and he tapped his foot with impatience.

"You shouldn't take a journey in your condition, Rikard, son of Sven."

"Is that what my wife told you, that I shouldn't take a journey?"

"Your wife? I haven't..."

"Don't lie. I'm sick of your lies, all of you!" he shouted with color flushing his cheeks. "You must know by now *what* she is, if there's any wisdom left in your withered skull," he barked. The pain, humiliation, and helplessness fanned his anger like the blacksmith's bellows.

"But I know *who* she is! She's hiding something for a noble cause," he said. "And you know about it. So, you're going to tell me, right now!" His chest rose and fell with the frantic beat of his heart, and he clutched his side as renewed pain jolted his body.

"Please," the druid said, "try not to aggravate your broken ribs further. We'll talk. But you must calm yourself." He drew up a chair beside him. Maeve, who'd stood stunned by Rikard's outburst, rushed to refill the cup. "*Tabhair beoir dó!*" the druid said. She lowered the water pitcher and walked to the keg, pouring him a mug of beer instead.

"I see you and your wife are well matched in temper and tenacity," the druid chuckled, garnering a glare from Rikard. "I meant that as a compliment. In fact, you're a complement to each other. Your bond was forged by fire. You both have risked everything to see the other safe."

"I didn't come all the way to ask for your wisdom on married life," Rikard interrupted. "I need to know..."

"She asked for a ship and a crew to sail north," the druid interrupted. "She was quite demanding. By threat of death, I wasn't to tell you."

"What?" he gasped. "That can't... She said that... How is that possible?"

"I can't be sure, of course. She didn't share her innermost thoughts, not in as many words. But if I were to read the signs, I'd say to keep you safe."

"And she forbade you to tell me, threatening your life?"

"I did!" Bergrún growled. She stood in the doorway, her eyes blazing red, and her voice brimmed with barely restrained fury. "I thought my words couldn't be mistaken, old fool, and neither my resolve!"

* * *

THE DRUID WHIRLED around, and Maeve took a step back. But Bergrún's gaze did not waver from Rikard's face. Like the first snowflake landing on a sea-drenched boulder, his confusion melted away, exposing the jagged angles of bitterness underneath.

"So, you planned a surprise?" he said, the sarcasm in his voice the thinnest sheet of ice over his burning fury. "A midsummer present, mayhaps? How kind of you, dearest!" Maeve edged away, but his hand shot out, holding her in place. "Stay!" he ordered. "I have a hunch this might involve you, too."

Bergrún stood stiff as a statue. Her eyes blinked, and her jaw worked as several emotions fought for dominance. Despite the warm weather, she wore a travel cloak and carried a pack over her shoulder.

"Were I to wave farewell at the pier?" he asked with scorn. "Or was I to receive a raven?"

"If I may..." the druid ventured.

"NO!" Rikard and Bergrún shouted in unison. The silence that followed lay thick as tar.

"I never meant to make this any harder than it already is," she said, straining to keep her voice even. "A clean break is best."

"And you would know all about breaking things?" He snarled.

His words struck her like a blow. The fight left her, her shoulders slumped.

"It was a dream, Rikard," she whispered, the words catching in her throat. "A beautiful dream, letting me forget for blissful moments what I was. But we can't close our eyes... not any longer. Five times you've come to grave harm, during the last fortnight alone, and twice you suffered at my hand. It's madness to take such a risk!"

"Call me a madman then," he barked, his knuckles white where he gripped the arm of his chair. "Because I knew the risk since you came to me in the hot pool. We all must die. I don't fear death... What I fear is not living!" He tried to push himself to his feet, but winced as the pain forced him back down.

"But I won't die!" she cried, shivering from head to toe. "I do not age. If you came to harm because of me, I'd carry the grief for eternity." She jerked as if to take a step closer, but her feet seemed rooted to the ground. "Seeing you die will destroy the last remnant of my soul. Woe to the world," she wailed, "if the monster is unleashed. If my dark powers reigned unchecked by human emotions..." she shuddered. "Let me take your love with me, forever unchanging. It's the only way..."

"I never thought," he gasped. His jaw went slack, and his hand slid from Maeve's arm as if his bones had evaporated.

"Of course you haven't, you dullard!" A broken laugh, bitter as winter's frost, tore from her lips before shattering into a sob. Her body trembled with the effort to remain standing. "How could you? You're too pure, too honorable, too good. The last people who've seen the demon at its worst now lie burned to a cinder in the castle ruin." She drew in desperate breaths. "Nothing can ever erase the darkness in me. Nothing!" Her choked cry echoed in the tiny space. "Only the memory of your love can hold my demons at bay."

"But what about me?" He called, his voice cracking. "How will I live on knowing your bitter sacrifice? You call me honorable, and then you rob me of the only honorable thing that matters—to stand by the person I love, even if the world around us burns!"

"Rikard, please, I can't!" she sobbed, burying her face in her hands. The witch swayed like a willow sapling in a gale wind. Maeve rushed toward her and, seizing her by the arm, steadied the distraught woman. One glance toward the druid was enough. He struggled to his feet and hurried from the room. Maeve guided Bergrún to the chair next to Rikard, giving him a sad little smile. He nodded, his eyes glistening.

"*Tá gach rud go maith*," the young woman whispered before leaving the two lovers alone, pulling the door closed behind her.

* * *

Nine days later, Bergrún stood aboard *An Faoileán*, holding on to Rikard's arm like a drowning sailor to a lifeline. They'd passed through the Iarntann Islands in the morning, and Njord's mighty breath sent the Seagull flying across the open waves. Twelve Éirans had volunteered to aid Rikard in his attempt to reclaim his homeland, Saoirse and Cormac among them. They'd convinced Dúnmuir's harbormaster with kind words and naked steel to part with the sleek vessel and left Éira in the dead of night.

So far, they'd only discussed the vague outlines of a plan. Their ship was still days away from Hrafney, and everyone gave Bergrún and Rikard space. The two hadn't left each other's side.

Standing at the railing, the witch closed her eyes, listening to the groan of the rigging. The deck planks hummed under her bare feet. She wore a loose blouse and a pair of soft woolen pants—a parting gift from Maeve. The women had talked for long hours, neither sure of what their future would bring. As the salty wind whipped Bergrún's hair, she felt adrift in currents beyond her control, and she'd made her peace with it. What would happen would happen.

No sense to worry about tomorrow, when today is all that matters.

CHAPTER TWENTY-SIX

Confrontation

THE MORNING DAWNED gray. Low-hanging clouds clung to the mountains, obscuring their peaks. Harold sat on his customary rock in the staging yard, looking up at the sky in the vain hope of seeing the sun. He yearned to feel its warmth before descending into the dark mineshafts below. He'd finished his portion of daily gruel, wiping the wooden bowl clean with his fingers. The Viking hadn't resorted to licking the bowl, but the constant hunger would soon erode the last vestiges of his pride. He'd lost at least two stone, and the fresh crossbow wounds on his leg throbbed worse on such wet days.

Einar stood across the yard in a hushed conversation with a group of men. They parted with a nod, and he walked toward Harold, sitting beside his friend. The older man had always been wiry, and he seemed to hold up well despite the hard labor and constant near-starvation.

"We should do it today," he whispered, his gaze fixed on the group of guards in front of the tool shed. "No sense in waiting any longer."

"Today is as good as any Hela-sent day," Harold growled. "Let's have a last stand for blood and glory!"

"Keep your voice down, or it'll only be blood... Your blood."

"You worry too much, old friend. Have I ever told you?"

"Once or twice... every stinking minute," Einar chuckled. "Watch, here he comes." Harold raised his gaze, his narrowed eyes alert.

Magnus Håkanson approached with hunched shoulders, clutching his wooden bowl like his life depended on it. He had a face that bards would sing about to scare young children in the audience. A chunk of his nose was missing, and a purple scar extended across his lips and chin, down his neck, and past his collarbone. Hailing from Starvinger in Norskvegn, he'd been among the first to abandon his chieftain and switch sides to Harold. Everyone knew the ruthless Viking's loyalty reached only as far as his coin pouch. He'd bet on Harold, and he'd lost everything, finding himself imprisoned due to his leader's erratic choices. Twice, he and Harold had come to blows, and twice he had been forced to retreat by the dwindling support for Hamarrfjord's fallen hero.

As he strolled by, offensively close yet without giving the seated men so much as a glance, Einar's leg shot out, tripping him. Magnus fell, his bowl of gruel sliding from his hands. Quick as a lynx, he sprang to his feet, murder in his eyes.

"*Skitr*, you *maðkur!*" he spat, the injury giving him a nasal voice. "You'll pay for this."

"For what?" Harold rose, his booming voice carrying far as he cracked his knuckles. "Is it my fault your soft Norskar feet can't handle our land? Are our rocks too hard for you?" he jeered, ensuring he had everyone's attention. Magnus crouched, pulling a shard of flint from under his tunic. The sharpened stone was a hand's span in length, one end wrapped in cloth.

"What are you gonna do with that?" Einar mocked. "Clean your nails?" He handed Harold a length of rope, an inch thick and a foot and a half long. A fist-sized stone was knotted into one end.

"Does he also wipe your ass, cripple?" Magnus taunted. "No one else seems to care for mighty Harold 'Fool' Svensen any longer!" He lunged, quick as a viper, but Harold sidestepped, bringing his makeshift mace around to hit his opponent's calf.

Magnus grunted, turned, and sliced, catching a piece of Harold's tunic. He ducked under the larger man's swing and rolled to his feet, ready for another attack. The thralls put their bowls aside and formed a ring around the fighters. Harold relied on his greater reach and brute force to score a few more glancing blows. His arm was in constant motion. The rope blurred, and the air thrummed with every swing.

Magnus used his superior speed to draw first blood, cutting Harold across the left arm and ripping two more tears in the man's tattered pants. Both men attacked with caution, wary of the other's deadly skill.

An uproar ripped through the crowd as a Starvinger prisoner shoved Harold in the back, shattering the fragile pretense of an honorable duel. Men started pushing and kicking, raining blows on anyone in their path.

Like a bushfire after a drought, the fighting spread across the courtyard, turning into an indiscriminate melee of fists, stones, and crude weapons.

"Back! Break it up!" the watchleader shouted, cracking his whip in the air. His men formed a line, banged spears against their shields, and stepped in to separate the fighters. Often, the guards ignored thralls fighting among themselves; it was a good way to relieve tension. Only when a brawl got out of hand, threatening the output of silver ore, did the soldiers intervene. They would whip the instigators bloody and have the rest work harder with reduced rations.

The prisoners retreated from the armored guards but continued fighting, moving together as a group, like maidens in a ring dance on the village green. With uncanny synchrony, they moved to the outside, surrounding the guards and blocking the exit. The guards rushed forth, shoved, and swiped with the blunt ends of their spears. They even lunged with the steel tips, all to no avail. The prisoners kept moving. A circle of punching, shoving bodies would break apart to let a guard's lunge find only empty air before reforming its menacing choreography an instant later. Only when Einar's son Eskil managed to trip the watchleader, seizing the surprised man's whip, did the dance freeze.

"Death to Toril!" Einar called. "For blood and glory!" the prisoners shouted in unison. They turned and attacked the outnumbered guards with deadly rage. They rushed them, seizing shields and spears with bare hands. Hitting the fallen men with stones and fists, they overwhelmed their oppressors. The men grunted. They snarled in rage and cried out in agony. Feet kicked and fists smacked against everything they could reach, providing the rhythm for the brutal symphony: the crack of bones, the bellowing roars, and the wet thuds of stone on flesh.

A horn sounded. From above, arrows rained down, finding prisoner and jailor alike.

"Retreat!" Harold shouted. "Take cover in the mine!" He seized Einar by the arm, pulling him along. An arrow had pierced the gaunt man's side, sinking inches into the soft tissue between ribs and hipbone. Einar grunted and spat as the archers above loosed another volley.

"Get me out of here," he snarled. "If I die, Harold Svensen, I'll kill you!"

* * *

RIKARD CROUCHED ON a rocky outcrop, the wind whipping his cloak. Below him, behind a stand of trees, lay the entrance to Hrafney's silver mine. Two weeks earlier, he'd left Éira on a stolen ship with a small group of twelve fighters. They'd sailed *An Faoileán* around the island, staying far from shore to remain unseen.

After landing on the eastern coast, he led them inland across the rugged highlands. They met a frightened shepherd who, with some persuasion, told them about the mine. Condemned criminals worked there as thralls, Harold Svensen among them. Bergrún agreed with Rikard's simple, if desperate plan: assault the mine, free the thralls, and bolster their ranks before marching on Hamarrfjord.

Their chances of victory hinged on stealth and surprise. But seeing Cormac sprint up the incline, Rikard knew that neither was an option any longer.

"Something is going on!" the breathless man called in Gaelisk. "Bowmen are firing from the rim."

"What did he say?" Rikard asked. He'd tried to learn as much of the foreign tongue as possible, but two weeks weren't enough. He hated the barrier between him and his men.

"There's fighting in the mine," Bergrún explained.

"Of course there is," he groaned. "My brother always had terrible timing."

"How many bowmen?" she asked Cormac.

"A score, mayhaps two dozen."

"Then there's no time to lose." To Rikard, she said, "We need to attack."

"Spread out in three groups," Rikard said. "Saoirse, Ciarán, you and I, we'll go through the middle and draw their attention. Let's hope our shields are strong enough. Cormac and Ronan, you'll split the rest. Come from the sides with arrows. By Hela, this is it. Time for blood and glory."

"For kin and jarl," Bergrún replied with a smirk after relaying the orders. But then she clasped his forearm and squeezed.

Moments later, they broke through the underbrush in a tight formation. Rikard and Ciarán walked in front, each holding a large wooden shield. Behind them, Saoirse fired jagged slag stones with her sling while Bergrún used the throwing knives the smith had fashioned, accelerating them with magic. As they'd hoped, the ambush drew the archers' attention. Half the men redirected fire. Rikard ducked, and Ciarán staggered as a barrage of arrows thumped against the wood.

The witch stopped her attack. She closed her eyes and hummed, causing the air to vibrate. Her voice grew louder, the rhythm gaining tempo, and a shimmering sphere formed around them. Distorting their view like a heat haze, the sphere expanded outward, deflecting the arrows. Bewildered, the archers stopped firing. They called to their comrades to turn and see the apparition. That's when arrows from both sides hit their line.

Shouts of surprise grew into cries of pain as steel tips hit flesh. Rikard's group advanced, pelting the panicking line with stones and knives. Cormac's and Ronan's groups fired another volley, then another. Pinned to the rim, the soldiers had no escape. Some took aim at the flanking forces, but without shields, armor, or cover, they fell to the last man.

* * *

BELOW, HAROLD STRAIGHTENED and looked to the rim. He'd sought shelter behind the rock he'd perched on earlier, using a slain guardsman's shield. All around, survivors stepped from cover. Some had made it into the mine's entrance, more had hidden behind the tool shed, but over a dozen thralls lay dead or wounded. Einar and his sons were the first to walk amongst the fallen, dragging wounded comrades out of harm's way.

"Seems this time, a plan of yours worked, my chieftain," Magnus mocked, giving Harold a curt nod. Hawking up phlegm, he spat. "Let's see if Thor was on your side, or if this was one of Loki's tricks." A fresh cut over his left eyebrow bled, and he swiped at it, smearing blood over half his face. Then he pulled a spear from the trembling hands of a fallen guard and buried the tip in the wounded man's chest.

The squeaking of rusted hinges drew all eyes to the massive wooden doors of the entrance. About a dozen people entered. Men and women in leather armor followed behind a tall young Viking. His wavy, flaxen hair lay plastered to his head, and he carried a shield sporting the stubs of several broken arrows. Beside him walked a woman with raven-black hair. They marched with confident strides toward the wary prisoners.

Harold bent, seizing a fallen pickaxe, and his fellow rioters followed suit, picking up weapons. Feet shuffled in the dirt. The tension grew as the newcomers drew near, until the black-haired woman raised a spear, unfurling a faded red banner with the snarling head of a gray wolf.

A deafening cheer rose from the men, bouncing back from the walls. The Vikings of Hamarrfjord were the first to bellow their battle cries. Heartbeats later, the Starvinger men joined in. Across from them, the Éiran fighters replied with an eerie sound vaulting between the deep-chested howl of a wolf and the shrill scream of an eagle. They spread out behind Rikard and Bergrún, thumping fists to their chests.

Rikard found Harold's eyes. In lockstep, both men took two strides into the open. As suddenly as it had begun, the cheers quieted, all eyes focusing on the two brothers.

Harold clutched the pickaxe in both hands, blood glistening on the metal. His long hair had been shorn off, and grime covered his haggard face.

Rikard wore the tunic and breastplate of an Inglan watchleader. He'd grown to match his brother's height, though his shoulders and arms were still lanky. He held a gleaming sword in a confident grip, the tip hovering an inch above the ground.

As Harold's eyes narrowed, Rikard instinctively slid his left foot back, widening his stance. The men shuffled for a better view, forming a wall of bodies around the brothers.

"I've saved your life, brother," Rikard shouted, his voice hard as the steel he carried. "My debt is settled."

"Aye, as you say, brother," Harold replied, rolling his head until the bones in his neck cracked. "But know this. I wouldn't have rushed to your aid if that... Agnetha hadn't forced me." He nodded toward the witch by Rikard's side, his voice firm, without fear or apology.

"Then we're even, because I wouldn't have rushed to your aid either if my *wife* hadn't convinced me." Rikard relaxed his stance, his tone mirroring his brother's nonchalance. "And her name is Bergrún. Bergrún Gullveigardóttir of Heillaður."

Einar Finsgúr snorted a strangled laugh, causing a round of uneasy chuckles from the men. Neither Harold nor Rikard joined in.

"Freya's blessing be with you! When she came to my bed, I hadn't learned of your vows." Harold declared with an edge of defensiveness. "I only took what was offered. I didn't force her."

"I know. She..." Rikard hesitated. "She did the same to me long before your return. I doubt any man who tried to force my lovely black witch would live to see the sunrise." Not an ounce of sarcasm tainted his words as he declared her nature to the assembled men.

Einar whistled into the stunned silence. He nodded his appreciation for Rikard's boldness, garnering renewed chuckles and cat-calling.

"Hear this, brother," Rikard shouted over the din. "We hadn't shared our vows back then. I bear you no grudge. Touch her again, though, and I'll cut off your hand, right below your chin."

Harold laughed, a bellowing sound that shook his torso. He dropped the pickaxe, closed the distance in a few strides, and pulled his brother into a crushing bear hug.

"You've grown, mighty warrior!" he shouted. "Good to see you. Good to have you back!" Bergrún shook her head as the men whistled and whooped, and Rikard hugged his brother back.

* * *

TORIL SOAKED IN the warm water, letting her muscles relax, when the village bell rang. For a heartbeat, she feared she'd misjudged the time. Was the bell heralding the beginning of the ceremony? She'd heard of bells on godhouses in the south ringing for special occasions. But this was the North. The sun still stood high in the sky, and the insistent ringing carried a more sinister tone. They were under attack.

Toril got out of the tub, pulled a linen tunic over her wet skin, and rushed to the window. The sky was blue, the sea calm. No hostile ships sailed toward their shores. She leaned out, searching the bay, but saw only seagulls bobbing on the gentle waves. The bell rang again, like the rapid hammer blows of a weaponsmith. An assault on land, then? Only one person would dare.

She pulled on a pair of leggings and wished for her sturdy boots. Instead, her wet feet wiggled into a pair of soft slippers that stood next to the mountain of fabric that was to be her wedding dress. At twilight, she was to marry Prince Filip of Danheimr.

Toril shook her head at the Norns' audacity to send her unwanted "guests," to spoil her victory. After years of planning, endless negotiations, ruthless scheming, and cold-blooded murder, she would face another grueling trial on the very day of her ascension. If she held her breath, she could almost hear Loki's laughter floating on the midsummer breeze.

A commotion sounded outside her room.

"Shield Olver," a young woman called in high agitation, "Mistress Toril is bathing. You cannot…" Her words were cut short by a thump and a cry before the door flung open. Olver entered, his face grim. Behind him, the servant girl picked herself up, rubbing her arm.

"Is it my dear cousin?" Toril asked, tightening a belt over her tunic. "How in Hela's name did he get out of the mine?"

"Both of them."

"Both?" she asked, blinking three times to make sense of his words.

"Rikard is leading the krigsband. They're marching in rank and file. They want to be seen."

"How many?"

"Three dozen, maybe. Shields, spears, light armor."

"But most have been in the mine for weeks." She wondered out loud. "They can't be in good strength."

"Don't underestimate them. Righteous fury will strengthen a man's arm. And that's not all." He looked at her, waiting for her full attention. "My men won't fight them. At least none of our kinsmen will."

"What?" she screamed. "How in Hela's thrice-cursed name has Harold managed that?"

"Not Harold. Rikard. He carries the banner of Leif Rødskæg and a flag of truce. He wants to talk. My men won't strike him. They honor the old ways."

"Your men are stupid!" Toril hissed. She sank into a cushioned chair and buried her face in her hands. "Stupid men and stupid Viking honor." Her voice hitched, and her body trembled.

* * *

RIKARD HALTED HIS krigsband on the village square. To his right, a newly erected frame of fresh-cut timbers marked the place where the chieftain's longhouse once stood. To his left, a group of men, too old or too weary to fight, huddled under the eaves of the stable. His Éiran fighters had spread out, on Bergrún's insistence, scouting the area behind him. They ensured no one would flank Rikard's forces unnoticed.

The young Viking leader stood straight with his hands at his side. He'd slung his shield over his shoulder and sheathed his sword. Harold stood beside him, holding Leif Rødskæg's banner aloft while Einar carried a spear with the white bedsheet of the silvermine's former watchleader. Together, they watched as Toril's troops descended from Rikard's house, standing rigid and coiled with the tension of warriors awaiting battle. Only the banners moved, snapping in the wind.

The defenders marched in two columns. Olver led the larger group of Hamarrfjord Vikings, while a plump man in eye-watering colors led a dozen Danske warriors. Toril walked ahead, her posture regal. She wore a green dress with silver embroidery. Her sleeves and hemline trailed over the ground. She looked out of place, as if she were greeting a foreign dignitary instead of going to war. Her golden hair hung in an intricate braid over one shoulder, and an ornate dagger glinted on her belt. When twenty paces separated her from her cousins, she raised a hand, and her entourage halted.

"Welcome home, Rikard, my dear cousin," she called, her voice clear. "I'm glad to see you well."

"Somehow, I doubt that," Harold shouted.

"If it weren't for the company you keep," she replied, ignoring Harold, "I'd embrace you with the sisterly love we once shared."

"How about a toast to his health?" Harold mocked. "I'm sure there's some Bog's bane to be found somewhere." The men on both sides booed, hissed, and jeered until Rikard's raised hand commanded their silence.

"I knew a girl once," Rikard said. "She was funny and clever. A good friend, a staunch ally, an inspiration in mischief and in valor. Some years ago, she succumbed to the poison of her ambition. Her body still walks this earth, but her soul has departed. I'm here to end her torment. Let her rest and be remembered as Rilly, Jarl Gustav's dutiful daughter, not as Toril the traitor."

"How dare you speak to my betrothed!" Prince Filip of Danheimr called. "I'll have your tongue for that insult!" His men readied their weapons but did not advance more than a stride. They looked to Olver Agnarsen, who shook his head, and the men fell back into formation.

"My father charged me with domestic rule and *justicia*," Toril declared. "We tried your brother for treason and found him guilty. In my mercy, I spared his life. How I regret my choice now, as he has poisoned your ear."

"It wasn't my ear that was poisoned, and Harold wasn't the poisoner. Still, I hope you do regret many of your choices. As the blood of Jarl Gustav and as one of the chosen leaders by our chieftain's word, I challenge you, Toril Ingrið Gustavsdotter, to a holmgang. We have heard enough of your words. Let steel speak now."

"You cannot!" Prince Filip spat. "We do not allow this barbaric tradition on Danheimr soil."

"But this isn't Danheimr soil," Einar Finsgúr called. "You haven't wed the traitor yet. So, keep your tongue behind your yellow teeth. We'll get to you soon enough."

A murmur of consent rose among the Hamarrfjord men on both sides, their gazes turning to hostile glares toward the foreign prince and his men.

"Name your champion, Toril," Rikard shouted in a tone of grim finality. "I have the right, as Olver can tell you. By the love of our people, do not let this turn into a clash of brothers where kin slays kin," he implored, quoting from the prophecy. "We can end this, here and now! Let Odin's wisdom, Thor's strength, and Loki's luck favor the hand of the righteous."

CHAPTER TWENTY-SEVEN

Downfall

BERGRÚN WATCHED THE verbal sparring match with the calm of a lone polecat crossing an open field under the eyes of circling goshawks. She'd argued against Rikard's march on Hamarrfjord, preferring a knives-in-the-dark assault, but hadn't been able to sway his opinion. The witch knew by now that the young Viking's stubborn sense of honor and duty was the metal from which he was forged. It was the reason she'd fallen for him despite her better judgment. Still, her skin tingled with unease, and her body felt taut as a bowstring. She didn't trust Toril and her ilk any farther than a corpse would walk once decapitated.

With her hands hidden in her sleeves, she let her gaze roam over the arrayed opponents, clutching the gleaming throwing knives. Prince Filip, Shield Olver, and Toril the traitor stood several feet in front of their troops. They were her first targets when the clash of words inevitably turned to steel. Would the Hamarrfjord-born Vikings fight for their jarlress and her lap dog once those two lay bleeding in the dirt? Or had Rikard's arguments already won his kinsmen over?

In that case, Bergrún needed to focus on the Danske warriors. Some carried crossbows, and all faced annihilation as retribution for the cruel treatment of thralls in the silver mine. They would fight for their lives like berserkers. The witch considered a distraction, such as conjuring a blinding light, when she heard her name spoken.

"Her name is Bergrún," Rikard said. "And she isn't my thrall any longer. She's my wife."

"Then you've fallen for her lies, cousin? I feared as much," Toril replied.

"How else would you stand here with weapons drawn, intending to have me disposed of? You marched on our home, Rikard Svensen, in the company of foreign mercenaries and condemned lawbreakers. You've committed treason. Yet still, you dare to call on honor and tradition."

"Are you unable to hear your own lies, Toril?" he shouted, anger breaking his calm demeanor. "Have you repeated them often enough so they sound like the truth in your ears?" He charged two steps forward, shaking his fists, but checked his stride with visible difficulty. "I haven't brought hostile forces onto our soil. With me are the allies our jarl, *your* father, ordered me to find. Éira is under the same threat as we are." He whirled around, pointing an accusing finger at Prince Filip. "Everywhere, Danheimr's vicious grasp seeks to conquer the people, eradicate their beliefs, and destroy their traditions. I've seen them hunting women and children like game for sport," he screamed. A ripple ran through the men as if his fury had hit them with physical force.

"No, Toril," he declared in a voice cold as ice. "I'm not merely here to seize the jarlship from you. I've come to defend our way of life from enemies abroad and within. If you search for criminals, take a glance in a looking glass!"

Cries of outrage rose above the renewed murmurs. The Danske warriors surrounded their prince, their weapons drawn. Rikard's troops reacted in kind, shouting insults. Olver turned to see most of his men yelling at the prince and his guards, their glares hostile.

"Then it shall be!" Toril called, straining to be heard. "Nothing is left of the cousin I once loved like a brother. We'll do it the old way—man against man—to the death!"

"My warriors stand ready," Prince Filip offered. "Pick whom you choose, my lady. Every last man will risk his life to answer these foul accusations! They'll defend your honor and mine!"

"How about yourself, Danske Prince?" Einar jeered. "Is your weapon too delicate for a true woman of the North?" The men's laughter and insults grew deafening.

Toril strode forward with her head held high. She stopped an arm's length from Rikard and stood ramrod straight until silence fell.

"Olver Bror Agnarsen is the First Shield of Hamarrfjord. He will fight for me!" she declared without looking at her consort. "And when you lie at my feet, bleeding into the dirt," she hissed, "will your men hold to your honor? Will they lay down their weapons?"

"I'll fight for my brother!" Harold called, stepping up to Rikard's side.

"On my word, only you have to die, dear cousin. And he!" He jerked his head toward Toril's champion and spat on the ground between them. "We'll spare the foreign princeling and his pack of dogs. There's a nice shed in the mines waiting for new dwellers."

"What about her?" Olver barked, whipping his head toward Bergrún. He marched up to Harold as if he would strike. The other man didn't flinch. Both stood with their chests out, sizing each other up. "Your witch isn't bound by honor like men, like our people, like a *human!*" Olver declared, shifting his gaze to Rikard. "She has murdered and lied since you first brought her to our shores. Who'll stop her from calling lightning out of the blue sky or have the earth shake at the right moment? I demand a fight of man against man without any unnatural interference!"

Bergrún sauntered up to Rikard's other side, a wicked smile on her lips. Her stride was measured, her gaze fixed on Toril's champion. She flexed her fingers, letting the hitherto concealed blades catch the sunlight.

"I'll be as trustworthy as your beloved mistress," she mocked. "At this moment, do you truly believe anything anyone says still has any consequence? I'd say let the runes fall as they will. Who stands last decides their meaning."

"No, Bergrún." Rikard seized her by the arm to hold her back. "We need to do this the right way, the old way, or we aren't better than them." His gaze found hers, and his striking blue eyes reflected the bright midday sun. She shook her head and inhaled a deep breath to quell her irritation.

Turning back to Toril's champion, Rikard added, "I agree to your demand, Olver Agnarsen. My wife and I will stay out of this. We'll remain secluded until Odin's judgment has been proclaimed." Bergrún gasped, clenching her fists, and Toril smiled, until he spoke again. "But only if Toril and her prince join us," he said. "His Danske men and my Éiran fighters shall stand guard, letting no one enter or leave." Placing his hand on his sword, Rikard concluded, "These are my conditions. Accept or die where you stand!"

* * *

"LET'S HAVE NO hollow speeches and pathetic rituals," Harold called half an hour later, feeling the weight and balance of the axe in his hands. "I've waited for this a long time, Olver Agnarsen. I don't want unnecessary foreplay to spoil my elation." He'd hefted a large ironbound shield of solid oak. No paint covered the surface, no runes decorated the rim. This was a tool for war, blunt and sturdy like the man who carried it.

"Then come at me, if you're done drooling!" Olver shot back. "The village has suffered the stench of your breath long enough." He carried a lighter shield of linden wood and a broadsword.

No one had built an island of black sand this time, nor did a wall of shields form a boundary. They squared off on a level meadow by the sea, where the wedding festivities were to happen this evening. On the western side, a twelve-foot cliff dropped to a rocky beach below. A large tent constructed from sail canvas marked the eastern boundary. Intended as a makeshift god-house to accommodate the ceremony of vows and union, it now served as the confinement area for Rikard and Toril with their foreign forces. The Hamarrfjord Vikings stood to the north and the south, separated by their allegiance to each of the fighters.

Harold and Olver stepped toward the center of the meadow from opposite sides. Circling each other like wolves, each yearned to rip out the other's throat. Olver moved with slow precision. Placing each step with deliberate care, he showed the grace of a man who'd shed blood, sweat, and tears in the practice pit for his skill. He held his sword tip low and his shield high to protect his chin and throat. His eyes never left his opponent, probing for the flaw, the single opening that would end the fight.

Harold was his opposite. He stood crouched like a caged beast, set loose upon its tormentor. His shield hung loose, an inch over the grass, and he swung his axe left and right like a pendulum. A low growl rumbled in his chest. He'd wrapped the crossbow wounds on his left leg, but still favored his right side, an almost imperceptible imbalance.

Harold let out a war cry and swiped his blade in a wide arc. Born from reflex, Olver stepped back, though more than six strides still separated the men, causing Harold to bellow a booming laugh. He turned his back on his foe and, raising his weapons high, he stoked the men's cheers.

Then, without warning, the fight began. Harold charged in a blur of pent-up fury. Bringing his axe down in a brutal, overhand chop, he aimed to split his opponent from crown to groin. Olver met the assault with the iron boss of his shield. The impact echoed like a smith's hammer across the silent square. The force of the blow sent a shudder up Olver's arm, demonstrating the raw power still coiled in Harold's weakened frame.

Harold didn't relent. He became a whirlwind, forcing Olver back with a furious barrage of axe blows and shield punches. His fight was a spectacle of aggression, honed by a raider's mindset. Each swing was a roar of intimidation, each block a scream of defiance. Dropping the shield, he grabbed his axe in both hands. The following blow cracked Olver's shield, splintered wood, and sent chips flying everywhere. The crowd gasped.

Harold pressed his advantage, overcommitting to a sideways swing meant to sever his opponent's head. For a fraction of a second, his full weight rested on his wounded leg. The muscles screamed in protest, and he faltered, his momentum lost in a spasm of agony.

That was the only opening Olver needed. His foot shot forth, kicking Harold's legs out from under him. A lunge followed, missing the heart but cutting a gash across his opponent's chest. Harold screamed in rage and agony. He rolled, avoiding another lunge. Then he punched with his left, finding Olver's jaw in a glancing blow.

Olver absorbed the force, rolled over his shoulder, and sprang to his feet, heartbeats later. Harold got up with much more effort. Blood stained his ripped tunic, and his body trembled. In an uncharacteristic attempt at showmanship, Olver swiped his sword through the air, letting the blade sing.

"Shall we?" he taunted, beckoning with his left hand.

* * *

Toril and Rikard sat at opposite ends of the high table, as far apart as the tent permitted. Flower wreaths and colorful buntings decorated the inside, creating an unreal contrast to the deadly fight mere feet away. Rikard felt like a child who, while fleeing from a pack of bloodthirsty wolves, had stumbled into Álfheimr to dine with the queen of the elves. Bergrún sat beside him, stiff as a steel dagger, exchanging stares with Toril that held all the warmth of an arctic snow blizzard. The prince fidgeted. His face shone beetroot-red, and sweat glistened on his forehead.

The air was thick with the sweat of two dozen armed guards, their faces grim. Rikard's Éiran fighters stood interspersed with the men from Danheimr. Standing at attention, only their eyes twitched toward the muffled grunts and shouts from the duel outside. So Svartálfaheimr, the realm of dark elves and evil dwarves, was a more apt description.

"Is that your White Christ," Bergrún asked, "in whose name you burn villages and abduct children?" She nodded toward the four-foot crucifix on a smaller table at the tent's head. Her tone was light, conversational, almost masking her tension. "He's smaller than I thought, and he looks ill."

"How dare you!" the prince spluttered. "I will not stand for this!"

"Apparently not," she mocked, "seeing that you're seated."

He was about to rise to her provocation, but Toril clamped her hand on his, giving him a tiny shake of her head.

"What do you kill for? Bergrún is it?" Toril asked. "Don't tell me you weep at night over innocent souls lost."

"I don't, because I don't hide behind a holy pretense. I am what I am. I've chosen my fate and I live up to it."

"Oh? But how does being a loving wife fit into your choice? I understood you better when you were riding one brother one night and the other the next."

Bergrún placed her hands flat onto the table, and the wood vibrated as the fire in her eyes ignited. Rikard laid his hand gently on hers.

"She was a thrall back then," he clarified, "using her body like a weapon to survive. But at least, she used her own and didn't buy a plaything for her lap dog to keep the leash hidden." Toril recoiled as if he'd slapped her across the face. "Anyone in the mood for refreshments?" he asked, rising. "It's getting quite hot in here."

He walked to the cask of ale and poured a mug, turning his back to the room. His hand trembled, and he jerked when a scream pierced the air that might have been his brother's.

* * *

HAROLD SWAYED. HE swiped blood from his eyes and shook his head to dispel the dizziness. More blood spurted from his broken nose. The cuts on his arms and legs burned in a constant blaze. He'd picked up his shield. The heft of his axe felt slippery in his tiring hand. Across from him, Olver's grin widened. He stood tall, his chest out. With his shield and sword hanging loose at his side, he proclaimed to the world that the fight was over. Harold was no longer a threat. He'd become a mouse with twisted legs, dancing for the amusement of a malicious cat.

The fight had moved away from the tent. Olver had herded his foe toward the cliff and the drop beyond. The villagers had followed. Forgetting their division, they formed a half moon, shoulder to shoulder, jostling to witness the duel's looming conclusion. They'd winced and groaned with every fresh wound Shield Olver's deliberate attacks left on Harold's bruised body.

Panting for air, Harold locked eyes with his executioner. Then his lips pulled into a mad grin, displaying bloodied gums. He screamed like a berserker and rushed his opponent in a hobbling gait. His left arm swung in an arc, and he let go of the leather strap, sending his shield flying. It hit Olver's raised shield a heartbeat later with a resounding crack. By then,

Harold had closed the distance. His axe knocked the sword from Olver's hand, his left fist connected with the stunned Viking's face, and the sheer momentum brought both men to the ground.

Harold landed on top, punching with all he had left. When Olver seized his hands, the raging fighter headbutted his foe. Harold snarled, and Olver groaned. They rolled over the uneven ground like feral dogs.

Now, Olver was on top. They'd come within mere feet of the rim. He had his left arm on Harold's throat and pressed down with all his weight. Harold couldn't push him off. He couldn't breathe. In a desperate move, he let go of the strangling arm and poked his thumb into his opponent's eye. Olver jerked back, and Harold pushed. Holding each other in a deadly embrace, they rolled over the edge and crashed onto the beach below.

* * *

Bergrún had calmed down. She'd bottled her rage up for the moment, storing it behind a wall of ice. Her senses grew heightened to painful levels. Every fleeting shadow, every shifting foot, every tense breath registered. Her eyes darted between Rikard and Toril. No one had taken his offer of refreshment, yet he remained standing in the corner, the mug of ale in his hand forgotten.

Her mind replayed the confrontation, marveling at the viciousness of the insults wrapped in the silken sheet of civility. She always knew Toril to be a conniving snake. But Rikard surprised her. He'd grown out of his naïve goodness into a man who wielded sword and tongue with equal skill. She wondered if that side of him had always been there and just needed time to ripen. Or was she to blame because of the time, the love, and the blood they'd shared?

She drummed her fingers on the table and saw Toril's eyes following the movement. What was going on in the traitor's head? Did she still believe she would outlive the day? The duel was meaningless. If Harold won, the witch would kill Toril, avenging Stina's death. The Danske princeling and his toy soldiers would pay for the violence on Éira. Bergrún knew that Harold and his men had been as cruel or worse on many raids, but right now they were on her side; they were *her* monsters while the Danskes were not.

And if Harold should lose, the witch would do precisely the same. She only needed to be quicker and deal with Rikard's honor-bound protests afterward. She reached into her core, feeling the beast inside her stir, uncoiling for the strike. Her grin widened.

That's when Toril spoke.

"What about my son?" she asked Rikard. "My Morton is still shy of his second name day. What will happen to him?" Rikard turned to Toril, and Bergrún followed his gaze, seeing the other woman's lips tremble.

"I bear him no harm," Rikard declared. "As long as I live, my little cousin will be under my protection. He's of the jarl's blood, and he'll hear of the honorable deeds of all his forebearers."

"I've named him after our home and my father, Morton Gustav Hamarrsen," she said in a quavering voice, "Not many know, but his father is..."

A deafening cheer from the outside interrupted her words. Everybody stood and turned anxious eyes toward the entrance.

* * *

MINUTES EARLIER, THE dueling Vikings had crashed onto the slope of fist-sized stones below the cliff. Olver's left hip hit the ground first with a sickening crack, but their momentum rolled them further down the incline. Both men grunted as the impact knocked the air from their lungs.

When they finally came to a rest, Olver hunched on top. Stars burst behind Harold's closed eyelids, and he spat blood, gasping for air. Olver pressed his elbow on Harold's face. His free hand fumbled to pull the dagger from his boot. Seagulls shrieked from above, chased into the sky by the fallen bodies, and the air stank of rotting kelp.

Olver managed to pull his knife free. He plunged the blade toward Harold's face, caught at the last second by the struggling man. Harold had both hands on the knife, but the blade sank closer. Olver pressed with all his weight. Again, Harold jerked his hand toward the other man's eye. This time, Olver caught the hand and slammed the arm to the side. Harold twisted and turned. His entire body was on fire, and pain blazed everywhere.

"Die! Die! Die!" Olver growled. With his teeth bared, he squeezed harder, driving the sharpened steel down to end his nemesis once and for all.

"How's little Morton?" Harold rasped, struggling to keep the blade from cutting his throat. "Does he have my eyes or just Toril's lies?" He spat the words in a venomous taunt.

The tip of the dagger had already pierced the skin when Olver froze. For a single, fatal heartbeat, his resolve wavered from the blow to his legacy. He recoiled before rage contorted his face. Pulling the knife back, he raised his arm to plunge it into his foe with raw, personal fury.

Harold seized his only chance. His left hand closed around a fist-sized rock. He smacked it against Olver's temple. The weight lifted as the struck man keeled over. Again and again, Harold pounded flesh with stone, finding neck, shoulder, ear, and forehead. When his opponent lay dazed, Harold seized a larger rock and shattered the bones in Olver's right arm. The man screamed, convulsing in agony.

Harold pushed himself to all fours. He'd spotted the fallen sword farther up the incline. Struggling to stay conscious, he crawled toward the weapon. When he returned, panting, Olver hunched on his knees, clutching his mangled arm to his chest.

"I yield," he gasped. A grimace of pain twisted his face. Each ragged breath sent a fresh wave of agony from his broken ribs. His dagger stuck out between the rocks, three feet away, unreachable. Crimson spilled from his torn-off eyebrow, and he licked his lips, his gaze lowered to the blood-drenched boots of his opponent.

"I can't hear you," Harold taunted, looking up to the men atop the cliff.

"I yield!" Olver screamed. He'd lost, and the humiliation cut deeper than Harold's blade.

"I fight for my brother," Harold shouted for everyone to hear. "To defend his honor!" He stood bent over, his left hand clutching the knee of his injured leg to hold him upright. Sweat and blood ran down his face, stinging his eyes. It dripped into the sand in a steady flow. His sword tip wavered, hovering inches from his kneeling opponent's throat.

"But I'm not my brother," he said, his voice becoming a low growl stripped of all performance. These words were for Olver alone. "My friends call me many things. My enemies call me worse. But honorable isn't among them." He barked a laugh, devoid of any mirth, his gaze on the heavens, before bellowing, "See you in Hel, Olver Agnarsen!"

Harold raised his sword over his left shoulder. Swaying, he waited until the beaten man lifted his gaze. Their eyes met, neither showing pleading nor mercy, only acceptance of what was inevitable. With a roar of fury and vengeance that carried pain, triumph, and dismay, Harold swung, taking his enemy's head off.

* * *

The cheers grew louder. Dozens of feet stomped toward the tent. Bergrún readied her throwing knives when their voices became discernible.

"Hail, Harold Svensen! Hail, Jarl Rikard!" shouted the men, followed by "Death to Danheimr! Death to Toril!"

The Finsgúr boys ripped the tent entrance open. Harold stood there. Leaning on Einar, he looked like Hela's favorite demon. Blood was everywhere. His face was smashed to a pulp. He gasped for air, displaying missing teeth. But his eyes burned with the vindication of victory. He swung his right arm, tossing an object. Olver's severed head landed in the dirt before Toril's feet.

"NOOOO!" Her scream of denial cut through the roars of triumph like an axe through an apple. She sank to her knees, seizing her consort's face in her hands before recoiling immediately.

"Kill them!" Prince Filip yelled. "Kill them all!" He pulled his ornamental dagger and rushed Harold like a rabid badger.

The tent exploded into violence. All pretense of honor evaporated, replaced by merciless butchery. The Danske guards attacked the Éiran, killing many in a heartbeat. Lulled by the sense of victory, Rikard's allies had lowered their guard. They were brave men and women, good friends, but inexperienced soldiers.

Einar pulled Harold back, and his sons stepped forth to confront the prince. He'd sliced Envar across the cheek before Eskil buried his dagger in the plump man's gut. By then, more Danske warriors attacked Harold's group. Bergrún had incapacitated several with her knives, but couldn't make out friend from foe in the throng.

"Save my brother!" Rikard shouted, dueling a Danske guard. She didn't dare until Rikard scored a decisive blow. The witch rushed in, blowing fighters off their feet. Horns blew. The sound, deafening in the tent, found its echo moments later in the village and up the hill at Rikard's mansion. More Danske warriors sprang from their hiding places.

"We need to..." Bergrún shouted, turning. She froze. She did not understand what she saw. Rikard was gone. In his place by the ale barrel stood Cormac with his shield raised and the spear lowered in a defensive position. Saoirse knelt beside him, bent over. And between them lay...

"RIKARD!" The witch's scream was nothing of this world. It pierced eardrums, ripped the tent cloth to shreds, and threw the people to the floor like a longship carving through a field of reeds. "RIKARD!" she screamed again, higher this time, tearing at the very fabric of reality.

Vaulting over the pile of fallen bodies, she rushed to his side, blasting the Éirans out of her way. He lay on his back, gasping for air. She sought his eyes and saw him blinking moisture away. He was trying to be brave.

Foolish boy!

Then her eyes fell upon the crossbow bolt protruding from his chest.

CHAPTER TWENTY-EIGHT

Pyre

BERGRÚN KNELT BESIDE Rikard, unable to move. She didn't know what to do. This couldn't be happening. For long heartbeats, she sat frozen while the world around her erupted in violence. Warriors yelled, and weapons clashed. Wounded men groaned, and shields burst. Nothing made sense, nothing mattered, except for the crimson stain on his tunic growing inexorably larger.

She ripped the cloth open, her hands shaking. The bolt had punctured his lung, causing a sickly wet gurgle to accompany every labored breath. Dark blood spilled from his lips. The shot couldn't have missed his heart by more than a hair's breadth. She needed to do something, anything.

Placing her hands on his soaked skin, she closed her eyes, letting the blood pool between her fingers. No spell came to her aid; no magic seemed to work. Her mind was blank, overwhelmed by the deafening ringing in her ears.

With panic rising, she grabbed the blood-slicked shaft, straining to pull it free. Rikard spasmed in agony. Her hand slipped. The barbed arrowhead remained stuck between his ribs. She couldn't pull it out. She couldn't! It wouldn't come free. She opened her eyes, searching his face for the key to salvation. But her vision blurred as tears gushed forth in a flood.

And then she was back in Fårosünd on the night of the raid. She lay in the dirt, helpless and spent. Fires burned behind her. Men screamed like beasts. A Viking rushed down the incline, his axe raised to end her cursed existence. His eyes glowed red. With his face contorted into a visage of rage, she barely recognized Rikard. She wanted to call his name, but couldn't find her lips; they wouldn't work. His blade fell.

And she sat on the cliffs, her feet dangling over the alluring abyss. Her soul had left on a tiny vessel, sailing into the west, never to return. The husk of her body shivered. The rocks called to her, and the sea beckoned. The wind urged her on, to shatter what had no purpose any longer. Behind, the village celebrated. Bonfires burned, flames shooting into the night sky, consuming life-sized scarecrows in her likeness. She jumped.

And she sat on a ship, Stina's head in her lap. The woman was dead, and her corpse cursed Bergrún's name with eyes like wheels of fire. Cold hands seized the witch's throat, squeezing. She couldn't fight, she couldn't breathe, she couldn't *be* any longer—except for the voice that had called her back from the brink over and over again.

"Take... my... hand!" Rikard wheezed. More blood spilled from his lips. She seized his fingers, clutching them to her heart, and holding on with all she had. His touch was her last grasp on sanity, the lifeline keeping her from drowning. But his hand was wet, his fingers started to slip, and she couldn't hang on.

Bergrún reached a shaking hand to wipe the crimson stream from his mouth. Forcing her thumb to move, she gently brushed over his lips. He closed his eyes and uttered a faint moan before willing a fragile smile into existence.

"Rúnie," he whispered, soft as the beat of a dragonfly's wings. His body shivered, and his eyelids twitched. But his gaze held her firm, letting her bask in the brilliant blue of a midsummer sky.

"I'm here, Rikard! I have you... I'll heal you... like on Éira, remember? Hold on, please, just a little." She tried to put confidence into her words, but her voice cracked. She couldn't draw in enough air. She needed to keep talking, to reassure him. Nothing else mattered. She was all he had left; he was all she had. "I'll find the word, the spell... I need to..."

He squeezed her hand with no more pressure than a raven's feather landing on a boulder.

"My... love," he breathed. And all air fled his lungs with the last syllable. He shuddered once. Then the pain vanished. The muscles in his face relaxed. He looked peaceful.

The shadow of his last smile still clung to his lips as the light in his eyes dimmed. His soul departed, passing by her in a final caress, gentle like a summer breeze. In that moment, she felt the fullness of his unwavering, self-less, and absolute love, before he left her behind in a world without sunlight.

* * *

HANDS SEIZED HER, pulling at her arms. Friend or foe, she didn't know, she didn't care. Her mind had collapsed, abdicating control, and her dark instincts took over. Her fingers shot forth like an eagle's talons, crushing throats and draining life with no more hesitation than grinding an ant under a booted foot.

Voices shouted, boots thumped, and weapons clashed against shields. In deadly struggle or cheers of celebration, she didn't know, she didn't care. She knelt in darkness, leagues underground, buried alive in a tunnel with only one path ahead.

She stood, cradling Rikard's body in her arms. She clutched him to her chest as if he weighed no more than a child. With unseeing eyes, she marched down the slope toward the harbor. Her stride was a jarring, unnatural gait. The ground groaned and buckled beneath her feet. With every footfall, the tremors grew more violent. Cracks ripped open, walls tumbled, roofs collapsed. Like ripples in a pond, the earth shuddered in ever-widening circles.

Her face looked hewn from granite, cold and unmoving. Vacant eyes stared ahead. Behind her, the tent erupted in purple flames. The wind picked up. Dark clouds coalesced over the village, writhing like a kraken's tentacles. Lightning split the sky, and thunder boomed, awakening a deep rumbling in the mountains beyond.

All around, the fighting had stopped, though not all the murdering had been accomplished. Blood-splattered men parted before her, like herring fleeing the shadow of a shark. Some, who stood too close, bent over in agony, clutching their guts as waves of menace radiated from her. Others covered their ears, trying to shield against the unnatural keening of damned souls that filled the air.

She placed one foot in front of the other, stepping over discarded weapons and fallen bodies alike, until she reached the harbor. A small boat rocked on the swelling waves. A faering like the one in which an elated couple had crossed the Inglan Sea after surviving a deadly chase. But that had happened eons ago, in another life, in another world.

With shaking arms, Bergrún placed Rikard into the boat. Her chest convulsed in a desperate fight to breathe, and the tremors grew worse. A fissure tore open in the valley of the hot springs, wrenching the brittle crust, and the earth's angry fire bubbled up. A radiant stream of molten lava oozed down the mountain slope. Sending flames and black smoke into the air, it devoured everything in its path.

The witch straightened Rikard's ripped tunic. The bleeding had stopped, leaving an ugly pool of darkness on his chest. That wouldn't do. Stepping back onto the field of death, she seized the cape of a fallen man. Then, she collected a spear, a shield, and a sword. People fled the village in panic. They rushed toward the harbor, but veered past it, not daring to approach. They found themselves caught between Hel's fire behind and Hela's demon in front.

More fissures rent the mountainsides open. The first fingers of the molten rocks had reached Rikard's manor, setting the outbuildings alight.

Bergrún arrayed the weapons with stoic precision: the spear to his left, the shield over his head, and the sword in his right hand. Before covering his chest with the cloak, she hacked off her raven-black hair. Gathering the strands, she placed them near his heart. She had nothing else left to give.

Time was up, the dream over. She had to let him go.

Bergrún kissed Rikard on the forehead. Her body spasmed, her vision swam, and her heart jerked in an erratic rhythm. His skin felt so warm and soft. She didn't want to move. Why couldn't she stay there, with him?

Calling on the last ounce of her fading strength, she pushed herself to her feet and launched the boat. The tiny vessel cut through the wave on a steady path, much smoother than the enraged elements should permit. Beyond the pier, the sail unfurled of its own accord.

The clouds broke, allowing one beam of sunlight to illuminate the sea. The sail bulged, the ship flew. Soon, the distance had grown to three hundred paces. The witch sank to her knees and screamed. The sound of a wrenching soul smothered all other noises, leaving a dead silence behind.

The boat ignited in brilliant flames of yellow, red, and orange, like the glow in the sky moments before the sun rose.

Even the people, fleeing for their lives, halted midstride and stood frozen for one heartbeat. They looked in awe at the dazzling spectacle ahead, until behind them, the mountaintop exploded. The island's volcano erupted, spewing barn-sized boulders into the air in a billowing cloud of poisonous gas. Rivers of glowing lava gushed from the crater, cascading toward the valley, like a flash flood during snow melt. The insatiable fires reached the village in minutes, consuming flesh, wood, and stone alike, erasing Hamarrfjord irrevocably from existence.

* * *

AS THE MORNING dawned, many hours later, Bergrún sat on a driftwood log, a dozen leagues from Hamarrfjord, her feet in the wet sand. A band of purple ringed the horizon, the sky brightening in the east. Sunrise wasn't far off. The wind had quieted, and the waves washed over the beach in an indifferent rhythm. The witch spat into the sand, her body balled into a fist.

How dare the vile Norns show me fake serenity and hollow beauty on a morning like this? Why hasn't the world ended? My world has, so why do the moon and stars and sun still traverse along their unrelenting paths?

She had no idea where she was or how she'd gotten here. Her mind had vacated her body after lighting Rikard's funeral ship. The tide of people fleeing the earth's cleansing fires must've swept her onto one of the vessels leaving the harbor. Had witless villagers rescued the demon who destroyed their home? Or had they, blinded by acrid smoke, mistaken a witch for a helpless woman? Why couldn't the wicked Norns leave their bony fingers off Bergrún, after taking everything from her?

She stared at the horizon. Beside her, a fire had burned out. She must've hunted a rabbit, skinned the animal, and grilled it on a stick without conscious thought. Rudderless, her body had fallen back into familiar patterns. Bile had risen in her throat when she came to and realized what she was doing. Her stomach heaved, retching forth emptiness. After wiping her mouth with shaking hands, she perched on the bleached treetrunk and resumed her vigil while the animal's meat charred to a cinder.

The witch closed her eyes, wishing to dissolve. The chill of the wet sand seeped into her skin, but she registered no cold. Every cell of her body should have been screaming with exhaustion after the unfathomable power she had unleashed, but all remained silent. Neither anger nor sadness stirred inside her. Emptiness occupied the hollowed-out space where a soul had once been. Had her life been nothing but a series of tragedies, inevitably leading to a grand finale of earth-shattering proportions?

"Or maybe your life's been a series of poor choices," a spiteful voice in the back of her head whispered, *"and your violent acts caused the tragedies?"*

Bergrún whirled around, her eyes wide. No one was near. No one else was speaking.

"The old witch on Heilladur, who took you in," the voice continued, *"she didn't choke to death on a chicken bone, did she? Your village didn't catch fire from a lightning strike."*

"Who's there? Who's talking?" she rasped. "Show yourself!"

"Did the stupid girls truly deserve to die for tricking you into bathing naked under the waterfall? And the blacksmith's son?" the voice asked, growing more agitated. *"He never even knew you."*

"What madness is this?" she wailed, her hands over her ears.

"*And, oh … your parents…*" the voice crooned with glee. "*They loved you, you know? Loved you right until the fire consumed them.*"

"Enough!" Bergrún shrieked. "Enough… I can't go on."

"*But you have to go on,*" the voice replied, sharp and unrelenting. "*While Death has been your lover, reaching for everyone you ever met, he's not coming for you, black witch. Never for you!*"

"I'm done! I got nothing left; I want it all to end."

"*Liar!*" the voice hissed. "*Everyone knows when you lie to yourself. Even innocent Stina knew!*" The words hurt like a rusty spike piercing her mind.

"Who are you? What do you want?" Her body shook, and her eyes stung, but no tears came.

"*What we always wanted: to go home, to avenge, to rule … and finally, to ascend.*"

"There's nothing for me there … NOTHING!" she screamed.

"*Liar!*"

"I'm not…"

"*LIAR!*"

"Leave me alone, please…"

"*Oh, but you are alone. Here in the darkness, you're all alone with your thoughts and your guilt and your pretend grief. Where are your tears, black witch? Won't you weep for Rikard's kin? His blood?*"

"Go away!"

"*Will you let his brother perish in the storm to come? The brother whom your brave, honorable, and heroic Rikard died to save?*"

"Why are you doing this to me?" she wept, her face in her hands.

"*And his cousin Toril? He fancied her when he was young, did you know that?*"

"I can't…"

"*Poor little Morton? Such a handsome baby boy. With his stubby fingers, his button eyes, and his mushroom nose. Didn't you always have a soft spot in your black heart for children?*"

"No!!! I'm dead. I'm dead… I'M DEAD!"

"*You're not!*" the voice barked. "*Rikard is. He died with a sword in his hand, making his forefathers proud—defending his people, as his mother had wished. So pull yourself together! Or his sacrifice meant nothing.*"

She recoiled as if someone had slapped her.

"*Harold is stupid. He'll lead the clan to Brótinholm, right into Danheimr's trap. Assert command and take them with you to Heilladur.*"

"Why me? I can't…"

"Because you started it. How many men died for your dream? How many villages burned for your ambition? Svartvik, Jarnholl, Skuggafjell, Fårosünd, and Hamarrfjord... How many more?"

"I never meant to..."

"Liar! You always have, and you always will. Your unholy fire will spread across the entire world unless you return home."

She cowered into a ball, unable to speak.

"Go home, Bergrún Lilith Gullveigardóttir," the voice said in a soothing tone, and the witch could've sworn to feel a gentle hand on her shoulder. *"Go home to Heilladur. Take Rikard's people with you. Lead them and fulfill your prophecy—becoming their queen without a crown."*

CHAPTER TWENTY-NINE

Queen

THE MEN HUDDLED around the campfire, exhausted, as the sun rose in the east. All conversation had died down hours ago, and many heads drooped as their owners gave in to their bone-deep weariness. Harold sat on an uneven stone, twisting the cork of his waterskin. His gaze was empty. Now and then, he blinked as the smoke from embers drifted his way. Or was it the sulfurous odors wafting on the wind that irritated his eyes? Someone coughed, and Harold turned his head toward the west. An angry red gleam tinged the indigo sky where the unabated eruption still raged.

When the earth had split open, swallowing Hamarrfjord in its fiery maw, the survivors sprinted to the harbor. Men, women, and children formed one stampeding herd. Thundering like wild horses, they forgot rank and origin. They dropped their weapons, abandoning their murderous desires, and flooded the ships moored to the pier.

Clambering over each other, they filled longboats, fishing vessels, trading knarrs, and everything that floated, pushing off in haste from the shore and the deadly inferno of the volcanic eruptions. Packed tight and close to sinking, the ships didn't chart a course but drifted along the island's southern coast, heading east with the gusting wind. They'd become refugees. And while they escaped with their lives—a fate many did not share—they felt far from elated. They took their fright and disbelief with them, seasoned with the suffocating stench of the volcano's noxious breath.

A dozen miles to the east, where a steep mountain slope formed a half-moon bay, Harold ordered his men to row the *Wave Dancer* into the sheltered waters. The shipwrights of Hamarrfjord had repaired the vessel during his weeks in the mine. Yet no one questioned his assumed command. Struggling to set the oars, the men pulled the longboat into the eddy and beached her on a bed of pebbles. Some boats followed while others drifted on. There might've been twelve in total, carrying what was left of an entire people who'd settled these shores centuries ago.

The refugees tied their ships to boulders and walked inland, where they dropped onto the grass in small groups. Some started gathering firewood, and others scouted for game, seeking distraction in mundane tasks. Harold and his men moved farther up the incline to a grove of stunted trees. Nearby was an overhang in the rocky cliff, like the remaining half of a large, circular cave, but no one dared to go near the mountain.

As soon as they'd found a place to camp for the night, Harold ordered sentries posted before letting Einar tend to his many wounds. The older man's deft hands cut away cloth, washed the deepest cuts with mead, and started sewing with grim determination.

When the men first sat down around the fire, they exchanged nervous glances. Some had coughed, as if to clear their throat. Still, no one dared to voice the questions that must've been looming in the forefront of everyone's mind: What came next? Where to go from here? Who should lead them? The battle-hardened warriors remained quiet. Keeping their thoughts close, they waited for another man to charge the wall of tense silence.

As the sun crested the horizon, a commotion sounded from the trees.

"Who goes there?" a sentry yelled. "Show yourself! No one is allowed..."

A yelp cut short his protests, followed by the thud of a body flung to the ground. A second sentry charged, crushing twigs and leaves under his stomping feet. But he, too, was tossed into the air, smacking against the trunk of an oak.

A figure stepped into the firelight. She was small, her clothes torn to shreds, her hair hacked off. She carried no weapons. Cuts and bruises covered the pale skin of her arms and shoulders. Her feet were bare, caked in mud and ash up to her knees. She stood there, rigid as a shard of obsidian, and regarded the dozen brutish men with no more trepidation than a she-wolf would exhibit finding a nest of newborn rats. Her eyes glowed red, and the men recoiled as her cold fury washed over them.

"Leave, all of you. Now!" she commanded. Her voice sounded hollow, like an echo from a bleached skull. No one moved so much as a finger. "Leave!" she shouted. The flames of the dying campfire blazed back to life, sending brilliant sparks twelve feet into the air.

The men sprang to their feet, fleeing in all directions. They stumbled over roots and rocks. Shoving each other, they scuttled to safety on hands and knees like woodlice discovered under a rock.

"Not you, Harold Svensen," she called. He hadn't moved, remaining stone-faced where he sat, his feet planted on the trampled grass. Meeting her diabolical glare, he straightened his spine, pulled his shoulders back, and cracked his knuckles.

"And neither you, Einar Finsgúr," she added. The older man had moved. He crouched, angled toward the darkness beyond, but did not leap from the circle of firelight.

"We'll sail for Heilladur," the witch declared. "You'll take command and organize your people. Warships must leave first to claim a foothold. Then the women and children should follow a few days later. Land on the northern shore, in Hagndal. From there..."

"Hold on, witch!" he called in a low growl, "Not quite so fast."

"Apologies," she barked, taking a step closer. The flames sputtered. "Is your head still muddled from the pummeling you've received? He has marked my every word," she hissed, pointing to Einar. Her nails were ripped, her skin rubbed raw, and specks of blood covered her skin. "He'll repeat my commands once the sea breeze has cleared the haze from your mind. Now get going!"

"And if I don't?" he asked, daring her. "You have no ships, no men."

The stone under him cracked, splitting in half, and he fell back with a yell. She strode up to him, straight through the flames that parted under her feet. Bending over him, she spat in his face.

"You're nothing, Harold Fisk Svensen!" she snarled. "You're a pale shadow of your father; you've been bested at every turn of your miserable life by your cousin, and you don't even breathe the same air as your brother did. I don't need you! Dozens of men are worth more than you. I'd squash you here and now if it wouldn't amuse me so much to see you squirm."

She grabbed him by the shirt and pulled the tall warrior to his feet.

"Let me make this simple, so your ratbrain can follow. You'll do as I say, or there will be pain without end." She pushed her arm out, and he flew backward, crashing into a bramble thicket.

* * *

HOURS LATER, THE sun stood low in the sky. Bergrún had returned to her driftwood log. Across the bay, busy ants scurried between the ships and the makeshift camps. Indistinct voices shouted brisk orders, engaged in agitated arguments, or called for loved ones with palpable desperation. The witch felt her unease rising. She dreaded the thought of interacting with these people, of re-engaging with the living. But even more, she feared the return of the voice.

Footsteps behind her. Sand squelched under a careful tread. She whirled around, ready to strike.

"It's me," Einar Finsgúr called, his hands raised. "I'm unarmed and alone. I want to talk."

"Are your ears worse than I thought, old man?" she growled. " I've told your master all he needs to know!"

"Harold is an idiot," he replied, stepping closer while holding her gaze. "I like to drink with him, I like to fight beside him, and I like to laugh when the bards make fun of him. He's many things, but he isn't my master."

"So you're here to throw him before the wolves?"

"Aren't we there already? You've bared your teeth and shown your fangs. Not even an idiot like Harold will forget that in a heartbeat."

"Then what's left to talk about?"

"Harold," he replied, letting the one word hang in the air until her eyes narrowed and the red gleam in their depth grew brighter. "Forgive my boldness, but you mistake the axe for the woodsman. He is a tool, and a blunt one at that. But I know how to aim him. Your powers are incomprehensible. But still, you'll need a fleet and someone to row."

He dragged another log of driftwood close and sat across from her without invitation. His perch was smaller than hers, and he let out a groan, lowering his gaunt frame. She hissed, and he dropped his act.

"What do you want?" she asked, her voice sharp like the crack of a whip.

"Funny. Too few people ever asked that. Harold never has, but I think it's the most important..."

She hissed again, sounding more wolf than woman.

"Frankly? I want to live, and if possible, somewhat better than I have in the last few weeks in the mine. I'm forty, and being the general of a conquering army, ruling over lush lands with soft beds and softer women, that sounds like heaven to me."

"I can send you to the afterlife right now!"

"If you couldn't, I wouldn't be here groveling, would I? You're like that volcano, a force of nature that no one can stop. People run, screaming with fear when you approach. But you can only chase them away. Herding them toward something, that's much harder."

"So, you're a shepherd? Shall I become your sheepdog?"

"That wouldn't work, given the whole wolf thing," he smiled, daring her to indulge in his humor. In response, her fingers convulsed, becoming claws. He gasped, doubling over in pain as her searing anger twisted his guts.

"Forgive me," he wheezed.

Her fingers relaxed, letting him gasp for air. His body shivered.

"If you are the goddess of darkness, let me be your prophet," he rasped after steadying himself. "I can persuade people to do what you want by convincing them of a greater goal. We must give them hope of a glorious destiny. Perhaps with a prophecy?" he hedged. His gaze became shrewd, and he tilted his head, giving her a strained smile.

"I don't trust you!" she declared, rising to her feet. "I don't care for your dreams and hopes any more than the waves care for the sand."

He, too, stood. Straightening his tunic, he wilted under her glare. His eyelids twitched, and his muscles vibrated with tension, like a convict awaiting judgment after his final plea.

"But if your plan works," she amended with a smile more vicious than a knife in the back. "I've never been much of a sculptor, but I hear some grow quite fond of their favorite tool."

"We need at least three days," he croaked, "to gather provisions, organize the raiding parties, and ready the fleet. We..."

She raised her hand, stopping him mid-sentence.

"Make it happen, old man! Don't bore me with details. And send your youngest to me. Erik, is it? He'll be my... page boy."

"Of course, Mistress Bergrún, of course!" He bowed and left, taking five strides before daring to breathe.

* * *

THE LATCH RATTLED, but the wooden bar remained stuck—the warped boards refusing to relinquish their hold. Cursing and grunting reached Toril's ears before a forceful kick shook the frame. Another kick and the door creaked open, letting the gray light of an overcast sky seep into the tiny shed. Toril crouched in one corner. Huddled into a ball, she'd tried to preserve her body heat. Mud caked her bare legs, and straw clung to her soiled underdress. Wearily, she raised her head to regard the figure standing in the doorframe.

"The men left three days ago," Bergrún said in a voice as sweet as honey. "Why don't you step out? No need for you to hide in here any longer. My ship leaves on the midday tide. I'd like you to join me. We'll have a week at sea in the best of winds. Good to have a female companion among these brutish men."

Toril lowered her gaze and rose to her feet, her muscles stiff. Her right cheek still throbbed where Harold had backhanded her. Without a word, she shuffled toward Bergrún.

"He got you good," the witch chuckled as the light touched Toril's face. "Count yourself lucky. There was a lot of killing going on in that tent. Perhaps his blow even saved you, since it sent you sprawling under the table. If I had seen you there..." she left the threat hanging open.

Toril remained quiet, waiting for Bergrún to lead the way. The witch looked her up and down, sniffing in disgust.

"You will wash before you come aboard my ship—your clothes, your hair, and your body. I can't have a filth-covered scarecrow share my cabin, can I?"

"Why?" Toril asked, anger flaring in her eyes.

"Because you stink!"

"Then kill me and be done with it, witch!"

"Oh no," Bergrún chuckled like a vulture finding the rabbit still twitching. "That wouldn't do at all. After all you've done? You deserve more than death!" Her voice dropped to ice, and her face lost all mock levity. "You've taken from me the only thing that ever mattered. I'll ensure you have a long and miserable life. And I'll be there with you every minute, reminding you."

Toril recoiled. She sank to her knees, vomiting as the witch's fury tore into her guts.

"I've a task for you," Bergrún declared, returning to her forced civility. "Your noble blood, not that it is very apparent at this moment, gave me the idea. You'll marry Harold."

"What?" Toril gasped. Hunched on all fours, she stared at the witch, her eyes wide with shock.

"Harold. Remember him? The cousin whom you fooled and thwarted all your life. Whom you fancied and despised. Whom you sent to die in the mine, and whom you let father a child on you. That Harold."

"I'll never!" Toril spat.

"Oh, but you will, believe me. It would be a true pity if some tragedy befell poor little Morton."

"You wouldn't," Toril gasped.

"I wouldn't?" Bergrún screamed, and the earth under her feet began to tremble. "I'd butcher him before your eyes, and I still hadn't paid you back in kind! I would bite off his little fingers one by one if I thought that would hurt you most."

She jabbed her fist forward, and a blast of air hit Toril in her midriff, sending her flying. The woman crashed against the back wall of the shed, cracking boards and perhaps bones. Bergrún advanced, seized Toril by her tattered undershirt, and shook her like a rag doll.

"There's nothing I wouldn't do, Toril Gustavsdotter, not anymore. You'd better remember that!" The witch let go, and the stunned woman collapsed into a heap, groaning. "Get up," Bergrún barked. "We have work to do."

The witch whirled on the spot and stomped from the shed. Two frightened warriors stood by a brazier, stoking the flames. With cloth-wrapped hands, they poked metal tools into the embers. Sparks flew, and the men shielded their eyes.

When Toril was too slow to get up, Bergrún growled in frustration. She stepped back in and dragged the former mistress of Hamarrfjord out by her hair. The woman screamed until the witch let her fall into the dirt.

Bergrún walked across the square and seated herself on a butcher's block, straining to slow her aggravated breathing before speaking again. "Your son is safe as long as you do as I say," she declared. "He's still innocent, and I don't harm children unless I have to."

Toril pushed herself to her knees. She looked to her tormentor, the tiniest flicker of hope in her eyes.

"Get up, woman, for Hela's sake!" the witch barked. "You're the chieftain's daughter. Your sniveling disgusts me." A cold wind swept across the square, swirling ash and dust around her seat.

Toril got to her feet, wincing. She stood rigid, straightening her hair over her shoulders and brushing hay off her soiled garment. She raised her chin. Her lips trembled, but her gaze fixed on her opponent.

"Harold will be king, then? King of the fabled lands to the north?" she asked, her voice still winded from the beating. "But a king in name only under your rule?"

"Not unlike Olver was to rule under your thumb," the witch chuckled.

"Then why make him marry me? I sentenced him to death. He wanted to kill me!"

"But that was then. Now we're building a new nation. You'll be queen and wear a crown, and the people will cheer. Isn't that what you always wanted? Isn't that your precious prophecy?"

"Only, I won't be queen. You will!"

"The Norns can be cruel," Bergrún mused in a return to her earlier act of civility. "I've seen my share of their foul weaving, believe me!"

"Why gamble? Who'll stop me from spreading rumors? Will you watch me all the time?"

"Oh, Toril, dearest, how I admire that tongue of yours. Your courage and wit, even in desperate moments like this... Your sharp tongue has always been your deadliest weapon." The witch stood and waved to the men. "Hence, regretfully, I'll have to ask these fine men to tear it out with hot pincers. My wedding gift, dear Toril, you're welcome."

Five years later

THE YOUNG MAN pushed the door open and barged in. His chest heaved from the hasty climb up the winding stairs, and a flush colored his cheeks. He stood in the door, his nostrils flaring, and held on to the latch with a shaking hand.

"He's dead," he exclaimed, flinching at the loudness of his own words.

"Who is?" Bergrún asked. She sat with her back to the door at the small table with the looking glass. Her raven-black hair lay coiled in an intricate pattern around her head, like a crown, and she wore a silken nightshirt, leaving her neck and her slender shoulders bare. Her pale skin seemed to glow in the soft candlelight. She regarded his reflection, her head tilted, and a half-smile played on her lips. Her onyx eyes were wide with innocent curiosity.

"The prince," he wheezed, catching his breath. "He's dead, and it's my fault!"

"Oh, him... But I knew that, Erik. I was there, remember? We gave his body to the sea this afternoon. Weren't you among the squires to ignite his ship with flaming arrows? That was your duty; you didn't kill him."

"That's not what I mean!"

"Then what troubles you?" She turned. Her garment was low-cut, revealing a generous expanse of her smooth skin. A silver amulet etched with mystic runes rested on her bosom. "Please, close the door," she said in her melodic voice. "Will you sit with me?"

"No," he blurted, shocked by the idea. "The heir is dead, and I'm to blame."

"Did King Harold blame you?" She moved to the bed, patting the space beside her. Despite his protest, he closed the door and walked to sit at her side.

"The king is in his cups again," he explained, his head hanging. "He's been drinking for days, ever since Prince Morton's death."

"Then why do you blame yourself?"

"Because I led the prince to the kitchen that day. You told me to!" He looked at her, his eyelids twitching.

"Me?" she asked with a note of surprise. "Oh, yes, you're right; I remember. I thought it wise for the young prince to meet the castle's staff, and for them to see him. It behooves a future ruler to understand how the many who serve the few live their lives."

"But I was with him when he died. The queen had charged me to look out for Prince Morton."

"Queen Toril charged you herself?"

"No, of course not! *She* didn't talk to me. One of her ladies did." He looked at her seeking reassurance. She smiled and laid her hand on his knee. "The prince wanted to try one of the pastries. The cooks were preparing trays of pocket pies with nuts and currants for the Midwinter celebration, and he said he'd never had one of those." Erik's words gushed forth in a flood. "Who was I to deny him? He was the crown prince, after all."

"Of course."

"But then he started coughing. He choked and spat. He couldn't breathe. His face turned blue, and then... and then he died!" Erik's muffled scream bounced from the bare walls.

Bergrún placed her arm around his shoulder and pulled him to her chest as if he were a boy of five winters and not a tall youth of fifteen.

"Listen, Erik. Prince Morton's death was a tragic accident. How unlucky that I was away and couldn't help." She stroked the young man's hair. "As soon as I returned, I examined his body. I didn't find poison, not in the usual sense of that word." She paused, and he raised his gaze. "It seemed that the nuts he ate unbalanced his humors. No one could've known."

"If no one knew, then why had the prince never eaten one of those pastries before?" Erik sat up straight, and she let her arm slide off his shoulder. "The cooks bake batches of them every year for yuletide."

"You're very bright, Erik," she whispered. "That's how you wooed me." Her cold hand slipped under his tunic, coming to rest at the small of his back.

"I... You did... I mean, it was you who..."

Her brows furrowed, and her eyes bore into him—pools of darkness with red sparks flickering in their depths.

"I remember you coming on to me while I was bathing," she breathed.

"That was *my* swimming hole," he protested with the indignation of a much younger boy.

"Yours?" she laughed. "Erik, your father is the duke of this province, and not even he can lay claim to the land. Everything belongs to our king."

"You know what I mean."

"What *I* know is that I was in the water, alone, unclothed, and defenseless, facing a strong Viking without the slightest chance to protect my virtue."

"You always do that. You look at me like that, and you use words I don't know, and you make me... You make me all fuzzy."

"Do you want to lie down?"

"No! Hela's tits... I'm sorry, Bergrún," he added, blushing. "But the King's firstborn son is dead. What'll happen to the king? To the land? To us?"

"King Harold has a daughter, has he not? And he can sire more children. He's still young—not as young as you, of course, but in his best years. Perhaps it was an act of fate that struck our King. Perhaps he grew too arrogant, saw himself as invincible, and challenged powers that were beyond his reach. This tragedy will make him become a better man, who accepts his place in this world and listens to those who have the realm's best interest in mind."

"How do you know such things of fate and powers?"

"I've learned through pain and sorrow, believe me." Her voice grew cold as midwinter frost, and her face became a mask of stone. "I've seen the Norns for who they are, felt their bony fingers trap me in their vile patterns again and again." Her words became a snarl, and her eyes glowed red. He recoiled. The bedframe vibrated, and a whirlwind rose, causing the candlelight to flicker.

Squeezing her eyes shut, she bowed her head and rested her face on her steepled fingers. Shivers ran through her body. For several tense heartbeats, she sat there, unable to speak. When the storm subsided, she looked at him with moisture pooling in her eyes. She swiped the tears away with the back of her hand.

"Erik," she said, forcing her voice to sound calm and even. "You will be the duke one day."

"I won't," he sulked. "Eskil is older than I."

"No one can know the path ahead with certainty. But I know, deep in my... soul, that you will become duke. Duke Erik Gunner Finsgúr—how does that sound?" He gave her a fleeting smile before the intensity of her gaze raised goosebumps on his arms.

"Do not make the mistake your uncle made," she said. "Do not challenge what ought not to be challenged. Listen to my counsel, and stay true to your word. Then all will be fine. Or as the locals say: *Tá gach rud go maith.*"

THE END

Author's Note

HELLO EVERYONE, AXEL here. I want to thank you for joining me on this adventure, which, underneath the clash of steel and the crackle of magic, is a journey into the human soul. Haven't we all felt out of place at times—unheard, unseen, yearning for appreciation and a chance to grow? We might not have resorted to the drastic measures of my protagonists—which is a good thing. But who hasn't felt a tinge of their anger about an unfair world and the limited horizons that fate granted?

I've always been fascinated with the space between good and evil, the patch of foggy marshes where you're alone with your instincts, and where each step bears the danger of sinking deeper into darkness. Yet, one doesn't reach safe ground unless one takes the next step. How does one find one's own way when concepts like good or evil, right or wrong, and true or false are so easily manipulated by societal trends and political pressures?

"Truth is what the powerful declare it to be," says Bergrún to Stina early in my story. I grew up in communist East Germany, a kind of dictatorship-light, where I've experienced how truth could be bent and facts twisted to suit propaganda. While the crumbling houses and polluted environment around us showed every possible shade of gray, the official mindset was strictly black and white. *"If you're not with us, you're against us,"* was the hammer that squashed any thought daring to challenge the dominant ideology. Sounds familiar?

Being an impatient teenager at the time, I felt, like Bergrún, that my fate was predetermined and that I, as an individual with dreams and ambitions, was nothing but a thread to be woven into the red fabric. Often I stood at the sea, watching ships leave for Scandinavia—far lands that were out of reach, and I wondered if there was a better world beyond the horizon.

So, is Bergrún a freedom fighter, a revolutionary, my alter ego? No. She is a fictional character who answers the cruelty of the world with her own cruelty. While I can relate to her anger issues, I don't see her as a shining role model. And that's the entire point of my story. She is a deeply flawed human being who often makes poor decisions. She has the power for villainous deeds and the compassion for acts of selfless kindness. In short, she has a choice.

Some fictional heroes are inherently good, like Superman and Wonder Woman. I personally find those characters less appealing to write. Even the unlikely heroes who stumble through their adventures and do good from the purity of their hearts, like Bilbo Baggins and Harry Potter, I've encountered too often.

Instead, I like to explore the question of limited choices and whether there can be redemption for someone whom the world labels as evil. In my first novel, *Mae – Death's Youngest Daughter*, a young woman became a black witch against her will. All her life, she struggled to fight her curse and do good, only to succumb to her dark urges. In *Kingmaker*, Bergrún is the flip side of that coin. She chose her destiny and uses every ounce of her abilities, including her dark powers, without apology. Driven by her ambition, she marches with her chin up and her shoulders squared. Yet, from time to time, she succumbs to the goodness in her marred soul, performing heroic deeds at steep personal costs—not unlike Severus Snape and Sandor Clegane.

I must admit that I never planned for my story to unfold this way. I had a much darker outline in mind when I started writing. But the more I got to know Bergrún and Rikard, the more I realized they were in charge of their fates (despite Bergrún's constant complaining about the Norns). As I observed them fighting their way through a forest of obstacles, I agonized with them about why they still cared. Making them human without the "Super," I could let them be tender one moment, bitter the next, and then silly a while later. Sometimes, I couldn't write as fast as their banter and conflicts played out in my mind. They made mistakes, as all humans do, and forgave each other, as too few can. In that sense, they're good people.

So there it is: I did my best, pouring my heart and soul into the story, and I hope you've enjoyed reading my novel as much as I enjoyed writing it. There will be (at least) one more installment in the *Heilladur Saga*, set roughly twenty years after the events of Mae. We'll reconnect with some familiar characters and meet plenty of new ones. Stay tuned for more twists and turns. And I hope the characters will stay with you long after the story ends, as they do for me.

For Blood and Glory, for Kin and Jarl
Kruse, Axel (author@project-witchcraft.com)

HEILLAÐUR
HAGNDAL
SVARTVIK
BRÓTINHOLM
FÁROSÜND
TRONDBORG
NORSKVEGN
ABERDEENIUM
HRAFNEY
HAMARRFJORD
EASTEND
INGLANDIA
IARNTANN ISLANDS
DÚNMUIR
STARVINGER
ÉIRA
GLEANN'AN
EARRAIGH
ÅALBRUG
DANHEIMR
FRIESEN
GÖTALAND
LINDVIK
GAUL

People & Places

PEOPLE & GODS

ABBY LYNN SVENSDOTTER: The older sister of Harold and Rikard, wife to Einar Finsgúr, died during Fårosünds raid one year before the story.

AGNETHA LUNDGREN: The alias used by Bergrún. She claims to be a healer from Götaland, hiding her true identity as a black witch from Heilladur.

ALDRED, BROTHER: A supposed Christian friar who arrives in Hamarr-fjord with Brother Eadmund, a spy from Fårosünd named **GREGER**.

ARNE: A young boy from Fårosünd whom Bergrún helps escape into the marshes during the first raid.

ASTRID MAIRE THURESDOTTER: The late mother of Harold and Rikard. During a Fårosünd's raid. She cursed Jarl Gustav with her dying breath.

BERGRÚN LILITH GULLVEIGARDÓTTIR: The protagonist, a powerful black witch from Svartvik on the west coast of Heilladur. She is slender and pale-skinned with raven-black hair and onyx eyes.

BJORGEN: A warrior from Hamarrfjord, described as a "lisping dimwit," who was killed by Bergrún's arrows during the raid on Fårosünd.

BJØRN JOHANSEN: A seasoned warrior and blacksmith in Hamarrfjord, a member of Jarl Gustav's council.

CIARÁN: An Éiran warrior who joins Rikard and Bergrún.

Cormac Ó Brian: An Éiran warrior and a former guard for the old Éiran clan chieftain, who joins Rikard and Bergrún.

Eadmund, Brother: A supposed Christian friar who is actually a spy from Fårosünd named Ivar. He attempts to poison the leadership of Hamarrfjord.

Edda Ingmarsdotter: Toril's loyal thrall and confidante. She is a stern task- and spy-mistress and a key figure in Toril's schemes. She has two sons, Frick and Frock.

Einar Godfred Finsgúr: A wiry warrior from Norskvegn, renowned for his fighting skills and sharp wit, brother-in-law and closest friend to Harold, father of Envar, Eskil, and Erik.

Envar Finsgúr: Einar's oldest son, a watchman in Hamarrfjord.

Erik Gunner Finsgúr: Einar's youngest son, who becomes Bergrún's page boy and protege.

Eskil Finsgúr: Einar's middle son, a warrior in Hamarrfjord.

Fenrir: A monstrous wolf in Norse mythology.

Fiadh Nic Chonaill: A reed-thin Éiran woman who is a skilled tracker.

Filip, Prince of Danheimr: The third son of King Olaf, betrothed to Toril as part of her alliance with Danheimr.

Frick & Frock: Edda's identical twin sons. Referred to as the "spiders," they serve as her spies and enforcers.

Freya: The Norse goddess of love, beauty, fertility, and war.

Frode Gundlofsen: A sailor on Harold's ship, brother of Snorri.

Garwyn, son of Faelan: The archdruid and keeper of Gleann an Earraigh in Éira. He seeks the help of Bergrún and Rikard to rescue his abducted grandchildren.

Grimarr: An aged, battle-scarred Viking warrior who acts as the thane of Fårosünd. Bergrún kills him at the start of the raid.

Grímnir: A warrior from Hamarrfjord who is killed by falling branches during the attack on healer Gunhild's hut.

Gunhild (Hilde) Kristinsdóttir: A thrall and healer in Hamarrfjord, originally from Heilladur. She is Stina's mother.

Gundloff: An old sailor from Hamarrfjord, killed by Bergrún's arrows during the raid on Fårosünd.

Gunnar: A trusted warrior of Jarl Gustav.

Gustav Haakon Larsen: The aging Jarl of Hamarrfjord, Toril's father, and uncle to Rikard and Harold. He is a strong but pragmatic leader trying to navigate the changing political landscape.

Haddur Borgersen: Brother of Sverre Borgersen. He leads a mob to attack healer Gunhild's hut, blaming the "Heilladur Witches" for his brother's death. He is sentenced to death by Toril's decree.

Hamar: The mute helmsman of the Wave Dancer.

Hannu Gundulfsen: A Viking from Fårosünd, chieftain Stígur Asmundsen's cunning brother-in-law and ruthless second-in-command.

Harold Fisk Svensen: Rikard's older brother, a fierce, ambitious, and traditional Viking warrior of the "old way." He is often at odds with his uncle and cousin Toril.

Hela: The Norse goddess of the underworld.

Holger Claassen: Watchleader under Olver and his second-in-command.

Ingvild Bramsdóttir: A black witch on Heilladur who took Bergrún in as her apprentice. Bergrún kills her, not knowing that the dark curse will claim her upon her mistress's death.

Kael Olfredsen: A sheep farmer from Eastend who was allegedly killed by his cousin, Killian, in a brawl after the Althing. Brother of Kaleb.

Kaleb Olfredsen: The man Rikard beats in a duel, leading to the challenge of a holmgang. Jarl Gustav grants all his possessions to Bergrún.

Kieran Peddersen: Kaleb's cousin, a giant of a man who fights Rikard in the holmgang as Kaleb's champion.

Killian Peddersen: Brother of Kieran. A sheep farmer from Eastend who was allegedly killed by his cousin, Kael, in a brawl after the Althing.

LEIF RØDSKÆG: Rikard and Harold's great-great-grandfather, the first jarl to unite the tribes of Hamarrfjord. His banner, a snarling wolf's head on a faded red field, is a prized heirloom.

LOKI: The Norse trickster god.

LYNGAR: One of Haddur Borgersen's men who participates in the attack on healer Gunhild's hut. He chooses enthrallment as punishment.

MAGNUS HÅKANSON: A ruthless warrior from Starvinger loyal to Harold.

MÉABH (MAEVE) UISCE GLAN: A young Éiran woman, Theron's sister, and Druid Garwyn's ward. She has a strong resemblance to Stina and possesses healing abilities. She helps care for Rikard.

MIKKEL: A warrior from Hamarrfjord who Bergrún's enchanted wolf kills during the attack on healer Gunhild's hut.

MORRÍGAN, THE: An Éiran goddess associated with war and fate.

MORTON GUSTAV BROR HAMARRSEN: Toril's infant son. His parentage is disputed between Olver and Harold. His name is part of Toril's plan for the future of Hamarrfjord.

MORWEN, SON OF GARWYN: Designated successor of the archdruid, grew up together with Theron and was killed by the Inglan invaders.

NORNS: The female beings in Norse mythology who rule the destiny of gods and men. Bergrún sees them as her primary antagonists.

ODIN: The chief god in the Norse pantheon, associated with wisdom, war, and death.

OLAF, KING: The ruler of Danheimr, who is expanding his kingdom under the banner of the White Christ.

OLVER BROR AGNARSEN: The Shield of Hamarrfjord, Jarl Gustav's first warrior, and Toril's lover and co-conspirator.

RIKARD THURE SVENSEN: The protagonist, a young Viking warrior from Hamarrfjord. His questioning of the endless cycle of violence puts him at odds with his kin. He has short, blond hair and sky-blue eyes.

RISSA: A giggling maid in Rikard's household.

Ronan MacGregger: A short, stocky Éiran man who is a skilled tracker.

Saoirse Gobha: A tall, muscular Éiran woman who is the village smith and joins Rikard.

Snorri Gundlofsen: A sailor on Harold's ship, brother of Frode, who is killed by Harold after being magically provoked by Bergrún.

Sól: The Norse personification of the Sun. The Moon is Sól's brother.

Stígur Asmundsen: The chieftain of Fårosünd and a blood enemy of Hamarrfjord. Bergrún kills him at the end of the battle for Hamarrfjord.

Stina Hilmarsdóttir: Healer Gunhild's daughter, a young thrall from Heillaður with auburn hair, green eyes, and a freckled face. She is repeatedly brutalized. Bergrún heals and befriends her.

Sven Arnulf Larsen: Younger brother of Jarl Gustav, Hamarrfjord's most famous raider. He is the father of Abby, Harold, and Rikard, and died at sea in a storm before the beginning of the story.

Sverre Borgersen: A guard in Hamarrfjord who repeatedly assaults Stina. The discovery of his death instigates the attack on healer Gunhild.

Theron Briarwood: The archdruid Garwyn's ambitious and resentful foster son in Éira, older brother to Maeve.

Thor: The Norse god of thunder, strength, and protection.

Thorstein: A massive, cruel warrior from Hamarrfjord who bullies Rikard. Bergrún kills him to save Rikard's life.

Tjorben Stígursen: A young boy, son of chieftain Stígur Asmundsen, who flees into the marshes during the first raid on Fårosünd.

Toril Ingrið Gustavsdotter: Jarl Gustav's cunning, ambitious, and manipulative daughter. She plots to secure the future of Hamarrfjord through an alliance with Danheimr, making her a primary antagonist. She has fair skin and wears her golden hair in braids.

PLACES

Åalbrug: Seat of King Olaf of Danheimr.

Aberdeenium: A major settlement in the north of Inglandia that Rikard initially plans to visit.

Álfheimr: The mythological realm of the elves in Norse cosmology.

Asgard: The mythological realm of the Æsir gods in Norse cosmology.

Brótinholm: "The Broken Islet," a group of islands akin to Orkney, home to the village of Fårosünd.

Danheimr: A powerful, expanding kingdom to the south, akin to Denmark, led by King Olaf.

Dansker: The people of Danheimr.

Dunscaith Castle: "Shadow Fort," the fortress in Gleann an Earraigh, stronghold of Inglan invaders, which Bergrún destroys.

Dúnmuir: A seaport in Éira controlled by Inglan soldiers.

Éira: An island akin to Ireland, where Rikard and Bergrún land after escaping the Danske ships. It's green, wet, and rich in magic but occupied by Inglan forces.

Fårosünd: Main village on Brótinholm, blood enemies of Hamarrfjord.

Friesen: A kingdom akin to the Netherlands, southwest of Danheimr.

Frisians: The people of Friesen.

Gaul: A kingdom akin to Normandy to the west of Friesen.

Gauls: The people of Gaul.

Geats: The people of Götaland.

Gaelisk: The language spoken on Éira and Heilladur.

Gleann an Earraigh: The "Valley of Spring" in Éira, home to the druid Garwyn and his people.

Götaland: The region in southern Sweden from which Bergrún falsely claims to hail.

Hagndal: Future seat of Harold the Conqueror on the northern shore of Heilladur.

Hamarrfjord: The home village of Rikard, Harold, the main location of the story, and the seat of the chieftain on Hrafney.

Heilladur: "Enchanted," an Isolated island nation akin to Iceland, Bergrún's homeland, known for its connection to nature spirits and magic.

Hel: The Norse underworld, ruled by Hela.

Hrafney: "The Raven Island," a group of islands akin to the Shetlands on which Hamarrfjord is located. Main location of the story.

Iarntann Islands: [Iron Teeth] The jagged islands guarding a treacherous channel into the Inglan Sea with submerged rocks and whirlpools.

Inglandia: The land akin to Great Britain, portrayed as a place of "wood witches and magic swords."

Inglans: The people of Inglandia.

Jötunheimr: The mythological land of the ice giants in Norse cosmology.

Lindvik: Minor settlement in Götaland, Agnetha's alleged home.

Norsk: The language spoken (with dialects) by the Vikings of Brótinholm, Danheimr, Götaland, Hrafney, and Norskvegn.

Norskar: The people of Norskvegn.

Norskvegn: A large land akin to Norway, sparsely populated.

Starvinger: Major settlement in southern Norskvegn where Harold spends the winter.

Svartálfaheimr: The realm of dark elves and evil dwarves.

Svartvik: Bergrún's small home village on the west coast of Heilladur, which she destroyed.

Trondborg: Major settlement in northern Norskvegn.

Valhalla: "The hall of the slain," Odin's majestic hall in Asgard, where slain warriors feast.

SPELLS & FOREIGN WORDS

AINNISEOIR: [Gaelic] "Wretch," a miserable person.

ALTHING: [Old Norse] A general assembly of the freemen.

ANGIST!: [Old Norse] "Anguish," the spell Bergrún uses to inflict chest pain.

AN FAOILEÁN: [Gaelic] "The Seagull," the name of the ship Rikard and Bergrún acquire in Éira.

ANOIS: [Gaelic] "Now."

AR MHAITH LEAT LABHAIRT LE GARWYN?: [Gaelic] "Would you like to speak with Garwyn?"

BLACK SISTER / BLACK WITCH: A specific and rare type of witch who does not age and must drain the life force of humans to survive. Also called "Death's Daughters," Bergrún is one of only five in the world.

BLÓÐHEFND: [Old Norse] "Blood revenge" or blood feud, a central theme of the story's conflicts.

BROTTU Í SUNDUR!: [Old Norse] "Break apart!" The spell Bergrún uses to shatter the compass dome.

CABHRAIGH LEIS DUL ISTEACH!: [Gaelic] "Help him get inside!"

CABHRAIGH LIOM, LE DO THOIL: [Gaelic] "Help me, please."

CAD ATÁ Á DHÉANAMH AGAT?: [Gaelic] "What are you doing?"

CAILLEACH: [Gaelic] "Witch" or "hag."

CÉ THUSA?: [Gaelic] "Who are you?"

ELJA: [Old Norse] A second wife or concubine in a Viking household.

FAERING: A small, open boat with two pairs of oars.

FUIL NA DRAÍOCHTA: [Gaelic] "Blood of Magic," the term for the magical bloodline the Inglan invaders are hunting in Éira.

HOLMGANG: [Old Norse] "Going to the island," a formal Viking duel to the death to settle matters of honor.

IS MISE...: [Gaelic] "I am..."

Já, herra minn: [Old Norse] "Yes, my lord."

Jarðsquake: An earthquake, a common manifestation of Bergrún's power.

Jarl: A Norse chieftain or nobleman, equivalent to an earl.

Karl: A freeman in Norse society.

Knarr: A type of Norse cargo ship.

Konungsdráp: [Old Norse] The killing of a king or chieftain.

Krigsband: [Old Norse] A Viking warband, ranging from a few dozen to several hundred. One raiding longship could hold approximately 30 to 40 men.

Maðkur / Maðkar: [Old Norse] "Maggot / Maggots," used as an insult.

Maidin mhaith: [Gaelic] "Good morning."

Ní h-é tusa, a Mhéabh: [Gaelic] "Not you, Maeve."

Níðingr: [Old Norse] A term for a villain, scoundrel, or person who has lost their honor.

Níl sí marbh: [Gaelic] "She isn't dead."

Non audet Normannus Éiram tangere...: [Latin] "No Norseman dares to set foot on Éira since that holy victory of the High King of the Britons."

Quis accedit?: [Latin] "Who goes there?"

Ráðast á! Bíta! Drepa!: [Old Norse] "Attack! Bite! Kill!" The spell Bergrún uses to control the she-wolf in the forest.

Ragr: [Old Norse] An insult implying cowardice or unmanliness.

Rífa!: [Old Norse] "Tear!" The spell Bergrún uses to rip the rigging lines of the mainsail apart.

Sisterbrother: Brother-in-law.

Skítr!: [Old Norse] "Shit!"

Springa!: [Old Norse] "Explode!" or "Burst!" Bergrún's most frequently used destructive spell.

SUMUS VIATORES … NORMANNI. QUAERERE COMMERCIUM: [Latin] "We are travelers … Norsemen, seeking trade."

TÁ AN DRAOI SA SRÁIDBHAILE: [Gaelic] "The druid is in the village."

TÁ GACH RUD GO MAITH: [Gaelic] "Everything is alright/good."

TÁIMID: [Gaelic] "We are" or "We will."

TÁIMID AG BRATH AR DO CHABHAIR: [Gaelic] "We need your help."

TÁ SÍ INA CODLADH: [Gaelic] "She is sleeping."

TABHAIR BEOIR DÓ: [Gaelic] "Give him a beer."

THANE: A man ranking above ordinary freemen, acting as the steward of the land or village.

THRALL: A slave or serf in Norse society.

TUSA AGUS BERGRÚN?: [Gaelic] "You and Bergrún?"

VERTU BLESSUÐ: [Old Norse] "Be blessed," Bergrún's farewell to Stina.

VINDSBRÚÐ: [Old Norse] "Wind's Bride," the name of Rikard's ship on the journey to Inglandia.

www.ingramcontent.com/pod-product-compliance
Lightning Source LLC
Chambersburg PA
CBHW070513310726
48976CB00002BA/428